From the distant thick of battle, Storm saw the marilith's snakelike tail rise into view. . . . Behind Maxer. Behind her beloved. He fought on, unaware. Sparks flew around him as, with powerful swings of his sword, he beat back the creature's three thrusting blades.

Storm slashed out behind her, felt her blade strike something, heard the same squalling scream that always sped her on her vain charge, and wept aloud as she leapt and ran. . . .

With almost loving gentleness, the snakelike tail curved, its tip twitching—and then struck. Maxer rose for a moment, eyes bulging in alarm as he fought to turn and hack at this new peril. The snaking bulk quivered, swayed fully upright, and surged powerfully.

"*No!*" Storm cried, knowing she would be too late.

She was always too late. . . .

A semi-secret organization for Good, the Harpers fight for freedom and justice in a world populated by tyrants, evil mages, and dread concerns beyond imagination.

Each novel in the Harpers Series is a complete story in itself, detailing some of the most unusual and compelling tales in the magical world known as the Forgotten Realms

D1474342

THE HARPERS

FANTASY ADVENTURE

STORMLIGHT

Ed Greenwood

First Printing: October 1996
Printed in the United States of America.
Library of Congress Catalog Card Number: 95-62253

9 8 7 6 5 4 3 2 1

ISBN 0-7869-0520-4   8567XXX1501

TSR, Inc.   TSR Ltd.
201 Sheridan Springs Rd   120 Church End, Cherry Hinton
Lake Geneva WI 53147   Cambridge CB1 3LB
U.S.A.   United Kingdom

To Helen in Houston,
for things Stormlike.

To Roxy, in the mountains or the big city,
for the spirit.

To Anja in Hannover,
for the kindness and thoughtfulness of Storm.

To Robert, Krystyl, and Susan,
for what Storm fights for.

itu ne cede malis sed contra audentior ito

*Whenever I think I can relax at last, someone hastens
to brutally point out to me that I've fresh work to do:
it's time to save the world again.*

—**Storm Silverhand**
Bard of Shadowdale

PROLOGUE

The sunset on the rugged flanks of the Thunder Peaks was glorious, but young Lord Summerstar did not give it a second glance. There'd be other sunsets to gaze at when he wasn't in such a hurry. He turned away from the window, not knowing he was turning his back on the last sunset he'd ever see.

But then, all too few folk know which sunset will be their last. And who's to say it isn't worse for those who do?

Once the sun was gone, the cold would draw down swiftly from the mountains, and folk all over Firefall Vale would go in to where it was warm, by a fire, and declare the fourth day of Flamerule in the Year of the Sword done.

Athlan Summerstar loved the vale—tucked away in the angle where the marching trees of the Hullack Forest met the western slopes of the Thunder Peaks—

and why not? It was all his! Even so, richer, prouder nobles and knights in Suzail dismissed it as a backwater, if they knew of it at all. Soon that would all change. Soon men would speak with awe of the Summerstars of Firefall Keep.

Soon, he would master the book that floated in the glowfield in the hidden room at the heart of the Haunted Tower. The book was almost as tall as he, open to two fascinating pages of runes that crawled and writhed under his scrutiny. The tome fairly crackled with magic. It must have been floating there in its hiding place at the heart of the oldest tower of Firefall Keep since the death of his eldest uncle, Orm Hlannan Summerstar—or perhaps it had been a treasure brought back from dragon hoards in far lands by Athlan's father, Lord Pyramus. Athlan wished he could ask his father about it—he wanted to ask his father a lot of things, but that warm, strong voice was silenced forever now.

The seneschal of Firefall Keep had ridden with his father for years. Shoulder to shoulder, they wet their blades in battles for king and country. Better than anyone else alive, the seneschal probably remembered the laughing, stern-eyed, neatly bearded Pyramus. . . .

Somehow, though, Athlan didn't want old Renglar to know about the book just yet. The scarred old seneschal had been a Purple Dragon for years before agreeing to serve the House of Summerstar. Whenever warriors of Cormyr came across any magical thing that had even a whiff of secrecy about it, they had a disconcerting habit of running to the same war wizards they grumbled so much about. This book might be no more than a patiently floating wizard's plaything, hidden away in Firefall Vale for years—but no doubt Renglar would judge that the "security of the realm" hinged on it. . . . Then the place would fill up with grandly robed old wizards who'd eat and drink like warhorses, pinch maids' bottoms, deliver stern lectures to the unwashed bumpkins around them, and look down their noses at everything in sight.

As he approached the book chamber, Athlan snorted at the thought. The great Storm Silverhand had shown him a lot of things when she trained him—things that would make those pompous wizards faint dead away and fall over backward like toppled dolls. Why, if even his fellow knights of the realm knew half the things the Harpers hereabouts worried about every night, they'd ride hard and fast back to Suzail and never again dwell so close to mountains where ancient dragons slumbered, and towers where ghosts walked, and—

He came to a sudden, shocked halt, and raised his lantern to peer about the long-hidden room behind the statue, just to make sure. It took only a few glances to confirm what he already knew: the book was gone.

There was the smallest of sounds, off to his left. Athlan whirled to face it, hand going to the dagger at his belt. He'd seen a thing or two to make the servants' whisperings about the Haunted Tower seem a little more than empty fancies, but . . . there was nothing there.

Athlan took a wary step back, and looked to his right. Nothing. A boot scraped on stone very close by to his left, and he whirled—in time to meet a dagger cutting hard into his tongue.

He tried to roar, or scream, or—but all he managed was a gurgle. Something smooth and sharp and icy slid into his spine, and on into his vitals, to burst forth from his chest dark and wet with his own blood. . . . He stared in disbelief at the slim sword—was that *all*? An instant and he'd be . . . dead?

The young Lord Summerstar sagged as the chill became a sudden fire that seemed to burn away all the strength he had left, and . . . Firm hands held him up.

The white fire blazed up and into his brain. He looked into the two dark, watching eyes of his murderer. Then the white fire told him things, and he wanted to scream.

He struggled to cry out, choking and heaving and . . . drifting away on the flowing white fire. It was too late for young Athlan. Too late . . .

The lantern fell from failing hands. It burst on the stones with a brief roiling of flame.

"Athlan Summerstar," a voice murmured in the sudden darkness that followed. "Head of a minor noble house. Harper, knight—and dreamer, like all of them. Perfect."

The body of the young noble seemed to shrivel. Trickles of ash fell from where eyeballs had once been.

The calm voice Athlan could no longer hear continued, "Almost worth spending a day as a floating book for. Almost." The flames brought the speaker childish memories of beautiful women and riding in the vale and so-so sword skills, and . . . complete, room-by-room knowledge of Firefall Keep.

"So there *are* ghosts," the voice said into the darkness, in tones of surprise—as a light husk of a body slumped to the floor. "And I guess I'm one of them."

*   *   *   *   *

The snake-woman screamed, a shriek of rage that echoed through the temple.

Storm Silverhand turned her head toward the sound. With a vicious backhand slash of her blade, she struck aside the cruel, long-eared face of the cambion she fought.

She saw Maxer's blade cut down on the snake-woman. A spurt of black blood caught fire. One of the marilith's shapely arms, still clutching its sword, flew away, spinning in the air amid flaming gore.

Storm whimpered as she turned back to strike away the cambion blade that sought her own throat.

"No!" she cried, knowing what was coming. "No!"

But she was spared nothing. With dreadful slowness, as she snarled in desperation and kicked away the last foe in her path, beginning her charge too late and too far back, she saw the marilith's snakelike tail rise into view. . . . Behind him. Behind her beloved. He fought on, unaware. Sparks flew around him as, with powerful swings of his sword, he beat back her three thrusting blades.

Storm slashed out behind her, felt her blade strike something, heard the same squalling scream that always sped her on her vain charge, and wept aloud as she leapt and ran and leapt again, knowing she would be too late.

She was always too late.

With almost loving gentleness, the snakelike tail curved, its tip twitching—and then struck. Maxer rose for a moment, eyes bulging in alarm as he fought to turn and hack at this new peril. The snaking bulk quivered, swayed fully upright, and surged powerfully.

"No!" Storm cried, running for all she was worth.

Before her horrified gaze, as the beat of her own heart pounded in her ears and the clangor of battle died away all around them, the marilith tore Maxer's head from his shoulders. The head leapt through the air, tongue lolling, and trailed a plume of dark blood down into the fray. Beyond it, the marilith grinned exultantly and shook the headless, convulsing body in celebration.

Storm's vain rush carried her closer. She wept in helpless rage and grief as the marilith's grin shifted to her and became gloating laughter. The whirling sparks and mists of the spell that would whisk it away were already rising in the air around it.

Storm raised her blade too late, knowing cambions

were leaping after her, hungry for her own death.

Something rolled by her feet, across the bloody flagstones of the temple: Maxer's head. His mouth was
open in a final cry that had been choked off forever. His
eyes were wide and staring.

And then, as it always did, despite her moan, the
grisly thing leapt into her lap, hissing wetly, "I *love*
you!" Still trailing blood, it sprang at her face, lips
pursed to kiss her—

* * * * *

Storm Silverhand awoke screaming, cradling nothing in front of her mouth. Her silver hair stood out
arrow-straight from her skull, and her bare body was
drenched with sweat.

"No! Oh, gods, no!" she sobbed, sliding down the far
wall of the room where she somehow always ended up.
Her trembling body was as wet as if she'd been for a
swim, and as always, her skin had shed blood as well
as sweat. Syluné was hovering anxiously over the
empty bed, surveying sheets and blankets that had
been slashed as if by frantic swings of a sword.

As she always did, Syluné watched silently as Storm
panted her way back to coherence, rolling over onto
her knees and sobbing. "Why did he have to die?" she
cried out. "Why?"

Wisely, her sister kept silent, even when Storm
raised her tearstained face. "I was so close! *So close!*
And I *could not* save him!"

Fresh tears choked her for a time, and she crawled
blindly back toward the bed, crying, "I should never
have left his side! I should have been there! I—ohhh,
Mystra, aid me!"

That last, despairing wail took all the energy she
had left with it; the Bard of Shadowdale fell on her
face on the floor and wept her way into slow oblivion.

* * * * *

When she awakened once more, Syluné's hair was softly brushing her bare shoulder. "Storm," the gentle voice came from above her, "a warm bath awaits you, and the sun is coming up. Rise, and put Maxer behind you once more."

"My thanks," Storm whispered, not moving, her cheek against the cold stone. She shivered, suddenly, and added, "Syluné? Stay with me just now . . . please?"

"It was a bad one," her sister said soothingly. "They seem to be the worst when they herald doom."

Storm sat up, her face pale but calm. "Oh, yes," she said wearily. "Somewhere, and soon, there will come another death that will matter greatly—another that I cannot stop." She gained and sighed. "A murder, of course. One more Harper will die."

One

STARFALL

"Look!"

The cry burst forth from one of the Purple Dragons as the honor guard stood back from the pyre. Heads jerked up, wearing the annoyed expressions of folk embarrassed by an unseemly outburst. Frowns melted away in awe.

Athlan's sister even broke off her sobbing to give a cry of near-delight. In the dusky sky over the distant Stonelands, a solitary light was plunging to earth: a falling star.

"Praise be," one guard muttered, "a good sign."

The Harvestmaster of Chauntea drew breath to thunderously acclaim this mark of divine favor. The old priest raised his voice in a tremulous declamation.

The gods—some god, at least—saw good or at least important times ahead for the noble House of Summerstar, here on the very edge of Cormyr. The assembled family members looked suitably gratified.

A moment later, the crackling flames rose with a sudden roar, hiding from them all the shrouded form that had been Athlan Summerstar.

The seneschal's gaze went from the racing flames to the icily beautiful face of the dowager lady. Even before he could have tactfully suggested such a thing, the matriarch of the Summerstars—Dowager Lady Pheirauze Summerstar—had ordered her grandson burned by holy handfire to banish any harmful magic. She now stood watching—calmly, even haughtily. But then, she did everything haughtily, carrying herself with the smooth sophistication that sixty winters of high station and great beauty had brought.

She stood at the center of the gathered family, tall and slender, and the firelight that found her danced on a face that showed more annoyance than sorrow. Athlan had failed her, tearing asunder her schemes of greatness for the Summerstars. She'd probably not live to see another male Summerstar heir ready to ride to Suzail and impress whichever king sat the Dragon Throne then. Worse than that, he'd failed her in a way that left her unable to get even with him . . . and Pheirauze Summerstar always got even.

Athlan's younger sister, Shayna, was suddenly the family heir now. Her stunning beauty had built to a peak, and her willfulness was making her dalliances with every second or third young and handsome Purple Dragon armsman in the vale increasingly difficult to hide.

Impossible to hide, more like, thought the seneschal. He'd soon have to call in war wizards to nose about in every corner and cranny of the keep. Murders of nobility might be hushed up, but never the sudden deaths of heirs or of any noble in a border hold. These days, Sembia was looking westward with ever-hungrier eyes. Renglar sighed.

No, the folk that the Purple Dragons privately

called "the Happy Dancing Mages" would come. This was murder, all right. No young noble heir goes alone into a so-called haunted tower of a castle and gets his tongue slashed to prevent any screams, a sword thrust through him from behind—and some spell or other that burns him to a shell—by accident!

Later, he said as much. Most of the ashes had been placed on the traditional saddle bowl and the dead lord's horse had been whipped into a gallop to strew them wide and far over the vale. The Summerstars retired to their quarters—no doubt to yell at each other over the details of Lord Athlan's will. They hadn't even bothered to accompany the priest of Chauntea on the solemn march down to the family crypt to inter the traditional lone handful of still-smoking ashes in Athlan's upturned helm. The seneschal and his guest, however, both did.

When it was all over—after the crypt doors had boomed shut and been sealed with a final benediction and the priest had scuttled away with the traditional gold goblet full of gold lions as payment—Renglar sighed once more and turned to his tall, solid, sharp-eyed guest. "Care for some wine? We need to talk."

"Yes, and we do," the tall man agreed simply. They went up the stairs together. "He meant a lot to you?"

The seneschal shrugged. "He was a good lad. Lots of dreams—and the dreams of young men light the fires that brighten Cormyr in years to come. I liked him, aye, and I put a lot of hours of sword-work in on him; all wasted now."

"Would he have grown into another Pyramus?"

Renglar shrugged again, and stopped to unlock a seldom-used door. "It was too early to say. He had a touch of the let's-use-magic-because-it's-quick-and-easy streak, and was drifting into poking into small magics because of that. Another Pyramus? I don't think so."

They went through the door. With a heavy clang and a rattle of chain, it swung to behind them. The seneschal of Firefall Keep took a torch from a wall-bracket ahead, and led the way. His guest followed, eaglelike eyes moving this way and that, missing nothing. . . . Then again, it might be his task to besiege this place some day.

Below those alert eyes, Ergluth Rowanmantle was growing stout. There were white hairs in his side whiskers, but the veined and corded hands that swung his mace of office were still strong. He wore a heavy broadsword in a plain battle scabbard at his belt, not the glittering rapier favored by his fawning counterparts who dwelt closer to Suzail. The boldshield of the district of Northtrees March was a sensible man and a veteran warrior, risen to his present rank out of competence and not gentle birth. There was not a man within a hundred miles that Renglar Baerest respected more.

They both knew a storm was coming, a storm of war wizards. The mages would skulk about, ask prying questions, use spells to peer into the mind of the seneschal to be sure he hadn't murdered his pupil and liege. If there were going to be glasses of wine drunk, and calm and reasoned words exchanged, now would be the best occasion, possibly the only chance, for a long time to come.

This little-used back passage led to a steep stair up. Both men took firm hold of their swords and dug into the climb, swinging their arms. They were puffing in unison by the time they reached the top. The two guards there saluted smartly as the seneschal and the local Purple Dragon commander passed between them and turned right, to another locked door.

"Simple quarters," Ergluth commented as Renglar let fall his chain of keys and swung the door wide. In the room beyond was a cot, a desk, a sideboard, and an armor stand. One wall of the room was all closets, and the seneschal waved to them.

"All the clutter goes in there, and I keep the place tidy out here," he said, and then grinned. The bold-shield's gaze had already fallen to the map on the gleaming desk—of course. Every room in Firefall Keep was on it, with Renglar's scribbled comments about needed repairs liberally adorning the layout. The seneschal laid a finger on one ink-outlined chamber.

"My Lord Athlan was found here, by a guard who's going to have to answer some hard questions from the mages. It's pretty clear the guard was passing through what we call the Haunted Tower—it *does* have some phantoms, plus the usual rats and bats, and isn't used—to meet with young Shayn— . . . ah, Lady Summerstar."

Ergluth carefully did not grin. "Yes," he announced to the world in carefully neutral tones. He stared down at the mapped heart of the Haunted Tower. "I think wine would be a *very* good idea."

The sideboard proved to contain a veritable arsenal of decanters. The seneschal soon steered a tall glass of Arabellan Dry into the boldshield's hand.

"To you, and to Azoun," Ergluth made the tradition-al toast.

"May one of us find his grave before the other," Renglar made the accustomed reply, even more dryly than usual. He might have retired from the Purple Dragons decades ago, but such habits weren't lightly forgotten. "I presume you see my problem at the proverbial single glance."

The Purple Dragon commander nodded. "Your slay-er must be someone who knew the young lord well—and the keep, too. Only someone familiar with both victim and ground could have found him there . . . too many corners for any light to give Athlan away. Your murderer dwells under this roof."

"Exactly," the seneschal said grimly, twirling his glass. With an absent astonishment, he realized it had somehow gone empty already. "But how long will it take our Happy Dancing Mages to see that, I wonder? And how many innocent folk will they upset first?"

"If they tangle with the old dowager," Ergluth said dryly, "my money's on her."

Renglar grunted in rueful assent and refilled both their glasses. "The roaming apparitions and the endless little noises in the Haunted Tower ought to keep them occupied for a tenday or more."

"During which time, they'll near be-damned eat you out of turret and cellar!" The Purple Dragon commander chuckled, and drank deeply. Coming up for air, he looked into the depths of his glass and said, "Yet you have no choice. The war wizards must be called in. Shall I do it? That'll earn you their deep suspicion but save you the wrath of the Summerstars."

"Of Lady Pheirauze, you mean," the seneschal corrected with a smile. "Nay, I know my duty. Let the Summerstars detest me. I serve Pyramus first, the realm second, Athlan third, and the rest of the kin a poor fourth. Best they be gently reminded of that.

"If they want me to walk away from vale, I've a place where I can sit out my last years watching adventurers ride by; hear tales race around the realm and come back again, all twisted; make bad wine and protect the realm by drinking it myself . . . and chat coyly with ladies not so young as to be cruel when refusing me."

Ergluth shook his head. "You make retirement sound good. I've kin who'll wear my feet down to stumps dancing every night, and keep me awake until dawn with the noise of young bucks rushing my nieces off their feet."

"You're not still angry with Shaerl for deserting us all to go to Shadowdale? I hear it's a beautiful place— now that Zhent troops aren't trying to burn it down or overrun it every second tenday."

Ergluth waved a dismissive hand. "Nay, she was fun. It's the pompous court boot-lickers among my kin that drive me wild. Be glad you've no noble kindred to embarrass you half so much."

"Truly, the gods felt I'd be better as a humble man," the seneschal observed. "I just sometimes wish they'd not had in mind a state *quite* so humble."

The boldshield chuckled in reply, and put his glass down. "Call in the wizards; I'll leave a rider in your gate tower should you want us here in haste."

"Let us hope no such frantic summons is needed," the seneschal said grimly. "If it is, there'll no doubt be a death behind it." He clapped his hand on the bold-shield's armored shoulder. "My thanks, whatever lies ahead. When you're gone, I'll send Janrath on a fast horse for the wizards."

"By sheer coincidence," Ergluth told the ceiling casually, "we should be riding along the same stretch of road, at just about that time, watching for arrows from the trees, brigands . . . that sort of thing."

"Sort of thing, indeed," Renglar agreed, and went to the door. "Thanks again."

The boldshield shrugged, and demonstrated that it was his turn to clap a comrade on the shoulder. "Whenever you need folk hacked to the ground, just call on the Purple Dragons. We also do parades, stand around beside doors looking menacing, and trample crops into the fields, given the slightest encouragement."

"So I've heard," Renglar said. "How are you at replacing slain young lords? Or dragging folk who killed them behind your horses at a fast gallop for a mile or so? My Athlan should not lie in ashes now. He should have served Cormyr until he was as old and fat as you and me."

"I hear you," Ergluth muttered. "If the spellhurlers

miss somehow, call me back in for a few more glasses of wine—and we'll turn Firefall Keep and everyone in it upside down and inside out for you."

He went out into the passage. The two veterans stood looking at each other for a breath or two, not smiling or speaking. Then the boldshield raised a hand in salute and went back down the stairs. The guards fell in before and behind him, as an escort of honor. When the seneschal heard the thuds of their boot heels joining those of his guest, he closed the door, leaned against it, and sighed heavily.

Athlan, gone forever. His fingers tightened suddenly around the glass in his hand—and it sang and shattered, spilling in shards between his fingers.

The seneschal watched the slivers bounce, dark with his blood. He set his jaw. Not bothering to stop the bleeding yet, he crossed the room to a certain closet door, and spoke to it.

"You heard? Janrath has orders not to hurry; you've got four days, mayhap five, before Ergluth gets a letter written and delivered to Laspeera. I need you to investigate everything the war wizards can't—or daren't. Do you agree?"

"Aye," said a muffled voice inside the closet.

The seneschal smiled grimly. "Good," he replied, and went back across the room to find a cloth to wind around his cut fingers. It took longer than he'd expected.

When he was done, he frowned and looked up, wine decanter in hand. "Well, you can come forth now, Arkyn—unless you *like* spending the night in a closet."

There was no reply. The seneschal's eyebrows rose, and then drew down into a darker frown. "Arkyn!" he called sternly. "Wake! Rouse!"

He went to the closet and pulled the door wide. The gruff jest he'd drawn breath to bark became a gasp of horror. The decanter found the floor, shattering in a thousand skittering shards.

The Harper agent was standing in his accustomed place in the closet, among the weather cloaks, but he wasn't wearing his usual grin.

Arkyn Hornblade was headless, encrusted with his own dried blood. Renglar's gaze traveled down the dirty brown trails to find the Harper's staring, severed head. It had been set neatly down between his boots.

"Gods!" the old seneschal gasped hoarsely.

The headless Harper moved, lunging forward for one heart-stopping moment before toppling to the floor. He landed with a heavy thud—but no blood flowed. Arkyn had been dead for hours.

The seneschal swallowed, spun around to strike the call-gong on the wall by the door—and froze.

A moment later he pivoted again, grabbing for the knife at his belt. If Arkyn had died so long ago, who'd answered from inside the closet?

Nothing moved. The dead Harper lay sprawled on the carpet, and silence hung heavy in the room. The seneschal spat out an oath and kicked open another closet door to snatch his hanging sword from its scabbard. With blades gleaming in both hands, he shifted from closet to closet, kicking open door after door. He panted in mounting fury, waiting for a killer to burst forth. There was no one lurking in any of his closets; the doors swung almost mockingly as he stared at them, breathing hard.

He roared out for the guards, and added to his bellow, "Bring me war wizards—and fast, damn you!"

Who had answered him from behind that closet door?

Two

HARPS AND FIREWOOD, WIZARDS AND GHOSTS

All summer long her hounds had been running along the old tree trunk fence. Last night, it had finally given way, collapsing with a dull double crack and leaving easy passage for deer. As much as Storm Silverhand loved to look out the window in the misty dawn and see deer prancing among the trees, she didn't want to see them out the other window—in her fields of lettuce and squash and asparagus. So, this early morn found her puffing down the back trail, a full-grown duskwood tree on her shoulders; one just right to fill the gap.

It was as long as three horses, and weighed almost as much. Storm's face was dark with effort as she bent to put it in just the right place. One of the wolfhounds raised its head and smiled at her. She tousled its ears affectionately. "Thanks for the help, Old Boldblade," she told it in mock disgust, and then headed for the rain barrel to wash off the sweat.

It was early, yet, and chill mists were still drifting along the ground like vengeful ghosts. Even so, the Bard of Shadowdale wore only floppy old boots, elbow-length gauntlets of heavy leather, and a fine sheen of sweat. Halfway to the barrel, she changed her mind about washing. By the looks of the fast-brightening sky, the sun was going to be hot today. It would be more comfortable, by far, to get a good lot of firewood chopped and split before full sunlight reached the chopping floor.

She sang an ancient elven song about a maiden who rode a stallion across half the Realms without realizing the horse beneath her was in truth her lover. He had been trapped in stallion-shape by the wicked spells of a rival. As she sang, Storm hefted her largest, sharpest axe, and set to work.

It felt good to put her shoulders fully behind a blow, swing hard, and see the wood cleave and leap. Storm laughed aloud and picked up the pace, flinging her finished work in all directions. The split segments could be tidied away later.

One shadowtop was particularly dry. It spun up from the chopping block almost into her face. Storm smote it away with the back of the axe head, sending it spinning end over end across the hollow.

"Hoy! Mind out!" an amused and familiar voice called.

Storm tossed hair and sweat aside from her face with one deft hand and grounded her axe with the other. The protest had come from a floating, disembodied head that hung in midair. The head trailed long, flowing tresses of a silvery hue that matched Storm's own. It was floating right about where the piece of wood must have flown.

"Why? It's not as if you're solid!" Storm replied, stretching.

"It's the principle of the thing," the floating head

replied tartly, and then added, "Nice ribs, there."

Storm put her hands on her hips and stuck out her tongue. Her sister laughed and added, "Besides—I could be."

"Principled?" Storm asked, plucking up her axe again.

"Solid," Syluné replied, floating over to hang at her shoulder for a better view.

"Huh," Storm said, exhaling with sharp effort as her axe came down on a duskwood trunk that had been drying for most of the season. It split crosswise, with a satisfying crunch. The bard kicked one end of it askew to have more room to split the other. "Why aren't you using your body, now that you've got one again?"

The Witch of Shadowdale made the little hopping motion in midair that meant she'd shrugged but forgotten she currently had no shoulders. "One has one's reputation to maintain. Besides, I'm used to being able to drift about, now—and my body's perfectly safe where it is."

"Reputation? My shapely behind!" Storm snorted, as wood clunked and flew again. "More like you didn't feel like helping to chop wood this morn, eh?"

Syluné smiled. "Now, would I admit that?" She slid around to hover by Storm's other shoulder as the first bright rays of the rising sun stabbed down into the hollow, over the tall stacks of split firewood. "And what would the wood-chopping Chosen of Mystra desire for morningfeast this fair day?"

"Fresh milk, dove eggs and sage, sharp cheese topped with hot nutmeg sauce, fried mushrooms and bacon slabs, a handful of radishes and another of grapes, and a mince tart or two, with a little mint wine to wash it down," Storm rattled off without hesitation or any pauses for breath.

Syluné gave her a withering look.

Storm said cheerily, "You asked. Did you leave your

body in the kitchen, as usual? Well, then—you can have it all ready by the time I'm finished here."

"I can?"

"Nothing's too much for the free-floating Chosen of Mystra," Storm replied grandly, bowing like a court noble.

"That gesture looks a little grander if you're wearing clothes," the Witch of Shadowdale observed.

"Such criticism is more kindly received from folk who're wearing *bodies*," Storm told her. "Now get out of here. There're two shadowtops crowning that pile over there, and I want to try a little axe-throwing *without* a clever-mouthed flying head in the way!"

Syluné thrust out her own tongue, and then flew idly away across the raspberry patch in the brightening morning.

Storm chuckled, shed her gloves, spat on her hands, and picked up the axe again, narrowing her eyes to judge the throw. The head of a doe rose above the two trees she was staring at, and gazed at her with soft, thoughtful brown eyes.

"Boo," she said. It knew her too well to be afraid of her, and came clambering down the bank to leap a stack of firewood and nuzzle her for anything sugary she might be carrying.

Storm sighed, picked the deer up, and trudged up out of the hollow, ignoring its startled kicks. "Back to the other side of the fence, little one," she told it. "It's not as if I don't provide you with your very own grazing garden already!"

Brown eyes met her own silver-blue ones, and the deer sniffed loudly.

"I see," Storm replied, as the animal kicked again. "No, you're coming with me. . . ."

* * * * *

The stone posts that flanked the rose-girded arch were graven deeply with swirling moons, stars, and harps; this was her farm, all right. The man in the dapple-gray cloak and mottled, smooth-worn brown leather armor put a hand into his shoulder-pouch and slowly drew out something silver. He showed it to the watchful wolfhound that stood in the entrance: a silver harp pin, gleaming on his open palm in the bright morning sun.

The dog nodded to him, for all the world like a respectful human gateguard, and stood back. The man gave it an answering nod and cautiously stepped past. The lane ran under a huge grape arbor and on toward a low-lying, grass-roofed farmhouse that seemed to grow out of the garden beyond. Birds were singing and flitting among the trees of an orchard to his right, and there was no sign of farmhands or livestock. Even the usual reek of manure was absent.

But then, anyplace that looked more like a woodland garden than a working farm almost had to be the abode of Storm Silverhand. The man picked up his pace. His soft boots made no sound on the grass path that led to flagstones and a little patio of hanging plants. A stone seat was built into the rubble wall of a raised herb bed, and—through another open arch, without any door that he could see—the path led into the cool dimness of a stone-floored kitchen.

He stood in the farmhouse, surrounded by its stillness. There was still no alarm, or hail, or any sight or sound of inhabitants. Birds flew about, a cat curled in sleep in the morning sun outside another archway, and . . .

Perhaps seven paces away, at one end of the huge, knife-scarred harvest table in the center of the kitchen, a woman's body was slumped back in a chair.

She wore only a light, filmy robe of flame-colored silk, and looked very dead. Her bare feet were sprawled among the legs of the next chair along. Her arms dangled loosely. Her head hung down over the back of the chair, so that her finely boned throat was uppermost, perched atop the chair back. Silver hair flowed down to curl in a smooth puddle on the ground. Her lips were parted, but no breath made her bosom move. She was as still as a statue ... or a corpse.

The man swallowed. The long, slender sword that swung at his side hissed out into his hand. Raising it before him, he crouched to look cautiously all around ... and then advanced quietly.

The cat did not move. In the garden beyond, birds sang and flitted about unconcernedly. Somewhere nearby, a tree toad began its lazy buzz. The bright sun that was coming in a dozen windows and doors laid long fingers across the smooth-polished flagstone floor and made the flowers inside and out blaze with bright glory. Their delicate scents came past him on gently stirring breezes as the man took one last careful step, looked all around, and then stretched forth a cautious hand to touch that magnificent fall of silver hair. He'd be able to recognize Storm Silverhand, they'd told him, by her silver hair.

He'd best make sure. Hefting his sword, he touched the glossy strands of silver. They were real, silken to his fingertips.

The man in leathers sighed, gently wove his fingers through the hair, and lifted the woman's head. Lifeless eyes stared into his—and just behind him, a light, furious voice hissed, "Beware! The dead sleep uneasily!"

The man jumped upright and whirled around, heart in his throat as his blade flashed up—to point at a ghostly, floating human head. The head of a woman with long, flowing silver hair.

"Gods preserve me!" he choked. "You're—" Without taking his gaze from the head, he gestured at the slumped body behind him.

The head advanced slowly through the air, eyes angry.

The Harper swallowed, and took a step back and to one side to have clear room to swing his sword. His eyes narrowed, judging just how distant the floating head was, and his free hand went to his belt. His fingers closed on—nothing. He felt around, finding the scabbard of his dagger empty.

Then he felt something else—something at his throat. Cold and smooth and very sharp, it was the edge of his missing dagger. Another hand took him by the opposite shoulder, clamping down like a claw of iron. A faint, spicy smell of sweat came to his nostrils.

"Tell me your name, and why you are here," a melodious female voice said calmly in his ear.

The man in leathers let his sword dangle from his fingertips and stood very still as he stammered, "I— Vrespon Flarnshan, at your service. I'm a Harper—my pin is in my shoulder-pouch—and I'm here on Harper business, sent from Hillmarch in Cormyr. Ah, where I dwell." His eyes darted to one side, and he tried to turn, but the hands that held him were as immobile as stone. Gods, she must be strong. "Have I the pleasure," he ventured, his voice trembling only slightly, "of addressing Storm Silverhand, the Bard of Shadowdale?"

"And if you are enjoying such a pleasure," the floating head asked expressionlessly, its tone a challenge, "what then?"

"Then I bring a message to deliver to her ears only. Words from the sorceress Aldaneth of Hillmarch."

"Who is a secret Harper," the voice by his ear affirmed, and the dagger and the grip were suddenly gone. "Catch!"

Vrespon turned—to see his dagger flashing end-over-end toward him! He plucked at the air, managed to catch it, held it up with a grin of triumph—and dropped his sword.

"He's a Harper, all right," the floating head said in tones of amusement as she drifted past him, heading for the body on the chair. Vrespon glanced up as he retrieved his sword, saw the head settle onto the throat of the slumped body, and decided he really didn't want to watch. He'd remember that exposed throat, those lifeless eyes, and the fright of the voice behind him for days . . . perhaps years.

"I am Storm Silverhand," said the melodious voice, "and I apologize for the fright we gave you. You may speak freely in front of my sister—Syluné, called by some the Witch of Shadowdale. What message do you bring me, Vrespon?"

The Harper turned, rose, and sheathed his blade— to find himself facing a woman, wearing high, battered leather boots. She was leaning against some cupboards, her arms crossed and an expectant look on her face. Vrespon flushed and hastily dropped his eyes to study her feet.

"Tell Storm from Aldaneth, these things," he recited, adopting a chant as the words tumbled out of his memory. "The noble Athlan Summerstar, of the Summerstars of Firefall Vale, has been murdered in his keep by mysterious means. Our agent at the keep, Arkyn Hornblade, has also been found slain. Laspeera of the war wizards spoke to me, requesting that the Lady Silverhand come to the keep and investigate. Wizards of war in service to Cormyr will be present, but will not know of Laspeera's request. They and the family expect Storm Silverhand to appear at Firefall soon, because she is named in Athlan's will—much to the displeasure of the elder Summerstars, I'm told."

Storm sighed. "Is there more?"

Vrespon kept his eyes on the floor. "No, Lady. I was told to escort you for as long and as far as you desired my presence."

A hand squeezed his arm. "You've done well. Are you afoot, or have you a mount?"

"My horse waits at the Old Skull, Lady," said the Harper said.

Storm sighed again, and it seemed for a moment that a shadow of weariness and despair crossed her face as she looked at Syluné. When she spoke, however, she sounded almost petulant. "Well, I'll have to go . . . though I *was* hoping to see what Flamerule looks like at my farm, for once."

"I'll watch over things here," Syluné told her, her head becoming spectral and sinking into her body. Vrespon turned in time to see it vanish, and stared, fascinated, as the slumped body raised its head, the whites of its eyes rolled up to reveal pupils—and winked at him.

The Harper jumped again. "Gods!" he swore. "Don't *do* that!"

Storm's deeply bubbling laughter rolled out from behind him, then, and Vrespon thought it was quite the most beautiful sound he'd ever heard.

* * * * *

The coach rumbled to a stop. Purple Dragons exchanged brief words, and then they were jolted into rumbling motion again. The clatter of the wheels roared back brief echoes as they passed through the clammy dimness of the gate tower, and into a cobbled courtyard beyond.

"Gods above!" one of the men in the back said. "Couldn't we have flown? My *tail*bone!"

"Belt up," one of his companions advised. "At least *you* have a seat with cushions."

"Now I know why messengers ride," a third muttered, "even into driving rain. . . ."

"I could have levitated the coach," a fourth man said haughtily, "and saved the horses, too—if I'd known things were going to be *this* bad. Unfortunately, I believed Runsigg when he said Cormyr had the best roads he'd ever walked on, and neglected to study that spell—"

"You belt up, too, Hundarr," the third speaker said sourly. "Runsigg was right; you obviously don't walk about much."

"Huh! His belly tells you that, even before—"

"Climb out and pipe down, the lot of you," an older voice growled. "You sound like a lot of wailing apprentices, not veteran wizards of war! Take a little pride in things, for the love of Laspeera!"

"Mother Laspeera provides all," one of the wizards replied mockingly as they clambered out of the dark, swaying coach. A line of Purple Dragons was standing stiffly at attention. Beyond them stood another, shorter line of guards in a different livery: an arc of three golden stars on a field of deep blue. The Summerstar armsmen, no doubt.

"Lady Summerstar and Sir Boldshield," Broglan Sarmyn was growling, "may I present to you the Sevensash investigative team, sent to you at the express command of Lady Laspeera of the wizards of war, on the instructions of the royal magician of the realm—upon consultations with His Majesty."

"Sevensash?" the cold-eyed, imperious old noblewoman drawled. "I see only six men."

She left a little silence, and turned to face Broglan, raising her eyebrows to bid him fill it. Gods, but she was beautiful. Beautiful like ice. Used to getting her own way in everything, this one, and dressed like the queen herself at a high court function, for all her sixty or more winters, and the minor—nay, unknown—stature of her house.

"We are, in fact, one member short, gracious lady,"

Broglan said smoothly, "though the name bestowed on us does not, in fact, refer to our number."

"And your missing man?" The bitingly bored tone made it clear that the Dowager Lady Summerstar cared not a whit for the fate of the absent wizard—only for how much she could make those present grovel and squirm.

"Ah—a woman, actually, lady, and at present engaged in giving birth. . . ."

"Congratulations," the Lady Pheirauze Summerstar replied with a cold little smile. She turned away before Broglan could even begin to protest that he wasn't the father.

Someone in the line of wizards snickered. Someone else was thinking that this old noblewoman was just perhaps a colder bitch than their absent colleague, Chalantra. Just perhaps.

They all watched the noblewoman walk away across the courtyard, her back as straight as a sword blade. The sway of her hips made more than one of her audience think again of her beauty, before Broglan turned briskly to the boldshield and said, "Ah—shall I present my mages to you, then?"

The solid, side-whiskered old Purple Dragon officer allowed just the slightest crook of a smile to creep onto one end of his mouth. "Suppose you do that, Sir Broglan. I know who you are, and you'd best know that I am Ergluth Rowanmantle, boldshield of the district of Northtrees March. I report directly to Baron Thomdor, warden of the Eastern Marches."

The boldshield's eagle-sharp eyes turned to look in the direction the old noblewoman had gone. "The lady you have all just—briefly—met is Lady Pheirauze, the matriarch of House Summerstar. The true family heir is her granddaughter, the Lady Shayna Summerstar, and the nominal head of the house is the other Dowager Lady Summerstar: mother to Shayna and daughter-in-law of Lady Pheirauze."

"That's Zarova Summerstar, is it not?" Broglan asked. "Who was born a Battlestar?"

The boldshield inclined his head in a nod. "That's right. In the absence of an heir who's been presented to the king, however, the master of this keep is its seneschal, whom you'll meet shortly. I'll leave him to introduce himself, but I'd best know your muster."

"So you can put names to the bodies, if need be," Broglan said, repeating the old joke.

The boldshield did not smile. "That's right."

The overwizard coughed, tried on an uneasy smile, and then growled, "Well, then: you see before you—in order, down our line—Hundarr of the Wolfwinter noble house." He looked to a tall, sharp-featured mage whose elegantly cut black hair was shot through with streaks of white. The mage inclined his head in a greeting every bit as haughty as the looks the Dowager Lady Summerstar had been dispensing.

"Lhansig Dlaerlin." A short, burly man with a broad face and an easy smile sketched a flippant, one-handed salute, his eyes mocking. The boldshield's level stare cut into those mocking eyes like two cold lance points, but made no change in their dark twinkling.

"Corathar Abaddarh." This mage was young, thin-lipped, and wintry-eyed, so eager to impress that he practically quivered, like a dog leaping to be let off the leash. He'd struck a dramatic pose, of course—and, as he felt the boldshield's eagle-eyed scrutiny fall upon him, he shifted rather self-consciously to another.

"Insprin Turnstone, recently transferred to us from Vangerdahast's personal Enforcers." An older wizard steadily met the boldshield's gaze, and nodded, as one to an equal. His face was weather-beaten, his eyes were the color of dull steel, and his black hair—what little he still had—had almost all gone gray.

Ah, yes, Ergluth thought. A pair of eyes and ears for

the royal magician, put into this group before its ambitious younglings took it right out of control. He returned the thin old man's nod, almost smiling. He could tell that a similarly knowing, not-quite smile lurked just below Turnstone's cheeks, too.

"Murndal Claeron." He was a darkly handsome man with a close-trimmed mustache and the sort of beard that puts two little corners to the chin before slicing up to join the sideburns. He had glistening brown eyes and a half-smile. Trouble. As ambitious as a hungry snake, and probably possessed of the same tactics.

"And, of course, myself." The boldshield swung his eyes back to Broglan Sarmyn. He was of average height and build. His hair was the hue of mud and going thin on top. It turned grizzled gray in his large but carefully trimmed sideburns, the man's only touch of visible personal style. Permanent worry lines creased a high forehead, and a touch of grimness hovered about the mouth. His robes were a year or two behind high fashion.

Ergluth knew Broglan's sort: a man uneasy in court society but decisive behind closed doors and out among the common folk. A good teacher who adopted the pose of the gruff, growling bear favored by so many swordcaptains of the Purple Dragons. A good man—principled, and with a love of the realm.

The others . . . well, more love of self and of mayhem than anything else, if he was any judge. A murderer loose in the keep, and we're adding *these?*

The boldshield gave them all a grave smile, and said loudly, half-turning toward his own men and the other armsmen in the courtyard, "Be welcome in Firefall Keep. May your mission meet with success. His Majesty has every confidence in you, and so do we all. Do not hesitate to call upon me, or any of my men, should you require aid." Then he turned fully to face the ranked guards, and barked, "Dismissed!"

The armsmen scattered like so many disturbed pigeons, clearing the cobbles in a whirl of weapons and trotting feet and jingling harnesses. The boldshield turned back to the wizards. "If you'd like, I'll conduct you to your quarters, where you may ease the rigors of so long a coach journey. You can meet with the seneschal before evenfeast, if you prefer."

"That would be acceptable," Broglan said with a smile, and turned to the other mages. The look in his hazel-gray eyes was a clear and cold command to utter not one word more until they were alone; smart comments about bucketheads in armor or rude backwaters would be neither appreciated nor received without cold rewards.

The rooms were dark-paneled, gloomy, and cold, like those in many a castle. Still, they were probably quite opulent by the standards of this place. Pelts had been laid in profusion across the threadbare patches in the carpet, until the floor seemed a deep, yielding grass-land under their boots. A row of doors led into private sleeping-chambers; Broglan raised his brows at this unexpected luxury, and made the silent gesture that bid the mages examine unknown territory for dangers. They curtly ordered the servants standing by their heaped baggage to begone, and began to roam about, peering under things and casting detection spells, listening here and sniffing there.

Not long afterward, they reassembled around Broglan. "Nothing," Lhansig muttered.

"A passage behind *that* wall, not far off," Hundarr said, pointing, "but probably not intended for . . . stealthy scrutiny."

"Concealed servants' door there," Insprin said, "and an old dweomer—probably a warning magic mouth."

Broglan nodded. "We won't worry about that. Any other dweomers?"

Heads shook in silent negatives. Their leader

sighed, and said, "I'm sure you noticed the baths, and after Insprin and I are done, you can all enjoy them in order of age. Next time, we'll reverse the order. No griping—they seem plenty hot right now." He reached for his belt, and said, "Choose your rooms; they all seem the same. Now, Murndal—tell me in brief what should interest us most about this mission."

Every inch the careful pupil, the handsome Claeron stroked one arm of his maroon silk overrobe, and said, "We have two murders, and reports from presumably competent priests that the bodies can't be raised, spoken with, or magically read in any way. They seem burned out from within, and utterly dead and lost to magic—worse than stones, which can at least be made to tell us something. Whoever did it, we want to find out how . . . or Cormyr, and Faerûn in general, may have far larger dooms upon them than merely two killings."

Broglan nodded in satisfaction, his face momentarily losing a little of its worried look. "I could not have put it any better. The manner of death is exactly our prime concern—though we should not, of course, admit that to anyone. Officially, we are here because the security of the realm demands that the death of any noble be investigated—and the violent death of any heir brings wizards of war to the scene.

"Please bear in mind that the dowager lady we met in the courtyard is precisely the type to go running to the king with complaints no matter what happens. Let's not be stupid enough, or allow ourselves to be goaded far enough, to give her anything reasonable to complain about. Let her make herself ridiculous. Don't give her any chance to make *us* look the fools."

He tossed his belt to the floor and undid the sash to let his overrobe fall open. "Now, the baths await. See to your rooms and baggage—and gentlesirs all, let us be very clear: this situation could hold peril, so I'll tolerate *no* pranks. Save your nasty magics for other folk, not your fellow mages."

Without another word, Broglan strode to the bath chamber. Insprin followed, and they heard the metal lids clatter up as the two older mages uncovered the heated baths.

With one accord the four younger war wizards turned to the heap of baggage and started pulling and tossing satchels and crates aside.

"So, laddies—pleased to be here?" Lhansig cooed in mimicry of a gushing matron, batting his eyebrows.

"Thanks to Mother Laspeera," Corathar said savagely, "I'll have to miss the Six Harpists concert, just to cool my heels in this backwater. *Thank* you, Mother Inthré!"

Murndal smiled. "I remember when she still called herself Laspeera Naerinth, before she married her mysterious man."

"Oh, yes. Do we still know nothing about him?"

"Well, he keeps to her quarters all the time—and I do mean *all* the time—cloaked and masked. The mask, they say, changes his features constantly, so that none know what he truly looks like. He can cast spells, but wears a blade. Some say he's a Harper, some—"

"I know, I know," Hundarr broke in sarcastically. "Some say he's a Red Wizard, some a Zhentarim, some a Halruaan outcast, and a few are even proposing he's a lich from long-lost Netheril. They say such things about every recluse in this land who knows a few light spells!"

Murndal sighed. "Yes, but this one does spend time scrying and working on spells. I've seen glimpses of the first and smelled and heard the less successful forays of the second. He's a powerful mage, all right, but he can't be a lich! Can you see Laspeera going to bed with a *dead* man? Or some sort of well-spoken, magically adept monster? I don't think so!"

"We're not here to *think*," Corathar said sharply. "That's the problem. We're always sent to places to look impressive and scare the chitlins out of folk, so *they'll* think—think twice, that is, about doing naughty things ever again."

"Well, *I* think we look very impressive," Lhansig joked, turning a cartwheel. "By the gods—you were all upside down, for just an instant there! How do you mages *do* that?"

Hundarr rolled his eyes. "Must you?" He turned to one of the doors. "If you must play such tricks, turn a few of those cartwheels in your bath—and call us in to watch, first!"

"One of these days Lhansig'll trip over his own tongue," Murndal murmured. "I wonder if we'll all be there to watch then?"

* * * * *

The wine and the roast boar had both been good, very good. They almost made up for having to listen to the barbs of the old Dowager Lady Daggertongue.

Lhansig chuckled and shook his head as he strode to the jakes—they probably called it a garderobe here, just to seem more sophisticated. It was the same brittle, empty way that Hundarr strove to be sophisticated. Lhansig rolled his eyes and hummed "I've Always Been A Lady Fair" as he shouldered his way through the door.

A single lamp was guttering, and the place wasn't any too well lit. The sea-serpent-mawed bowl he was seeking ought to be around here . . . yes. He contentedly fumbled with the laces of his codpiece—and so never saw the hand that drove his head forward against the wall, hard.

Lhansig Dlaerlin reeled back, dazed. Deft hands plucked his tunic up and over his head, blinding him.

He was struggling to draw breath when two very sharp things burst through the cloth and into his eyes . . . and there was no longer any need to scream.

White fire surged through the brain of the man who was always smiling and joking, and he opened his mouth in a last, soundless laugh as all he had ever been was sucked away. It did not take long.

Quick hands laid a silver harp pin on the wizard's breast—and then whimsically plucked up his unlaced codpiece and perched it on Lhansig's nose. It was a gesture worthy of the man, after all.

* * * * *

"Great gods above!" Broglan gasped, rising from the body, looking old and sick as well as worried. "The effrontery of this!"

The somber circle of shocked faces around him remained silent. Insprin, on his knees by Lhansig's motionless form, looked up and said quietly, "Nothing my Art can find."

"Then put his codpiece back and cover him," Broglan said in sudden, savage anger, face going red, "before one of the guards comes in here, and the jest spreads all over the keep!"

"S-Some jest," Corathar said, white to the lips.

"Death is never far away, lad," Insprin said almost absently. Corathar turned a glare of mingled hatred and fear down at the older wizard. Not seeing it, the veteran mage added, "This was a clear warning to us."

Broglan looked down again at Lhansig's eyeless, staring skull. The flesh had been burned away, leaving the death-grin of the bones beneath. He shivered. "Even the Harper badge told us nothing?"

Insprin shook his head, and plucked the pin from Lhansig's breast. One of the younger mages drew in his breath, as if expecting deadly magic to be unleashed—but nothing happened. Insprin shot a reassuring look in that direction, and mutely held up the badge.

It gleamed in front of Broglan's nose in the flickering candlelight, and he took hold of it. "Why a Harper badge?"

"One who was slain here—Hornblade—" Murndal said, "his was found on him, the seneschal said."

Broglan Sarmyn frowned, looking worried again. "This must be the work of Storm Silverhand. We were warned about her for good reason. She must be here already, lurking in the keep!"

He strode to the door, and then turned and snapped grimly, "Insprin, inform the seneschal and the boldshield about Lhansig's . . . demise. Have the Purple Dragons search the Haunted Tower. I'll go to farspeak the royal magician."

Three

STANDING STONES AND AUSPICIOUS ARRIVALS

The wards flickered one last time before settling down to a steady glow. Satisfied, Broglan Sarmyn seated himself at the table, sighed, and unwrapped the bundle he'd laid there. Black velvet unfolded into a circle with a diamond-shaped cushion at its center. On its puffed softness lay a flat-bottomed but spherical chunk of glossy black obsidian as large as Broglan's fist.

He took a deep breath, glanced around the room warily, and tapped the stone with a finger, murmuring a certain word under his breath.

The stone quivered and slowly lifted away from its cushion, wavering up into the air to hang above the table at about the level of Broglan's nose.

Broglan stared at it less than happily, the worry lines on his forehead deep again, and said, "Broglan Sarmyn, speaking from Firefall Keep. Lord High Wizard?"

"I hear you," the royal magician's voice rasped from the stone. It sounded sharp—but then, through speaking stones, it always did. "What news?"

"One of my team has been slain, presumably by the same creature or magical attack that killed the Lord Summerstar and the Harper agent," Broglan said heavily. "Lhansig Dlaerlin is no more—and we're no wiser as to how it was done. A Harper pin was left on his chest for us to find, and the body was arranged in such a way to mock us."

"Burned out, and barred to all magic, as before?"

"Aye." It was a measure of how upset Broglan Sarmyn was that he forgot to use any of Vangerdahast's titles. His next words made that agitation very clear. "What should I do?"

The stone turned slowly in the air and emitted a sound that might have been a sigh. "I can't spare the time just now to investigate," the distant Vangerdahast said bluntly, "and I'm leaving this in your capable hands. I realize this is something that could kill you all—and baffle Laspeera, myself, Elminster, and every last one of his ex-apprentices, for all I know. I won't tell you anything grandly foolish about knowing you'll pull through, and such nonsense. Just do the best you can, Broglan. If you have to flee from the place or bring Firefall Keep crashing down, do so. Try to stop short of butchering the entire Summerstar clan, if at all possible."

"I—I'm heartened to know that you understand," Broglan said hesitantly. "I have just two more questions. Firstly, how far can I trust the local boldshield, Ergluth Rowanmantle?"

"Absolutely, so long as you do nothing he sees as a threat to the realm. The man is loyal through and through, and is far more . . . perceptive than most Purple Dragon commanders. Next question."

Broglan took a deep breath—this was it, there was

no ducking the matter now—and plunged right in. "It looks like we're going to have a senior Harper who also happens to be of the Seven Sisters on our hands, here, any moment now. Storm Silverhand is named prominently in Athlan Summerstar's will."

"Did he deed the vale to her, or just the keep?"

"Neither—quite," Broglan replied. "There's nothing that diminishes the authority of the crown of Cormyr . . . but she is guaranteed freedom to arrive, leave, dwell, and hunt in the vale as she pleases, unless or until a subsequent royal decree deems otherwise. I think Athlan was aiming to protect his lands and kin by surrounding them with a Harper training facility, if anything happened to him."

"You think he knew he was going to die soon," Vangerdahast asked, "and specifically how, or at whose hand?"

"It's impossible to say. It feels like he was just being cautious—unusually cautious, for one so young."

"Indeed," the royal magician agreed. "As for Storm—watch her. There's not a lot any of us can do to stop her. Just be polite to her, and watch."

"But what if she's our murderer?"

"Why would she slaughter some back-country noble in another land? Use your head, man—if Storm took any interest in Summerstar at all, it's because he was mixed up in something the Harpers didn't approve of . . . slaving, dealing with the Zhentarim, or the like. All the more reason to be wary. Doesn't this Firefall Keep have a haunted quarter, or something?"

"A 'Haunted Tower,' Lord," Broglan replied.

"And what better way for someone at the keep to hide—or explain away—funny goings-on? 'You didn't really see that—it was ghosts!' "

"I see where you're leading, Lord. It could be someone striking out against Lord Athlan because he uncovered the secret, or threatened to."

"Exactly. And if Storm is a danger, get away from there and get word to me, above all else! That spell-reflection amulet I gave you ought to protect you against at least one attack, if she offers you violence. If that happens—don't waste your chance to flee, even if means abandoning the others, or a pretty young lady of the realm, or all the Summerstars and their horses and servants too! Got it?"

"I understand, Lord—and I thank you."

"Speak to me whenever you feel the need," Vangerdahast said briskly. The stone crackled once and started to sink toward the cushion. Broglan sat back wearily and watched it fall.

Encouraging words, but no aid. He was on his own, at least for now. How many more deaths would it take, how many more war wizards would die before the royal magician sent serious aid? And would that aid, if it did ever come, reach Firefall Keep in time?

Broglan rubbed at his eyes. He did not see the darkness that shifted in one of the shadows beyond the wards to slink away to the next shadow. One of the wards flared for an instant, as if powerful magic had been used nearby, but Broglan did not see that soundless flash, or its cause.

Sometimes mighty mages are just as tired and careless as the rest of us.

* * * * *

"My thanks for your work in getting to me so quickly," the Bard of Shadowdale said, turning in her saddle and slowing her mount to lay a hand on Vrespon's knee, "but I must leave you here."

"Leave me?" the Harper in worn leathers asked warily, looking around at the desolate, rolling wilderness. "Here?"

"Just ahead—at the top of this hill."

"I wondered why we were riding up rather than just going around," the Harper muttered, the lift of his voice making his words a question.

Storm tossed silver hair out of her eyes and gave him a level look. "If I am to do any good at Firefall Keep at all, I must get there at once—or at least, far sooner than they expect me. You half-killed your horse getting to me as swiftly as you did. I want you to rest her on the way back. Ride mine. Consider it yours now." She lifted one leg, put both hands on her saddle, and propelled herself a good dozen feet off to one side, to land crouched and facing him. The horse continued its patient walk up the grassy hill.

"You're going to *walk* to Firefall Keep?" Vrespon protested. "Dressed like that?"

Storm chuckled. "No, I'm going to gate there—and what's wrong with what I'm wearing, anyway?" She put hands to hips and tossed her head in mock indignation. Gods, but this lad *was* young. Right now, his eyes were shining in delight. He mustn't get many chances to do anything exciting, or be a part of any adventures. Ah, well—time to give him something to remember. Inspiring the young is part of the Way of the Harp, after all.

She strode on up the hill, still wearing her floppy old boots. She'd added torn and dirty trousers and a field smock that was more dirt and dung than garment. The rents they sported demonstrated repeatedly that she had nothing on underneath . . . and Storm hadn't even brought a dagger, let alone a purse or even a pouch to hold a meal or gear. Though she hadn't given it an order or even a glance, her horse trotted after her like a large and contented dog.

They reached the crest of the hill together, and Vrespon gaped in surprise. The little bowl that dimpled the hilltop wasn't visible from below—nor the small ring of standing stones that filled it. The ancient, moss-covered sentinels of craggy, fissured dark rock reached to the sky like the fingers of some long-forgotten, half-buried god. They stood in a tight circle, enclosing nothing.

Storm strode toward them without hesitation. "I take it you didn't know these were here?"

"No," said Vrespon, still looking amazed.

"And I take it you'd like to be back in Hillmarch as soon as you can, without a long ride through or around the mountains, entertaining bandits along the way?"

"Y-Yes," Vrespon replied warily.

"Then get down from that saddle and hold your horse quiet," the lady of the Harp told him, and tore a long strip from her trousers. Stuffing that scrap of fabric into one of her boots, she calmly took off the rest of her filthy clothing and tossed the smock to him. "Cover the horse's head with it," she directed. "They hate this, and always bolt if they see that instant of falling, amid the stars."

"What instant of . . . falling?" the Harper messenger asked.

Storm whipped what was left of her trousers around the head of her mount, and led it ahead into the stones. "Come and see," she called back to him, and when he hesitated, beckoned in the sultry fashion of a tavern dancer. This time, he did not look hastily away, but neither did he advance.

"What is this place?" Vrespon asked, bewildered— but he was asking the empty, wind-whipped air. The space between the stones was empty.

He swallowed once, took a last look around at this uninhabited corner of southeastern Daggerdale, with the Moonsea Ride a ribbon of mud in the distance. He squared his shoulders and led the horse steadily on into the stones . . . not hurrying, but not hesitating either.

* * * * *

Storm was suddenly elsewhere, and her feet were wet. The gelding snorted nervously and danced, its hooves splashing up water around her. The bard held its bridle firmly, patted its flank in reassurance, and led it out of the pool just below the well.

Two startled pairs of eyes looked up at her from the grassy bank. The man and maid lay in each other's arms, the remains of their luncheon and books of poetry strewn around them.

"Sorry," Storm told them gravely, and arched her eyebrows impishly. "Pray, continue."

She marched past them, flopping boots and snorting gelding and all, as the man hissed a startled oath and shot a look at the pool where they'd just—appeared, out of thin air!

As he stared, a man in worn leathers appeared. Another hooded horse splashed where, a moment before, there'd been nothing but roiling waters.

The man with the horse looked at him, and he stared back, his astonished lady-love still nestled against his shoulder. "What's going on?"

"Ask *her*," the newcomer protested, sounding almost hurt. He pointed ahead and down the hill, where the lady with the silver hair had gone. "Ask her!"

"Phernald," the maid quavered, suddenly finding her voice, "shouldn't we—?"

"No! Whatever it is, *no!*"

With those last, shouted words, the man was on his feet and sprinting for the safety of the trees. He dragged his lady with him, heedless of the fate of her finest gown as he hauled her through brambles. Poetry, wine, and all lay forgotten behind them.

"Oh, Phernald!" she wailed as they disappeared.

Vrespon shook his head, hauled the smock off his mare's eyes, mounted, and urged her into a trot to catch up with the Bard of Shadowdale.

When he reached Storm, he said almost accusingly, "You scared the wine right out of those two, you know!"

She was thoughtfully draping around herself the woefully inadequate strip of material she'd stuffed into her boot earlier. Perhaps, Vrespon thought, all senior Harpers were crazy.

This one certainly seemed to be. She turned and smiled at him. "I did apologize," she said, "and they'd finished their meal but not gotten beyond whisperings, if you know what I mean. . . . There's no harm done. They've just enjoyed an invigorating race through the forest, that's all!"

The Harper stared at her for a moment longer, and then burst into shouts of astonished laughter. Both horses snorted and shifted, and Storm told him severely, "Stop that—you're frightening the horses."

"And I suppose you're through frightening *me?*" Vrespon demanded in mock exasperation.

Storm clapped him on the shoulder. "*That's* the spirit," she said. "Now you know how to cross the Thunder Peaks from east to west, from the Farlight Stones to Muskrin's Well, here. It doesn't work in the other direction. Don't forget, now."

Vrespon shook his head. "Muskrin's Well . . . I must be a little north of . . . let's see. . . ."

Storm took him by one ear, swung him close, and kissed him. "It's been a joy," she said lightly, "but I must go. Take Lazytail, here." She steered the gelding's bridle into his hands and walked away.

Vrespon stared at her. "You're going to Firefall Keep like *that?*"

Storm frowned. "Of course not. I'm a *lady.*" She snapped her fingers, muttered something—and the tattered strip of cloth draped about her suntanned skin became a high-bosomed, filigreed glossy court gown, pleated and slit, with flaring sleeves and lace panels. She struck a pose, spreading silken-gloved hands to show off her finery. "Like it?"

Vrespon's jaw dropped. After a moment of making inarticulate sounds, he closed it firmly again, and nodded. In truth, he'd never seen so expensive, elegant, and, well, *beautiful* a gown. The wild woman who'd ridden with him was suddenly every curving inch a Cormyrean lady of stunning beauty and monstrous wealth.

He was still nodding when Storm gave him a cheery wave and vanished again.

* * * * *

Even the Chosen of Mystra have limitations. Of the Seven Sisters, Storm outstripped only Dove in her mastery of magic. There would be no more teleporting until she got some time to study—and, oh, yes: something to study with. She glanced around to be sure that she was unobserved, murmured an incantation, and moved one hand in a sweeping, circular gesture of beckoning.

Obediently a bulging strong chest burst into being in midair, floating in front of her. A moment later, the strain of overloading popped its lid open, revealing satchels, duffels, coffers, and trunks within. Storm smiled and started around the rocky ridge where she'd arrived, with the luggage floating along behind her. If she'd remembered the place rightly, Firefall Keep should be just over this next rise.

The next few days were probably going to be full of the unpleasant tensions and bloody actions that adventurers call fun, once such doings are safely in the past. Storm smiled. Ah, well—it was what she was here for.

Beyond immunities most folk could only dream of, the Bard of Shadowdale had surprisingly few tricks left. Depending on her wits and strong arms had always been her way, rather than spending long years in dusty towers learning spells for everything. Some folk thought the Seven Sisters no more than a pack of deceitful manipulators. Such a view was closer to the truth than the idea that they were nascent goddesses, transforming the Realms around them at will.

This little business of uncovering a murderer or two, for instance. Contrary to popular belief, the bold and brave Storm Silverhand couldn't call on Mystra directly to find out things; that had always been one of the Forbidden Things. Moreover, since the ascension of the young mortal Midnight to the Mantle of Mystra, the Lady of Mysteries really didn't know much more than her Chosen. She was still learning how to use the powers available to her . . . a process that would probably continue until long after her present Chosen were dust and fading memories. So this wayward bard was going to have to do her own detecting.

At a gentle stroll, Storm came over that last rise. A broad and pleasant smile filled her face. The keep rose dark and imposing ahead of her, more a border castle than a country manor. There were plenty of armed and watchful men on the walls and at the gates.

Storm walked on until the walls loomed up over her. She fully expected the keep to be one vast, patient trap, with the murderer waiting for her—as well as a reception committee of suspicious, resentful Cormyrean nobles.

The Purple Dragons at the portcullis of the gate tower could see her face clearly now. They were studying her closely, shifting their halberds to the ready and taking paces to one side to get clearer looks at the luggage floating serenely along behind her. She neared them. Two moved to either side of her, halberd points held respectfully down—but ready. Two more barred her way, and in front of them stepped their swordcaptain.

"Halt, lady traveler. You are come to Firefall Keep, a house in some present turmoil. We are commanded in the king's name to keep its gate closed to the uninvited. Surrender to us your name, I pray."

Storm gave the officer a smile that made his eyes melt above the bristling mustache that hid the rest of his face. "I am Storm Silverhand, the Bard of Shadowdale."

The man gave her a quick bow and trotted away, into the keep, leaving her to stand in the hot sun. The two guards who'd stood like a wall behind him stepped forward in unison, forming an unbroken wall of armored flesh to block her advance.

Storm lounged back, sitting on empty air as if it were a comfortable throne. She looked around at the warriors sweating in their armor and scrutinized each one in frank admiration. The guards shifted uncomfortably from foot to foot, unaccustomed to such boldness. They glanced sidelong at her beauty. This one seemed every inch the high court lady, outstripping even the Dowager Lady Pheirauze in elegance, and far outdazzling her in beauty.

Storm assumed a more comfortable position on empty air and started to sing—a sad ballad. The song told of a soldier who rode into battle, knowing his love, from whom he'd been parted for a long year of fighting, had gone into the arms of another man. Her voice rose, rich and enchanting. Though the guards coughed and tossed their heads and pretended not to be caring or even really listening, they leaned forward to hear better, and broke off all of their muttered, side-of-the-mouth comments about her.

When she swung into the sequel, tears began to appear in certain eyes. She sang of the dead soldier's ghost coming into the garden of his former love, where she sat sadly with her new babe, the father having abandoned her. When she came to the soft, almost whispered passages where the spectral soldier pledged to watch over and guard the child as it grew up to be the son that should have been his, some of the men were weeping openly, tears running down their faces and their shoulders shaking.

"Bewitching my men, lady?" The swordcaptain's tone was not hostile, but it was loud enough to cleave through her singing and jolt the armsmen back to the here and now. They stared at her almost resentfully, but Storm sent each of them a personal smile and a silently mouthed thank you.

The officer added gravely, "You are expected, lady, and I am instructed by the Dowager Lady Pheirauze Summerstar to bid you fair welcome, so long as you keep the peace of this house. Pray, pass within."

As he escorted her—and her floating luggage—through the echoing gate tower and into the sun-drenched courtyard beyond, Storm saw what she'd been expecting. The wait had been used to assemble a small but stiffly resentful group of splendidly dressed Summerstars. The war wizards there gave her steadily hostile looks. The folk in livery blinked in awe. At the head of these servants stood the seneschal, who gave her a low bow and said, "Be welcome in Firefall Keep, Lady Silverhand. May I present the Dowager Lady Pheirauze Summerstar?"

A strikingly beautiful lady who'd seen a few more than sixty winters glided forward in an exquisite gown of mauve silk. The puffed sleeves and shoulders made her seem tall and imposing—every bit as menacing as the hulking guards at the gate. She extended her hand for Storm to kneel and kiss, as an inferior.

Storm took it and her forearm and shook heartily, as if the dowager lady were a fellow warrior at a camp-fire. "Well met, Pheirauze," she said cheerfully. "You've certainly turned out splendidly from the perky little miss I remember!"

Someone in the gathered Summerstars snorted, and Pheirauze whirled around, but could not discover the culprit. She turned back to Storm with menacing slowness, and said carefully, "I'm glad to hear I've fulfilled *your* expectations. I'm gratified you came so quickly to share in our bereavement. My grandson would have made you most welcome. You are most timely come; a feast is just being set in the great hall. Will you dine with us, *great* lady?"

"With a right goodwill," Storm said heartily, ignoring all the cutting barbs and insults she'd just been handed. She swept around the dowager lady, sliding out her arm as she did so to catch the crook of Pheirauze's arm and jerk her around. They ended up walking together, hip to hip. Storm set a brisk pace across the courtyard. The tall, silver-haired vision in high court dress led the shorter, older lady in mauve, who trotted grimly to keep up. "What's for dinner?"

Someone among the Summerstars chuckled—or was it a giggle? As the two grand ladies entered the keep, Pheirauze's coldly furious face glared back over her shoulder, seeking a villain. It was becoming a popular occupation in Firefall Keep, it seemed.

Four

FEAST AND FOLLY

Candlelight glimmered from end to end of the great hall of Firefall Keep. The air was sharp with the smoke rising from two lines of candle-wheels, which hung above the tables on long, dusty chains. The flickering light danced on dozens of shields, halberds, and suits of armor along the walls, but the loftiest reaches of the hall, above the balconies and minstrels' galleries, were as dark as the night sky. A long table ran down one side of the vast chamber, providing the softly scurrying servants a sideboard to hold steaming covered platters and frosty bottles from the cellars.

The two main tables stood at the midpoint of the hall, well removed from the brightly lit daises at either end. The tables formed a huge V-shape, with chairs along only their outer sides. The two open ends reached toward the long sideboard, outlining an area where dancers might dance, jugglers juggle, players act, and minstrels play.

There was no one in that open space tonight. It didn't take Storm long to figure out why: *she* was this night's entertainment. Extra candles had been set in man-high candelabra behind her seat, halfway down one wing of one table; the only other well-lit spot was at the meeting of the two wings, where the two dowager ladies of the Summerstars, mother and daughter, sat facing each other.

The nobles who called Firefall Keep home were all gathered here this night, sitting along both wings of the high table. One wing began with the Dowager Lady Zarova, mother to Athlan, known as a woman of serene silence in court gossip—and no doubt cowed into her present timid state by the older dowager lady, Pheirauze. Beside Zarova sat her daughter, now heir of the house, and from her the seats of the lesser Summerstar kindred ran out to where the seneschal sat, with Storm on his right, and only a few ladies-in-waiting and scribes beyond her.

Storm looked again at Shayna. The young Lady Summerstar was truly as beautiful as folk in Cormyr said: slim, graceful, and by the looks of things a trifle shy—not overproud. Waves of glossy chestnut hair tumbled over delicate shoulders. Her skin was almost white, her eyes large and liquid green. A stunning beauty indeed.

As she gazed at the new Summerstar heiress, Storm felt the weight of cold, hostile eyes upon her. She looked in their direction. Across from Zarova sat Pheirauze. She was flanked by a slimly handsome young nobleman, who sat shoulder to shoulder with a lionlike, bearded rogue of a man of about the same age as the dowager lady. His eyes, as they met hers, were both hot with invitation . . . and cold with dislike.

Storm gave him a slight smile and glanced farther down that table. Beside the sneering sophisticate sat a pair of fearsome old battle-axes. In the candlelight, their jewels glittered like falls of frozen water. The old ladies fixed Storm with identical toadlike glares of hauteur and hatred. The bard gave them both broad, pleasant smiles, and felt a touch of inner amusement as they stiffened in mortification. These two must be the maiden aunts. Beyond them, a handful of kindred gave way to a solid row of war wizards. They faced Storm watchfully—no doubt ready to hurl spells at the well-lit target if she did anything threatening. Storm smiled inwardly. It was going to be one of *those* even-feasts.

"Have you . . . dined in polite society often, Lady Bard?" asked Uncle Erlandar, curly bearded and suave. His large emerald earrings flashed as they dangled over his steaming soup. His tone made the question a biting insult.

"Many a time, Lord Erlandar," she replied sweetly, "from the table of divine Mystra herself to the breakfast-table of His Majesty, King Azoun. Sometimes, I've even enjoyed myself." She sipped at her peppery soup and thought it was a pity some enthusiast had ruined the subtle flavors of mingled fowl and turtle with the burning buzz of an overly lavish poison. *Someone* was going to be disappointed when she didn't fall on her face into the soup . . . and she'd lay money it was someone sitting at this table right now.

"I'm surprised," Erlandar said, his voice dripping false honey, "that a minstrel from such a backwater as Shadowdale has had so many opportunities to pluck strings in exalted surroundings . . . but of course, one must never cast aspersions on the veracity of a lady's claims—no matter how lowborn the lady."

"She *is* from the Dales, dear," Dowager Lady Pheirauze said with bright concern. "Folk of such . . . ah, unfortunate backgrounds may not realize the importance we place on honesty here in Cormyr."

Storm chuckled as deeply and heartily as any man,

and told her goblet, "Yes—Azoun has spoken to me on
several occasions of how much he values the all-too-
rare commodity of loyalty and honesty among his
nobles." She lifted her eyes to regard the diners across
from her, and saw glittering amusement in the eyes of
several carefully stone-faced war wizards. Cold glares
awaited to the left, so she looked instead down her own
table. The Lady Shayna was looking down at her plate
as she ate, her face crimson . . . and it was not Storm's
replies that were embarrassing her.

Erlandar thought he'd espied an opening in Storm's
observation, however, and was roaring, "Do you *dare*
insult the collective honor of the entire nobility of
Cormyr, Lady—ah, whatever your name is? Do you
actually have the gall to hold yourself in judgment of
all the Forest Kingdom?" His words were echoed by
hisses of contempt from the two maiden aunts,
Margort and Nalanna Summerstar. "By the gods, you
lowborn women push us far, sheltered in your immu-
nity from challenges of honor by the sword!"

Storm laughed easily. "Do I understand you correct-
ly, Erlandar Summerstar? Are you . . . challenging
me?"

"Bah!" he snarled, flicking his fingers in her direction. "I don't make war on women!"

"Ah," Storm informed her goblet, "but I've heard
from many lasses in Suzail that you *do*—and very
energetically, at that!"

Down the row of war wizards, someone sputtered as
mirth overmastered him. The Dowager Lady
Pheirauze immediately leaned forward to try to see
who it was, and said sharply, "Oh, Erlandar, don't be
tiresome. She only makes you seem ridiculous; waste
no more words on coarse country wenches."

A momentary silence followed these words. Another
male voice drawled into it. "There is something I'd like to
know, Lady Silverhand—and I mean no impertinence."

The speaker was the young and handsome
Summerstar male who sat between Pheirauze and
Erlandar. This would have to be Thalance, the cousin
of Shayna . . . and, of course, to the dead Athlan.

"Yes, Sir Thalance?" Storm asked, her words a
warm, musical invitation.

"I've heard many legends about you and your sisters. Is it true that you're hundreds of years old, and
serve the goddess Mystra?"

"Yes, to both of your queries," Storm replied, setting
down her empty sipping-bowl of soup.

"So you really have gone all over the Realms and
been at many important battles and known famous
folk and . . . all?"

"Yes," Storm said simply.

"Why is it, then, that you aren't ruling a realm
somewhere? Why do you live on a farm and go about
harping to earn a few coppers now and again? And
why do the Harpers you belong to meddle in all sorts
of lands, and not rule openly?"

"Good questions, all," Storm told him, and then
counted off her replies on her fingers. "I don't want to
rule anyone, so I don't. I do love growing things and
being able to walk among forests and gardens, so I do.
I love music, and meeting people, so I harp. And the
Harpers want to help people and fight evil by turning
out secrets before they become bigger, darker things—
they don't want to rule, either, and so don't."

"I've heard that the Harpers serve a dark and evil
god," Erlandar cut in, "and that you and your sisters
are immortal because you drink the blood of men you
entice." His eyes were dark with anger.

"My, people do say a lot of silly things, don't they?"
Storm replied lightly. "I often hear that the nobles of
Cormyr summon fiends to build their castles, and breed
slaves until the offspring look to make promising
heirs—and that King Azoun sleeps with every woman

over the age of sixteen between Baldur's Gate and
Telflamm . . . but of course such tales are ridiculous."

More than a few eyes flickered along the tables;
Azoun's courting was a matter of vivid legend in the
realm.

Erlandar half-rose in his seat, glaring in challenge
across the open space, and said, "*Now* you insult our
king! Truly, wench, you go too far!"

Storm saw the seneschal, the Lady Shayna, and one
of the war wizards wince at the word *wench*. Storm
kept her easy smile and said, "Is it to be a duel
between us, then, Uncle? Wet trout in the pigs' mud-
wallow, at dawn?"

"I'm not your uncle," Erlandar snapped, "and I don't
duel women or anyone of lesser rank. Is that the only
response you know when someone objects to your wild
words?"

Storm shrugged, spreading her hands. Her goblet
flashed in the firelight. "Perhaps I misjudge you, Lord
Summerstar," she said mildly. "I assumed it was the
only response you'd understand."

Someone muttered something grimly affirmative
under his breath, somewhere along the tables. This
time, both Erlandar and the Lady Pheirauze leaned
and craned their necks like gawking youths in an
attempt to discover the speaker. Shayna Summerstar
and her mother drained their goblets in unison, and
rang forks against the bases of them to summon
refills. At the same time, steaming platters of roast
boar were set on the tables. Storm appreciatively
sniffed, and helped herself heartily.

As forks flashed into boar, Broglan Sarmyn of the
war wizards cut into the silence with a hearty sally.
"Pray, forgive me, Lady Silverhand, if this is a question
one does not ask, but why were you 'Chosen' by the
Divine Mother of Magic as one of her mortal servants?
You're not—so far as we know—of the first rank of

archmages, or even particularly powerful in magic."

Storm raised an eyebrow. "There is never a crime in asking such things . . . but seldom a clear response, either. I truly don't know how much I should reveal of the nature of the Chosen. Why don't you offer a prayer to the divine lady I serve and we both—I presume—worship, and see what she makes clear unto you?"

"Of course," Broglan said politely, unsurprised. "I shall do so later this night." He lapsed into silence with a satisfied air, his purpose accomplished. As they'd spoken, the Lady Pheirauze had leaned over to hiss something in Erlandar's ear—something about adopting a less confrontational manner.

Erlandar leaned forward, raised his glass to Storm to get her attention, and said in coldly polite tones, "I'd forgotten that as a guest here, you may be unfamiliar with your surroundings. You've probably wondered where the name 'Firefall Keep' came from, for example . . ."

Storm, who knew very well how the keep had won its curious name, said nothing, but favored Erlandar with an encouraging, wordless smile.

"Well, this great fortress we Summerstars call home is named for the vale it stands in—but the vale got its name centuries ago, when our house was founded. A nest of red dragons laired high in the nearby peaks—wyrms so fierce and hungry that elves dared not dwell in the vale, despite whatever bargain had been struck between the old Purple Dragon and the elven Lord of Scepters."

Erlandar's voice rose in volume and passion as he chanted the well-known sentences that followed—and he rose with it, standing with arms spread. He stared almost defiantly across the table at Storm. "Dragons that suffered no elf to stride uneaten in the vale welcomed men even less—or perhaps, welcomed them into their gullets even more. When the founder of our house, Glothgam Summerstar, led his men into the vale, he won past repeated swooping attacks. In time, the dragons retreated to their caves high in Mount Glendaborr—caves you can still see today, if you don't mind facing the ghosts of dragons! There, they worked a mighty magic."

Erlandar leaned forward, fixing his eyes on Storm as if his very glare could slay her. "Then, as now, Turnwyrm Brook flowed down the heart of the vale to join the Immerflow, and Glothgam was camped beside it. As he and his men were watering their horses and bathing, the brook's flowing waters became a roaring river of flame! Many died screaming in this Firefall, but Glothgam did not quail. The wyrms swept down from on high to see what death they'd wrought—and he called on the powers of the enchanted blade he bore, the Sword of the Summer Winds, and soared aloft to meet them, slaying three before the others fled. 'Twould make a handsome ballad, Harper!"

Storm nodded. "It has."

"What?" Erlandar cried in astonishment. "So why've I not heard of such a song?"

"The song centers on the sword, not on Glothgam," Storm said quietly, "and speaks of the greatness the blade could bring Cormyr. Years after minstrels first sang the song, rebels borrowed its words so they could recognize each other at midnight meetings. When the rebellion failed, the king of the time outlawed the ballad—and the Summerstars of the day were only too happy: they'd grown very tired of visiting thieves tearing down every third panel and tapestry in the keep, looking for the lost sword."

"That sword," Erlandar snarled, "is indeed rumored to still lie hidden somewhere in this keep. Do the Harpers know anything of its whereabouts?"

Storm shook her head, trying hard not to yawn. There were *so* many tales of lost enchanted blades that would save the world—or make the finder ruler of some handsome part of it—if they could only be found. "I'm afraid not, Lord Summerstar . . . but I do thank you for Glothgam's tale, simply but strongly told." She smiled. "Would you like to become a minstrel?"

Erlandar scowled. "No," he said, obviously biting back other words that had sprung to his mind. He sat down again, shoved aside a platter of boar that had grown cold, and angrily signaled a servant to bring him fresh meat and more wine.

Silence followed Erlandar's last angry bark. Servants scurried, bringing out bowls of green mint-water and table fountains of sweet syrups.

The seneschal and the worried-looking Broglan Sarmyn simultaneously began speaking, trying to carry the conversation brightly onward. They spoke as one, deferred to each other uncomfortably, and tried again, launching into a discussion of the last great royal hunt. It had left from the vale to try to reach Mount Glendaborr. En route, many monsters had been slain. The true nature of the 'ghost dragons' that drifted half-seen around the nearby mountains was obviously a matter of hot local controversy, and an argument erupted that almost everyone except Storm and the senior Summerstars joined.

The Bard of Shadowdale settled into carefully watching other diners, looking for the slight gestures of a stealthily cast spell or the shifting of muscles that might herald the hurling of a blade. She was paying particular care to the coldly smiling mask that was the face of the Dowager Lady Pheirauze. The matriarch was obviously aware of her scrutiny, and was letting nothing slip—if anything ever did.

Storm did, however, notice when Thalance slowly and quietly drew his chair back, to sit sipping wine and listening . . . and a little later, silently set down his glass and slipped away.

The seneschal obviously thought the debate about the ghost dragons was far too familiar ground to still hold any interest. He turned to Storm to remark quietly, "I must leave briefly to attend my duties, Lady Silverhand—but before I go, I think it best to tell you just a little more about the Summerstars than you've yet been privy to. I'd like to avoid armed battle here in the keep between you and any of them, if at all possible."

"I, too," Storm murmured.

Renglar Baerest smiled tightly, and said, "Know, then: the Lady Pheirauze has never remarried, but persistent rumors have linked her to no less than three generations of the Illance noble line. I'd not speak disparagingly of that family—nor allude to any closeness between it and herself—if I were you."

He inclined his head toward another Summerstar. "You have already measured Erlandar; be warned that he likes to crush women or bed them, and will not rest, now, until he's served you with one fate or the other. We see little of Thalance—he's faded away on us again now, I see—but I'm told the local loose ladies and young drinkers do."

He sighed, and added more quietly, his voice just barely above a whisper, "The Lady Zarova has tried to take her own life more than once, when her mother-in-law was particularly . . . difficult. Before wedding Pyramus, she was of the noble house of Battlestar, who dwell on the West Shore, not far outside Suzail. She'll be intensely uncomfortable if you ask her anything in front of Pheirauze or Erlandar."

The seneschal glanced down the table at the two senior Summerstar nobles as he named them, and noticed the eyes of the elder dowager lady were cold, hard as daggers, and fixed firmly on him.

With a smile, he turned back to Storm and said, a trifle more loudly, "An unexpected pleasure to meet a fellow gardener; we must talk again. I've heard how lush you and your neighbors keep Shadowdale."

"And I'm interested in the herb-plantings I saw on my way in," Storm replied promptly. "Yes, let's trade secrets . . . and seeds." They exchanged nods of agreement, and the seneschal rose, bowed, and left the hall. The eyes of the Dowager Lady Pheirauze followed his every step—and when he was gone, turned swiftly back to meet those of Storm, who had been watching her.

Storm raised her goblet to Pheirauze in salute, added a merry smile and a nod. Then she glanced toward the war wizards. They seemed to have forgotten their guest for the moment. With heat and scornful disputation, they discussed the legendary and recent hauntings of Firefall Keep.

"Any fool—save perhaps yourself, Hundarr—knows phantoms can't carry or disturb swords and coins and such! If things were stolen or shifted about, we're talking some other sort of undead!"

"Well, Sir Exalted Expert, what sort?"

"Gods take you, Hund—"

"Goodsirs!" Erlandar said firmly. "Entertaining though this may be—and I'm not one to miss a chance to hear a mage make a fool of himself—I've heard about enough nonsense for one night! I doubt our guest appreciates knowing what fearsome thing lurks in the Haunted Tower! It's enough to know that something fell and sinister is there—something that slew young Athlan, pride of the Summerstars. Keeping out of the Haunted Tower is the best policy for us all to follow." He swung his head to deliver a cold, heavy glare across the table, and added, "Even clever and beautiful Harpers."

Storm laughed lightly. "Another of your challenges, Lord Summerstar? They come so thick and fast—almost like the courting comments of an ardent man!"

Erlandar Summerstar grinned slowly. "Aye, so they

do . . . strange the similarities, eh?"

Storm smiled back at him, but let her eyes show her true feelings. If she'd thought to leave just a little of that soup, she could have kissed the man and passed the poison on to him. . . .

Erlandar winked at her, and then leered again. No, Storm thought, poison was too gentle. It had to be a sword—deftly wielded, to make his end slow and painful. . . .

Erlandar winked again. Well, Storm thought, painful at any rate. . . .

* * * * *

Renglar Baerest, seneschal of Firefall Keep, stood in the courtyard of the fortress he had come to love, facing a silently floating strongchest. It belonged to a woman who might well be able to shatter the keep and hurl it down stone by stone until only windblown dust was left. Seneschal or not, he might well be making a terrible mistake—but he had to be sure.

Swallowing, Renglar took a step forward and laid a firm hand on the side of the chest. It promptly and silently sank to a gentle grounding on the cobbles, and opened itself. The seneschal stared down at the satchels, coffers, duffels, and trunks crammed into it. He sighed and began carefully lifting them out and placing them on the blanket-padded service carts he'd brought. It was a long way to the quarters he'd chosen for the most distinguished—and dangerous—guest to visit the keep during his tenure, but this was one job he was going to do alone.

He'd have insisted on that even if any of the servants *had* dared to help him.

* * * * *

"We call it brittle tart," Lady Margort Summerstar said stiffly. "And serve it with dry wine at the end of most high meals." She paused for a moment, and then asked coldly, "You do have dessert in—oh, wherever is it again, dear?"

"Shadowdale," her sister said with a sneer, rubies glittering as she leaned sideways to speak by Margort's ear.

"Ah, yes, *thank* you, Nalanna," Margort continued. "You *do* have desserts in Shadowdale, don't you?"

"Once or twice a year," Storm said solemnly, "when dragging the plows around all day and whipping ourselves to go faster leaves us enough energy to eat an extra course. Then we enjoy crushed apples, or sometimes just handfuls of sugar. We're too poor and backward to have oxen, you see."

"Ah," the Lady Nalanna Summerstar said in tones of satisfaction. "I thought so."

"Lady Silverhand," the Dowager Lady Pheirauze said coldly, "stop toying with my kinswomen. I expect better behavior from my guests."

Storm raised her brows as she set the last bones of her roast boar aside. It had been delicious—poisoned again, but delicious. "They do seem to keep disappointing you, though, don't they?"

"We do not," Pheirauze observed frostily, "have many guests here in the vale."

"Aye," Storm Silverhand replied, tossing a stray lock of long silver hair back over her right shoulder to join the rest of the glossy flow there, "that I can well believe."

One of the war wizards snickered, and Pheirauze stiffened. Only pride kept her from looking away from Storm's steady gaze. An instant later, anger broke that reserve, and the dowager lady's head snapped around. By then, though, the mage had recovered his control, and all the war wizards wore frowningly thoughtful faces.

Damn them, Pheirauze thought. Just once, she'd like to wipe that smug standing-above-everyone-but-caring-about-the-realm worldly confidence off their faces. Just once. She wondered what it would take. . . .

* * * * *

Renglar Baerest, seneschal of Firefall Keep, puffed one last time into the room with the soft gray tapestries. Lady Maerla's Room, it was—the most remote and smallest of the guest apartments, and hard by the dusty passages that led into the Haunted Tower. It was a fitting place for Lady Silverhand to sleep. Maerla had been a Harper and a quiet, strong-willed woman who'd dabbled in magic, the family history said. She was an adventuress who'd married a Summerstar out of love.

It was also said in the family that Maerla's room was haunted—more strongly than the entire Haunted Tower, if folk Maerla disapproved of tried to sleep in her bed. The seneschal thoughtfully regarded the soaring gray canopy of that central sleeping-place, bowed, and told the empty air around him, "Pray, excuse this intrusion, Lady Maerla. As seneschal of the keep, it is my paramount duty to see to the security of us all, so I must search the belongings of the lady who'll be sleeping here this night: Storm Silverhand, a Harper of some repute. Forgive me."

The silence was deafening. Renglar shrugged, bent over the largest trunk, and lifted its lid. Thankfully, the Lady Storm felt confident enough in her power not to bother with locks, and the old amulet he wore ought to ward off at least one spell trap. Its feeble powers might not protect against a second magic, though— which is why he was starting with the things least likely to be protected. An old, scratchy gray wool cloak covered everything. Renglar took careful note of the way it was folded, lifted it aside, and cautiously plucked out what lay beneath.

A belt bristling with sheathed daggers, several slim-heeled boots that a Purple Dragon would look ridiculous in . . . and a spare sword. Best leave that sheathed for now; it probably did bear magics. The next item glowed with faint enchantments even when closed and undisturbed. By its shape, the seneschal recognized the smooth wooden case as the home of a harp.

Well, of course. She was the Bard of Shadowdale. Renglar turned to the next trunk. It seemed to be full of tattered silk . . . well, no.

He held one garment up, frowned, turned it around—and swallowed. He let it fall onto the lid and plucked up the next one. And then the next. His frown deepened. These were not the sort of gauzy underthings respectable women wore.

His frown turned into a smile when he saw what lay at the bottom of the trunk, beneath thirty or more scarves, sashes, and silken nothings: a leather war harness. It was the plain, sturdy sort that a working soldier would wear, as slashed, mended, and sweat-stained as most. Renglar restored both trunks to the way they'd been and turned to nearest duffel.

Being a seneschal in Firefall Keep involved more than one man's share of odd tasks. Like this one: unwrapping a canvas bundle to reveal a garment that seemed to be made entirely of lengths of fine chain. He'd give a lot to know when she'd have occasion to wear a gown like *this*. . . .

No, he couldn't think of any prudent way to ask her. Renglar sighed, and reached deeper into the duffel.

Wait—what was *this*?

* * * * *

"Weather magic has always been a temptation," Storm told them, "but the teachings of Baerauble—if any of his own words have survived—should tell you why it must be avoided. Weather magic affects more than one's own land. Things can quickly escalate into wars that ruin realms and break the power of both combatants. I've seen it happen."

"Oh, of course," Hundarr Wolfwinter agreed derisively. "You've lived since before there were sunrises, and seen it all . . . of course. Still—"

He broke off, staring, even before Broglan Sarmyn could voice a rebuke. They all followed his gaze to the source of his amazement: a huge silver platter bristling with the slim spires of wine and liqueur bottles. The platter and its burden were both splendid, but hardly unusual at a feast such as this. What was unusual was that it was drifting slowly across the empty space between the tables, approaching the senior Summerstars.

"Pah!" Erlandar half-rose, his hand going to the dagger at his belt. "Wizards' tricks!"

"But no," Broglan protested. "None of us has—"

"Ah," Storm said firmly, "but one of us has."

She raised her eyes to look steadily at one of the war wizards and said softly, "Clever, Corathar Abaddarh. A deft little spell that very few would notice you casting . . . but is such a working prudent, given the situation here? The talk of hauntings, and the bereavement of the Summerstars? The danger we may all face?"

The platter crashed to the floor in a thunderous shattering of glass. "I'm not a child, lady, to be told off so," Corathar snarled, eyes flaming, "and I'll thank you to—"

His face paled, and he fell silent. The platter trembled, rose slowly, and proceeded on its interrupted journey. The shattered bottles rattled nervously atop the silver.

"Enough!" Storm said sharply. "Consider us all impressed by your little cantrip, and end your magic at once!"

"I'm . . . I'm not, now . . ." Corathar stammered, swallowed, and then managed to add, "lady, this is not my doing!"

Storm looked along the row of war wizards, and then at the Summerstars. Frowning perplexity showed among the former, and growing, suspicious fear filled the eyes of the latter. Even Pheirauze looked uneasy. "Stop it," Storm said firmly, "whoever is working this!"

The platter continued on its unhurried, drifting way. Storm sighed and vaulted the table in a swirl of silver hair, reaching out both hands to grasp the platter with its cargo of toppled and shattered glass.

She murmured the words that should have spun away all magic as her hands closed on the chased and fluted silver handles. Instead of the peaceful silence that should have followed, the world exploded in roaring flames.

White-hot and hungry they howled. Fire raced up from the floor to scorch the lofty beams of the feast hall. It rushed out of empty air and entirely hid the lady bard from view.

Wizards gasped curses and lady servants screamed as the flames roared on. In the rafters, a banner burned through and fluttered down in a lazy ribbon of sparks. Still the flames roared on, until Shayna was sobbing and even Erlandar was on his feet staring up at the ceiling of the hall and cursing in fear—fear that the whole roof would come crashing down on them.

Then, as suddenly as they had come, the flames were gone. They left behind cracking tiles, groaning stones, and the reek of burnt wood and human hair. The diners all stared at the thing of tottering bones and ashes that should have held a melted platter—and gasped in unison.

Droplets of silver and glass lay like glistening rain on the blackened and shattered tiles, yes. But standing at their heart was a faintly smiling, weary-eyed woman. Her silver hair was curling and writhing lazily around her, a forest of roused snakes. The ends of those silver tresses were blackened and shriveled, but Storm Silverhand was otherwise unharmed. They could see that clearly enough. Most of her clothing had gone with the vanished flames. Her gown was now no more than ashes and blackened tatters, clinging to limbs that seemed . . . unharmed!

The others stared at her. Storm returned their look, arms still spread to grasp a platter that no longer existed. She said mildly, "My roast boar was quite well cooked already, thank you."

Her eyes darted from diner to diner as she spoke, seeking traces of guilt or disappointment or baffled fury in their eyes . . . but she found only smirks or looks of horror on the female faces, and the beginnings of avid admiration from the males.

There were two exceptions. Broglan of the war wizards looked even more worried than usual—genuine concern, she judged. And the elderly steward of the hall was aghast. Black beard and mustache trembling in his haste, he swept a cloth off a bare section of the serving table, and hurried toward her, raising it like a shield.

Storm thanked him with a smile. He reached her, gabbled out mortified apologies—as if what had befallen her was his fault—and whipped the cloth around her as an improvised gown. What was his name, now? The seneschal had rattled it off, complete with a list of the battles the old man had fought in, in his days as a Purple Dragon . . . Ah, yes: Ilgreth. Ilgreth . . . Drimmer.

"My thanks for your swift-witted kindness," Storm told the old man, laying a gentle hand on his shoulder, "but I prefer garments a trifle less drafty. Perhaps you'll conduct me to my room?"

Drimmer nodded almost beseechingly. He waved at

her to accompany him, and then turned and scurried away. Storm followed, staring thoughtfully at his back. He'd flinched at her touch . . . but then, that was understandable when he'd just seen flames roaring up around her. Who knew what might have burst from her fingers?

A few paces away from the table she turned, favored all of the guests with a broad, easy smile, and said, "Save me some wine—I'll be back!"

Then she turned her back on them all, tore off the tablecloth and swung it over her shoulder like a shawl, and strode away in Ilgreth Drimmer's wake.

He hastened to one dais, turned at its doors, and gulped at her fashion rearrangement. "If you'll follow me, gracious lady," he said faintly, whirling back to face the door, "your chambers are this way. . . ."

The route he led her along was a long one, but Storm trailed him for only three passages and two rooms before she caught up with him, laid a firm hand on his shoulder, and said, "Catch your breath, good steward, and talk to me."

Ilgreth slid frightened eyes around to meet hers. With a puff of ash, a strip of blackened gown fell away from her shoulders. He quickly looked away again. "Talk? What about?"

"Lord Athlan's death—and anything untoward that's befallen since," Storm said crisply, ignoring the ongoing ruin of her gown. Another scrap drifted away from the still-sturdy cuff about her left wrist.

"I—I don't know where I stand, Lady," the steward replied frankly. "How far will what I tell you travel?"

"Do you mean, will I reveal that you told me things?" Storm asked, eye to eye. He nodded, and she said firmly, "Not at all. I heard nothing from you except: 'This room is yours, lady.' "

His face split in a sudden grin, and his eyes dipped involuntarily to survey her smooth curves—which made him blush and the smile hastily vanish again.

Storm laughed merrily and said, "Look all you want! *I'm* not ashamed of this body—but it still amazes me how many men are!"

That make him look quickly away again and sputter through his mustache, "Have done, *please,* lady. We're almost at a guard post."

Storm sighed, wove the tablecloth around herself, and assumed a stately stride at his heels. He slowed, matching her mood. They swept past the startled guards in silence. They were two rooms beyond, at the midpoint of a long hall lined with statues, when he spoke again.

"There have always been deaths in the keep," he muttered abruptly, so that Storm had to bend forward over his shoulder to hear. "Mainly among us—the servants, I mean—and always in the Haunted Tower. Warnings to us, to keep out. Once it was a chambermaid and a hostler who'd gone there together, if you take my meaning. They were found by the daily guard patrol, lying in each other's arms—headless."

He walked on a few more paces for emphasis before adding, "We never found the heads."

They passed through another door and turned left down the hall beyond. Drimmer looked cautiously up and down it before continuing. "Lord Summerstar was different—as was this last one. They were both found burned out inside, like something had sucked their innards away. Well, no; *burned* them out from within, more like. I saw ashes trail from the body when they laid my Lord Athlan on the table to be shrouded."

" 'This last one'—the Harper, you mean?"

The steward came to an abrupt halt. "Ah—no, lady . . . haven't they told you?"

Storm sighed. "Obviously not. Why don't you tell me, then?"

Ilgreth Drimmer nodded. "There's been a third gone,

just before your arrival, lady. The war wizards think you struck him down."

"Why?" Storm asked calmly.

The old steward's eyes flicked sideways to assure himself that she was as level-hearted as she sounded. She was. He replied, "A Harper pin was found on the body—and it was not the pin belonging to the dead Harper. I fear Sarmyn thought it was a boast from you."

"Whose body was this?"

"One of the war wizards who came here to learn who slew Lord Summerstar . . . Lhansig Dlaerlin."

"I've never heard that name," Storm said with a wrinkle of her brow. "What can you tell me about him?"

The steward shrugged. "I saw him only a handful of times, and briefly. A wizard who was always smiling . . . a sly one. 'Twouldn't surprise me if he knew more secrets than many folk wanted known."

Storm nodded, managing not to sigh. Everyone's favored foe. "And how was he found?"

"The man was struck down in a garderobe, after a feast," Drimmer said, "burned out, like the others."

"Nowhere near the Haunted Tower?"

"Nay, lady. Just outside the hall where you've been dining," the old steward said. He fumbled with his keys. "These chambers are yours, and I should tell you that the wizards've ordered a doorguard to stand right here as soon as you retire."

"To keep me from creeping around Firefall Keep in the dark hours," Storm murmured, "in case I should fall and hurt myself."

Ilgreth Drimmer's mouth twisted into a wry grin. "In a manner of speaking, lady, yes. I'll just light another lamp in here, and—"

He broke off with a queer, sobbing sort of gulp, and stood very still. Storm had to thrust him aside to see what he was staring at.

The center of the room held a fine, gray-cloaked bed whose backboard soared up into an overhead bunting. It faced the door through the open doors of a small antechamber. Her luggage, most of it opened, lay at the foot of the bed. In its midst sat the seneschal of Firefall Keep, waiting for them.

He would wait forever, now. Renglar Baerest sat atop the duffels in Storm's open strongchest, his booted legs spread. Between them his chest and gut had been torn open, clothes and all, to reveal a slumped chaos of entrails and gore in which a lone, delighted fly was buzzing. Over this carnage the seneschal grinned at them, two staring eyes fixed forever on the doorway where they stood.

Those eyes were the only scraps of familiarity left on a head that had been otherwise burnt away to a bare, charred skull. A fall of ash lay thick upon the shoulders of the corpse, and it wasn't hard to see where it had come from.

Drimmer made a few broken, whistling sounds, and Storm saw that his mouth was moving. He was trying to say something, but finding no words.

"A fourth death," she murmured to herself. "Cormyr used to be quieter than this."

The old steward started to tremble. Storm's arms went protectively around his shoulders. "He went in battle, Ilgreth," she told him gently, "as he would have wished."

The old man sobbed, trying to nod. Tears ran down his face as he turned to her, blindly took hold of two locks of her hair, and snarled, "He was my *last* friend, lady! The last man left who swung a sword with me for the realm! Oh, *gods look down!* May they give you the power to do what I beseech you to!"

"And what's that, friend?" Storm asked, cradling him to her breast as if he was a small child.

The old man raised blazing eyes to her, and hissed

through his tears, "Find the one who did this to Renglar! Find him—or it—and *tear them apart!* And if it takes my hand in aid, even if it costs my life, too—call for it!"

"Sir, I will do so," Storm told him, looking deeply into his eyes. *"This I swear."*

A flame of hope kindled in Drimmer's old eyes. "Gods bless you, lady," he whispered. "Gods bring you victory."

Storm looked at the seneschal's skull-smile and his fear-filled, staring eyes. She swung her gaze back to meet the steward's own. She managed a wan smile, and said, "They don't owe me a victory, Ilgreth. But they do owe one to four men no longer with us—and perhaps many more if the cause of all this isn't soon found and stopped."

As the words left her mouth, the seneschal's skull suddenly toppled from his shoulders, bounced once on his thigh, fell to the floor, and rolled to her feet.

As its dead eyes gazed up at them, Drimmer burst into fresh tears. Storm held him, and then, softly, lifted her voice in the first mournful cry of the "Soldier's Farewell."

At her feet, Renglar Baerest went on grinning.

Five

DEATH OLD AND NEW

"Legendary godservant, my left elbow!" Erlandar Summerstar snorted. *Elbow* was not the word he'd first thought of. "She's a saucy wench who wraps herself in a few protective spells and knows a few tricks."

"Good uncle," the Dowager Lady Zarova Summerstar said firmly, "can we speak of other things? Unwelcome a guest as she may be to some of us, my son's written wishes did bring her here. I am more shocked at what befell her than I am at the discovery that if her clothes burn away, she's naked. I trust none of these mages here would deal in such deadly magic—and yet who else could have done it?"

All of the diners stared at her; the younger dowager spoke so seldom that some of the servants in the hall had never before heard her voice.

Her daughter Shayna, heiress of the Summerstars, nodded. "I, too, would like to hear what the gentlemen

of the Sevensash have to say for themselves," she said
firmly. "Lady bard or no lady bard, flames nearly
brought down the roof of this hall, and I would know
why."

She turned her head, emerald eyes flashing, and
caught the frowning gaze of Broglan Sarmyn.
Pheirauze and Erlandar added the weight of their
regard, and Broglan suddenly found himself dancing
on the ends of six hard gazes, and finding them all too
much like daggers.

"I-It's no doing of any of us," the worried-looking
senior wizard said hastily, looking from one hostile
Summerstar to another. "We're just as . . . mystified as
any of you."

"Why?" Pheirauze said cuttingly. "We're not the
experts in magic here—you are. We've dined in this
hall for more nights than I can count, year after year,
never seeing flames roar up out of nowhere—until
now, when you are here: a row of war wizards, skilled
in battle magic. What else but your guilt am I—are
any of us—to conclude? I've half a mind to summon
that Purple Dragon commander here to send a complaint about you to the court, forthwith."

"Lady," came the deep voice of Ergluth
Rowanmantle from behind her, "I am here."

The diners turned in their chairs, startled.

"I don't recall summoning you," Pheirauze snapped
at him, nettled. "Why—?"

"Nevertheless," the eagle-eyed officer said flatly as
he strode forward, "I am here. My duty to the king
requires it of me. I bring a question: where is Thalance,
and when did he leave you?"

"Why?" the elder dowager lady almost snarled.
"What are you accusing him of?"

"Nothing, lady," the boldshield told her, towering
over her chair. "I need to know where he is, so that I
can protect him."

"Against what?" Erlandar asked, eyes narrowing.

"Against whomever—or whatever—murdered your seneschal in my bedchamber," Storm Silverhand replied, stepping out from behind the Purple Dragon. Instead of a gown, she wore a well-used leather war harness—armor that bristled with swords and daggers in plenty.

The steward of the feast hall quavered behind her for a moment, a neatly folded tablecloth shaking in his hands. He then scurried to the sideboard to serve sherries and wines to the assembled company.

Most of them looked like they needed such bracing refreshments. They stared at Storm's warrior garb, even more astonished than they had been after the flames.

"What?" Erlandar repeated, glaring at Storm in open-mouthed disbelief. "What're you playing at?"

"I'm not the one who's been playing at things around here, Lord Summerstar," Storm told him crisply. "Renglar Baerest is sitting on my luggage with his guts torn out of him—and his skull burned bare and empty. After what befell Athlan, is the word 'murdered' still unfamiliar to you?"

Shayna gave a little scream, and her face twisted. Her hands flew to her mouth. Down the line of pale war wizards, someone's face—Hundarr's, was it?—creased in revulsion. He gagged over his empty plate.

Ergluth Rowanmantle went to stand watchfully behind the Summerstar heiress, never taking his eyes off the other diners. He'd been staring at faces intently since Storm's first words, trying to catch sight of a suspicious reaction. Of course, he reflected grimly, he couldn't watch the absent Thalance.

The stout, bewhiskered boldshield loomed like a mountain over Shayna. His eyes were cold as his gaze met the shocked, angry glares of Erlandar and Pheirauze Summerstar. His hairy, muscular arms were crossed in front of his chest—but the fingers of one hand rested on the haft of his mace of office. The fingers of the other were on the pommel of the heavy broadsword he wore. "Where is Thalance?" he asked quietly.

Pheirauze flushed crimson. "How dare you imply—" she began, voice rising in a magnificently trembling cry of outrage.

"I imply nothing, Dowager Lady," Ergluth rumbled, drowning out her words without seeming to raise his voice in the slightest. "I leave such subtle nonsense to those who have the leisure for it—such as the nobility of Cormyr. I ask a simple question, in the king's name, and expect a clear and swift answer of you: *where* is Thalance?"

"I—I know not," Pheirauze snapped, blinking. "I'm not the lad's keeper!"

"Lucky him," someone among the war wizards murmured quite clearly.

The boldshield turned and snapped, "Find Thalance Summerstar at once! Guard him, hold him in one place in the name of the king, and report back!"

"Sir!" the Purple Dragons by the door chorused. They rushed out, leaving only two of their number behind, standing on either side of the door. For the first time, the Summerstars noticed that these guards were hefting loaded and ready slings, and looking alertly at all the diners.

The war wizards were beginning to look scared now. Neither Storm nor Ergluth were surprised when Broglan Sarmyn suddenly rose and leaned forward, fingertips on the table and face contemptuous. "Threatening nobles in their own home is hardly prudent—and never polite. If a man lies dead in a bedchamber, who better to ask how he got there than the occupant of that room? Boldshield, the outlander among us is one of the folk we wizards of war are taught to beware—one of the bringers of trouble we're charged with keeping the realm clear of. If anyone is to answer questions about murders, let it be her!"

Silence was his only reply. He turned to glare at the Purple Dragon commander. "To answer your question: I saw Thalance rise and leave, not long ago, and have no trace of an idea as to his whereabouts now. But I have a question for you: was there a Harper pin on or beside the Seneschal's body?"

"There was not, Sir Broglan of Sevensash," Ergluth replied curtly, his eyes more like the keen gaze of an eagle than ever, "and what if there had been? I know of over two hundred Harpers who've perished in Cormyr in the past decade . . . yes, in this 'safe,' loyal, law-abiding realm." He put one of his great battered hands down on the back of Shayna's chair, seeming not to notice her staring wide-eyed up at him, and leaned forward to fix the leader of the war wizards with a gaze that had grown dark and stony.

"Now," he continued heavily, "how many wandering Harper pins do you think their deaths have produced? Have you ever heard of a Harper marking a corpse as some sort of 'Harper kill' by leaving a pin behind? I've not—and yet why do we stand here debating such things? We've a Harper in our midst. If you suspect this leaving of pins might be a Harper tactic, why don't you ask her?"

The power of his words was such that even Pheirauze looked to Storm.

She kept her eyes on Broglan's as she told them all, "No Harper, so far as I know, has ever put a badge on a dead person except as mark of honor for the deceased, when the dead person is a Harper. And to answer the question you've not dared ask, Sir Wizard: I've not, within any of your lifetimes, slain anyone in this keep . . . yet."

There was a stirring. Not even Erlandar quite dared to contest what some of them held to be empty and overblown legend: that the lady standing before them, or any of the Seven Sisters for that matter, had really lived any longer than other folk. They used potions to appear youthful long after age should have stolen their teeth and sleek agility, as many a wizard did . . . surely no more.

Storm looked a wintry challenge at Erlandar, but when he said nothing, she continued crisply, "I've heard something of what Lord Athlan's body looked like—and that of the wizard Dlaerlin, too—"

Broglan Sarmyn's head snapped up and his eyes narrowed, but he said nothing. Storm brought her gaze to meet his as she continued.

"—and I've never seen anything quite like the . . . wounds left behind by whatever or whoever is doing the slaying. You'd all best be *very* wary. Not only do you stand in personal danger, but if the cause of these deaths gets out of the keep, Cormyr—and all civilized lands—could well be doomed."

Storm turned back to Broglan. "I want to examine Athlan Summerstar's body," she said quietly. "Now."

Broglan seemed about to refuse, but the boldshield raised a hand and pointed warningly at him, and he shrugged and said, "The Lord Summerstar was burned upon the orders of Lady Pheirauze. Given the manner of his death, her wishes seemed only prudent. All we have left of him is a handful of ashes."

"Take me to that handful," Storm said quietly.

Broglan bowed his head, gathered the other war wizards with glances, and left the table. He headed at an even pace for one of the doors of the hall. The boldshield followed.

Storm paused only long enough to say to Shayna, "My deep apologies for disturbing the peace of your hall so often this even, gracious lady. The viands, and your care and kindness in the offering of them, are appreciated."

She sketched a bow. The startled heiress returned it. Without another word, Storm turned and went after the boldshield. Cold and thoughtful Summerstar eyes watched them go.

In the passage beyond the feast hall, the ring of war wizards closed in around Storm and the Purple Dragon. Ergluth Rowanmantle raised his hand in a signal, and there were suddenly Purple Dragon armsmen everywhere, melting out of the gloom along the walls to form an outer ring of watchful warriors around them all.

Storm smiled tightly as the war wizards collectively stiffened. "What is the meaning of this?" Broglan snapped, but he sounded more weary than surprised.

"That's what we're trying to discover, mage," Ergluth explained with hearty patience as they strode on into the darkness. "That's what we're all trying to discover."

The leader of the war wizards didn't bother to reply. He led the way in stony silence. Down a musty stair they went, and across a hall lit only by the faint blue radiance that surrounded an old statue of a Summerstar lord. Another stair led down from that hall, turning several times, into a dank and deserted lower level. This was not the way the boldshield knew, and his eyes were narrow with suspicion before the doors of the Summerstar crypt came into view ahead.

Broglan Sarmyn turned to Storm and said, "Lady Silverhand, beyond these sealed doors lie the fallen who have borne the name Summerstar down long and proud centuries. I've never been inside it, but I must remind you and Lord Rowanmantle that the seal was put there by a local priest for a good reason: it keeps undeath in, as well as thieves who fear such walking dooms out. I do not recommend—"

What the wizard chose not to recommend, they never learned. At that moment, a silent blue-white pale figure rose up behind him and reached down long, clawed hands to rake Broglan's face and throat.

Those talons were like smoke. The startled wizard's face shone through them as he stammered out a spell.

At the same moment, Storm felt a terrible cold slice through her from behind. A man's voice by her shoulder hissed, "Stop, it, witch! End your spell, or my next thrust will be through your heart!"

The bard looked down at the blue flickering that was shaping a point just below her right breast. "A spellblade. Murndal Claeron—it is Murndal, is it not?—do you know the price of wielding the weapon you have so boldly used?"

The war wizards had all turned to face her by then, their hands up to hurl spells. The boldshield had his blade half out. Following his lead, the armsmen reached around to put daggers to the throats of the mages. Everyone watched in frozen, wary silence as Storm turned to face the mage who'd struck her from behind.

Murndal made a frightened sound and tried to slash the spellblade sideways, to reach her heart. Storm stepped easily away from it, so that it sliced its way right out through her ribs instead. Spinning gracefully around, she touched it once, and the wizard was suddenly holding nothing but a few blue sparks that flickered and drifted from his hand.

"Let us have peace," she told her attacker then, towering over him.

Murndal of the war wizards cowered away from her, his mouth dry and his fingers cold with fear.

Silver fire was swirling around the wound in her side, and curling out from between her lips as she spoke. Her eyes were suddenly two pools of soaring silver flames, and Murndal could not help screaming as she took him by the arms. He felt the crackle and surge of powers he could only guess at.

Storm said gently, "I've worked no spell, ambitious one . . . and I can see that the crafting of that weapon was beyond you, too."

She let go of the trembling mage and turned around again. "Broglan! Mind your manners!" she snapped. "Spellblades? The backlash could have killed this young mageling of yours—and a dozen more folk, if he'd dragged it out at the wrong moment! What were you thinking of?"

Broglan stared at her, naked fear on his face. He licked his lips. The haunting that had startled him and scared Murndal into attack was gone, scattered by his hasty spell. Now Storm Silverhand, every inch a Chosen of Mystra, with the divine silver fire of legend curling out of her very eyeballs, was staring angrily at him.

"Y-Your power, and how we might stop it," he whispered, unable to think of anything to say but the truth.

She sighed, and tossed her head. Already the wound in her side was smaller, and the terrible silver radiance was blazing and flowing along it, fading away from her face. "Well, at least I'm hearing some honest words from you," she said calmly. "Do you think you could open the crypt now, and forget such nonsense as this for a while?"

Broglan stared openmouthed at her, and then turned to the crypt doors. The shaken war wizard took a deep breath and bowed his head for a moment. He raised his hand, murmured something, and touched the line of wax marked by the three runes that the Harvestmaster of Chauntea had impressed on it. A small fire blazed up around his fingers. At first a green-white, it became a deep and restless red and raced along the wax.

When it had traced around both of the doors, it died away. Broglan drew in another deep breath, stepped back, and indicated the unsealed doors.

"Open them, and lead the way in," the boldshield ordered him.

The war wizard shook his head. "The haunting—there could be—"

Ergluth gave him a look of cold disgust. "Wizard," he growled, "go in, and take that lantern from yon armsman with you—or I'll soon be telling Vangerdahast that the leader of his Sevensash investigative team had the great misfortune to fall onto my sword while we were exploring the haunted Summerstar family crypt."

Broglan gulped. "Y-Yes, Sir Boldshield," he said, and did as he'd been ordered.

The lantern bobbed away reluctantly into a large and eerie chamber, its walls broken by many niches containing stone coffins. Several larger coffins, their lids carved into semblances of sleeping Summerstar lords and ladies, stood in a fan-shaped array radiating out from a large central table.

"Hundarr," Broglan asked in commanding tones, pointing, "is that table clear?"

The war wizard nodded gravely, took a stance, and cast a spell of detection with as much showmanship and grand oratory as he could muster. Storm, Ergluth, and several veteran armsmen hid their smiles; several of the more junior Purple Dragons didn't bother.

Lost in his moment of glory, Hundarr missed the displays of mirth. He strode around the crypt, looking this way and that, and finally announced, "Faint magics—possibly preservative enchantments—around those three coffins, this one, and that one over there. The rest of the chamber, including the table, is clear, Sir Broglan."

The senior war wizard gave him a tight smile. "Good." He turned to Storm and Ergluth. "Well?"

"Which of those coffins contains Athlan's handful?" Storm asked. The wizard laid his hand on the newest, and she said, "Bring it forth, and pour it out on the table. Lanterns well clear, good sirs."

Broglan raised his eyebrows, but did as he was bid. Storm looked down at the small heap of cinders, turned her head away to sigh, and said quietly, "I'm told you carry a spell you're very proud of, Sir Broglan . . . one of your own devising, that returns things to their last shape. Will you cast it on these ashes, please?"

The war wizard looked at her in surprise, more for her knowledge of his prize enchantment than for what he'd been asked to do. He said, "The body my spell will fashion can be no more than an empty shell, feather-light and very short-lived. Whatever you want to do, do it quickly."

Storm merely gestured for him to continue. Broglan met her eyes doubtfully for a moment. He took several small items from the sleeves and lapels of his robe and, with slow and exacting care, cast his spell.

The ashes on the stone table gradually drew together and shaped themselves into a sprawled body. Storm regarded it critically as it changed from a thing of black flakes tinged with white or brown to an almost corpselike shape of dull gray.

"How long can you hold it thus?" she asked.

"Not long," Broglan said flatly. Tiny beads of sweat sprung into being on his forehead. Ah. That short a time, then. She went straight to work.

The shape of Athlan Summerstar lay on his back, naked, a smooth nothing where his face should be. Storm indicated this. "Is that your spell, or had he no face when he died?"

"That's what it looked like when he breathed his last," Broglan said tersely. "I've never seen one of these reconstructions with no eyes before—but my spell could not have been miscast, or you'd have no image at all to look at."

"Could the face have been burnt away?" Storm asked sharply, bending by the ash-image's ear.

Broglan looked surprised, and then said, "Yes. Yes, certainly. That would almost have to be the reason for no trace of eyes. They must have been gone before he died."

Storm nodded somberly. "That's what I thought," she said quietly, and bent over the shape again.

"I see a dead man, lying on his back," Ergluth Rowanmantle said, standing at the crypt doors. "Can you see more?"

Storm nodded and pointed. "See the mark, and the darker area? A sword came out of his breast there. So our mysterious murderer drove a blade through a young and energetic man from behind, and did the burning after."

"But why?" the boldshield said. "Concealing who the victim was is the only reason I know besides disease banishment to set fire to a man's face. . . . And we knew immediately who the victim was."

"What if someone—Athlan himself?—has taken the shape of another Summerstar, say, and tried to leave the body of someone else behind, burnt to conceal the fact that it *wasn't* really Athlan, as we're all assuming?" the war wizard Corathar asked excitedly.

"You've been reading too many dead-knight chap-books, lad," Insprin Turnstone said wearily from beside him. "Now belt up, and listen to the lady."

Storm was bent over the ash-shape, frowning as she thoughtfully bit her lip. "His knees and elbows are both scraped," she said. "He fell on stone, in some haste or with some force . . . and this bruise on his cheek, here, means . . ."

"Yes?" Broglan and Ergluth prompted, in unison.

"He fell on his face, onto something shaped and metal. The less likely cause is that his cheek was struck by the quillons of his own sword or the blade of another,

as Athlan's uplifted weapon was driven into it by a hard
parry or by the force of a meeting with a wall or attack."

She looked up. "Broglan? What did your spells tell
you when you tried to touch the mind of your slain
mageling?"

"Nothing," the war wizard told her bleakly. "To
magic—all the magics we could think of, that any of us
can cast—he was 'not there.' Unreachable, absent . . .
blindbarred."

Storm nodded, and whispered something over the
silent shape. A pulse of light raced away from her lips,
passing swiftly through the thing of ash. When it was
gone, though, the ash-corpse looked just as it had before.

Her eyes flickered. The boldshield took a cautious
step forward. "Can you bring the dead back to walk
among us, Lady of Mystra? Then Athlan could lead the
House of Summerstar once more, and we could banish
all this strife and upset."

Storm laughed shortly as she circled the shape,
looking at the soles of its feet. "For all the tales of the
dead rising at a wave of a priest's hand," she said slowly, not looking up, "death is still the final and
inescapable fate of all—or at least, one very few find a
reprieve from. Not this one, I'm afraid—something
bars my every spell."

As the last words left her lips, the ashes gave forth
a queer little sigh and collapsed.

She looked up. The wizard Broglan was shaking
with weariness. Feeling her scrutiny, he looked up and
managed a smile.

"That's—not an easy spell to hold," he said.

There was a stir outside the crypt, and they all
looked up as the Purple Dragons standing wary guard
stepped back to allow the entry of more of their fel-
lows. They bore something in a covered strong chest,
and were preceded by the grim and white-lipped old
steward of the feast hall.

"My thanks for guiding my men hence," Ergluth Rowanmantle told the old man gravely.

Ilgreth Drimmer nodded wearily and leaned back against the wall, silently waving away the thanks.

Broglan had already swept Athlan's ashes carefully back into their coffin, leaving the stone table clear. He joined the steward against the wall, too tired to do more than watch.

Storm pointed. The armsmen lifted the sheet out of the strong chest and swung the shrouded bundle onto the funerary table.

"Renglar?" Ergluth asked quietly.

Storm nodded. "I hope he'll do Athlan one last service," she said.

"But none of the spells you tried back in your bedchamber could reach him," the Purple Dragon commander said.

Storm gestured to the armsmen to draw back the edges of the sheet. "There is one spell left."

"A wizard's wish?" Ergluth ventured. "Can your will overcome the burning he suffered?"

Storm shook her head and took the seneschal's blackened skull into her hand. "No," she whispered. "Hush, now."

Then, looking into the two shrunken and dusty eyeballs, she breathed some phrases, put her finger to her own eyes, and touched the fingertips to Renglar's sorry, staring orbs. She turned, still holding the skull, and waved at the war wizards and armsmen to stand clear. The skull stared endlessly across the crypt. Something in the air where it was looking stirred, danced into life, and flickered.

A dozen men held their breaths as one and stared intently.

"Storm—?" Ergluth asked quietly, his hand on his sword.

"Nothing to do us harm," she replied, eyes never

leaving the stirring air. "We'll be seeing the last thing the seneschal saw before he died."

As if obeying her, the flickering disturbance suddenly coalesced into a sharp, stationary image: a darkly handsome man with a crooked-bladed dagger in one hand. He reached it forward with a cruel, maniacal grin.

There was a murmur. "So that's our slayer," Ergluth said sharply. "Take a good look, men."

Storm moved and made a slight sound beside him. He glanced at her. The Bard of Shadowdale had started back. One of her hands had gone to her lips—lips that were suddenly chalk-white, and trembling.

Broglan saw her face too. "What's wrong, lady?"

"None of you recognize him?" Storm asked, almost whispering.

There was a general shaking of heads. "Nay, lady," Ergluth spoke for them all.

Storm let out a long, shuddering breath, closed her eyes for a moment, and then opened them to stare one last time at the grinning image as it started to fade. "That's Maxan Maxer, once my consort."

" 'Once'? He left you?" Ergluth asked, raising an eyebrow.

Storm gave him a wan smile. "In a manner of speaking." The image faded into a ghostly shadow. When it was quite gone, the bard turned away and added, her whisper loud in the silent tomb, "He's been dead for years."

The sound that she made next was very much like a sob.

Six

WHEN EVERY BED HAS ITS WIZARD

 A table stood in the center of the finely panelled study shared by the Sevensash war wizards. The table was fashioned of shadowtop wood, its curving legs sculpted into stylized tree roots and its oval top inlaid with plain, smooth-polished duskwood.

Far too plain, Hundarr had judged it with a sniff.

Broglan disagreed. The small globe of winking lights he had placed to rotate lazily in the air above the table wasn't meant to be an ornament. Rather, the globe was there as a warning. It was linked to an invisible web of enchantment that spanned the floor, ceiling, and walls of the room. If any active spell effect moved into the study or was unleashed there, the globe would fall and shatter in a shower of harmless but dramatic sparks, telling everyone that magic was on the loose.

The leader of the war wizards ducked his head out of his bedchamber door and glanced at his spell globe.

It still spun above the table, patient and undisturbed—a scant few feet from an elbow propped on the polished duskwood.

The elbow belonged to Murndal Claeron, who sat at ease in an old, overstuffed chair, his feet up on a footstool. The young wizard was frowning over a spellbook, but Broglan could tell by the way he hummed and absently tapped his fingers that he was ruminating, not intently studying the magic.

Broglan strode across the fur rugs to sit on the adjacent lounge. Murndal raised his eyes and nodded in greeting, but said nothing.

Broglan was not so reticent. "I've been thinking about the lady—and the spellblade."

Murndal sighed and laid aside his book. Broglan raised an eyebrow. The young man's nonchalance was a mask; his hands were trembling. "She'll have her revenge on me," he said, voice low and urgent. "I know she will."

"Perhaps," Broglan said. "Almost any mage would, true—but she seems . . . different. She was more angry at me than you. And her ire seemed to come because we'd broken the rules of courtesy, rather than from surprise or outrage. Moreover, if I saw what I thought I did, she's healed already, long since. Folk released from pain can forget its cause more easily."

"Who's to say what she thinks?" Murndal said, almost bitterly. "She doesn't strike me as particularly sane."

"If you'll forgive the intrusion—and further, some blunt speech," a deeper voice put in from behind them, "you are judging her so because she doesn't act or speak as you expect her to." Insprin Turnstone took his own seat beside Broglan, steel-gray eyes glinting. He added, "Ambitious mages are the only folk of power you've taken measure of, Murndal. She's not ambitious . . . and, I suppose, not much of a mage."

"Murndal's point is a fair one, though," Broglan said. "Being alive for so long and serving our Divine Lady of Mysteries directly all that time—what would that do to one's mind?"

"Are we in a position to judge her?" Insprin asked mildly.

Broglan frowned. "Another good point," he admitted.

Murndal sighed. "While you debate the state of her sanity," he growled, "I could be *doomed!* Have you any spell or item you can protect me with?"

Broglan laughed a short and mirthless laugh. "Against Mystra's silver fire? Nothing can withstand that save the goddess herself. There's not a mighty staff or earth-rending spell I know of that can protect you if she really desires your death. But consider this: she can rend anyone thus, and has walked Faerûn for centuries, with six of her sisters similarly armed . . . and there are still folk left alive to people Cormyr, and Sembia, and far Waterdeep, and a dozen other lands besides. So rest a little easier, Murndal."

"All the happily resting citizens of those lands haven't plunged a *sword* into one of Mystra's Chosen— the one who also happens to be a leader of the Harpers," Murndal said bitterly. "Folk she hasn't noticed yet are perfectly safe, but I stand in rather more danger!"

"Our plan was still a good one," Broglan said, "and I noticed no such fear when you volunteered—*volunteered*, mind you—to be the one to strike with our spellblade. Weeping now is wasted wind . . . and it undercuts your bravery in everyone's eyes."

Murndal sighed gustily and fell back into his chair, spreading his hands. "All right, I'm a dead man," he growled. "So while she plots a suitable manner for my execution, what'll the rest of you be doing?"

"Doing?"

"There's a murderer, or more than one, at work in

Firefall Keep," Murndal reminded his superior with some asperity, "or have you forgotten Lhansig and his codpiece? I know you spoke of the killings being Storm's work—but she can't have slain the seneschal . . . unless you think her capable of enchanting the wits of both the steward and the boldshield!"

"I do think her capable of just that," Broglan said, "but I'll admit that Baerest's demise doesn't *feel* like her work. But did you not see Thalance Summerstar leave the table in plenty of time to have done the deed?"

"That fop? Take the seneschal? With luck, perhaps, b—"

"Not luck," Broglan said tartly. "Magic. The man's skull was burnt bare . . . not the work of a lucky sword thrust."

"But Thalance hasn't the *brains* to—"

"Oh?" Insprin put in. "And just how do we know that? We've seen him twice, mayhap thrice. By all accounts he's seen every chambermaid and unattached lady in the vale. That may be the work of a fool, but it requires no small amount of cunning."

"None of the Summerstars need to be cunning," Broglan reminded them, "when they've got the Lady Pheirauze to do it for them."

"Yes," Murndal said thoughtfully. "I could just picture them all running to and fro at her bidding. . . ."

"So what are you saying Pheirauze gains by slaying her own grandson?" Hundarr Wolfwinter broke in. His sharp tone made it clear that he'd heard enough commoners criticizing the ethics of a noble house.

"A lot more power around here, for one thing," Insprin said gravely. "Where Athlan would be expected to rule his house his own way, youthful mistakes and all, Shayna will be expected to take advice from her elders . . . particularly in matters of marriage."

"And what would you know of the expectations at court?" Hundarr asked coldly.

"All too much, I fear," the thin, gray-haired old mage calmly replied, ignoring the bait.

Broglan turned. "Enough, Hundarr! Even we low-born men have eyes and ears and brains! I've seen no sign that either Lord Vangerdahast or the king are stupid enough to divide the citizens of Cormyr into but two groups: cultured, clear-thinking, loyal nobles and howling-dog, brutish, dangerous commoners. I hope you won't make that mistake either. Too many proud families of Cormyr are extinct today because of it."

Hundarr Wolfwinter stared back at him silently, a clear challenge in his eyes. Neither man moved or spoke for a long minute. Then Broglan shrugged, turned away, and said, "The fact remains that Murndal has asked a good question—what is our course, in the hours and days ahead?"

"Watch and wait," Insprin said flatly, "with eyes open and battle spells ready, to see what Storm Silverhand stirs up as she roams through the keep."

Broglan nodded. "That's exactly the road I've been following," he admitted. "If we spend our days interviewing servants and scrying at their thoughts to ferret out murderers who I doubt are lurking in their ranks, our distinguished lady bard will be scouring the Haunted Tower *and* poking about in the private wardrobes of Lady Pheirauze before long."

Broglan leaned forward and said to Murndal, "I've got a little task for you."

"Me?" Murndal asked, more surprised than suspicious.

"I gave you the only cloak of concealment I brought, to keep the spellblade hidden until you were ready to use it," the leader of the war wizards explained. "It's bonded to you now."

"And so?" Murndal asked warily.

"You saw how upset the vision of the seneschal's slayer—if that's who it was—made the lady bard? She left the crypt in such haste that no priest was called to reseal the doors."

Murndal nodded slowly. "You want me to go there and cast an unsleeping guardian to see if anyone enters or leaves."

Broglan inclined his head in a nod so slight that it seemed for a moment to be no nod at all. His hand dipped into the breast of his robe. "I also want you to leave this there."

Murndal studied the silvery metal wand. It was tipped with an emerald and sprouted sharp metal fins, collars, and rune-inscribed horns. As he watched, it pulsed slightly, as if a deep-buried power were awakening in it. He lifted his eyes hastily from its rising glow. "What is it?"

"A decoy, of course. It has no powers save the ability to be traced by us at a distance—and to be violently destroyed by Insprin or myself, at a somewhat closer proximity."

"So if our murderer—or anyone else—snatches it from the tomb, we can follow, and visit an explosion into the very hands that would try to use the thing against us."

Broglan nodded.

Murndal looked around the circle of curious, watching faces, broke into a sudden grin. "I'll do it." He rose. "Now?"

" 'Twould be best," his superior told him. "The sooner this lies in the tomb—on the table, perhaps, or 'fallen' beside it—the faster we can ensnare Lhansig's slayer."

Murndal strode to his chamber. Shrugging himself into the cloak, he asked with a frown, "The guards?"

"With that cloak, a minor problem," Broglan replied. "I'm about to send everyone on short missions at once, to give our patient Purple Dragons something to watch."

The war wizards grew matching grins of anticipation. With a smile that was almost a purr, Broglan said, "Corathar and Hundarr, go to the old steward of the hall to borrow two of his tall braziers; don't press him if he refuses. Insprin, there's something vital—and for the time being, *very* secret—that you have to hunt down in the keep library . . . or perhaps in the seneschal's papers. I'll be needing at least one of those doorguards to go and get the boldshield for me—and the other to take custody of this execrable liqueur for me; it seems to bear some enchantment or other that's interfering with our work. Murndal, stand behind me and awaken the cloak."

He waved at them to get gone. With nods and grins, they obeyed. The leader of the war wizards turned and held out his hand to the globe above the table, giving it a steady glare. Under his scrutiny, it began to flash and pulse, sending strange shadows leaping around the room. They almost entirely obscured the faint shimmering in the air right in front of him—Murndal in the cloak.

Broglan nodded in satisfaction and turned to the door. "Mystra and Tymora both be with us now," he muttered, and laid a hand on the bar that kept non-wizards out.

So it was that Murndal Claeron slipped out of the room quite unseen, and down the only hall that wasn't rapidly filling up with wary Purple Dragons. Curse that boldshield! He'd foreseen something like this, and posted what looked like at least three armsmen for each of the guest mages. It also seemed that, for the time being, he'd taken on the seneschal's crown-appointed duties, and would be resident in the keep until the killings were solved.

Murndal stifled a heartfelt oath and hurried away from the jostling and chatter, hoping no narrowed eyes would notice the slight shimmering the cloak trailed in

its wake. He was around the first dogleg corner and into
deeper dimness ere he realized that this hall led into
the Haunted Tower. He paused for a moment, looking
back and then ahead—and then shrugged. What could
a few phantoms do, after all? And with that open stair
at the center, he could get to the crypt quickly indeed.
After that, the kitchens awaited. That repast had been
marvelous, and surely there must be some left . . .

* * * * *

The lady in the long gown looked back over her
shoulder, opened her mouth in a soundless scream,
snatched up her trailing skirts, and ran on, fading
away in midfrantic stride.

"Haunted Tower, indeed," a voice said disgustedly.
"*That's* not going to keep anyone away." Two hands lifted to work magic.

The spell was newly gained, and so the casting, as
always, was just a trifle awkward—but there were no
charging adventurers or other foes to make haste necessary.

Soon enough, the blue mists were swirling. Out of
them, with a cold rattle of laughter, came the first of
the skulls. With eyes of flame, it winked at its creator,
and swooped off to the right as it was bid. The watcher smiled grimly as it plunged back into the mists, and
made the fog drift into a ring around him.

When the watcher was surrounded with a roiling
barrier, he began to pace. No curious armsman or
mage was likely to pass screaming skulls and mists
that flickered with lightning. And this haunting, however harmless, would last until all the magic was
drained from the enspelled daggers that the
Summerstar fools had seen fit to inter with their fall-
en. To leave such things to rust away in a crypt! Truly,
nobles *were* mad!

Well, there'd be fewer of them soon enough. It was time to plot and plan in earnest . . . no matter how hard that was becoming.

Hard indeed. A tremulous sigh echoed within the roiling ring of mist.

The fire brought spells, and the skills to cast them. It could bring also important knowledge, and useful powers akin to spells—whatever mental properties the victims had possessed. But with such treasures came annoying memories.

Floods of memories, bright and sharp and roaring and . . . oh, so heavy. Crowding and clamoring for attention, always, jostling along in an alluring flow that could spin one way, breathless, into being a man shivering on his first battlefield, side torn open, as the wolves came trotting nearer; then a woman shrieking under the brutish cruelty of her lord, in a room where the rippling blaze of candles brought no warmth nor comfort; and then a man again, watching from the battlements on a day of chill fog, as a falcon came streaking down to tear a dove from the air in a flurry of bloody feathers, and . . .

On and on, for one heart-wrenching moment after another, until strength came to rise up out of the endless flood and know what was truly befalling here and now. The seneschal had known damned near every chamber and passage of this old keep, and the ways of the vale beyond. What he hadn't known was familiar to the Harper. Even those with paltry lives were best subsumed when met with—for a body emptied by the fire was forever mindless. Even if some meddler transformed an errant finger into a whole body, that body would be a brainless husk . . . and brainless husks could be trusted to keep secrets.

Secrets that must stand for a time longer, until no alarm among the Harpers or the Zhentarim or the Red Wizards or those who defended the crown of Cormyr

could spell doom for the rising power in these two
hands—the power that *must* triumph.

Dimly, through the ever-increasing, racing chaos of
stolen memories, the watcher could recall the *taste* of
divinity. It had a tang like the iron of blood in a mortal
mouth . . . and yet, so much more. He ached to know
that taste again, ached to be revered, and worshiped—
and feared. It would come again. It *would* come again!

Usurpers commanded the priests who should still
be his. Usurpers wielded the power that was rightful-
ly his. Usurpers made decrees and blundered through
divine dealings, speaking where he should have spoken. All of this would end. Hands clenched in the dimness of this chamber at the heart of the Haunted
Tower. Aye, all of this would end.

It would take much more power, though. The power
of that servant of accursed Mystra.

His hands itched at the thought. Ah, to wield what
she had. But he must take care. Subsuming the
essence of a mortal was all too easy with the fire at his
command . . . but she could destroy him even without
the aid of the others she could call on. He must be very
careful.

It was prudent to skulk within spell-spun walls of
magical mist, to hide behind gibbering skulls and
other madnesses folk wouldn't dare pass. Prudent, but
hardly subtle. He must take great care in the days
ahead.

And he must feed again. He'd gained the wits and
wariness of a hardened Harper and the wiles and local
knowledge of a veteran warrior—but his magic was
still all too feeble. There were only five war wizards
left. The two older ones might have something of worth
. . . but slaying them was sure to bring more mighty
mages, who'd arrive well prepared for trouble.

What choice was there? For him to regain his rightful place, many must die. He needed to do more than

shapeshift and subsume. He needed true power—the power to withstand the mightiest of spells once more, such as the wish magics of mortals. No one in this vale, perhaps in this realm, had what he needed. . . .

But Storm Silverhand came close.

He must move softly. Best to take the powers of some more mages first, and at least one better fighting man, before making any move against the woman with the silver hair. The Purple Dragon commander was probably the best target outside the ranks of the war wizards—but getting to him would take careful planning.

The watchfulness of veteran soldiers and Storm Silverhand, though, were nothing when measured against the peril offered by the probes of a competent priest. There was a Harvestmaster of Chauntea about, and other clerics who'd known adventure, and seen life, and learned things.

At all costs, he must avoid being recognized for what he was. Thoughtful hands stroked a chin. Yes, the form of an attractive maid might be safest for what would have to come next.

Perhaps, after ascension, he'd take a Twisted Skull as his symbol. Lips twisted wryly in the darkness. That would be a worthy jest, seeing as he was having to change from one forlorn form to another all too often these days. It would be a good sigil to make mortals know terror. He'd made mistakes before—mistakes that had cost him nearly everything, leaving him a thing like a howling shadow, able only to fly and moan and claw . . . and subsume.

Aye, subsume. It was time, and past time, to feed again. The memories rushed past in an endless torrent, but he heeded them no more. He'd mastered them, and grown stronger . . . and it was time to seize more.

The dark figure dwindled and took on fullness—

smooth, buxom curves of flesh, half revealed by a low-cut, ruffled bodice above a dark sash and slit skirts. Bare feet padded on stone. An anxious-looking maiden blew a kiss to one of the skulls, and stepped into the mists.

On their other side, a pale form waited—a warrior with no eyes. It howled soundlessly, raising the stump of a shattered sword with menacing intent. Another of the real phantoms of the keep.

The chambermaid laughed and strode right through it, using the light it radiated to adjust her garments more provocatively. Still laughing, she went on into dusty darkness.

It was time to feast again. . . .

* * * * *

"Mystra guard me," Storm muttered as she set the door bar in place and went wearily around the room, checking for intruders. She'd already looked for secret entrances and moved the bed to one side, just to be safe. Now exhausted, she wanted to relax within that safety, however false or flimsy it might really be.

She yawned, and felt suddenly homesick. She wanted to be in her own bed, with the green growing things of Shadowdale all around her. "You're getting old, lass," she told herself. "Wanting to stay in one place and become a part of it—that was the sign Mystra warned of."

. . . The Mystra who is now gone, she reminded herself silently. The Mystra who'd dared to challenge Helm, and so left all her Chosen to go unguided into this new age. And how she needed guidance. The man she'd loved—and seen brutally torn apart in battle, years ago—apparently roamed this backcountry keep burning out men's brains.

Sudden tears rose raw in her throat, threatening to

overwhelm her. "Maxan," she gasped aloud. Memory brought his smiling face in front of her again, and she remembered the warm strength of his arms. . . .

Storm shivered, fought down a sob, and shook her head in denial. She waved at empty air to bid the memories of her dead man begone and leave her in peace.

She was suddenly tired of it all. When such good men were torn away from her and all Faerûn, who could care about self-important magelings and sneering Summerstars? Let them all go down, and . . .

Storm shook her head as she turned back the covers. Nay. Nay, not so harsh. Shayna Summerstar and Ergluth Rowanmantle were swimming in her mind's eye. Behind them, coming up with that weary smile, was Renglar, the seneschal. They mattered. All of Cormyr mattered.

"It matters to me," she told the silent room. She unbuckled the dagger sheath on her left shoulder. "It always matters to me." She tossed the sheathed dagger onto the bed and reached for the matching one on her right shoulder. "That's the problem," she told it with a rueful smile.

The bedchamber, which had maintained a dignified silence during this soliloquy, continued to do so. Storm stripped off her war harness, rubbed at the places where the leather straps had chafed, stared at them critically in an oval wall mirror as tall as she, waved cheerfully to the wizard she suspected was scrying her through the mirror, and went back to the boots she'd stuffed full of discarded daggers.

Driving one into the door frame and another into the foot of the bed, she murmured some words over each. Then she did the same to a pair driven into either side of the frame of the mirror.

Two spells well spent. If any living thing but herself passed between a pair of daggers, it would receive both blades, flying full tilt, and the spell would jolt Storm awake.

She shook her head at having to take such precautions, sniffed at one armpit, and murmured, "I *am* getting a little musky."

Whatever Pheirauze Summerstar might think of her, it seemed the keep servants considered her a guest to be honored. Under its padded metal cover, the bath proved to be deliciously warm. Storm propped her long sword within reach, shed her scanties, and sank thankfully up to her chin in the waiting waters. Warm ripples almost went up her nose; she chuckled and resisted the momentary impulse to play at being a sea-serpent and rise from the waters to bite and drag down a hapless floating wooden back-scrubber. She was just too tired.

"Syluné," she said aloud, " 'tis I—the bold bad Bard of Shadowdale. How goes it?"

As she'd hoped, her distant sister heard her own name spoken, recognized Storm's voice, and used a spell to let them farspeak mind to mind.

Dozing in the water, lazily running handfuls of scented soap shavings over her limbs, Storm chatted silently about the current sad state of mastery and maturity among Cormyrean war wizards, and the grim, unfolding run of murders. "It looks bad, I fear."

In return, Syluné told her how things were growing on the farm, and of the latest happenings in Shadowdale. She did not bid her be careful, offer assistance, or remind her of half a dozen things to be wary of. Storm was thankful for that, as always, but was startled to hear her sister observe quietly, "Something has upset you more than usual. Give, lady."

Storm sighed, but did not bother to hesitate or deny. "I used the 'last thing the eyeballs saw' spell on a decent old warrior slain in my bedchamber," she told her sister aloud, "and it seems our killer is, or at least wears the likeness of my man, Maxer."

"Oh, *Storm*," was all Syluné said, but there was a long lifetime of compassion in her voice.

Hearing that, Storm felt fresh tears well up, and added firmly, "Oh—one thing more. Our Happy Dancing Mages are so sure that evil lady Harpers are dismantling Cormyr stone by stone that one of them used a spellblade on me, and spilled some of Mystra's fire."

"Not something you can afford to dispense endlessly," Syluné observed, understanding at last why Storm was so weary. Her exhaustion was obvious; speaking aloud during farspeech was something the bard did only when she was very tired. "You'd best sleep. Fare thee well."

Storm found herself climbing out of the now-cool bath. Her sister's mental equivalent of a kiss tingled on her cheek. She padded to where towels awaited, and then to bed.

Chosen of Mystra don't need to sleep, but someone seemed to have forgotten to tell Storm's body that. She'd been wounded before, and swung a sword for hours in battle with her own blood raining down around her in tongues of silver flame . . . but she'd been younger then.

Now it felt good to lay her unsheathed long sword ready on one side of the broad empty bed, and curl up against the pillows to stare into the night. She lost herself in the silent songs that lived in her memory, ballad after ballad, as the wee hours trailed quietly by.

It wasn't long, of course, before Maxan's face swam up to her again. He was laughing across a campfire somewhere deep in the High Forest as he tossed a bowl to her. She reached out to catch it, and found herself cradling nothing and staring at the empty bed around her.

"Oh, Maxan," she whispered, "why did you have to

leave me so alone?" With sudden speed, she snatched a
pillow onto her raised knees and hugged it to herself
before the tears came.

* * * * *

Even a woman who carries centuries of sorrows can
run out of tears and drift into dry-eyed melancholy.
Tossing aside her sodden pillow, Storm decided not to
get off the bed and get a decanter of something fiery.
Instead, she began to sing softly again, keeping to ballads she and Maxer had not enjoyed together. Perhaps
knowing everyone else had troubles, too, would make
her feel better. . . .

Some time later, she was silently singing the final,
mournful verse of "The Old Wandering Knight" when
there was a sudden burst of blue-green light, a rush of
displaced air—and something limp and heavy crashed
down atop her!

Even as she thrust it away and rolled to her feet,
calmly commanding her discarded underthings to
blaze with the radiance they'd been enspelled to emit,
Storm had a good idea of what she'd see.

She just didn't know whom. So she stood with a boot
in one hand and her other hand thrust into it, on the
hilts of a quartet of daggers, and peered narrowly at
her bed in the growing light.

On the pillows where she'd lain was someone else—
someone who'd never move again. Someone who could
never have teleported himself to where he now
sprawled, facing her.

It was one of the young, clever war wizards . . .
Murndal Claeron, that was the name . . . in his robes
and the tattered remnants of a cloak. His boots bore
the dust of little-used passages—in the Haunted
Tower, no doubt—and his skull seemed to have been
burned out from within. The eye-sockets that stared at

her were black, empty pits, and the gaping mouth
lacked a tongue. As she watched, a trickle of ash fell
from it to the linens where she'd been lying moments
before.

Storm sighed to mask her involuntary shudder.
Someone obviously believed in less-than-subtle warnings. "Scream," she snarled aloud, in case the someone
was listening for that very reaction right now, and
drew in a deep, tremulous breath. So much for relax-
ing; she had a long night of work ahead of her.

She started for the bed, automatically reaching to roll
her sleeves back out of the way. She chuckled a trifle
harshly: dressed like this, she didn't *have* any
sleeves. . . .

Seven

KNOWN BY HIS RING

Dark and savage rage was rising in Broglan Sarmyn as he stalked up to the closed door of Storm's bedchamber.

Murndal had never returned to the study.

It was early indeed for insistent servants to be rousing Broglan from the chair where he'd finally fallen asleep, waiting for the young wizard's report. They rushed him down chilly corridors, heedless of his stiff, aching limbs and urgent need to relieve himself. All of it was at the behest of a shameless outlander Harper who hid her insolence behind the title of Chosen of Mystra! Hah! He could style himself First Prophet of Azuth if he'd happened to have so brazen an ego, and take on the same airs. . . .

He was a dozen angry paces from Storm's door and the expressionless Purple Dragons flanking it when a shadow stepped away from the wall in front of him.

With a start, he recognized Ergluth Rowanmantle, the boldshield of Northtrees March.

"What is this—a court meeting?" Broglan snapped. "This had *better* be worth rousing me at this hour." Close on the heels of his words came the faint cry of a rooster from the vale beyond the keep walls. "Bloody Harpers," the wizard added—and of course, the bedchamber door in front of both men swung open at that moment.

"A favorite expression of mine, too," Storm agreed mildly, waving at them to enter. She wore a fine court gown, complete with earrings to outdazzle those of the old Summerstar aunts. A pectoral flashed and gleamed all down the low front where her gown was cut away.

Broglan found himself looking where that pectoral was designed to make him look. He harrumphed and fixed a gimlet eye on the Bard of Shadowdale. "You *summoned* me, Lady Silverhand?"

"Both of you, actually," Storm told him calmly. "You'll find the reason why in the bed there. Lord Rowanmantle, if you'd be so kind?"

Ergluth gave her the weary look of a man who knows just what unpleasant thing is coming. With one hand, he turned back the bedclothes. Murndal Claeron lay on his back, spread-eagled on the linens, his head dark, burned out, and hollow.

Broglan stared, openmouthed, and found no words to say. Empty, sightless eye sockets stared up at him, and the mouth was a similar gaping void. Something with talons had shredded the enchanted cloak, but he could see no sign of the false scepter.

"Suppose you tell us," the boldshield said, after a swift glance at the white-faced leader of the war wizards, "just how this mage came to be here."

"I'd also like to know that," Storm replied. "Whoever sent this unfortunate to me in the wee hours—he appeared in midair, and fell right on top of me—must be familiar with a spell unknown to me: magic that can teleport the dead."

Broglan made a wordless sound of denial and disbelief.

"He was on a mission for you?" Storm asked quietly. "Where was he going when he left your study?"

They waited, but Broglan merely shook his bowed head and covered his eyes. The boldshield made a certain gesture; his men withdrew and closed the door, leaving the three of them alone in the bedchamber with the sprawled corpse.

"All the younger magelings found it necessary to go and do urgent things at the same time yestereve," Ergluth said grimly. "No doubt their scurrying was to achieve one purpose: allowing this luckless boy his chance to slip away unseen. Where did he go, Broglan?"

The war wizard shook his head again.

"He went into the Haunted Tower, didn't he?" Storm asked quietly.

Broglan's head snapped up; his eyes were wild. "No!"

"He may have been heading elsewhere," Storm continued relentlessly, "but to get there he had to avoid Ergluth's guard posts. And to do that, he got himself into the dark ways where he could travel unhindered." She sighed. "He was heading for the crypt, wasn't he?"

Broglan said nothing, but they could tell from his sudden stillness that she'd hit upon the truth.

Storm shook her head. "Well, another wizard is dead, and can tell us nothing." She walked away from the bedside, adding, "I doubt he can be restored, short of direct divine intercession. . . . Mystra doesn't tend to do such things even for great mages, to say nothing of ambitious novices. He's gone."

She turned to face them both, and asked with exasperation, "Sir Broglan, isn't it about time we started to

work together? While you indulge in your little plots
and secrets, your magelings go on dying. I can't fight to
protect someone I don't know is out there, roaming the
keep like a thief."

That stung. Broglan's head jerked around to face
her fully, and his eyes blazed. Still he kept silent. The
Purple Dragon commander put his hand on the hilt of
his sword, took a slow step away, and turned to watch
the wizard narrowly.

"I worked on Murndal's body most of the night,"
Storm said, "trying to learn something—anything—
from it. His cloak bore magic before someone—our
slayer, no doubt—tore it to ribbons, and he carried the
usual components for spellcasting. His boots say he
walked in dusty places, and he tried to defend himself
with a dagger that's gone, now . . . and that's about all
he can still tell us."

"Shall I order the scouring of the Haunted Tower?"
Ergluth asked.

Storm shook her head. "From what I've seen, our
murderer would not be found . . . and could roam the
keep while your armsmen were searching the tower. It
is a place with its own phantoms, and thus would give
chances for them to mistakenly hurt each other. You
were going to issue crossbows, were you not?" Ergluth
nodded silently, and she shook her head. "A recipe for
disaster," she told him, "though I admit I haven't
thought of anything much better."

"So you have no counsel for us?" the boldshield
asked.

Storm spread her hands. "I'd like to cast some silent
watch spells on you and your senior officers, and on
Broglan and all of his war wizards."

Ergluth raised an eyebrow. "And just what do 'silent
watch' spells do?"

"Allow me to see out of the eyes of anyone I cast it
on, for about a twelve-count, when they call my name

aloud," the bard told him. "Once only, and only if they call desiring to summon me, not if they merely say my name in normal converse."

Ergluth nodded. "This seems wise," he said. "Will it take you to the person calling on you?"

Storm shook her head. "I'm afraid not," she said. "If they look around, I may be able to see enough of their surroundings to teleport to them. Otherwise, it at least lets me see who's attacking them."

"You don't sound all that hopeful," the Purple Dragon commented.

Storm gestured to the bed. "What length talons did that? I think we're dealing with a shapeshifter."

"A Mal . . . Malinaug—er, Malaugrym?" Ergluth asked, stumbling over the unfamiliar word.

The bard shrugged. "I can't tell that yet, one way or the other." Her eyes went to the war wizard. "Well, Broglan? What say you?"

"To your spell? No. Absolutely not," the mage replied. "No war wizard of Cormyr dares allow someone else to spy on him!"

"Ah," Storm said, "but it's quite all right for you to spy—to use your word—on others?"

"What d'you mean?" Broglan snarled, eyes afire again.

Storm waved a hand at the man-high oval mirror on the wall, its frame still bristling with daggers. "Which of your men was watching me last night? Did he like what he saw?"

Broglan flushed scarlet. "Madam," he began icily, "I assure you—"

"I doubt you can in truth assure me of anything," Storm said quietly. "Yet it is not my purpose to humiliate anyone or argue; I merely want us all to be better protected by working together. What can I promise, or do, to make your 'absolutely not' become a 'yes'?"

"I—nothing," Broglan said heavily. "I must protect

my men and myself against possible treachery. If Lord Vangerdahast ever heard of my allowing a possibly hostile outlander to gain any magical influence—or even potential influence—over a war wizard . . ."

"He'd huff for a few minutes and then tell you never to do it again," Storm said smoothly, "without clearing it with him first. Am I right?"

Broglan shook his head. "A reprimand would be the very least I could expect," he muttered.

"Broglan," Storm said crisply, "worrying about your career prospects is a bit pointless if you wind up dead—forever dead—because you ran around afraid of offending rules. If you want to die blindly for your realm, go join the soldiery. I've seen plenty of Purple Dragons do just that."

Ergluth Rowanmantle's brow darkened. He shrugged. A tiny smile plucked at the corners of his mouth, and he turned away, murmuring very softly, "The worst lashing a man can suffer—under the tongue of an annoyed lady bard . . ."

Neither of the others paid him any heed. Broglan's voice was rising in anger. "Since you arrived, Lady Silverhand, you have persisted in ignoring the rightful authority vested in officers of the Crown of Cormyr, treating us as lackeys—or ridiculing us as fools and empty blusterers, trusting in your Harper rank and your gender to escape the consequences of such insults! I've had quite enough of it, and my patience is now at an end! Either you'll show a little deferential obedience and cooperation, or you'll be shown some shackles and a cell to wear them in! Now, tell us straight: who is this murderer? You recognized that image you conjured up from the seneschal in the crypt. Who is it? I command you to share that information with the boldshield and myself. *We* are the only lawful investigators of the unjust and protectors of the right in Firefall Vale."

Ergluth Rowanmantle waited for the stormy reply that was sure to come. In the terse silence, the mage's hands tightened on a certain wand at his belt.

Surprisingly, Storm smiled. "Ah, you're awake at last. Good. Are you listening?" As Broglan sputtered, her eyes went to Ergluth. He nodded.

Storm walked to the bed, put her arm around one of its ornamental posts to lean against it, and told the nearest wall, "Long ago, I came to love a man—the man whose likeness you saw last night. Maxan Maxer was his name, a good and law-abiding man from Turmish. He was quick with a blade, and one of the most thoughtful beings I've ever met. He was always anticipating, thinking ahead, and arranging things to flow easily."

The bard's voice grew husky. She stared off through the wall, seeing things far away and long ago. "We lived and laughed and adventured together for years, until he fell . . . in the Year of the Bright Blade."

"You thought him dead?" Broglan snapped, every inch the inquisitor.

Storm looked at him coolly. "I saw him die. We were in a ruined city north of Escalant, fighting tanar'ri. Cambions and dretches had been scouring the countryside, seizing farm folk and bearing them off to an old temple there."

"For some sort of dark ritual?" Broglan asked, sounding disgusted. "I must have heard this tale a hundred times."

Storm shrugged. "Do you want to hear my words, or not? If I offer truth and you dismiss it, war wizard, there is very little I can do to help you. If you think me false, there are spells that can detect lying, and—unlike some—I'd gladly submit to them."

She looked at him in clear challenge and kept silent until Broglan dropped his eyes and muttered, "Go on."

Storm nodded her head as if she were a queen

solemnly agreeing to something distasteful. She said, "All of the foul ones served a marilith who sought more power. She believed—perhaps rightly—that the ritual she'd discovered or devised would yield to her the life-forces of sacrificed humans so that she could grow far more powerful than others of her kind ... and come to dominate them. We fought our way into the temple and disrupted her ritual."

"Was that ritual the cause of the spell storms I've heard about, that made southern Thay perilous?" the boldshield asked, frowning.

"Not the ritual, but our breaking of it," Storm said. "It had been going for a long time, and the energies burst out in waves of enchanted fire and wild magic. The temple roof fell. Many humans and tanar'ri alike died. My beloved hewed his way almost to the marilith, striking ahead where I could not reach, being engaged with too many foes."

Old anguish made her voice harsh. She looked away, eyes falling to the silent body on her bed.

"A tanar'ri drew six blades and fenced with him. I heard her hiss in glee: 'A worthy opponent to slay!' Maxer proved a worthier opponent than she'd thought, lopping off several of her arms. As I cut my way free of the last cambions around me, I heard her shriek with rage, and saw her writhing, racked with pain. She stopped toying with my beloved."

Storm took a deep breath and turned to face them again. "She ran her snakelike tail up around his neck from behind ... and tore his head off. I saw his body jerk and spray out lifeblood. . . . I saw his head roll across the temple. Before I could avenge my love, the marilith fled in spell-smokes, still clutching his body. When all was done, I could find no trace of his head, either."

"So if this is not him, risen from that death," Ergluth said slowly, "it is someone or something who knows you—and that seeing your man's likeness will cause you distress."

Storm nodded grimly.

Broglan stared at her, and then at the Purple Dragon commander, drawing back from the boldshield almost as if he'd been betrayed. "So *now* we're chasing *phantoms!*" he roared angrily. He turned in a swirl of rumpled robes and stormed out.

The lady and the soldier stood looking at each other for a moment. Ergluth said softly, "Our war wizard hates and fears what he can't understand or overmaster."

Storm shrugged. "Being human, how could he do otherwise?"

That tiny crook reappeared at the corner of the Purple Dragon's mouth. "How could he not, indeed? Cast your spell on me, Lady Silverhand—we two, at least, will work together in this."

Storm smiled suddenly. "It's nice to meet someone reasonable in this keep," she said, laying a hand on his arm.

" 'Sweet reason oft in short supply,' " he wryly quoted a famous Cormyrean poem, and sat down on the blanket-chest at the foot of her bed. "If you don't mind my boldness," he said carefully, "there are things I'd like to know, about—the fate of Gondegal, and how Cormyr really turned back Sembia from invading in the early days, and if Princess Alusair has joined the Harpers, and . . ."

"Hold, Lord Rowanmantle!" Storm broke in with a smile. "We've too much at hand to sit about talking now. Perhaps when all this is over. For now, don't thrust as Broglan did—or, I warn you, I'll become a lonely, flustered woman and forget all my answers."

"Flustered?" Ergluth snorted. "Lady, you are near to being a goddess! You've walked these lands for centuries, and seen and done more than I'll ever do. Right,

I'll behave, and not probe like a lord high inquisitor. And in return, pray, spare me your talk of being 'flustered' or a weak woman. I sit here in awe of you!"

"Really?" Storm said, giggling and bouncing like a little girl. "That's nice!"

Ergluth rolled his eyes up at the ceiling, and was rewarded by her full, throaty chuckle. "If you'd like the body removed now," he said carefully, "my men . . ."

* * * * *

Orling the Bold proudly touched the silver harp pin on his breast, his heart full. High Lady Dragonbreast herself had pinned it there, and kissed him, not an hour past. He could still taste the cinnamon of her lip glaze.

Reflectively running a tongue over his lips, he closed his eyes and rocked in pure pleasure. Soon the celebratory revel for the new-honored Harpers would begin, and Twilight Hall would be plunged into dancing and drinking and dalliance. And he must be ready.

He hefted the harp in his hands and ran a gentle finger over its strings. Two were badly out of tune, and a third just a trifle. He opened his eyes to start tightening, looking at the silently glowing glass display case that rose proudly on its plinth in the center of this little antechamber. Within was a ring. It had always floated there, turning slowly. It winked at him as some curve of its sculpted dragon caught the light. Something from Cormyr, wasn't it?

Orling smiled at the ring, noting silver, gold, and electrum in it as it turned. He plucked at his lowest string. Then he blinked, gulped, and nearly dropped his harp.

The ring was gone. The case still glowed, as brightly as it had before, but now it was empty. Completely empty. He peered at its bottom to be sure the ring hadn't just fallen, but before he really looked, he knew the ring had vanished. Silently, without flash or fuss—it was gone, right before his proverbial eyes.

Orling the Bold drew in a deep, unhappy breath. Whom was he going to tell? And would they believe him?

* * * * *

There was a sharp rap at the door. Broglan looked up. "No armsman nor servant knocks like that," he said softly. "Be ready for trouble."

Insprin nodded and took two wands from the table by his elbow. He handed one to Corathar and the other to Hundarr. By the time he'd joined the two younger wizards in a rough semicircle around the door, Insprin had his own wand out.

Broglan took the center position in the curved line of mages and drew his wand. Satisfied that all four wands were trained on the door, the leader of the war wizards called, "Enter!"

The door swung open. Storm Silverhand took a step into the room, earrings glittering above her gown. Out of the corner of his eye, Broglan saw Hundarr look at her with new respect. She swung the door shut behind herself.

"Come no closer," Broglan said coldly. Storm turned, one eyebrow raised—to face four ready wands. "We would know why you are here."

Storm squarely met his gaze. "It is imperative that we work more closely together, Sir Broglan. None of us can afford more deaths. You—all of you—must agree to my placing silent watch spells over you, as Lord Rowanmantle has done."

"Rowanmantle's a fool for a pretty face," Broglan snapped, "and such blandishments fail here. I've given you my refusal already; be aware that each time you force me to repeat it will bring a sharper and more hostile reception. Things would be much simpler if you were not here, Lady Harper."

"I agree," Storm told him, every inch a court lady as she took two smooth steps nearer. "They'd be much simpler indeed: you'd all be dead by now." She shook her head. "You may soon be anyway if you refuse even this simple measure of protection."

"The answer remains no, lady," Broglan said coldly, "and the door remains there, awaiting you. Pray, begone, or you'll force me to banish you from Cormyr in the name of the king! What's going on in this keep now is far too important for us to listen to silly and dangerous requests to submit to your spellcasting!"

"Oh," Storm said quietly, "were you under the misapprehension that I was requesting anything, sir? Allow me to correct that: I am not now asking you to submit to my spells. I am commanding you to do so."

Broglan stiffened. "You're in Cormyr now, Harper," he snarled. "You have no authority to *command* anything! You've already shown us that you can threaten . . . war wizards of Cormyr ignore threats!"

"Pardon me, sirrah," Storm told him smoothly, "but I do have that authority. I speak to you now not as a Harper bard, but as Marchioness Immerdusk—of Cormyr."

Broglan frowned. "What nonsense is this?" Beside him, Insprin opened his mouth to say something, but the leader of the war wizards quelled him with a dark glance.

"That is the title given me by the king of Cormyr," Storm said calmly. "Is there some problem with your hearing, sir, or comprehension?"

"The Lord Vangerdahast schools us well in what ranks and titles are borne by citizens of the realm," Broglan said icily. "In particular, when new titles are created—for the suddenly ennobled sometimes let things go to their heads, and create trouble. Lady, desist in this falsehood: all of us here would know if King Azoun had created you a marchioness—a rare rank in any case; why, I believe there are no more than eight marchionesses in all the realm."

"Azoun did not name me to any noble rank," Storm told him, gliding forward. Four wands lifted as one, and she looked coolly along them and came to a smooth halt. "My title was conferred upon me by King Baerovus Obarskyr."

"*Baerovus?*"

"It was some time ago," Storm said, "but Lord Vangerdahast's lore-learning should bear me out. I adopted the king's bastard son, Casplar Hundyl Immerdusk, as my own. I reared him, versed in the principles of law and loyalty. By ennobling me, Baerovus was able to give his unacknowledged son a senior rank at court. Casplar became the first lord chancellor of Cormyr, scribe of the laws—and so the noble house of Immerdusk was founded."

Broglan looked like a man bewildered. He frowned, shook his head as if to clear it, gabbled for a moment incoherently, and then said grimly, "Whether this be true or not, the wizards of war have never taken orders from the nobility of the realm, lady!"

"Oh?" Storm said. "They certainly did in my day."

Broglan gave her a wintry smile and a little shrug, and said lightly, triumph in his tone, "Times change, madam. Sad, isn't it? Now, if you'll excuse us, we've a few things to do that are slightly more urgent than standing about arguing matters of rank—the door, as I recall, still lies in that direction." He drew himself up and smiled at her.

Storm matched his grim smile and said, "As Vangerdahast is wont to say: not *quite* so fast, Sir Broglan." She saw Insprin and Hundarr both hide grins at that, as she put her hand very slowly into her bodice and drew forth something small. A ring.

She held it up. "Azoun did give me this," she said, "to use if I ever needed to command any lord, officer, official, or common citizen of Cormyr, in his name. It compels you to obey me as if I were the king."

Four pairs of eyes bulged in astonishment. Vangerdahast had seen to their training properly; they all recognized it, though there could scarcely be more than a dozen such items in all Faerûn.

What impressed the wizards so much as it gleamed on her palm was a Purple Dragon ring. She held it up, turning it so they could all see what adorned the gold band: a tiny sculpted dragon of electrum, heat-tinted to a delicate mauve and surrounded by a disk of silver. "Will you test its veracity, Sir Broglan?" she asked, almost reverently.

Broglan's face held awe as he stretched forth his hand to take it. The three other wizards drew in close to watch as he held the ring in his open palm, touched it with one finger, and said hoarsely, "Azoun rules."

Immediately, a clear and cultured voice—King Azoun's—arose from the ring. "As the war wizards guard," it responded.

Eyes widened among the watching wizards. They looked at Storm with more respect than she had ever seen in their eyes before. She crooked two fingers in a beckoning motion, and Broglan reluctantly tipped the ring back into her hand. "Are you prepared to obey me, Broglan?" she asked him quietly. "Or will you be forsworn before your king?"

"I—I . . . what precisely do you want? I have very specific instructions on some points," Broglan said, face twisting anxiously. "I—I can't just . . ."

With a firm hand Storm pushed aside the wand that was leveled at her chest, stepped up to him, and said, "You have a speaking-stone hidden away hereabouts. Use it."

Broglan blinked at her. "Pardon?"

"Confer with Lord Vangerdahast," she said briskly. "Get his permission to work with me, if you feel you need it. Or talk to His Majesty, if you'd prefer—but in the meantime, it can hardly hurt to show me Athlan's notes, which I know you've hidden here some-where. . . ."

Storm had turned to survey the faces of the watching mages as she spoke her last sentence—and was rewarded by Hundarr Wolfwinter, who glanced involuntarily at a certain tome on the bookshelves behind Broglan's chair.

Without another word, she stepped around the senior war wizard, the skirts of her gown hissing past. She snatched down the book Hundarr had looked at. It was the work of but a moment to thumb its latch, flip open the cover, and discover that it was a hiding-tome rather than a real volume. Curled up in its central well were a few pages of ink-scrawled parchment.

Storm flicked the topmost page open between her thumb and finger, seeing only the words, "Beware the Walker of the Worlds," before book, parchment, and all were roughly snatched away from her.

Broglan stared at her, eyes blazing. "Lady Silverhand! Kindly wait until I *have* spoken with Lord Vangerdahast, if you *don't* mind!"

She sighed theatrically and said, "Well, get *on* with it, then."

Behind them, one of the younger war wizards snorted in amusement. When Broglan swung around to see which of them it was, Storm pounced on the black velvet bundle that now lay on his table.

By the time he turned back from glaring at both of the younger mages, the fist-sized sphere of obsidian was already rising smoothly up from its cushion at the center of the black velvet circle. A slight smile on her face, Storm sat in his chair, her arms folded on the table.

"What do you think you're *doing?*" he almost screamed, lunging at the table—and then bringing himself to a halt, inches away from crashing into the furniture. The speaking stone came to its own stop not a breath away from his nose, and began to turn lazily in midair.

Storm lifted amused eyes to meet his. "Is this some sort of trick question, Sir Broglan? What does it look like?"

"Broglan?" a voice rasped, out of the stone. "Is that you?"

"Vangey!" Storm barked. "Good to talk to you again! Why don't you ever swing out to Shadowdale to see me?"

There was a moment of silence, and then the sharp voice spoke again, in tones of cold dignity. "The Lord Elminster and I did not part on the best of terms," it informed her, "and I've no wish to sneak into his very yard and perhaps bump into him."

Storm made a rude noise. "He's forgiven you, Vangey—he forgave you the very same nightfall, and that was *years* ago. Forget it, man!"

"The question is not whether he has forgiven me," Vangerdahast's voice came out of the stone very precisely, "but whether *I* have forgiven *him.*"

Storm rolled her eyes. "Well, if you haven't, you should have. Isn't it about time you set aside all this overblown pride and *grew up?*"

The obsidian stone in front of her sputtered and then snarled, "Whatever you wanted me for, good lady, this interview is at an *end!*" It quivered once, and then sank toward the tabletop.

"What have you *done?*" Broglan roared.

Storm made a gesture. The speaking stone stopped and floated back up to its former position again.

"Not until I'm finished, Old Thunderspells!" she told it crisply. "Your team has a serious problem. None of

us—from ambitious young Hundarr, here, to you at
court and Azoun up at the palace—can afford to have
you getting up on your high horse and overplaying the
high-and-mighty old wizard role. The safety of the
realm is at stake. Even if it weren't, you'd do well to set
aside the nose-in-the-air, fit-me-for-a-statue stuff, or
you'll start to believe the role. Worse, you'll start to
shrink and gnarl down to fit *it!* Royal Magician of
Cormyr, indeed!"

All of the wizards were staring at her now, aghast.
Hundarr was quivering in the grip of a rage even
greater than Broglan's. The leader of the war wizards
stepped back one deliberate pace—half to keep himself
from throttling this outrageous woman, and half
because he expected the stone to spit lightning around
the room.

The stone flickered and pulsed with sudden light.
Then the four wizards heard Lord Vangerdahast's
voice say quietly, "My apologies, Storm. What is happening at Firefall, and how can I help you?"

Jaws dropped in disbelief all around her as Storm
said crisply, "We're facing an entity who can shapeshift
and burn out the brains of its victims. They're blindbarred to all magic we've tried thus far. Since the two
initial deaths, it's slain two of your junior wizards and
the seneschal of the keep. On my arrival here, I
enjoyed a feast that was one long parade of poisons
and magical traps, too. You've got problems with a rot-
ten noble house, and this slayer who can walk right
through the ranks of the noble and powerful in Cormyr
and keep going. The boldshield—Ergluth—is willing to
do whatever it takes, but Broglan here has to have
your permission before he'll even be civil to me. Will
you tell him I'm his commander for a tenday, so we can
get to work . . . before it's too late?"

"Lord High Wizard!" Broglan shouted. "There's—"

"Broglan, I presume you heard her," the voice rasped

out from the stone. "Obey her as you would me, and tell all of the mages under you to do the same."

"I—yes, Lord High Wizard," Broglan said with a sigh.

"May I cast spells on your mages?" Storm asked.

"Gods, woman," the stone said, a hiss of exasperation in the voice, "I can see why you want to, but that's one rule I *never* break . . . only war wizards can enspell other war wizards, and then only for certain specific things—else the Dragon Throne would've faced attacks from hostile mages long since . . ."

"These are not normal times," Storm said quietly, "and I'll not misuse this grant of power. More than that, I'll drop in on you soon and scratch your ears and the small of your back the way you like, and dare not trust anyone else to—"

The stone harrumphed very loudly, and said, "Consider both the offer and the grant of power accepted. I don't think we need say anything more about such matters, do you?"

Storm smiled. "I guess not. Fare thee well, Thunderspells."

"Don't *call* me that, blast it! A man has to have some dignity," the stone said, quivering. It started to sink down toward its cushion, "And keep safe, Storm. Deliver our kingdom to us and save the day and all that wind and roar . . . but keep safe."

"You, too," Storm said gently as the stone settled onto the black velvet. She gave it a last smile, and then looked up at the four silent men above her and said brightly, "Now, this won't hurt a bit. . . ."

* * * * *

Orling the Bold unhappily strummed his harp, eyes on the bright—and empty—display case beside him. This was the last string that needed tuning. When it was done, he'd have to go tell someone about the ring vanishing. That would be the end of his night of revelry, over before it began—and perhaps of his career as a Harper. Or even his life, if they took it really amiss.

Orling gulped as he plucked the last string repeatedly. He certainly didn't feel 'Bold' right now, or even just 'bold.' No one would believe he'd not even touched the case, and the ring had just up and—

He blinked at the case again, and let out an uneasy laugh. His forehead was suddenly wet with sweat, and outside the room he heard the first trumpets echoing through Twilight Hall to start the fun. He looked in wonder at the case, shaking his tense fingers to loosen them and hardly daring to believe his eyes.

The ring was back. Floating there, turning slowly, as it had been for years. The little electrum dragon, the silver orb under it, and the plain gold band. Orling smiled.

The ring was back, as silently as it had gone. It winked almost mockingly at him—turning just as it had been turning for years.

* * * * *

The poison was rather more subtle this time, but it was still there. In the stuffed pheasant, the lemon juice and the pepper overwhelmed the burning, oily taste that Storm'd come to expect from the kitchens of the keep. There was nothing wrong with the good, sharp stonemountain cheese on her side dish, and the white sauce for the birds was simply exquisite.

Storm ate with gusto, washing down bird after bird with wine, and enjoying the sniping attacks of the Summerstars down the table. It was good entertainment—even if the chilly atmosphere was made even colder by the retention of the same seating arrangement, with empty seats where the seneschal and the two dead wizards had sat. Uncle Erlandar had also decided to miss the meal for some undisclosed reason or other. Pheirauze was preoccupied, and that left the mice free to play.

Just now, the two maiden aunts were taking turns sharpening their tongues on the outlander guest.

"Have your . . . kind . . . lived in Shadowdale long, dear?" Margort asked with kindly condescension.

"Humans?" Storm asked brightly. "Oh—for centuries, now."

"Oh, surely not as long as there have been Summerstars in Firefall Vale, dear," Nalanna put in. "We're a very old family, you know."

Not far from them, Thalance rolled his eyes, favored Storm with a sympathetic look, raised his glass to her, and drained it, all in one smooth motion. He got up from the table. Both of the dowager ladies favored him with frowns, but neither said anything as he loped down the feast hall and departed.

"A Summerstar was at King Galaghard's side when he went in to see the Last Elf, on the eve of the battle where he broke the power of the Witch-Lords," Margort said haughtily.

Storm nodded. "I remember that," she said, tapping her goblet. "I wanted to see Othorian myself. He was very rude to Thanderahast, as I recall."

"You don't expect us to believe that you were *there*, dear? I mean, *really!*" Margort said in pitying tones.

Pheirauze said coldly, "I'm sure this could go on all evening, but in defense of our . . . distinguished lady guest, it must be said that all she has done is answer your questions, Margort and Nalanna. Is there some point to this . . . inquisition? The lineage of our house *is* a matter of record, you know."

Margort darted a glance down the table, and hissed, "Not in front of her, Pheirauze!"

"Yes, in front of her," the elder dowager lady said

with a sigh. "I'm tired of this. Next you'll be telling me that old tale about her sleeping with Pyramus again!"

"Yes!" Nalanna squeaked.

Margort nodded, and said fiercely, double chin quivering, "That's it *exactly!* She's here to try to steal the vale and the keep and all away from us!"

"What?" Pheirauze shot an incredulous look down the table at Storm, who shrugged and spread her hands in a baffled gesture.

"There she goes!" Margort cried, bouncing up and down in agitation and pointing with a wrinkled hand whose wrist dripped long ropes and hoops of gems. "Acting all innocent! Why, *I* caught her sitting up in the Twilight Turret with Pyramus—late one fall, it was, when the sunsets were long. And they didn't even act ashamed!"

Heads turned all along the table to look at Storm, who smiled faintly, and waved a polite reply to all the curious stares.

"I confronted him, later, with Nalanna, and—"

"Yes!" Nalanna said, bobbing her head up and down in violent assent. "With me!"

"—he said they were lovers, and that he was going to *marry* her!"

"So you fear we have a Lady Storm Summerstar in our midst," Pheirauze mused aloud. "I'm sure the aunts have only the interests of our family at heart," she said to her guest. "To save a lot of time and sidelong comments, could you satisfy them—and, I confess, the rest of us—by telling us straight out if any such wedding ever did take place?"

Storm looked down the table, from the fascinated faces of the war wizards to Shayna's fearful gaze, and saw the young heiress clasp her mother's hand. She smiled inwardly at the two aunts, who were practically falling into their platters as they leaned out impatiently to hear what she'd say. Then she shrugged. In cases like this, the whole truth, however brutal, was best.

"Pyramus was very kind, and both a good man and a good lover," she announced clearly, "but we did not marry. How could we, after he'd secretly wedded Princess Sulesta, Rhigaerd's daughter?"

In the uproar that followed, the Dowager Lady Zarova quietly fainted and fell on her face into her soup. The Dowager Lady Pheirauze looked as if she wanted to, as well. Across the table, Storm could see at least three war wizards struggling not to laugh.

* * * * *

"S-Storm, help *me!*"

The scream cut through her reveries. Storm leapt out of bed, thrust both feet into her boots, and sprinted for the door, snatching up blade and gown from the table as she went.

She was well along the passage, with startled Purple Dragon armsmen pounding along in her wake, when she looked down at herself and realized that she wasn't yet wearing anything to belt the scabbard to.

Not that she was going to be in time. Her spell had shown her a dark and dusty room somewhere in the keep, and a beautiful woman's face—for just an instant, before flames leapt from both its eyes. The magic was shattered.

Shattered with a backlash that made her head nearly split. Hundarr Wolfwinter's brain was now ashes.

She sprinted on into the darkness anyway, snatching her blade out of its scabbard just to be safe. A moment later, she tripped over the wizard's sprawled body.

Parchments flew from Hundarr's dead hand—some of Athlan's notes, by the look of them—and as she rolled over and came up running again, Storm twisted and snatched one out of the air.

"The dragon of the keep, watching over me," she read—and then flung it away as something large slashed at her with talons. She dodged and ducked and drove her sword through glowing nothing. It was an illusion.

Cold laughter welled up ahead of her. She sprinted toward it. A moment later, the floor gave way beneath her boots. She was falling. A deep, grating rumble overhead told her that the stones tumbling down on top of her were no illusions at all.

There were six—no, seven. All of them were as big as she was. Storm hit rough stone, and bounced bruisingly. She struck once more and felt ribs splinter like kindling. Then the first of the huge blocks crashed down on top of her.

As bones shattered and the breath was smashed out of her, the last thing she knew was the sword shattering in front of her face.

Then the other blocks came down.

Eight
THE KISS OF EVIL

The pain drove her back to wakefulness—raw, shattering pain. Tears glimmered in Storm's lashes as she tried to see past the rock that had crushed her chest. Every breath was a searing, tearing agony of bubbling froth and grating ends of bone. Her back was broken, and her right leg seemed to be either missing or shattered to rubbery nothing just above her knee.

Into every life, a little pain must fall. . . . By the gods, fall was right. She'd had a bad one.

Patiently, Storm called on the fire within her—rising, cool, cleansing, divine fire of Mystra. She sent it flowing into places where pain throbbed, or stabbed . . . or where she felt nothing at all.

The fire went where she bid, rushing into crushed and mangled places. The sudden, sharp jabs of agony made her hiss bloody huffs of breath, shouts such as an angry, wounded badger might make.

She smiled at the thought, her eyes dark with pain. From just beyond the crushing rock, Maxer—or something that wore Maxer's face—grinned back at her. Seeing that face hurt most of all. Tears blinded her.

"Not quite dead yet?" It—no, *he*; the manner as well as the voice were male—laughed, and said, "An oversight easily corrected. Give me a kiss for old times' sake, Beloved."

With those mocking words, the face of her dead lover leaned down over hers . . . giving her the revulsion and anger she needed.

Storm blinked back tears and glared up at it. "You're not my Maxer. Your charade disgusts me, whoever you are. Such tricks won't make me lower my guard."

That brought on a real laugh. "Lower your guard? Why bother when you're smashed like a hurled egg? Oh, that's rare!"

The false face of the man she'd loved so much, and missed so terribly, mastered its mirth and leaned close again to whisper, "Your back is broken, isn't it? Who'd have thought kicking a wedge away from a few blocks of stone would destroy one of the legends of Faerûn? You're going to die, my pretty one . . . and I'll feed on all you have been, and all you would have been. Just as soon as you're weak enough. . . ."

Storm closed her eyes, shuddering as fresh agonies blazed out within her. Boast and taunt just a little longer, shapeshifter. Give me the time I need to grow whole again . . . and then strong once more. . . .

"Ah, but you still hope for a rescue, I see," the murderer said. "You Chosen have always been so arrogant, so secure in your power—and so unused to hiding that triumph in your eyes. I saw that look!"

Brutal hands rocked the stone atop her chest, forcing half-knit bones to grind and turn in their sockets. Storm shrieked in torment, tears bursting from her eyes and blood from her nose and mouth.

Cold laughter rolled around her again as the stone rocked back and forth, back and forth. The false face leaned close over her again.

"Dying yet? Not quite? No? Time for a little more fun, then!"

As the stone jostled more violently, Storm gasped, opened her eyes, and flexed the fingers she'd need. They moved slowly, still numb, but—well, they'd have to do.

She waited, gathering her will. As that face bent over her again—and actually opened its jaws to bite her!—she whispered the phrase that unleashed her Galkyn's bolt spell. Silver fire leapt within her as the magic surged forth.

At this range, she could not miss. The shapeshifter was lifted off his feet, squalling. Magic thundered into him, tore open his front, and rushed down his body and out his nether end.

Storm watched him crash against the far wall of the rock-filled pit. With more satisfaction than she'd felt in the fall of a foe for quite some time, she called again on the silver fire.

It roiled and cascaded within her. She set her teeth and pushed with all the strength she had. Tears came, but the stone block atop her stayed where it was.

She sank back with a groan, lips trembling. Perhaps the stubborn immobility of the stone was a good thing. Sudden shouts came from overhead, and a rock whistled down into the pit, cracking off the wall just beside the shapeshifter's head.

The murderer ducked away—straight into the path of another slung stone. He reeled, gasped out a curse, and crawled toward the rocks that lay atop Storm, seeking their shelter.

Storm heard a barked command, and almost smiled. The pursuing Purple Dragons must have found the pit and decided this stranger was the murderer. They

were busily employing their slings right now—and
buying her the time she needed.

The murderer must have thought so too. He snarled
another curse, cast a spell, and soared up out of sight.

Storm bent all her will to healing herself, gasping
and shuddering in agony as limb after limb jittered
and ballooned back to its proper shape, shifting the
massive blocks of stone. She'd not have much more
time. . . .

The first armsman made a short, despairing cry as
he pitched down. Close above Storm, he struck the
wall with a wet, pulpy sound, and said no more; his
limbs convulsed once or twice after his body landed on
the rocks and slithered down their far side.

Storm drew in her breath, thankful for the small
mercy of the corpse's location, and found the strength
at last to shift the stone atop her. She expanded her
lungs and begin to heal them and the splintered mess
that was her rib cage. The expected second Purple
Dragon corpse fell limp and silent, his neck already
broken, and crashed down hard on the upraised edge
of her stone.

The impact made her gasp in fresh agony—but the
stone rolled slowly away from her, crushing the armsman with sounds both brittle and wet. Storm shuddered, but dared spare no time for sorrow or revulsion
. . . her foe would be back for her soon enough.

A third guardsman fell into the pit, roaring out his
despair. Storm was still too weak and pain-racked to
do anything to save him. He fell at her feet, smashed
on the rocks, and stared at her beseechingly before his
eyes grew dull and distant. In an ear that could no
longer hear, Storm whispered, "You shall be avenged."
She bent over the man to draw forth his sword. By the
smiling mercy of the gods, it was unbroken.

Not so the dagger—but the man had a second one in
his boot. Storm was fumbling it forth when another

armsman crashed down beside her, limbs jerking in agonized spasms.

A familiar form jumped up from a crouched landing on the soldier's gut.

"On our feet so soon? My, but Mystra must love you!" the man who was not Maxer said merrily.

Storm pounced, her borrowed blade flashing. "*I'd* love the world around me just a trifle more if it held just a few less meddling Malaugrym!" she snarled, thrusting. Her steel caught in cloth that tore as her foe twisted away. He was as fast as she, maybe faster.

A dodge, a duck, and they were both sure of that. He was fast enough not only to leap clear of her seeking steel—but to mutter out a spell.

Luckily for Storm, the pit was full of loose stones. There was a sliding and clicking of rubble behind her as the big stone that had crushed her once—a boulder as tall as a troll—lifted into the air under the bidding of her foe's magic. She spun around as it rose. The shattered body of a Purple Dragon peeled limply away from it.

"There are far greater powers in the worlds than that clan of proud, self-important feuding fools," he said mockingly from behind her. The stone thundered down.

Without looking, Storm thrust viciously behind her at that voice. She spat out silver fire at the stony death above her. The blood-smeared boulder shattered into a thousand shards.

"Such as?" she snarled, and spun around. Her blade touched nothing but air.

From a safe dozen rocks distant, he was murmuring another spell. Storm flung her dagger at him.

It spun end over end, straight at his face. It clattered off stone. He was suddenly not there.

Storm went into a crouch of her own, bringing the sword up in front of her and trying to watch everywhere at once. The air glimmered. She spun around. He appeared out of it. She dived into a thrust, and was rewarded with a startled gasp and blood on her sword tip before he was gone again.

She rolled to a stop beside one of the crushed Purple Dragons. Storm sprang away from the blood-slick stones. If he was going to be blinking in and out all around her, she needed good footing. She stabbed at empty air, danced a few steps, turned, and stabbed again.

He chuckled from nearby. "The Sharn battle the Phaerimm, and the Phaerimm fight everyone. Others mightier than these walk the worlds, you know . . . or should know, daughter of Mystra. You've not heard of such? Die ignorant, then." He was gone again.

Storm whirled. The air around her shimmered and grew a cold fang. The bard twisted away, smashing the blade frantically aside with her sword. The dagger that had hurt her spun away from the bloodied hand of her foe—before the air shimmered and hid him again. Storm cursed heartily and whirled her blade around; it struck something. She heard a grunt of pain. An instant later, her sword struck stone with numbing force. She reeled, fighting for balance on the shifting scree underfoot.

A face loomed above hers as his body struck aside her sword arm. Lips that burned kissed her cheek with obscene delicacy.

With her free hand, Storm clawed at those eyes. Amid shimmering, the face was gone again. Her fingers felt the place where his kiss had burned away flesh, exposing her jawbone. Angrily she ran in a swift circle, hacking at air—until she saw him appear across the pit. He leaned against the wall with almost casual hauteur.

"Who are you?" Storm spat, raising her blade.

The man who was not Maxer laughed. "I am the wolf

in your dreams," he said. His limbs grew fur. "I am the child you pass in the street." His smile melted into a woman's face more beautiful than her own had ever been, with moon-pale eyes and long, sweeping black hair. Then it dwindled into the leering visage of a dwarf.

"I can be everyone, everywhere. Soon, I'll be much, much more than that." He left that quiet taunt hanging in the air as he became a Purple Dragon armsman, the mage Broglan, and one of the Summerstar maiden aunts.

With narrowed eyes Storm watched him. She murmured and made small gestures as his shapechanging display unfolded. Her spellcasting earned a mirthless grin from him. She finished one spell, and nothing happened. Without delay, she began another. His grin became a frown—and she was suddenly alone in the pit.

An instant later, a view of the keep battlements unfolded in her mind, only to fade almost immediately and be replaced by the lightless interior of an empty bedchamber, lamplight from the courtyard flickering through its windows. The scene changed again twice before Storm's second spell was done. She kept her mind firmly shaping it—and then let it take her to the latest scene.

The servants working the night through in the kitchens were in their usual bustle, with steam rising from the stew pots here, there, and everywhere. They darted about putting this tray of goose pies into the ovens and taking that tray of stuffed silverfin out. One servant looked down, startled, as a shaggy black dog suddenly appeared in his way, growled warningly—and then vanished again.

He'd have been more startled by far, Storm thought wryly, if he'd seen the true shape of the creature who'd appeared to him as a dog.

The cook looked up, saw her, and dropped his tray of pastries.

Shouting in horror, he fled as the crash echoed around the room. A gravy pan made a deafening *whonga-onga-onga* clatter. A curse came behind Storm. She turned, blade up, just in case someone was in the mood to hurl cleavers.

She was in time to see a steaming pan of gammon pies flung to the floor by a man who sprinted over them even before they landed. Another man backed away from her, white-faced. The gleaming platter that hung on a cupboard beside him shone back her reflection clearly: a tall, wild-eyed woman with silver hair, garbed only in blood. Teeth and bone glinted in the hole burned in the side of her face, and there was more blood all over the sword in her hand. She smiled ruefully, closed her eyes until her tracer magic showed her the next place clearly, and let the other spell take her there.

Mystra's Kiss, but those pies had smelled good.

She was in another dark chamber now—a lady's robing room, with a flicker of shimmering air at its far end where a black dog was just disappearing.

The gown hanging to her left was the one Dowager Lady Zarova had worn to the last feast. Storm heard soft weeping from beyond the door at the end of the room. She closed her eyes to find the next place her foe would appear.

Zarova was tossing in the throes of a nightmare, but the shapechanger appeared at the foot of her bed only long enough to murmur something—something magical, no doubt—and was gone again. Storm reached mentally . . . where was he going? Wh—ah. A turret room. The chamber at the top of the Twilight Turret!

Her magic took her there. As her feet touched the bare stone floor, it became spongy and somehow warm. Black, eel-like tentacles rose around her in a small, hungry forest. Cold laughter came from a stout stone pillar across the room. She struggled for two long strides toward it before the entwining tentacles held her fast.

The pillar became Maxer. He stood and watched her, a broad smile on his face. "Centuries of service to the goddess of magic," he gloated, "only to be caught in so simple a spell-trap!"

He took a step nearer. His arm grew long, dark, and serpentine, until it resembled one of the many tentacles coiling ever more tightly around her. He reached out almost caressingly.

Storm spat silver fire.

The tentacle darkened and curled involuntarily away, trailing smoke. The smile on the murderer's face turned brittle. "I'll be back, Lady Storm," he said softly, "a little later. About when you've used up your fires."

Storm held his gaze and let the fire suddenly blaze up around her. Blackened tentacles fell away into ashes. The sword in her hand melted into glistening syrup and flowed out of her fingers. Letting it fall, uncaring, she took a slow, deliberate stride toward him, only to be caught fast in another dozen tentacles.

He smiled coldly. "Sooner or later you'll run out of those blasts. Then I'll be back, and you'll know what it really is to burn! In the meantime, I've heard there's a griffon stabled not far away in the vale. I'd dearly love to gain the power to fly!" His words became wild laughter, and then ended as if cut off by a knife. He vanished, leaving her alone with the tentacles.

Storm let herself relax into their choking, tightening grip. She bent her will to seeing where he was now.

Her tracer was fading; she saw only someplace dark before the strangling tentacles broke her spell. Grimly, she let out the divine fire again, consuming the things as if they were smoke. She kept walking until they were all ashes around her . . . black flecks that eddied and were gone.

She shook her head. The man—if it was a man—was as mad as he was powerful. Somehow he could drain abilities from those he killed and take them for his own. Why taunt her and lead her on wild chases through kitchens and . . . oh.

He was slaying particular victims to lure her here and subsuming their powers until he grew strong enough to take her.

It would be simple enough to flee his trap, but better by far to stop him here and now . . . before he dropped out of sight and quietly subsumed most of Cormyr.

Storm shook her head. Well, he'd be back soon enough. She went to a window and thrust its shutters wide. The lamps in the courtyard below flickered in a quickening night breeze; she felt it glide over her skin as she looked south and west over the darkness of Cormyr. The stars twinkled in their endless watches.

"Oh, Mystra," she whispered. "Guide me. I see a sphere of fire around this place . . . do I see your will, and is this needful now?"

She felt the awesome weight of dark eyes in her mind, regarding her unblinkingly. Suddenly she saw herself watering plants back at the farm, and picking out weeds with her fingers. It was a hot day, and she wiped away sweat—but went to the pond for more water despite the beating sun. The plants needed it. . . .

The vision faded. Well enough; she had a clear answer: it was needful.

Slowly and carefully, Storm let out unseen tendrils of the fire within her, stretching them out in a sheet that flowed around the turret and down the outer wall of the keep. Ever thinner she stretched them, letting the invisible fire flow, feeling the vitality within her ebbing away as the net spread wider.

Along the walls of the keep she went. She seeped down into the earth beside old, mossy blocks of stone, welling into every crack and crevice. She closed her eyes, trembling with the effort, and embraced the stone sill, pressing her lips and body against it, willing the fire to flow. Deep into the earth, to enfold the cellars and deep wells and all with reaching fingers of force. Up again, beyond the stables and the granaries and the far wall, up the outside of the south wall. Racing now, the sheet of fire joined the spreading edges she'd laid on the stone earlier. It widened into a bowl enclosing Firefall Keep in unseen silver fire.

"Mystra," Storm gasped, dimly aware that she was sinking down the sill, the stone scraping away flesh as she went to her knees on the cold and dusty floor. She shaped the fire up into a tongue, now, an arch of unseen force that reached down to give her bowl a handle, like a basket. The handle thickened as she built up fire along its edges, ready to slam it down and complete the sphere once her quarry returned.

She was shaking, now. Weakness replaced the surging fire. This was a mightier magic than many an archmage could hope to craft, and it was costing her dearly. Once the keep was sealed, the silver fire would bring her no instant energy—she'd need to eat, drink, and sleep again. It would shield her from no more spells, and bring her no more new ones once those in her mind were cast and gone. She'd already lost the means to farspeak the other Chosen, and to hear folk around Faerûn speaking her name or the Rune of the Seven. If she was hurt, healing would come very slowly. So long as the silver fire thrummed and flowed around Firefall Keep, trapping her foe in it with her, she'd be little more than an ordinary mortal.

Just Storm Silverhand, a lady with silver hair, a smart mouth, some skill with a sword, and a not-bad voice—against a shapeshifter. "How," she asked the night ruefully as she dragged herself back to the window, "do I get myself into these things?"

As if her words had been a cue, a griffon that was half-man swooped like a great bird into the courtyard. It struggled to grow human arms. Storm smiled grimly, let her hair hang down to cover her face as if she'd collapsed over the sill, and sent the fire flowing to seal up the last gaps in the sphere.

Merrily the murderous shapechanger circled the lamps, causing the guards there to cower down behind raised halberds. With a roar, he rose, sweeping up toward her.

He was going to circle the turret. This was it. Storm set her teeth and made the sphere of fire pulse, letting the surge roar painfully through her breast. It flowed freely; the sphere was complete.

The griffon's head became the laughing face of a man as he raced toward her. Through her hair, Storm watched his eyes widen with delight at her apparent helplessness. Then he veered up and to the left, racing around the turret, out of sight—and into her barrier.

Storm felt him strike the silver fire. The strain made flames sputter from her nose and mouth. She threw her head back and gasped as she felt the fire claw at him, and his clawing, slashing struggles to break through it.

She could hear it roaring, now, and see the glow of its blaze around the tower. Burn, then, murderer! Burn!

The Bard of Shadowdale dug long fingers into the window sill and snarled, her face a mask of sweat. She strove to sear the shapechanger to nothingness. From behind the tower came a tattered cry of pain.

Let there be no mercy.

Nine

DEATH AND A DARK MASTER

Silver fire roared and raged, blinding him. He struggled to grow eyes on stalks before his own were burned away forever. That bitch of a bard was too near for him to be defenseless. . . .

He thrashed against flame that seared and ate at him, melting flesh like bubbling wax from bones that slumped in their turn. Defeated, the shapechanger flapped the seared, blackened stumps of his wings frantically, hurling himself back over the courtyard.

Trailing fire, the griffon-man fell heavily onto a balcony on the turret next to where Storm clung to her window. He rose, reeled, smashed aside flimsy shutters, and fled into the keep.

The man snarled softly as he ran through dark rooms on unsteady cloven hooves. Throbbing pain danced through his shoulders. Whatever spell the Mystra-woman had used on him, he dared not taste it again.

When he tried to change shape, it felt as if he were sliding through soft mud. The world grew faint and dim. He could not tell where his limbs were, or how they'd obeyed his shaping. Yes, he dare not wade into one of those spells again.

With an arm that was partly a tentacle, he shouldered through a doorway, and found himself looking into the startled face of a guard. An old man with a mustache, who was opening his mouth to shout—

The shapechanger closed it for him forever, stabbing savagely with the crab-claw he'd managed to grow on what was left of his right wing. The guard wasn't expecting an extra arm to be there. With his face torn off, he wouldn't be expecting anything ever again.

The shapechanger slammed the body brutally and repeatedly into the wall, listening to bones shatter. He thought about where to go now. Someplace to rest. Someplace safe, to mend. . . .

For what seemed a long time, he cowered in the darkness of the Haunted Tower. At last, his body obeyed him again, flesh flowing and shifting with its old ease. The stabbing pains were gone, but his feet and shoulders still ached. Damn that woman! She'd seemed such an overconfident, overkind idiot, too. . . .

Not like that cold-as-a-blade dowager, who . . . well, now: Pheirauze Summerstar! Well, why not?

He grew eyes that gleamed in the dark. He shrugged and became the black, sleek body of a panther. Looking around once, the great cat stretched, sniffed the air, and padded off into the keep, seeking a certain bedchamber.

* * * * *

"That will be all, Narlargus," the Dowager Lady Pheirauze murmured, the crack of command surfacing once more in her voice.

The old servant bent his lips to kiss her hand—a gesture he knew she loved. As he rose from the bed, he kept his eyes downcast. Daring to survey her as she lay at ease among the candles, with their light dancing over her jewelry, would earn him a whipping.

Catching up his robe from the floor, he bowed low and backed away from the bed. Surprisingly, she spoke again when his hand fell upon the door ring.

"My thanks, Narlargus."

He froze, but no more words came. After a moment, he turned. She'd never bothered to thank him before.

Still keeping his head down, the old servant knelt, touched his forehead to the floor, and then rose and withdrew, closing the door carefully—and very softly—behind him.

Pheirauze felt something like regret as she heard the door settle into place for what would undoubtedly be the last time. She would miss those long sessions with her loyal dresser—even if it had been years since they'd loved the night through to watch the sun come up, when she'd used a candle flame to burn her mark on his thigh.

But if there was one thing the cruel gods had taught her in her long life, it was that all things, however precious, must pass away.

She stretched among the candles, and raised her eyes to regard the cat-headed man who stood silently in the shadows. Narlargus had not even noticed him, but Pheirauze had felt the feline gaze upon her. The cat head turned swiftly to regard the now-closed door, and then back to meet her gaze once more.

"I know who you must be," she calmly told the silent shapechanger. "And what you've come for. If I promise I'll not scream, or plead, or fight, or raise any alarm, will you tell me what you hope to gain by my death?"

"I hope to learn from you where old gold lies hidden," the voice out of the shadows came smoothly. "The wealth of the Summerstars. Yet I confess that I am here *now,* when it seems that I face true battles ahead, to gain the wits and drive and cunning I see in Pheirauze Summerstar."

"It is almost all I have left," she replied calmly, watching those cat eyes roam up and down her still-beautiful body. "Almost."

He lifted an eyebrow that no cat would have possessed. "You do not fear me?"

She lifted her smooth shoulders in a shrug and said, "A little. But I fear a slow, lingering death more." She spread her hands in welcome, gestured up and down at herself, and added, "Come. I've been expecting you—and if I can't run from you, perhaps I can live on in you. My hips and shoulders pain me almost constantly, now, and my hearing on the left side is almost gone. I want to feel youth and vigor once more. So come to me now. Slay me—but let it be slow, so that I can teach you of what I wield before I'm gone. You won't be sorry you did."

"Can I trust you?" the cat-headed man asked, rough wonder in his voice.

"The bellpull is there," Pheirauze told him, her eyes very large and dark. "Loop it up out of my reach if you prefer. Behind yon hanging you'll find a bar to keep the door closed. There are two concealed ways into this room, and the doors to both are locked." With one finger, she lifted a swirl-shaped golden pendant from her breast. "Their keys—the only keys—are here."

Warily, the cat-headed man took a step forward, his eyes darting about the room. Slowly he grew a tentacle and reached for the bellpull, and two more to seek out the door bar; Pheirauze watched in fascination, swallowing once.

"Does any magic await me?" he asked softly, gesturing with one circle of a tentacle at the bed. The bellpull rose up to the ornate canopy above her bed, and the bar settled into its sockets.

"I keep no magic in my bed," the dowager lady told him calmly, "but if you fear traps, choose a spot on the floor yourself."

He shook his head slowly. "That will not be necessary. Lady, you will be remembered with honor."

"It is all I ask," she whispered as he rose over her and grew gentle fingers to encircle her wrists. "It is more than many can expect."

His grip was like immovable iron on her wrists and ankles. Pheirauze shuddered then, at the first, tentative touch of fire—but the firebringer found that he could be gentle and slay slowly. What was even more surprising was that he truly wanted to.

* * * * *

Gods, but she'd been willful! Briefly he'd had to fight down her wants and schemes to keep hold of his own. He forgave her that, and almost any villainy she might have planned, for what she'd yielded unto him. Pheirauze Summerstar had always been able to speak to the minds of humans near her, and even dominate some of them!

He laughed exultantly and looked down almost fondly at the shrunken husk that lay beside him, limbs spread but somehow still proud. Not wanting to crush any part of it, he bent with infinite gentleness to kiss the fire-scorched lips before rolling up off the bed.

In silence for a time, he looked down at all that was left of Pheirauze Summerstar. He half smiled, shook his head, and swept a row of guttering candles onto the bed.

Two strides took him to more candles. A funeral pyre was only fitting for a lady of such splendid spirit; matron of her clan and wielder of such power. Power now his!

He laughed aloud, threw aside the door bar, and ran

out into the passage, becoming a hound as he went
down the hall. Behind him, the bed burst with a loud
roar into sudden, towering flames. The Purple
Dragons would have to scramble to save this part of
the keep. By then, of course, the man who was more
than a man would be long gone.

* * * * *

Storm toweled the last of the bathwater from her
limbs and strode toward the bed, where she'd laid out
fresh clothes. On the way, she glanced at the tall oval
mirror on the wall, and saw that her cheek looked as
smooth as it felt; the deep burn was gone. Well, thank
Mystra for the small things as well as those that shake
all Faerûn. . . .

Linen briefs and halter, green hose and stays, her
traveling boots—who knows where her hunt for a
shapeshifter might lead her?

White shirt, leather tunic, sword belt, and gloves.
Gods, but she looked like she was off to some forest
war! Storm shook her head and sang softly, "Forth
went the maiden, sword by her side . . ." Striking a
pose, hand on hip, she stretched like some great cat
and went to the door.

"Too fair to crawl, but too 'fraid to ride. . . ." she continued. Mouth open to sing the next line, she paused,
sniffed the air—and snatched open the door.

Smoke. She was out and down the hall at a run
before she'd even selected a curse. Somewhere in the
keep, there was fire.

* * * * *

Running feet pounded past the door, and men shouted. There was a distant crash, more shouts—and then
more hurrying, booted feet.

"*Move,* damn you!" an officer barked right outside the door.

The noise brought Shayna Summerstar awake. She sat up, blinking, in the close darkness of her canopied bed. There was a sharp smell in the air. She sniffed. Smoke.

Smoke?

Gods, was the keep afire? Since the Harper lady had come, men had been dying and there had been tumult and much whispering among armsmen and wizards alike. . . what *else* would the days ahead bring?

She rolled out of bed, put a bare foot on the soft rug, and took a step sharply to the side, to bring her other foot down on cold stone and jolt herself fully awake.

More men ran past. "The whole floor's ablaze!" someone shouted.

It *was* a fire. Shayna swallowed and went to her wardrobe. She'd need boots, and her jewel-coffer, and—

She swung the wardrobe door wide, and stared into the eyes of her grandmother, Pheirauze. But those familiar eyes were looking at her out of a man's face!

"Come," said a voice that was almost her grandmother's. A firm hand took hold of hers.

"Yes," Shayna said quietly, not even remembering to whimper.

The man with her grandmother's eyes thrust aside her best gowns as if they were rags, and led her to a dark place at the back of her wardrobe—and through it, into blackness beyond. The young Lady Summerstar scarcely knew when he slid a panel closed behind them, and drew her on down a narrow, damp passage that led straight into the Haunted Tower. . . .

So it was that when frantic chambermaids led two Purple Dragons into the bedchamber to take the flower of the Summerstars to safety, they found her gone from her bed, with no clothes taken and no sign of where she could have gone. The bed was simply—

empty. One of the maids shrieked and ran from the room, and another dissolved in sobs, but the two armsmen poked and peered all around the chamber, swearing horribly.

. . . The man whose face was slowly changing led the Lady Shayna on into darkness, away from the tumult. The sharp smell faded behind them, and the noise with it, as they went. The floor was cold under Shayna's bare feet, and the air chilled her through the thin silk and openwork lace panels of her nightgown. It seemed as if a mist lay on her thoughts. It was a warm, comforting mist, which did not lift even when they came to a chamber of real, luminous fog.

With a hunger she'd seen on other mens' faces before, the man turned to look her up and down. Somehow, this place of eerie, empty darkness was a haven of comfort as long as she stared into those dark eyes . . . eyes that seemed to hold two dancing red flames.

The fiery gaze held her bound—and a voice cut like a knife through her head:

I AM YOUR DARK MASTER. ADDRESS ME THUS.

"Y-Yes," she said, lips trembling. She was suddenly more afraid than she had ever been in her life. As she stared into those dark, gloating eyes, a word swam unbidden into her mind: thrall. Thrall . . .

YES?

Yes Dark Master, she said in her mind.

He smiled and nodded.

Shayna found herself smiling and nodding too. Somehow the title fit the figure standing in the darkness before her.

Then a door in her mind opened. Through it tumbled images, phrases, and iron-hard feelings that burned her and flayed her, surging through her and battering down any self-will she'd managed to cling to.

Grandmare Pheirauze?

ALWAYS, CHILD. I SHALL BE HERE, WATCHING
OVER YOU ALWAYS.

[Fear.] *Must you?*

OF COURSE. WE HAVE WORK TO DO, YOU AND
I.

[Confusion.] *Who are you, really—changing man?*

YOUR MASTER. PHEIRAUZE LIVES IN ME. WE
HAVE WORK BEFORE US—SHE, I, AND YOU: WE
MUST OVERCOME THE WOMAN WHO SERVES
MYSTRA.

The Lady Storm?

YES. YOU MUST HELP LURE HER TO ME.

Why do you need her? You have me!

I MUST HAVE HER POWER, SHAYNA. POWER
YOU LACK.

[Disappointment.] [Fear.] *If I bring you Storm, will
you still want me?*

OF COURSE. I SHALL ALWAYS WANT YOU.
JUST AS YOU SHALL COME TO WANT—AND
NEED—ME. BUT FOR NOW, OBEY: COME WITH
ME.

The eyes of flame turned away from her. Shayna
trembled, and found herself trotting along in the wake
of her Dark Master. He grew long, wriggling arms like
eels and hurried along passages she'd never seen, ways
in her own home that she did not know.

After a long but swift journey, the changing man
abruptly halted, turned, and fixed his fiery eyes on
hers.

DO YOU WANT TO SERVE ME?

Yes. Oh, yes, she told him, nodding frantically
despite the silent scream that rose somewhere inside
her.

THEN OBEY. A tentacle snatched something down
from a high ledge—something cold and sharp: a dagger. Its hilt slapped into her palm, hard and reassuringly heavy.

Shayna held it, scarcely daring to breathe. Another
tentacle did something, and the wall ahead rolled
open. Flickering torchlight flooded into the dark passage. The Dark Master stepped into the light and was
gone.

COME TO THE DOOR. His command rolled
through her.

Shayna did so, gliding forward on bare feet. The
blade trembled in her hands and excitement rose in
her breast. The Dark Master faced her, but between
them was the back of a guard in chain mail. His sword
was raised, and he was in a wary stance. His attention
was fixed on the man who had something that looked
like glistening eels hanging from his shoulders. The
master did not look at Shayna.

STRIKE AT MY COMMAND. STRIKE NOW.

A sudden image in her mind showed her just how.
YesyesNOW!

The knife flashed. Shayna struck swiftly. She drew
the blade firmly across the unseen throat. A sudden
splash of hot blood over her hands.

The man turned and gurgled. His elbow crashed
into her ribs. Trying to ignore the pain, she stepped
back, let the guard fall, and watched him die.

His eyes stared up at hers in horrified recognition.
The light in them faded, and they rolled up to stare
forever.

Her master smiled at her. To her horror, Shayna
found herself smiling back. He gestured for her to let
the dagger fall. She did so, standing stock-still as his
tentacles became long, glistening tongues that lapped
and licked every spot of blood from her hands and
arms.

The smile broadened. The eyes became those of
Pheirauze Summerstar once more.

AN EASY THING, WHEN I BID IT. BUT YOU
MUST HAVE MORE PRACTICE. GO NOW TO THE

STEWARD, ILGRETH DRIMMER.

Shayna stiffened. *That fussy old fart?*

YOU WILL DO AS I BID. HEARKEN . . .

The lady who was now head of House Summerstar grew pale as the voice only she could hear continued. This was a test. She'd do it willingly or as an automaton under iron control, but carry it out one way or the other. Slowly, uncertainly, she gave him a smile.

* * * * *

The guardcaptain had curtly ordered him to keep to his room until released to do otherwise, and Ilgreth Drimmer was a man who followed orders. The smoke grew thicker, and he could hear distant coughing and cursing. He dared not do more than stick his head out into the hallway to see what might be happening.

There was, of course, nothing to be seen. The same nothing he'd looked at a score or more times already. He paced back and forth before the open door of his room, worrying about what might be lost if the fire spread—things he could be, nay, *should* be snatching up and carrying out to safety even now! He was going to have to . . .

For perhaps the twentieth time, he strode determinedly to the doorway to begin the vital work only he knew how to do. He might not be able to fight fires, but no Purple Dragon was going to tell . . .

"Ilgreth?"

He came to an abrupt, staring halt. He opened and closed his mouth several times, finding it did not work no matter what position he put it in.

Shayna Summerstar was leaning against the door frame, a thin silk nightgown clinging to her in several places. She was smiling at him in a way that Ilgreth had never dreamed he'd see from her—or any other beautiful lass of her age.

"The fire is well under control, they tell me," she said in a low, husky voice, unfolding herself from the door frame and gliding forward. Her gown fell open.

Involuntarily Ilgreth looked down, and then up, and gulped again. He kept his eyes firmly on her face, but knew his own face was blazing. Try as he might, nothing would come out of his mouth.

"So it provides me with the distraction I've been waiting for," she continued, drawing the door firmly closed and wedging a chair against it. "Think no more about flames, but about this instead: I have always loved you."

Then she was pressed against him, soft and warm. "For years," she told his throat, "I've looked for a chance for us to . . . be together."

In mute disbelief, Ilgreth stared at her.

Emerald eyes smiled up into his. "Take me to your bed," she whispered. "I've waited so long."

"Ah, uh—a-ho!" Ilgreth burst out intelligently, finding his voice at last. "Lady, are you *sure* you're—"

"Ilgreth," she said, pushing him back onto the bed and planting a knee on his chest. "I'm *very* sure. Humor me. . . ."

"Ah, yes, of course, lady," Ilgreth said faintly, wondering when this dream would end, and where he'd find himself when he awakened. . . .

* * * * *

The man with the tentacles and the face that was slowly changing sprawled at ease in Lady Shayna Summerstar's abandoned bed. A goblet of fine wine was in one hand and the decanter he'd filled it from in the other. He was smiling and nodding at something that was unfolding in another bedchamber.

He suddenly stiffened, spilling wine on the coverlet, and sat up. Newly gained memories of similar things had stirred within him—reminding him of a certain someone who knew far too much.

He tossed goblet and decanter carelessly away and snapped his fingers decisively before the items crashed to the floor. He was gone out the open door in a trice, striding hard along the passage outside, toward the source of the smoke.

* * * * *

"How are we—?" The guardcaptain was too breathless to say more, but the soot-blackened armsman nodded in understanding.

"Winning, sir—the two chambers beyond are as wet as duck ponds, and the fire's more smoke now than flame. As long as the roof-timbers don't catch . . ."

The weary, sweat-drenched officer nodded grimly. "Good. Hand me another bucket, and we'll go look at th—"

He reached back for the next bucket in the slopping line, but paused in astonishment. Beside him, old Narlargus slumped against the wall, and the bucket he held gently poured its contents out onto his boots and down the steps.

There was a smoldering, ashen stump where his head should have been.

Armsman and officer looked at each other and then back at the corpse sliding slowly down the wall, trailing a black smear of ash. They gabbled prayers and oaths, and fled in terror.

Storm Silverhand shortly came striding up the stair, cast a grim glance at the slain servant, and broke into a run. She was soon splashing along a passage whose walls were stained with soot, and whose floor stood an inch deep in water. Voices came from a room ahead, and Storm turned into it.

Weary Purple Dragons stood staring at a pile of

ashes on the floor. "Is the fire out?" Storm asked.

"Aye, Lady," Ergluth Rowanmantle told her, "that's not what we're worried over, now."

Storm looked a silent question at him, and he raised grim eyes to meet hers. "This was the bedchamber of the Dowager Lady Pheirauze Summerstar," he explained, "and *that* was her bed."

Storm looked down at the pile of ashes. "And she was in it when the fire . . ."

"The flames started here, so far as we can tell by the marks," he said, "but that's not what—well, look here." He gestured with the tip of his boot at gold puddles on the floor among the ash. "This was an anklet, and, here, a row of rings. These—all of these—are what she called her 'gold glisters'; the jewelry she never removed."

"She died here," Storm agreed, nodding.

"Lady," the boldshield said wearily, "have you ever seen a fire that left puddled gold behind, but not a single bone? She's gone, *completely*—and yet she must have been in this; I've been told she couldn't get some of those rings off over her knuckles."

"There's a man on the stairs back there," Storm told him, "a servant, by his livery, who has his head—just his head—burnt away. He was carrying water buckets when it happened."

Their eyes met. Two mouths tightened into identical thin lines.

"Our murderer, it seems," Ergluth said softly, "has s—"

"My lords!" The breathless shout came down the passage from a servant who coughed out smoke. "Lord Boldshield?"

"In here," Ergluth said sharply, turning to the door.

A man in the livery of the house ducked in through the door, a torch in his hand. "Sir," he panted. His eyes went to Storm and then darted away again. "There's something you must see. Pray come quickly!"

Ergluth wasted no time on questions, but gestured for the man to lead them; the folk in the room emptied out into the passage after him. They had shouldered through a doorway and started down the stairs when the Purple Dragon commander asked his first question.

"Will we need our swords out?"

The man shook his head, and then turned on the landing below them to do it again. His face was grim. "Nay—too late for that."

He stopped at an open door where two Purple Dragons were standing guard, and gestured within. Storm and Ergluth looked at each other.

"The steward," the warrior told her. "Ilgreth Drimmer."

Something hard came into Storm's face, and she laid a hand on his arm. "I'd like to look at this alone for a breath or two, if you don't mind," she said quietly.

Ergluth shrugged. "It won't make any difference to him," he said wearily. "Go ahead." Then he laid a hand on her arm, and murmured in her ear, "Was he a Harper? Is that it?"

Storm whispered back, "No. I just . . . have to say farewell to this one."

Ergluth waved his hand at her to go forth and do so, and muttered to the armsmen coming up behind him, "This is getting as bloody as a battle."

Storm took the torch from the servant who'd fetched them, and stepped cautiously inside. Nothing seemed disturbed in the room but a wicker laundry-basket, fallen by the foot of the bed that Ilgreth Drimmer lay upon. A door at the back of the room was ajar, opening onto a narrow passage where the dim blue light of false dawn was just beginning to show at the windows.

The steward lay sprawled on his back on the bed, a dagger in his breast. His face was slack in death, but nowhere could Storm see the burns left by the consuming powers of the shapeshifter. Had someone else slain the man to settle old scores, trusting to the tumult of the other deaths to quell all hue and cry?

Storm looked at the steward's hands, and took up a single strand of hair from under his nails. A long hair—too long for most men. She bent over Ilgreth's face and wiped at his lip with a finger. The tip of her finger came away red. Lip-rouge.

A woman, then—or a shapechanger posing as a woman, to gain entry here unopposed, and get close to the man. She frowned—and then gasped in astonishment.

Where the steward's red robes had been pulled away from his throat and pinned thus by the dagger, his neck was exposed—and there, glinting up at her, was a silver harp.

Storm reached for it. There was a sudden shout from the door. She looked up to see one of the guards staring past her at the other doorway. She whirled to look there—but saw only empty passage.

Vaulting the bed, the pin in her fist, she sprinted to the door and looked both ways, silver hair swirling. The dark, narrow hall was empty.

She turned back into the bedchamber. "What was it?" she demanded. "Who was there?"

The armsman looked at Ergluth, who'd come into the room at the head of a crowd of Purple Dragons. The commander gave him a grim nod.

"A man in a cowled robe, Lady," he said, "with a staff in his hands and eyes like red flame."

"Anyone seen such a person hereabouts before?" Ergluth demanded. There was a general shaking of heads and negative mutterings. "Our shapechanger," he concluded.

Storm nodded. "Wearing the shape of a Zhent or Cult wizard, it seems."

Ergluth looked down at what she held. "So he was a Harper."

The Bard of Shadowdale shook her head. "I doubt it. Sympathetic to the Way of the Harp, perhaps, but I'd have known if he was in our ranks. And this was laid at his throat with no chain or pin to hold it there. No, this is another taunt to me—a double thrust."

Ergluth raised a brow. "A death and Harper blame for it?"

Storm shook her head again. "Two deaths; this one, and whatever Harper he slew to get this." She handed him the pin. "Put this in a place of stone, far from things that can burn or folk who can be affected by magic—a dungeon cell will do. I'm going hunting."

"How does one hunt a shapeshifter?" Ergluth asked grimly. "He could be anyone in the kingdom!"

Storm turned to look at him. "Not quite. I've raised a barrier he cannot pass—at least, not without my knowing it. He can be anyone only in Firefall Keep."

"You've shut him in here with us," one of the Purple Dragons gasped.

Storm's eyes met his. "That's right," she said softly. "I'm very much afraid some of us will soon learn what the phrase 'died for the good of the realm' really means."

* * * * *

Not far away, Shayna Summerstar trembled in the darkness against a wall, staring again and again at the blood on her fingertips.

WELL DONE. WASH IT AWAY AND BE AT PEACE. SEE HOW EASY IT IS TO SLAY?

I hate it. I hated tricking that old man.

IT WAS NECESSARY.

Why?

I WANTED YOU TO—THAT'S WHY.

Shayna shivered again, but said nothing.

NOW COME TO ME. YOU'LL FIND ME MUCH BETTER COMPANY THAN AN OLD, OVERWEIGHT STEWARD.

Shayna bit her lip, felt a protest well up within her—and then found herself pushing away from the wall and walking toward him. There was a deliberate strut to her stride as she went, swaying her hips like a tavern-dancer.

She could not even scream in protest. When she came around a corner two hallways later and looked into the eyes of a startled guard, she winked, smiled, and then strutted provocatively past him. He did not see the blood on her hand. She took the stairs beyond two steps at a time, hurrying to be with her waiting, smiling master.

Her Dark Master.

Ten

TO DREAM OF A DRAGON

 Storm yawned once more and stumbled, bruising her shoulder against the passage wall. "Careful, lady," the guard just behind her said, reaching out a hand.

"Aye. You should get some sleep," said Ergluth, at her elbow.

Storm shook her head. "I don't need . . . can't need . . ."

Then it struck her. Of course she'd need sleep, now, like any other mortal, with Mystra's silver fire flowing out of her endlessly to fuel the barrier. That was why she was so exhausted, her legs rubbery and blundering. For the first time in centuries, she desperately needed sleep.

"You're right," she said abruptly, and handed her torch to the nearest guard. "It's . . ." She lifted her head, trying to remember where her bed was.

"We're heading there now," the boldshield told her. When she gave him a hard look, he shrugged and added, "It's along our way."

Wearily, Storm nodded. It seemed only a moment later that she was dropping the bar into place across the inside of her closed door, yawning once more, and turning to make sure the room was empty of lurking shapeshifters.

It was, or seemed to be. Storm shucked her gloves, unlaced and kicked off her boots, undid her sword belt and let it fall, and hauled the tunic off over her head. The rest could wait.

The bed felt so soft. . . . With an effort, Storm sat up, blinked sleep from her eyes for just a few moments longer, and carefully cast two of the precious spells she had left. Wards flickered into glowing life around the bed, shimmering where the silver fire streamed out through them. No spell, and no body—however it changed its shape—should be able to reach her now.

Storm sighed, shook her head at the thought that she couldn't cower in a bed for very long . . . and then she was swimming in warm white mists.

Dark things loomed out of them as she moved forward, flying now. The black fingers of giants, frozen into vainly reaching stone things . . . then a fire-darkened skull so large that she passed through one of its eye sockets . . . and a red, scaled head rising up through the mists to fix her with an old and very wise eye . . . a dragon? What was a dragon doing in her dreams?

She fell down an endless well, tumbling. Bodies with eyes and mouths aflame rose past her. Grinning things changed shape around her, and the dragon's great eye looked endlessly down on her from the top of the shaft. Why a dragon?

Suddenly Storm stood in the Summerstar family crypt, lit by flames that floated without torches to feed them. All around her, the bodies of the long-dead fallen were thrusting aside their coffin lids and rising stiffly out of their shrouds. Ignoring her, they walked to the walls and punched through them, every blow of

skeletal fists making the room tremble and boom as if
thunder had rumbled.

The space beyond the walls was a room she knew:
the great hall of Firefall Keep. Storm stepped out
through a hole made by a tall, broken-skulled skele-
ton. She found herself standing in the open area
between the wings of the long table, during a feast. All
the places at table were occupied by sneering
Summerstars and disapproving war wizards. The staggering corpses disappeared like smoke, leaving her
alone with the laughter of the diners, who pointed at
her and howled with mirth.

Looking down, she saw that she wore only black tentacles . . . tentacles that rose up, twining around her
limbs, until they reached her throat and began to
squeeze. She choked, fought in vain against the glistening constriction, and then everything she saw was
rimmed with green and gold, wavering until the
watery world went away, and all she could stare at was
the dragon's lone, watching eye.

"*Why* a dragon?" she snarled in bewilderment and
awoke. She sat bolt upright, drenched with sweat.

Ergluth and four Purple Dragons were calling anxiously to her from around the bed, the drawn swords in
their hands flashing and spitting back sparks from her
wards.

"What—what befalls?" she asked in weary puzzlement.

The eaglelike eyes of the boldshield peered into
hers. His face was graven with lines of concern. "This
barrier—is it yours?"

"Yes, of course," Storm snapped. "Why did you wake
me by thrusting steel into it?"

"We heard you call something about dragons," he
replied. "Several times, you cried out—once at full bellow. When we came in, someone was standing by the
bed, holding a dagger. He was shrouded in spell-mists,

with laughing skulls flying all around him like birds.
We couldn't see who it was, but he was trying to get
past your wards. When he saw us, he sent mists,
skulls, and all at us. Things've only just cleared, now
. . . there must be a hidden way into and out of this
room."

"I've found several," Storm said, yawning, "but I
thank you for trying to guard me, just the same." She
fell back onto the pillows, waves of weariness rolling
over her, and managed to say, "I was too sleepy to think
of this before . . . Ilgreth was the first to die and not be
burned. Keep him safe, and the dagger that slew him,
too, until both can be examined with spells to tell us
who might have killed him."

"I thought of that," Ergluth Rowanmantle said grimly, "and left him in the care of two of my most trusted
guards while I sent for Broglan. When he got to the
steward's room, one of the guards was dead on the
floor—burned to a husk—and Drimmer, dagger and
all, was gone. It seems one of my trusted guards was
. . . someone else."

"We've got to stop him," Storm murmured, falling
back into welcoming drowsiness, "before he slaughters
half your command."

"Lady," Ergluth told her grimly, "I've lost eleven men
since sunset, all slain at their posts . . . to say nothing
of the two who'll be months coughing the smoke out of
their lungs from fighting the fire. You'll get no argument from me. . . ."

He fell silent then, and shook his head. A gentle
snore told him she was no longer hearing his words.
Well, let her sleep. Without her, Firefall Keep would be
a house of ghosts right now, every last one of them
naught but ashes. He looked from armsman to armsman, all four of them veterans. "Protect her," he said
gruffly. "Sword anyone who comes into this room and
tries to get at her—even if you think it's Broglan, or

me—who fails to give you the password. I'll be back before highsun."

The four guards nodded, looked at each other, and went to the door to drop the bar behind him. Then they went slowly and carefully around the room. They checked under the bed and above its canopy, one searching while the others watched. They found nothing. Casting a look at the silver-haired woman on the bed, they leaned on their swords and tried to think how they might walk out of Firefall Keep alive.

Not many scenarios came to mind.

* * * * *

Master, I failed.

Shayna Summerstar let her master feel her bitter disappointment as she put the dagger high up on the ledge above her wardrobe, where no prying eyes would find it.

NAY. YOU DID WELL. YOU STOOD AGAINST THE WARDS AND TESTED THEM—FUTILE, BUT FEARLESS. I LIKE THAT.

Shayna felt a glow of pleasure at the praise, but tried not to show him just how much she needed his approval.

I could have had her! She was asleep—I could have found some way past the wards, if there'd been time! But the guards came . . .

I SENT THEM.

You sent *them?*

I MADE THEM THINK THEY'D HEARD SOMETHING ODD IN THE HARPER'S ROOM. THEY DID THE REST. THEN I SENT THE MISTS THAT HID YOU, AND LED YOU TO THE HIDDEN WAY OUT.

But why? *I thought you wanted her dead!*

OVERCOME, I SAID. STORM SILVERHAND MUST DIE ONLY BY MY HAND, AT A TIME WHEN

I'M READY TO TAKE HER POWERS.

Why? Her mind-voice was small and miserable.

SO THAT I CAN BECOME A GOD he replied matter-of-factly.

On her way back to her bed, Shayna stopped in mid-stride and began to shiver uncontrollably.

* * * * *

When the war hound trotted down the hall, paws clicking on the stones, one of the guards knelt and said, "What're you doing here, boy? You should be back at—"

He reached out to scratch its head, but the blade of a drawn sword reached past his hand to hover in front of the dog's nose. "You heard him, Tith," his fellow guard said almost regretfully. "Trust no one, he said . . . and why would a hound be wandering around up here, anyway? Begone, you, or—"

The dog growled and sprang back, away from his blade—but it left two tentacles behind, lashing out at the ankles of both guards.

They cursed, slashed vainly, and fell hard on their behinds. The dog that was not a dog swarmed in over them, taking their frantic thrusts through its shoulders as it stretched out two sets of impossibly long jaws and bit their faces off. The blood of three beings mingled together on the floor for an instant before fires rose from the bodies.

The dog reared up among the blazing bones and became manlike . . . a dog-headed man with two thin, hooked blades of bone where its hands should have been. It thrust them between the doors, and sharply up, lifting the door bar. Then the blades of bone slowly lengthened, moving the bar away from the door so that it could be swung open.

A third hand grew from the belly of the thing that

was not a man, and did just that, revealing the bed beyond. Standing on it, eyes red-rimmed and unshaven jowls set grimly, was the boldshield of Northtrees March, with a loaded crossbow in his hands. It snapped.

The quarrel thrummed across the room, plucked the dog-headed man off his feet, and drove him hard against the far wall of the passage.

"Come on," Ergluth Rowanmantle told it, dropping his bow and unsheathing his sword. "You want me? Come in and get me!"

But the eyes that met his were as dark and knowing as the old Summerstar matriarch's had been. The shapeshifting thing let his flesh melt and flow until the crossbow quarrel fell out. He favored Ergluth with a wide-fanged and mirthless smile, and vanished down the hallway.

The white-faced boldshield hissed a heartfelt curse. Somehow it knew he dared not leave the bed, and the protection of the magic shield he'd raised there. The shieldstone was a Rowanmantle family secret only his oldest, most loyal armsmen had known about, and both of them . . . had been on guard outside his door.

Ergluth Rowanmantle looked out at blackened bones and cursed again, not caring if he raised echoes this time. How was he ever going to get to sleep after this?

* * * * *

Highsun came and went, and the four guards grew restive.

"Gods, but I'm hungry," one of them growled. His stomach added a wordless roar of agreement. His companions smiled ruefully.

"It won't be empty bellies we'll have to worry about," one of them said, "if he comes back and finds us gone from our posts. It'll be our throats—after our backsides do a dance or two with the lash."

There were weary murmurs of agreement.

A quietly amused voice from behind them asked, "What if I go with you to the kitchens? Will he lash my behind, too?"

The armsmen whirled around. Storm Silverhand was sitting up in bed, her wards dissolving around her in twinkling, drifting motes of light.

"Beg pardon, lady," one of the Purple Dragons began hastily, "but—"

She raised a hand. "None necessary. I've had sleep, and now food is my need. Stand clear now; I'm going to do something with magic that I don't want you to get caught in."

She watched them back warily away, closed her eyes, and felt for the rushing stream of silver fire. Yes! As she'd thought, it couldn't restore spells she'd cast . . . but if she diverted just a touch of it, for just a moment, it could duplicate a spell she was still carrying, if her mind could hold the extra load. She might be no great realms-shaker as a mage, but one thing all Chosen of Mystra had were minds that could carry heavy loads. They learned to, or soon went insane. Hmmph; perhaps the less thought along *that* line, the better. . . .

Done! "Thank you, Mystra," she murmured aloud, watching silver fire that only she could see swirling around her. Now to do it again. . . .

She'd already decided she'd need one for Ergluth Rowanmantle's room, another for the wizards' study, and a third for Shayna Summerstar's bedchamber. The heir of House Summerstar was the most important being to protect in this place, after all—even if the boldshield was the most useful. She called on the fire to make herself a third watchful eye, leapt off the bed, and snatched up her boots.

"Food!" she bellowed, "and then your commander, to

release you from your orders while you still have strength to yawn."

Good-natured chuckles answered her. The guards drew in protectively around her as she hauled on tunic, sword belt, boots, and gloves once more, and set forth.

In the passage outside, they stumbled across signs of fresh carnage. Stumbled across, literally; the smoking, headless bodies of two sprawled Purple Dragons, limbs twisted in agony, lay underfoot as Storm stepped out of the bedchamber. No one chuckled after that.

* * * * *

"This keep has become a battlefield!" Corathar snarled, eyes large with fright. "We dare not step outside without an armed escort and all our spells ready, for fear this shapeshifter could be anywhere!"

Insprin Turnstone shrugged. "Our duty to the Crown is clear; we must do whatever we can to destroy this murderer. See to your spells, and let us all be glad there's but one monster, and not an invading army of them!"

"Are your veins full of *ice?*" Corathar snarled, voice rising in horror. "Don't you know what I'm saying? Death waits for us in the jakes, in our beds, at any step we take in the passages—everywhere!—and all you can do is—"

"Enough, Corathar," Broglan Sarmyn said severely, coming out of his sleeping-chamber with an old, brass-bound grimoire in his hand. "Fear is as deadly a weapon as a foe's spell or blade. Resist it, as Insprin does, by keeping your mind on what must be done." He sat down, reached for the decanter and a glass, and added, "Speaking of which—"

He broke off as there came a rap upon the door. All three mages caught up their wands, and Broglan called, "Yes?"

The door opened a cautious handspan, and a Purple Dragon they knew said, "The Lady Storm Silverhand to see you, gentlesirs."

"Oh?" Broglan exchanged wary glances with the others, and gestured at them to stand on either side of the door, well back. "Show her in."

The door opened wide. He could see six Purple Dragons outside. Out of their midst stepped the silver-haired Harper, clad as if to go hunting in the forest. She gave him a calm nod as she stepped into the room, hands spread wide and empty.

"Well met, Broglan," Storm said. Without pause, she turned to look at the two mages on either side of her, and repeated her grave greeting, naming them both.

Three sets of eyes narrowed. "How do we know," Broglan asked slowly, setting down his glass untasted, "that you are truly the Bard of Shadowdale—and not some deadly shapeshifter?"

Storm shrugged. "You don't. On the other hand, I doubt our deadly shapeshifter would know just where I promised to scratch old Vangey when next we met—do you recall?"

"Yes," Broglan said with a sigh. "Forgive my ill manners, Lady; pray sit down. The doors, Insprin?"

"I'll gladly sit and chat in a moment, Sir Broglan," the lady bard told him, "but there is a casting I must do first." And without further ado, she raised her hands and made a complex series of passes in the air, murmuring words the wizards could not quite hear.

Broglan flushed in anger, and opened his mouth to protest—but she was done, and smiling sweetly at him. He shrugged, reached for his glass, and said in acid tones, "I suppose you'll get around to telling me just what you've done when you have, say, some idle hours?"

Storm chuckled. "You war wizards certainly lack for

fun," she told him merrily. "All this grim silence and snapped orders, and keeping your laundry lists deathly secret! Aren't you even going to offer a lady a drink?"

The worried-looking senior war wizard sighed. "On one condition, Lady Storm: that you drop this giggling maiden act. I'd appreciate the teasing more if I wasn't scared witless, and facing the first truly important threat to the realm that I've seen in years. Treat us as equals."

"Will you in turn accept the authority Lord Vangerdahast gave me over you?" Storm asked quietly, meeting his eyes.

Broglan sighed again, and then said quietly, "Lady, I will. Corathar? Insprin?"

"We will," they said in rough chorus.

"Then let us drink to seal it," Storm said, extending her hand.

"There's only the one glass," Broglan protested.

"So fill it, and we'll share," Storm told him crisply. "The spell I just cast here is called a 'watchful eye.' Like a magic mouth spell, it is triggered by certain conditions—in this case, by any attack in this room that unleashes fire or draws blood, or by entry into this room through any way but the doors I know of. I'll write down the word of activation for you; don't speak it aloud until you really need to."

"What does uttering the word bring?" Insprin asked from close behind her.

"The spell creates sound and moving images of what befell in its area of effect when it was triggered—hopefully showing us just what was said and done after an attack occurred."

"So the survivor can see who killed the rest of us," Corathar said sarcastically.

"Corathar!" Broglan snapped angrily, but Storm held up her hand.

"A fair reaction," the lady bard said quietly, "being as

you've given this mage under you no comfort." She sipped from the glass Broglan was holding and then offered it to Corathar.

"Drink, sir," she said quietly, "and know this: giving in to fear doesn't help. Let it keep you awake, and wary, and thinking, yes . . . but don't let it master you. Watch old Insprin, instead of envying and hating him; he knows this."

Corathar's eyes blazed, but he sipped from the cup carefully, and then passed it to Insprin, who murmured in mock-quavering tones, "Eh, Storm! Not so much of the 'old,' hear ye?"

It was just the right thing to say; they all burst into sputtering laughter, and rocked together in shared mirth for a moment.

Broglan took back his glass before the last of the wine got spilled. "We know we face a shapeshifter—something called a Malaugrym, Lord Vangerdahast ventured—so what will seeing a shape assumed by this killer tell us? Why set the spell?"

It was Storm's turn to sigh. "My magic is little better than yours, gentlesirs; not all who serve Mystra can rend mountaintops. I can't bring this foe to stand and fight, so I'm trying to learn all I can of him." She shrugged. "He seems able to shapeshift at will . . . so I'd like to catch a few more of his shapes."

"Are you sure it's a 'he'?" Broglan asked quietly.

Storm frowned, and then sprang up, almost bowling Corathar over. "Mystra *aid* my wits!"

She was across the room in two strides, snatching the door open, and snarling, "Shayna!"

Behind her, as the three war wizards stared in astonishment at the racing bard, the air shimmered slightly as the watchful eye spell activated.

A secret panel slid aside in the ceiling above the table where Broglan sat, and three glossy black tentacles reached down for the wizards. Each eely intrusion ended in a bony joint from which three human fore-arms sprouted. Behind each tentacle came a many-fanged mouth, surrounded by a nimbus of purple light. The hands reached for the necks of the mages, but the mouths opened in silent eagerness as they drew near the tops of the wizards' heads.

Corathar saw the monster first, and screamed.

"A Sharn!" Insprin said in awe, as he looked up and triggered his wand. Magical bolts burst from it in blue-white pulses, curving to follow those reaching arms.

Corathar screamed again and triggered his own wand.

Broglan dived for the floor as fast and as frantically as he'd ever done anything in his life. . . .

Eleven
THE TAPESTRY TORN

Magical radiances flashed and spat as Broglan rolled over and over in frantic haste, terrified the beast would fall on him. Blue-white magic missiles streaked overhead and tore into the glossy black monster. Corathar was shouting at the thing in wordless, furious fear, and there were answering, startled shouts from the corridor outside as Purple Dragons came running.

The armsmen couldn't get to the monster protruding from the ceiling without hacking through the finest war wizards ever to come to Firefall Vale. Grimly, Broglan found his feet and his own wand. They were going to have to do this themselves.

Insprin was backed against a wall, calmly emptying his wand into the beast. The black hands reaching for him recoiled and convulsed in an endless dance of pain.

Corathar was producing more noise than damage, firing his wand wildly as he dodged and fled from relentless clutching hands. Only frantic struggles had kept him alive this long; his robes were already torn away at both shoulders.

Broglan sighed inwardly and abandoned the young mage to whatever fate the gods had in store for him. Blasting down this beast was more important. His own wand pulsed in his grasp as he made it roar forth deadly fire.

Glossy black arms shrank away. Drooling jaws snapped and snarled in retreat. All three wands were firing now, and the purple radiance around the sharn was gone, seared away by the raw fury of the magic hurled against it.

Then the hole in the ceiling was suddenly empty. The thing had fled. Broglan shouted for a halt, and let his hands fall to his sides. He quickly discovered how violently his hands were trembling.

* * * * *

The blazing pain was behind him, and he could think again. The glossy black blob hissed out agony from mouths that drooped and flowed back into it as it grew thinner . . . and taller . . . and became a man again.

The shapeshifter panted slightly in remembered pain as he stood in the cool, dark places of the Haunted Tower, idly watching a spectral gowned form glide past. An eerie chord of wild, high harp music echoed briefly through the empty room behind him, but he did not flinch or turn; he feared no phantom—nor armed mortal, for that matter. Prudence sometimes forced retreat upon every mortal.

The folk of Firefall knew about him now and walked the halls ready for battle. Firefall Keep was becoming a fortress armed against him. It was time to find some magic and gain the upper hand again.

From Pheirauze, he'd learned how pitifully few

enchanted items of consequence the Summerstars
owned. A few light globes, a healing hand that Athlan
had hidden away somewhere, a brazier that needed no
fuel . . . little that could readily serve in a battle. He
needed more—something that could blast hands and
feet off an arrogant Chosen of Mystra and leave her
helpless to his subsumption.

The Summerstars might have all too little magic, but
the place to find items of power in Cormyr—away from
the palace, with its alert guards and war wizards—was
in the hands of nobles. And the greatest concentration
of nobility . . . moreover, the place of most danger to
them, and where they might most need to impress or
coerce others . . . was the grand city of Suzail.

He'd best give this persistent servant of Mystra the
slip and go hunting nobles. She'd dare not raise a general alarm in the kingdom, or the panic might bring on
war between neighbors all over the realm. He'd have a
little time while war wizards scurried here and there,
trying to keep secrets. Yes . . .

He laughed aloud in the empty, echoing darkness
and became a war hound again, padding across the
cold stone with paws that still trembled from the rav-
ages of those searing wands. Well, that would pass
soon enough.

By now, they'd suspect any beast flying over the battlements or slipping past gate-guards. The sluice gate
below the kitchens, where refuse and garderobe
washouts went down a long pipe to the midden by the
barns, was the wisest route.

Unseen, he found the dumping room, became a
water-snake, and slid into the unpleasant liquid. It
would be the work of only a few moments to—

Gods! There was a sudden flare of silver fire in the
sludge around him; he thrashed in helpless pain as it
raged, burning away scales and flesh beneath.

He struggled on, but the flames rose up with an

earnest roar, and flesh melted before them. Gasping, he turned quickly, before it was too late. Pain rode him and clawed at him as he wriggled frantically back up the pipe, out of reach of the flames.

Had the Harper bitch seen him? Or had she merely cast a spell on the pipe to wait for anyone trying to travel it?

He waited a long time, mastering the pain and rebuilding his body where it was torn and melted. He was lessened, but he could do nothing about that. Nothing save go back into the keep . . . and feed.

First a test had to be made. Slowly and cautiously he descended the pipe again, growing a long, slender tentacle to probe ahead. All too soon it met with the familiar flare of silver flame.

He drew back hastily and departed, becoming a hound again . . . a wet hound with a tentacle coiled under the dripping fur of its belly. He found the nearest window and stretched the tentacle west toward the heart of Cormyr—a tentacle that soon felt the searing kiss of flame once more. He was walled into the keep by a barrier of goddess-fire!

The shapeshifter growled. He heard a nearby scullery-maid call out to another about hearing a dog, and left hastily, seeking a chamber with rugs to dry his paws on.

When he had done so, his half-hidden tentacle sported a human hand that could open doors. He went on, seeking a room where he could be alone.

* * * * *

Halfway up a curving stone stair, Storm Silverhand sagged against the wall, gasping, her face a sheet of running sweat.

"Mystra preserve me!" she panted, wiping at her brow with the back of a glove.

If she was going to be battered so each time the foe
tested the barrier, he might kill her just by going around
the keep trying to force his way out! She mustn't let him
know how thrusts against the sphere hurt her. . . .

Clenching her teeth, Storm pushed herself away
from the wall and went on, climbing the steps like an
old woman. Her legs were weak and unsteady. She
tried to act as if she were merely idling her way up the
stair, deep in thought, but she could not hide her pale
face or the sweat that still coursed down it, dripping
from her nose and chin.

"Gods!" she swore under her breath; even her ears
were filling up with it. Perhaps she could tell folk that
sweating like a waterfall was a fashionable thing for
half-crazed bards to do. . . .

*　*　*　*　*

The man who was not Maxer sat alone in the dusty
darkness of a disused back storeroom, old jars and
salt-barrels all around him. His eyes were closed, and
he hummed softly, as one of the spells he'd gained from
those fools of wizards unfolded. Yes, the invisible barrier enclosed all of Firefall Keep in a great sphere . . .
no doubt to keep him in.

Ah, but of us two, who is the hunted, and who is the
hunter?

Let it be a barrier for both her and me. If I lace *this*
spell around it, just so, and then cast that one . . .

The silver fire flared into visibility for the briefest of
instants, but seemed to accept his spells, binding them
into itself without faltering or backlash. Good. Now the
Chosen One of Mystra was caught here, too—his helpless prey in an ever-deepening trap.

The shapechanger opened his eyes, stood up, and
smiled. They'd face each other soon enough—and he'd
get what he'd come here for. Oh, yes.

With that confident smile still on his face, he stepped out into the passage and strolled openly across the keep, heading back toward the Haunted Tower, to await dusk and his next move. He'd never thought this road he'd chosen would be so much *fun*.

He crossed the portrait-hung Hall of Honor—full of stuffy-looking Summerstars glaring down out of frames that hadn't been dusted for a tenday . . . and why was that, now? Could it be for fear of a certain tentacled prowler?—and headed up the Gargoyle Stair.

Halfway up it he heard a hail from above, and saw a Purple Dragon, drawn sword in hand, standing at its head. "I know you not," the armsman said, frowning. "Who are you, and why are you here?"

With an easy smile, the man on the stairs spread empty hands, and continued to mount the broad, plum-carpeted stone steps. "I am Maxer," he said, "a . . . friend of Lady Storm Silverhand." He raised an eyebrow. "Do you harp?"

The guard's frown deepened. "I do not," he said coldly, "and I've no love for Harpers—or anyone else who skulks about evading the dictates of rightful authority. I ask again: why are you here?"

"So the harp isn't to your taste," the smiling man said, approaching the head of the stair. He raised his hands as if conducting an imaginary band of musicians—making sure the armsman did not see the rising, moving hump between his shoulder-blades—and asked, "What instrument do you play, pray tell?"

"I'm not one for music," the guard said shortly, raising the point of his blade to menace the throat of the ascending stranger. "I don't play—or play at—anything."

"Ah," the smiling stranger said softly, "I'm sorry to hear that." The gentle smile still on his face, he lashed out with his newly grown tentacle, snaring the guard's throat.

The Purple Dragon reeled and fought for breath, hands tearing futilely at what was strangling him. The shapechanger lifted him delicately clear of the ground to render his kicks useless. With casual amusement, he watched the man's face darken. The valiant boldshield was going to have one less witness to report on the murderer loose in the keep—and one fewer Purple Dragon sword to swing at dangerous shapeshifting beasts.

The smiling man's eyes caught sudden fire. The choking armsman tried to scream as he stared into those flaming orbs, and managed only an agonized whistle before two needles of flame lanced out. His head caught fire from the inside.

The smiling man drank in a flood of memories from the squalling, spasming body—dark visions of battlefields and tankards and willing lips, mostly. When he was done, he cast the husk casually aside. It slid down the wall as he strode on, licking his lips and murmuring from time to time.

The memories he'd stolen jostled with those he'd already taken, whirling and surging together in a wild cacophony of unrelated, overlaid images. . . .

With dismay, the shapeshifter realized he'd forgotten who and where he was for some time, drifting along in a tumbling journey through the unfamiliar, stolen memories of others. He was striding down a passage that led to the Haunted Tower and must have walked straight through the floor occupied by guests—such as the war wizards.

He shook his head and saw a servant glance out of a room, frown in concern, and draw its door swiftly closed again. Filled with sudden, savage glee, he sprang to that door, grew talons, and raked the wood, laughing wildly when he heard a terrified cry from the room inside.

"I am the Eater of All!" he howled exultantly, dancing on down the corridor and lashing the air around him with a restless tentacle. "I am the Slayer of Mages, the slaughterer of doves and children and helpless little kittens. *Fear me!* Obey me! *Run from me while you can!*"

* * * * *

The late afternoon sun brightly lit the battlements of Firefall Keep—a good thing for those brave enough to stand on the heights, given the chill breezes that blew from the mountains.

Those winds whipped the chestnut-hued hair of Lady Shayna Summerstar into an unruly plume. She didn't care. The ruin of her coiffure was not why her face was tight and tense as she stared at the tall woman with the silver hair—hair that serenely held its shape, defying the winds. Shayna admired this Harper. She felt shame and resentment as question after question politely probed at her secret.

"I know that even now, a Summerstar is aiding the foe who slew your brother and your grandmother," Storm was saying, her eyes two dark pools Shayna could not escape. "Is it you?"

Dark Master, aid me! With an effort, the young heiress kept her face calm, trying not to show how frantic she truly felt. "I am shocked that such an idea would occur to you or anyone," Shayna said with just a touch of ice. "I am, after all, a Summerstar."

"So is Thalance, the scourge of Firefall Vale," Storm said with just a hint of grim mirth about her lips. "So is Uncle Erlandar, reportedly thrice the rogue in his day than Thalance will ever be."

Shayna made no more reply to this than to sardonically raise an eyebrow. Inwardly, though, she screamed, *Master, can you hear me? What shall I do?*

Because Storm was more than a mortal, and the cry was so impassioned and so close, she heard the mental call. Keeping all trace of that hearing from her face, she said, "You can't hide forever, Shayna. House Summerstar needs a leader as bright and clear as Athlan tried to be. Those who consort with beasts end up as beasts themselves—or, far more often, end up the food of beasts."

With those softly barbed words, she turned and walked away.

Master? Master!

Shayna watched the woman she admired so much stride along the battlements, dwindling into the distance. Storm disappeared down the stair she'd come from. Still, empty silence was the only reply to Shayna's entreaties.

She drew a ragged breath. Storm *knew*. She must know. . . .

Too late, her worried fingers found the hilt of the knife sheathed in her bodice, and she drew it out. Bright and sharp it flashed, throwing sunlight defiantly back up into the sky. With this blade, one could slay a Harper. But would it fell a Chosen of Mystra, wise and spell-shrouded from centuries in service to the goddess?

Could she go after Storm Silverhand, the Bard of Shadowdale, and put this gleaming thing in her throat? Did she dare? Did she *want* to?

Sudden tears broke forth and ran down her cheeks. Shayna shook her head and sobbed against a crumbling crenelation. No, a thousand times, no. There walked the sort of lady she dreamed of being. . . .

She found herself looking over the battlements. Down, down . . . it was a sickeningly long way to the treetops below. Shayna Summerstar started to shake. She was alone, and trapped, with death drawing nearer—oh, gods, why had she been such a fool?

But what choice had she had?

Athlan's choice, she told herself. She looked down over the battlements again. Then she shook her head, went to her knees against the old parapet of her home, and started to cry in earnest as a soft and magnificent sunset came down over Firefall Vale.

* * * * *

The man who was not Maxer shook his head to banish the ever-crowding memories. He wearily descended a flight of steps into the great vaulted hall at the heart of the Haunted Tower.

Let me take charge, Pheirauze Summerstar said in his mind. *I can handle such things.*

NO DOUBT, he grunted mentally. He sank down into a high-backed seat that still bore the stains where one Summerstar had killed another on it, a century ago.

He thrust the knowing voice of the dowager lady firmly from his thoughts and hummed to himself, feeling bloated and tired. This subsumption was useful, but burdensome. His mind was awash in the thoughts and passions and scenes of others, crowded until he could scarcely think—unless battle brought him fully to the here and now.

Battle. Yes, it was almost time. Let night fall and grow long, and the guardians slumber. Then he'd fare forth again in beast-shape and slaughter servants and guards without subsuming, whittling down those who could stand against him until his awed quarry would have to challenge him.

Yes. That would be best. First the hun—

He looked up, startled. A glowing figure appeared on the balcony above him. It was robed, bearded, and gaunt. As he watched, it gabbled something silent, pointed its hand down at unseen foes, and hurled a bolt of soundless, ghostly light. He tensed and almost sprang from his seat, but the apparition faded. It and its spell were but harmless phantoms; visions of the Haunted Tower.

But what if a phantom were not harmless? What if he could create his own automaton to surprise Storm Silverhand with attacks when her power and attention were bent on an annoyingly successful shapeshifter? What if she faced more than one foe?

Yes . . . he did spring up this time, and strode through an archway toward another part of the keep. He needed a servant, one who'd scarce be missed. . . .

Some places in Faerûn attracted and fostered and preserved hauntings—battlefields, aye, but what was it about places like this dark and gloomy tower? It was so rife with ghosts that the family who dwelt here had abandoned it. They spent their lives walking around it, not talking of it. Was there some magic here he couldn't feel, or something else he could use? He must return when the next victories were his, return and find out. . . .

Right now, he needed a servant. One like this one. A water-bearer, spending his days groaning under the weight of buckets. He was bent over now, dipping water from the well pool into a jug, with loud splashing sounds. He did not even see the hands that descended to his ears and flashed fire between them.

The man staggered, squealed in astonished pain, and grabbed blindly at the edge of a nearby tapestry, trying to claw his way erect.

The old, rotting tapestry tore away in his hand, and he fell on his face into the water. The fire flashed again, and Mathom Drear, cellarer of the ewer, shuddered once and lay still.

Delicately, the shapeshifter seared the brain, burning away all thoughts but obedience and love for . . . a certain mind like *this*. He smiled, turned, and hastened back to the Haunted Tower, his mindless slave dripping along in his wake.

"Mathom Drear," he muttered, surveying the empty-eyed face. "Gods, what a name." He'd have to strengthen his control over the mind that now held only thoughts of him, and no memories of its own; an exacting task. . . .

He made the cellarer sit on the stained high seat. He stared thoughtfully at the mindless man. Once the shapeshifter's newly gained memories surged and swirled, threatening to overwhelm him, but he snarled, bit his lip until the blood flowed, and fought the maelstrom down.

"Let there be two enemies seeking Storm Silverhand," he said aloud, his voice echoing in the dark, dusty room. "The Foe, and . . . Hungry Man." He laughed. "Aye, I'll make you hungry for her doom!"

He stroked his chin, considering just how to feed the mindless husk with spells and energy, to make it capable of striking a Chosen of Mystra and holding her—just long enough for her true foe to overwhelm her!

"Yes!" he shouted. YES YES YES! The memories swelled up with a roar and burst through his tattered control. . . .

An observer, had one dared to venture into the dark and lofty hall at the heart of the Haunted Tower, would have seen a slack-jawed man sitting in a chair, staring endlessly at nothing. Another creature danced around it, cackling in wild, deranged glee . . . a creature who was sometimes a darkly handsome warrior, and at other times a stout, nude woman of mature years. Then again, it was also a warrior in the armor of the Purple Dragons, and at other times a young, sly-looking man in plain robes—and a war hound, or a water snake, or a griffon, or a handsome, imperious young man, or a grim old seneschal, or another young man, or . . .

The shifts in shape became faster and wilder, with tentacles and glossy black biting mouths rearing up out of a dancing blur. Always, the cold laughter went on, high and wild and free from all reason.

What *was* it about this Haunted Tower?

Twelve

TRUST AND OLD WINE

When a weary Storm Silverhand returned to her chambers, the Purple Dragons at the door saluted her as a fellow warrior, clapping their hands to their chests. She smiled, matched their salute, and strode in through the open door—to find a war wizard waiting for her. He smiled tentatively, looking every bit as tired as she.

She raised an eyebrow. "Broglan Sarmyn? Smiling at me, an ancient marchioness?"

He sighed. "Aye, Harper tricks and all. We dare not go further, lady, as uneasy allies. No sooner had you left us than the beast attacked in the shape of a Sharn—"

Storm raised both eyebrows at once, truly surprised.

"—and all I could think of, as we fired all our wands to beat the thing off, was that if you'd been there to hurl a slaying-spell or to hold it where we could empty all our magic missiles into it, it would be dead now, and our troubles over."

Their eyes met, and Broglan continued slowly, "Lord Vangerdahast did tell me to obey you as I would him . . . but, lady, I have measured him, many times, and it has taken me longer to measure you." He extended his hand, looking even more worried than usual. "Will you—command me?"

Storm took that hand. "Only if I have to, Broglan. I'd prefer to stand shoulder to shoulder with you, not distantly bark orders through a speaking-stone, like a certain Royal Magician of Cormyr."

Broglan smiled ruefully. "Yes, I'm one of Vangerdahast's tame dogs, and—as we all do—I sometimes chafe at glib orders from afar."

Storm smiled. " 'Tis the human thing to do," she replied, taking off her gloves. "What is your counsel now?"

Broglan drew himself up. "Lady, the first dishes have already been served, but if you'll have me do so, I would escort you to evenfeast."

"I'd like nothing more!" Storm said heartily, feeling suddenly how hungry she was. "Let's go!"

"But, lady," the war wizard said, blinking. "No gown? No gems?"

Storm waved a hand dismissively. "I feel better dressed like this," she told him, "but if you'll be more comfortable . . ."

She hauled her tunic off over her head. Broglan beat a hasty, embarrassed retreat—not fast enough to avoid receiving the wadded-up garment in his face. He caught it reflexively, in time to see Storm dabble perfume behind her ears, down the open front of her shirt, and up her sleeves to the elbows. Winking at him, she snatched out a pendant from a coffer and hung it down her breast.

She strode toward him. He extended his arm to her and swallowed as her hair shaped itself, a smooth forest of silver snakes moving in unison, into a spectacular upswept high-court plume.

"Useful power, that," he commented as they swept out past the guards and went down to feast.

They shared no further conversation, falling quickly into a somber mood. The passages were empty; their footfalls echoed in a waiting, wary stillness. The keep felt like a cowering prisoner waiting for the executioner.

At the doors of the great hall, a dozen guards stood, a tired-looking Ergluth Rowanmantle in their midst. He gave them a grim smile and waved the doors open.

The hall looked very much as it had on Storm's first night—save that most of the seats now stood empty. Shayna Summerstar's seat was vacant. At the point of the table, Uncle Erlandar and the Dowager Lady Zarova Summerstar faced each other. Erlandar was flanked by Thalance and then the wizards Insprin and Corathar. Beside Zarova was Shayna's empty seat, and beyond that the two aunts.

Broglan conducted Storm to the seat beside Nalanna, who favored the new arrival with her usual cold and haughty glance. Smiling faintly, the war wizard took the seat across from Storm. Both of them found themselves looking down the empty tables. From them, two wings of empty places stretched out into gloom. They exchanged rueful glances.

Broglan turned his head in the other direction and said smoothly, "I apologize, Dowager Lady, for the lateness of our arrival. We had business of state to conclude before dining."

"Bedded her at last, did you?" Erlandar muttered under his breath, in tones just loud enough to carry clearly to them all.

Margort and Nalanna smirked in unison, but Zarova said quietly, "No more such words, thank you, Erlandar. You should not judge others by your own vices."

Erlandar flushed and seemed about to say something, but shrugged and reached for his goblet instead.

"Is the Lady Shayna unwell?" Storm asked gently, ignoring Erlandar's remark.

"She has chosen to dine in her chambers," Zarova said firmly, "and, as heir of this house, is entitled to her eccentricities." Her tone made it clear that further discussion of the subject would be unwelcome.

"Roast rothé in white wine and 'shroom sauce," the understeward murmured as platters were set down in front of the diners.

"So," Erlandar growled. "Have you found out who murdered Pheirauze yet?"

Steely silence fell as Broglan and Storm looked at each other. He spread his hand, indicating she should reply.

"We have a shapeshifter in our midst," the Bard of Shadowdale announced calmly, "of unknown origin. It, or he, has slain Lord Athlan, the seneschal, some of the war wizards, and many of the armsmen."

"You forgot the steward," Erlandar boomed.

Storm shook her head. "No, Lord Summerstar," she said, "someone else killed Ilgreth Drimmer."

"Oh? Well—d'ye know who?"

"The Lady Shayna," Storm said quietly.

"What?" The startled roar came from both Thalance and Erlandar, who half rose from their seats. All of the Summerstars stared at Storm with barely checked shock and rage—and Storm saw that Broglan was gazing at her in open-jawed dumbfoundment.

"Brawn in cinnamon sour sauce, with onion tarts," the understeward murmured imperturbably, gliding between them all at the head of another cluster of servers.

"Stay your swords, gentlesirs," Storm said with just the slightest snap of command in her voice. "Her mind was not her own when she did the deed, but in the thrall of the foe. I tell you this so that you may all be warned in case he takes control of her mind again while you stand near."

"I don't believe it," the Dowager Lady Zarova said, her voice trembling.

"Yes, you do," Storm said gravely, "or you'd not be so desperate to deny it. I apologize unreservedly for all the outrages I have offered you, both now and previously, but you of the blood of Summerstar must awaken and realize that you now dwell in a battlefield—or the *next* time we gather for a feast, there'll be a few *more* vacant seats."

In shocked silence, they stared at her.

Storm added, "Go nowhere without guards, none of you—even you, Thalance: invite them along, man!— and carry weapons if you know how to use them. Linger nowhere alone, even in garderobes. Bathe together, or not at all—'tis better to stink unwashed than to own the stink of death."

Thalance shook his head, a half-disbelieving, half-admiring smile on his lips. "You're serious, aren't you?"

Storm leaned forward. "Lad," she replied, "I am *very* serious. The Lady of Mysteries gave me powers that have kept me alive for centuries, in far more perilous lands than this. I fought this shapechanger and only *just* prevailed. If I fall, I charge you in Azoun's name: get to horse, and ride as hard as ever you can to the king—or, better, to the Lord Vangerdahast, and tell him all. Don't rest on the way, or you'll never awaken— and be ready to fight beast after beast on your ride."

"I'll not listen to more of this," the Lady Zarova said grimly, rising from her seat. "Thurdal, serve me the rest of my dishes in my quarters!"

"And ours!" the aunts said in outraged chorus, flinging the contents of their glasses at Storm. She nodded to them, ignoring the wine coursing down the side of her face, and said, "The pleasure was mine, charming ladies."

"Trollop!" Nalanna snarled as the three ladies

whirled away from the table to storm out.

Erlandar shook his head and reached across the table to take up the decanter from beside Zarova's glass.

"Uncle Erlandar?" Storm asked with a smile. "You, too?"

"No," he said gruffly, fixing her with a look, "I'm staying to hear it all—whatever you've got to say. After that bit with the flaming platter in here the other night, lady, I believe what you say about battles."

He plucked up Zarova's unused dabble-linen and tossed it to Storm. "For the wine you're, uh, wearing," he said.

As Storm thanked him and wiped her face dry, the understeward glided in again to announce, "Lambs' kidneys in a sherry sauce, set about with chestnut and parsnip fritters."

It only took one taste of this most recent dish for the familiar oily fire of poison to spread out through Storm's chest. Grimly, she called on the silver fire to purge it, having no choice but to weaken the barrier for a moment.

Broglan saw her eyes flicker and close for a instant. The rise and fall of her breast halted, and sweat glistened suddenly at her temples, but he said nothing as she slumped back in her chair, opened her eyes again, and gave him a grim smile.

"Stuffed stags' heads with sage, apples, and sandalwood," Thurdal continued serenely, as more platters arrived.

"As the ladies have left us," Thalance said carefully, "I find us poised on the threshold of a unique opportunity: the chance to speak openly and plainly for once, laying the usual courtesies and silent subjects aside. Lady Storm, I must confess that I am eager to hear more about this foe you speak of—and something of your own experiences, down the centuries."

Storm smiled thinly. "As with most lives, the bits others find exciting are few and far between, set in long stretches of more mundane things. I break a lot of harp-strings."

"No, really," Thalance said, frank admiration showing in his eyes. "If you are centuries old, how is it that you look no more than twice my cousin's age? And is it true, what I heard about your being a marchioness of Cormyr?"

"The divine fire of Mystra keeps me young," Storm replied quietly, "and I should add that at the moment it is also protecting the realm—but endangering everyone at this table—by keeping Firefall Keep enclosed in a barrier to keep the foe within."

Erlandar looked around, as if he expected to see a flaming wall dancing in the air. "Barrier? Where, and for how long?"

"As long as we need it, I hope," Storm replied. "And yes, Thalance, I am the Marchioness Immerdusk—so I fear I dare not go out on the battlements to watch a moonrise with you. Ladies of exalted station, I must remind you, have reputations to protect."

Her last sentence was delivered in a perfect mimicry of the cold, cutting tones of the elder Dowager Lady Summerstar; Thalance snorted with mirth, but Erlandar said heavily, "Pray don't mock Pheirauze, lady, for all her faults. She was . . . the storm wind that shaped me."

Storm bowed her head. "My apologies, Lord Summerstar. I have an impish streak that often gets the better of me."

"Is it true you spent years in the South as a tavern-dancer and pleasure slave because of that streak?" Thalance asked eagerly.

The war wizards leaned forward in interest.

Storm was even more amused by the lift of the understeward's eyebrow as he glided in between them to murmur, "Venison haunch in crust."

Thurdal kept his face otherwise carefully expressionless, and Storm gave him a broad smile as she replied, "Yes—and I enjoyed most of it, too. Did you know that many elven men can be transported to the heights of passion by stroking the tips of their ears?"

Erlandar shook his head in exasperation. Storm helped herself to the haunch—one of her favorites—generously. "No, I didn't, lady, but frankly I care not. Elven men aren't likely to be high on my list of conquests—or anyone else, for that matter, if this shapeshifter decides to slaughter *me!* What else can you tell us about . . . well, Shayna, and just what this foe can do?"

"Our foe can somehow drink knowledge and abilities—spells he can cast, for instance—from his victims. This power has something to do with the burntout state of the bodies we've found," Storm told them. "As to Shayna—well, she refers to this shapeshifter as her 'Master,' and can talk mind to mind with him . . . presumably another power he's gained."

"You said he had her in thrall," the wizard Insprin said quietly. "Can this foe do the same thing to the rest of us?"

Storm shrugged. "I don't know," she said, "but surely his killings could be fewer, and he could show himself less, if he could control anyone from a distance."

"Azoun's eyes," the understeward announced, carefully not meeting Storm's gaze.

"What's 'Azoun's eyes'?" Corathar whispered, eyeing the steaming tureen set down in front of him.

"Oysters in spiced ale," Storm told him, leaning forward conspiratorially.

Erlandar's gaze went involuntarily to the pectoral gleaming on her breast—and his eyes narrowed. "That jewelry you're wearing . . . isn't it the same design as one I see often on Queen Filfaeril?"

"Yes," Storm told him, filling a bowl with a hearty helping of Azoun's eyes. "It bears some magical defenses."

"Such as?" Thalance asked.

Storm smiled thinly. "It's unwise to reveal such things when anyone may be your foe, but I'll show you just one." She pushed back the sleeve of her open shirt, unbuckled the dagger strapped to her forearm, and fastened it high up by her shoulder, to hold the sleeve up.

Extending her bare arm out across the table, she said gently, "My Lord Erlandar, I know that the death of Pheirauze troubles you—and you ache to have something to smite and carve with your sword. So strike at me now, with all your strength and savagery!"

Erlandar frowned at her. "This is—not right, lady," he said in protest, shaking his head.

"Please," Storm said. "Thalance needs to see a little magic."

She held up her other hand in warning. "Only pray balance yourself, as if you might miss, to avoid a fall."

Erlandar stood up, still frowning at her, and his blade slowly slid out. "It's a trick, then—the magic will make me miss."

"Try to cut my arm off," Storm replied gravely, "and you'll see. You will not be harmed."

Erlandar shrugged, and then raised his blade. With a smooth lift of his shoulders, he swept his blade down in a cut across her forearm. The steel slid through her flesh as if it were empty air, and left no wound behind. Her arm was untouched. Thalance stared at it in fascination.

"An ironguard," Broglan said, and Storm nodded. "Try again, Erlandar—really hack; you'll feel better."

The eldest Summerstar man gave her a hard look, and then growled and swung his blade down again, hacking and hewing like a man possessed. In the midst of the flashing steel the understeward came in at the head of another line of servers, glided to a stop, and waited politely until Erlandar lowered his blade, panting—and Storm withdrew her unmarked arm.

"Old coins," Thurdal announced gravely, setting down the lead platter.

When the servers had done the same and turned away, Corathar leaned forward and whispered, "Right—what're 'old coins'?"

"Egg, cheese, and marrow pies," Storm and Insprin told him, more or less in unison. The bard was still standing, calmly rolling her sleeve down, when the unmistakable crack of a crossbow firing echoed across the hall—followed by the loud, rising *thrum* of a streaking quarrel.

With an angry buzz, it zipped between Thalance and Broglan, burst right through Storm's body, and splintered against the far wall. Everyone at the table whirled around—except Thalance, who kept his awed eyes on the lady bard. Storm herself was already gazing at her would-be slayer.

Everyone else saw a Purple Dragon hurl down his crossbow and flee, the doors banging wide in his wake. The passage beyond was strewn with the bodies of other guards.

"Gentlesirs, the foe," Storm announced calmly.

The doors at the other end of the hall, behind them, burst open, and the boldshield hastened in with his sword drawn, Purple Dragons all around him. They glanced quickly around the tables and then ran on down the hall, toward their dead comrades.

As if in unspoken accord, everyone at table turned to look at Storm. She was unhurt, no mark left in her breast—where the pectoral glittered almost tauntingly. Calmly buckling her dagger back into place, she looked up and said brightly, "Oh, did I forget to mention that this collection of baubles is also a protection against missiles?"

"Gods, lady," Erlandar growled, "you're a laughing lunatic to top all!"

Storm tossed her head as she shook her sleeve back down into place. "I fear so. Folk always seem to remember my kinder side, and forget what an imp I am." She bowed to them gravely, and added, "My apologies."

There was a general shout of relieved laughter. The understeward glided serenely into the midst of it to announce, "Marsemban tarts, roast pheasant, and roast quail in a sauce of cheese, saffron, and white wine."

"All right," Corathar said disgustedly. "*What* are Marsemban tarts?"

There were chuckles, and Erlandar rose, said grandly, "May I? Pastries topped with parsley and potato, containing diced salmon and crab in a sauce of almond milk, wine, leeks, and persimmons."

There was a smattering of applause—but then, there were few diners left to give it. Erlandar and Storm both sat down.

The old Summerstar noble said, "I must thank you, lady, for making what I feared would be a grim meal indeed into something . . . entertaining."

Storm shrugged. "Death comes for us all, and unpleasantness, too," she told him, filling her glass with amberheart sherry. "Some of us are given very little time to live, so why not enjoy all we can and share that joy with others? It's better than melancholy moping, to be sure!"

"Magely philosophy?" Broglan asked with a smile.

Storm shrugged. "I'm more an adventurer than I am an all-knowing sorceress, Broglan. Far from it; Mystra wants her Chosen *not* to be tower-girded tome-studiers." She saw Insprin and Corathar leaning forward again in keen interest, and added, "It's Mystra's Way to let us all forge our own paths in life; we know only what we can learn ourselves . . . and I've spent far more time with a sword in my hand down the years, than a spellbook."

Broglan nodded slowly. "Do you . . . speak of such things often?"

Storm shook her head. "Only with Harpers—or, most recently, with the foe, as we fought," she told him. There were gasps and dropped jaws up and down the table.

Erlandar swore. "Gods, but you're a cool one," he murmured, shaking his head and reaching for his decanter.

"I'm not, you know," Storm told him intently, her tone making him look up and meet her gaze. "I've just had more years of learning control and acting than the rest of you."

"Chicken livers in spiced cream broth," the under-steward said then.

Corathar made a face. Thalance ignored the tureen placed before him. Erlandar, Insprin, and Broglan, however, lifted the lids and ladled out generous portions.

As soon as her first spoonful touched her lips, Storm waved her arms and snarled, "*Don't* eat this!" Insprin dropped his spoon, and Broglan spat out the spoon that had just entered his mouth. Erlandar—who'd just swallowed—stared at her in horror.

"Oh, Mystra *aid* me!" Storm moaned in exasperation, and dived over the table, scattering dishes and decanters in all directions.

Erlandar was already turning purple around the lips when she leapt on him, knocking noble and chair over with a crash and coming down on top of him. In frantic haste, she glued her lips to his and called forth the silver fire. She'd just have to hope the foe didn't test the barrier now. . . .

He didn't, thank the gods. The Summerstar noble

bucked and squirmed under her, trying to speak. He then fell still, and slowly raised his hands to cradle her in his arms, as tenderly as any lover.

When Storm lifted her head from his at last, he was grinning at her, eyes shining. She gave him a slap and rolled off him.

"You old rogue," she said affectionately. She looked up to the others. "Let those livers be cast into the braziers without delay! What's in them could kill anyone who takes a mouthful. An earlier dish held poison meant just for me, but this time it seems the foe decided to leave me as alone as he could, by eliminating everyone else.

"Corathar, please hasten to the boldshield and tell him two things: he must check on the Lady Zarova without delay—and he must consider the understeward dead, and anyone who looks like him to be . . . the foe."

As the young wizard hurried from the room, Erlandar looked up at her with something like worship in his eyes. She reached out a hand and hauled him to his feet.

"Consider yourself honored, Lord Summerstar," Storm told him. "You're one of the few mortals to taste the divine fire of Mystra—and live."

"Lady," the old noble said huskily, "I shall worship the Mother Of All Magic henceforth, to my dying day."

"Dare we touch anything else on our plates," Broglan asked faintly, "or is it too late?"

Storm spread her hands. "Poison's not so easy to get or make as some think, but I doubt . . . well, let me taste a bit of everything, and then you can eat and drink all you like."

"Right now, Lady Storm," Insprin said heavily, "that won't be much. What with crossbow bolts, and men lying dead by yonder door, poison on our platters, and the fire of Our Holy Lady of Spells, I'm . . . no longer hungry."

There was a general rumble of agreement.

Thalance grinned and said, "I feel a trifle ill, lady—kiss me?"

"Perhaps later," Storm told him with a grin. "*I'm* still hungry."

Broglan's eyes narrowed. "This silver fire," he asked, "it can't sustain you while it's holding that barrier, can it? You have to eat, to stay strong enough to go on—that's it, isn't it?"

Storm's eyes met his gravely. "Broglan, you see far too well for your own safety. Say nothing of this, any of you—or the foe will know of another gap in my armor."

"There's something else I should tell you, lady," Broglan said awkwardly. "We kept Athlan's notes from you. Frankly they don't hold much of use. They were largely what any novice mageling would write of his discoveries, plus a lot of dream visions, and—"

Storm frowned and held up a staying hand. "Did he dream a lot about dragons watching him?"

"Why, yes," the war wizard replied, matching her frown. "Do you know what it meant?"

Storm shrugged. "No. Not yet. Please say on."

"Well, the only thing we found of real interest is a few passages about the subsumption you spoke of—stealing powers from beings one kills. It seems that, long ago, Athlan discovered instructions for gaining this ability—instructions we can't find. He wrote that he found the process in notes made by a mad recluse, Glondar of Hilp, once a war wizard of Cormyr."

"And where did Glondar learn of it?" Storm asked softly.

Remembering, Insprin shook his head and shivered. The bard glanced at him, and then back at Broglan.

The leader of the war wizards looked grave. "Ah. Well. Glondar claimed, or so Athlan writes, to have come upon it in notes left by men he came to believe were avatars of two gods: Gargauth and . . . Bane."

* * * * *

In a chamber of dank darkness, sudden light flickered and glowed, eddying about a motionless figure slumped on a stone bench. Cold laughter arose as the radiance settled down to a steady glow.

"Soon," a tentacled thing told the slumped man. "Soon you'll be ready, my Hungry Man. And then—" His voice rose and danced with glee. "Then it will be time—" He chortled and began to shuffle about the room, the shape of his body flickering and changing wildly. "Time to feed!"

The cold laughter rose again, high and sharp, echoing around the chamber until it rolled out through the empty passages and rooms of the Haunted Tower.

After a moment, another sound joined it. Slobbering, the Hungry Man began laughing, too.

Thirteen

DRAGONS IN THE KEEP

"All of this is edible," Storm said, looking at the grim-faced men around her. "Take it, just as it is, to some place in the keep you can defend. Go to the pantries and take what raw foodstuffs you can find, too. You'll need water more than anything. Erlandar, where in Firefall Keep are a few secure rooms—no secret passages and no cracked walls or ill-fitting doors? The rooms must have water, and space enough to improvise a privy."

Lord Summerstar frowned, looked at Thalance, and then said, "Well, there's a pump-room by the kitchens. . . ."

He looked a question, but Thalance shrugged. "The only other pumps I know of are by the stables. There're wells in the Haunted Tower and in the courtyard, but I don't suppose we could defend either of those."

"The kitchens it'll have to be, then," Storm said, "but try to choose rooms that you can't be smoked out of if our foe sets the ovens or pantries alight with everything that'll burn."

"So we build ourselves a cage and cower in it," Thalance said, acquiring a frown of his own. "I can see how that'll prevent this shapeshifter from catching us alone . . . but doesn't that give him free run of the keep, and keep us all in a known space he can hurl magic into whenever he pleases?"

Storm nodded. "All of that, yes. Consider warriors expendable—as most Purple Dragons already believe their commanders do—but necessary to guard the few war wizards we have left."

Thalance glanced at the two mages, wondered briefly what horrible fate might have already befallen the third. "And what will they be doing?"

"Trying to identify and keep track of our foe by means of wizard eye spells, so that I can shrink down my barrier around him and put him in a trap. This won't be quick or easy, especially after he guesses or learns what we're trying to do. The mages will need to sleep in shifts and be watched over constantly . . . we don't know how far the foe's mind powers can reach."

"Into our midst, you mean," old Insprin said calmly.

Storm nodded.

Broglan shook his head. "I don't like it," he said, looking around at the tureens and platters, "but I can't see any better way of doing things. We should act like we're taking this food back to the kitchens to start with, and all go to these rooms together. Then we'll have to shuttle our spellbooks and all down from our rooms."

He looked at the two Summerstars, and added, "If I may presume to give orders to you two, my lords, you're going to have to learn how to use wands that hurl magic missiles, so that you can defend us while we're packing up, dismantling, and such."

Thalance and Erlandar both nodded soberly. "We

can take orders," the younger Lord Summerstar said quietly. "I'm just glad to have some sort of plan to follow, at last."

He looked down at the silver-haired woman at their feet, where she was settling the last lid onto a tureen, and asked, "Lady Storm, will you lead us?"

"No," she said, rising smoothly. "I have to go and think—and, to cover all of you, hunt shapeshifters while I'm at it." She smiled at them all, and then said briskly, "I believe that side table over there, if you upend it, can bear all the food at once; if two of you carry it like a litter, the rest can guard. Just remember to set it down at once if you're attacked."

"You're going off by yourself?" Broglan asked. "Lady, is that wise?"

Storm rolled her eyes at him. "Broglan, if I'd stuck to what was 'wise' down the years, I'd be long dead. Mystra would have given up on me, and I'd have lived and died a house drudge in some village or other in the North, safe and growing daily more bent and crabbed and frustrated. If I were wise, I'd never have come here—I'd have stayed safely at home working on my farm until word came that Cormyr was awash in blood, and the king and Lord Vangerdahast were able to change their shapes at will, and the realm was whelming for war! Speak to me not of 'wise,' all right?"

"Yes," Thalance told Insprin, "she's definitely a marchioness."

"Definitely," the thin, gray-haired elder wizard agreed.

"Right," Storm said. "Be about it, then. Broglan, before the lot of you leave this chamber, tell Ergluth or whichever officer is at the doors where you're going—and ask him to tell Corathar where to find you when he returns." She started away.

Storm turned, silver hair swirling about her shoulders, and added, "Of course, bear in mind that when you see him again, it *might* be the foe walking into your midst—but then again, it might just be a scared young mage, of lesser powers than the rest of us."

"I'll test him by asking about his noble past," Erlandar offered.

"If the foe can take the memories of those he slays," Storm reminded him, "he already has those of Athlan, and Pheirauze, and the gods know who else in this kingdom!"

"Get gone," Broglan growled, "before you raise our spirits too high, and make us overconfident!"

They chuckled hollowly, and Storm turned away again.

Thalance watched her go and murmured, "There goes a woman I'd go on my knees to wed . . ."

"After me, boy," Erlandar told him. "I'm th—"

"No," Broglan said firmly from beside them, startling them both into silence. "After *me*."

* * * * *

With unhurried confidence, the Bard of Shadowdale strode past the guards—after all, if your enemy can be anywhere, why run? She went up the first flight of stairs she found, and then down the next staircase toward the cellars, only to double back and climb again. There was an unused closet she'd seen on her way to the fire . . . a gown-room, by the looks of it.

There it was. Storm looked up and down the deserted passage. She cautiously hooked open the door, and found herself looking at the dead, burnt-out husk of a Purple Dragon. She sighed and caught the corpse as it toppled past her, cradling the dead warrior to lay him gently down. The sightless eyes of an empty skull stared up at her.

"Helm or Tempus guard you, soldier," she murmured, and dragged him into the nearest room along the passage—a dusty, sheet-draped guest bedchamber. It would not do for anyone to find him right outside the closet she'd chosen.

She cast swift glances up and down the passage again, but the fear that now gripped servants and armsmen alike meant that they went nowhere alone. No one had even replaced the burned-down torches along this hallway. She wondered briefly if the foe had subsumed the servant who usually did that task, and then shrugged and started to undress.

When she was bare, she dropped her pectoral into one boot, snatched up the scabbarded sword and bundled everything else up around it, and stuffed them all down behind a bucket at the back of the closet. Then she stepped into the small room after them and firmly closed the door, shutting herself into the darkness.

She did not need light to work her spell, just a moment of peace to call it forth. In a drifting moment, she would become an unseen, flying phantom that could wander at will around the keep, spying out shapeshifters and their mischief.

A moment of unguarded dreaming . . . she was adrift amid fire, both amber flames and silver. Out of them swam the red-scaled head of a dragon, watching her. Its great, dark eye blinked at her . . . and then seemed to dwindle through the mists . . . no, it was growing *smaller,* and turning to become—a vivid, glistening teardrop on a brassy handle: an ornate metal scepter surmounted by the dragon's eye. She slid past it. It was gone in the mists, and she was starting to be able to see the dark walls of the gown-room around her.

As she rose, featherlike, to fly out into the keep, Storm shook her head in puzzlement. What *did* the dragon have to do with this?

* * * * *

"Saw through my scheme, did she? *Hah!* 'Twas but an idle tactic! No one shall escape me! None shall leave Firefall Keep alive! Hahahahahahaha!"

The figure shouting those echoing words lashed out with hands that spat lightning from each finger, scorching the stones of the dark chamber around him. A phantom flew away, as if startled by the outburst, and was chased by deep, bellowing laughter.

The capering, tentacled man making that sound suddenly fell silent, and asked in the icy, patrician tones of Pheirauze Summerstar, "What buffoon disturbs my home?"

He whimpered for a moment, and then said in quite a different voice, "Have they fallen yet? Well, see to it, man! See to it!"

And he raised his hands and hurled fire—a raging, white-hot ball that roared across the chamber and crashed into the far wall, sending flames flying about the room. The man sighed.

"Please," he said in infinitely bored tones, examining nails that swiftly grew into talons. "Spare me."

Then he howled like a hound in despair. He set off at a run, cackling and howling by turns, blasting stone walls, steps, and statues around him with golden-green flame. Stone exploded into rubble on all sides as he raged, trying to sing and bark and spit out words all at once.

"I'm rich, sire, and you cannot trouble me anymore!" he called to a mirror that had gathered dust for over a century—before he shattered it with all the fire he could muster.

"Yes," he breathed a moment later, voice hushed but trembling with emotion. "A Summerstar would do *this....*"

"All I know is," he snarled, interrupting himself with a harsher, deeper voice, "we as wear the Dragon spends all our spare time dyin' for the king, that's all!"

"What gods-accursed plan . . . ?" he asked the empty air as he capered down a hall.

He whirled around. "He made it," he told the passage with quiet fury, "as if we had never been."

"I-I-" he said in anguish, and went to his knees. His face melted and ran like butter in the sun. He howled with all the strength in his lungs, *Why can't I remember my name?"*

That agonized shout echoed down the empty rooms for a long time. "Name, name, name" came faintly back to him, as he held his head in his hands and sobbed.

Or tried to. As he clasped his cheeks, his head melted away from between his cupped hands, and ran down onto the floor, glistening like blood. Though the room was dark, it reflected back a dancing radiance as it flowed across the floor: the flickering shadows of silver flames.

* * * * *

"Take it," Insprin Turnstone told the young noble. "We can worry later if that's mold."

Thalance Summerstar nodded, turned awkwardly with the heap of long, curl-ended bread loaves the wizard had thrust into his hand, and started back on his way. Insprin waved four of the Purple Dragons to follow him and turned back to the dusty corners of the pantry.

Everything was a mystery. Why can't people *label* their jars?

It's not as if they'd wizardly secrets to keep, Insprin thought sourly, running his fingers through his graying hair. The question before him right now was—is this oil that's gone off, or is Calishite olive oil *supposed* to smell and taste like this?

Urrgh. Forget it; the Calishites could keep it! He put the stopper back and reached for the next jug—only to freeze in midreach as a merry giggle sounded from just over his left shoulder. He turned slowly, fearing each breath would be his last.

Shayna Summerstar was leaning against the pantry wall, a dusty bottle in her hand. Chestnut hair spilled down over her ivory shoulders, and the old wizard almost licked his lips. Gods, but she was beautiful. "The kitchen wine cellar's around *here*, silly!" she said, friendly mirth in her eyes. "What're you trying to drink the fish-oil for?"

"F-Fish oil?" was all old Insprin could think to say, as he felt for his wand.

Shayna's emerald eyes went down to it as he tore it forth. "Is anything wrong, sir wizard?" she asked. "I'm sorry if I startled you—I only wanted to offer you some wine! You looked so hot and bothered after Thalance left, and . . ."

She frowned. "How'd you manage to get him to fetch and carry, anyway? It's more than *I've* ever managed to get him to do!"

"Forgive me, Lady Summerstar," Insprin said gravely, holding the wand trained at her from about two paces distant, "but I must ask this: is your mind your own?"

She gave him a puzzled smile. "Is it *what?*"

They looked at each other in silence for a long moment, and then she said quietly, "You're serious. Well, of course it's my own. This isn't some strange ritual greeting war wizards use, is it?"

Then she seemed to notice the bottle of wine in her hand for the first time, and added, "Well—do you want some wine, or not?"

"No, thank you, Lady Shayna," Insprin said, taking a careful pace away from her. "Forgive me for being suspicious," he added, "but in my admittedly brief time here at the keep, I've never seen you be so—ah, *forward*. Outspoken, instead of shy, and open and easy

with a war wizard you've scarcely met." He looked at
her narrowly. "I'm not sure I'm speaking to the real . . ."

Her smile fled. "I see now," she said. "Lady Storm
met with me, yes, and spoke to me of the shapeshifter
loose in the keep. You think I might be some sort of
monster." She shrugged. "I don't know how I can prove
myself to be the real Shayna. If, as you say, we knew
each other better, you could ask me questions about
my younger days, and so be sure, but . . ."

She sighed, and turned away. "This isn't turning out
the way I meant it to," she said in a low voice. "I waited until you were alone, thinking this would be a won-
derful chance . . ."

"Chance?" Insprin asked quietly, wand still aimed
steadily at her. "Chance for what?"

Shayna Summerstar turned back to face him, and
then peered quickly past. Assured that they were still
alone, she said in a low voice, "I must now lead House
Summerstar, and put away thoughts of gowns and
feasts and . . . handsome men. I—I'll lose those things
before I ever even get to touch them with my fingertips! Snatched away, so I can never have a lover,
never—"

Insprin raised a graying eyebrow. "Why not?" he
asked. "Being head of a noble house doesn't mean setting the world aside, lady! Not in Cormyr, anyway!"

Shayna looked up at him. "You don't see, do you?"
She took a step forward, and he raised the wand tensely.

A pained look passed over her face. She snatched at
the tip of the wand and thrust it firmly between her
breasts, where her gown was cut away to show a fall of
lace. "There! If I'm some sort of monster," she told him
fiercely, "blast away!"

He looked into angry green eyes that were very close
to his, swallowed, and asked carefully, "Lady, what is it
you want?"

"You, Insprin Turnstone!" she hissed furiously. "Do I
have to go to my knees and beg you? I need a man to
teach me what loving and kindness and comfort are all
about . . . a man who dares not carry tales around the
realm, and who has magic to keep unwanted children
from me! The only man I've ever really loved and
admired was my father—and you are *so* like him!
Kind, and thoughtful, and yet quiet, keeping your own
counsel until those around you really need it. I think I
could love you . . . and yet I know I can't wed you, so I'd
like to be in your arms for—for whatever times we can
steal from the world together!"

She gazed into his eyes and almost whispered, "Of
course, if you find me repellant, or my asking ridiculous, I'll understand, and say nothing . . . except to beg
you to forget I ever spoke these words. Only please,
please don't laugh at me, or call me a child!"

Insprin lowered his wand and put one hand to her
magnificent hair, stroking it with infinite gentleness.
"Lady," he said softly, "no lass who thinks such things
can be anything but a woman, whether she's known a
man yet or not. I-I do find you young, and I confess I'm
more startled than flattered, but if you'll allow me to
walk with you awhile, and talk, perhaps you can per-
suade me that you really want *me*, and know what
you're getting yourself into . . . this keep is not the
safest of places right now, you know."

"Precisely," Shayna said, "and if I die this night, or
on the morrow, or the day after, I'll never even have
known a *kiss* from any man who was not my kinsman,
and just being polite or kind!" She took his arm firmly,
set down the dusty bottle, and said, "Right then—
walk, you said, and we will. I'll walk to the end of
Firefall Vale and back, wizard, so long as you take me!"

"Ah . . . I was thinking more of a tower where we
could be alone," Insprin replied, holding his wand
down by his side. Abruptly she caught hold of his

sleeve and turned him, trying to kiss him—only to feel the point of the swiftly raised wand hard against her breast.

She glared into his eyes, her quickening breath warming his chin. "Fire the damned thing, I said," she whispered fiercely. "Find out that I am Shayna Summerstar, and then heal me, wizard, and then make love to me!"

He never knew, later, if he bent his lips to hers, or if she thrust her mouth forward, but her kiss was hot, and tremblingly eager, and sweet.

When he drew away at last to breathe, he said very quietly, "You mean it, don't you?"

"I do," the young noblewoman in his arms said simply. "Do you still doubt it?"

"No," he said, just as plainly, and took her arm. "Let us leave this place, and go wherever you want."

Shayna sighed as if a great weight had been taken from her, and smiled, her eyes bright. "Now we're getting somewhere, Insprin! I know just the place!"

"Oh?" Veteran war wizard that he was, Insprin still had hold of his wand and his presence of mind—but the lady in his arms giggled and said, "No, it's not my grandmother's bedroom or some dungeon cell! Come on!"

They hastened through the wine cellar, avoiding the pantry and its gathered guards, and past the granaries to a back stair. Three halls and a passage later, the way ahead turned dark—and the wizard slowed.

"Isn't this the Haunted Tower?"

Shayna gasped with exasperation. "Wizard," she hissed, "this is my *home!* Mine, now that I am head of House Summerstar—and I can't help it if folk call this whole central bit haunted! We just have to pass through it here, to reach the far wing!"

Insprin's eyes narrowed, and he stepped back from her and cast a quick spell. She made as if to interrupt, and then said, "Finished? Satisfied? Come *on!*"

The shield was a feeble one, but it would keep off the first slap of a tentacle or stab of a tail-sting . . . unless it came from *her*. Insprin sighed—we all have to take some risks in life, after all—and drew Shayna into his arms once more.

She laughed softly in delight and anticipation, and led him into the darkness. "It won't be long now," she said, guiding his arms around her slender waist, to where her gown seemed to have come undone. "I want to feel your hands . . . no, don't stop, I want to get there . . . I've a cabinet full of sherry, and a fire laid ready to light, and—"

Master? Master, I have him. Where are you?

[CHAOS]

Master?

AH *THERE* YOU ARE MY PRETTY ONE HEIGH-HO THERE'S A BLADE BRIGHT AND READY BUT THE STORMS ARE SO FIERCE, MILORD, THAT WE DARE NOT TRY TO KISS ME NOW YOU WENCH, YOU BRAZEN DOG! WOE BETHRUST IT ALL! THERE'S AN ANKLE THAT MUST BE HIS, IN ALL THIS BLOOD, AND . . .

It seemed to Shayna Summerstar then that a bright sword of silver flames cut open a door in the back of her mind, and images tumbled in, rushing and overwhelming her, all shrieking and moving and overlaid and shifting at once. . . .

With a snarl, she tore away from the wizard, leaving bits of her gown behind, and barked like a dog. Insprin went pale and backed away from her warily, but the face she turned toward him was streaming with tears. Emerald eyes implored him to stay with her even as she snarled and babbled wordlessly and clawed at the empty air.

"Insprinwizard!" she gasped, as if rising from deep water, "don't leave meeeeee!" She was gone again into a nightmare world of howling and shrieking and staggering. Abruptly she raced off into the darkness of the Haunted Tower, crying out despairingly, *"Don't leave meeeeee!"*

Insprin took two running steps after her but stopped. He looked around at the dark walls and the scraps of cloth in his hands, cursed softly, and turned back. He ran for all he was worth, his aging heart pounding in his ears. The jaws of the trap could close on him any instant.

The child was trapped, in torment. Alone, and frightened—and the heir of a noble house he was sworn to protect so long as she lifted no hand in treachery to the Dragon Throne. For Shayna to survive Broglan's spells and the silver fire and the bard's sword, he had to find Storm, swiftly, and tell her . . . tell her everything.

"Storm!" he called, when he could find the breath. "Storm Silverhand! I need you!"

He lost his footing on a stair, stumbled painfully, and with a rueful laugh rebounded off the wall at the bottom. Of *course* he needed Storm. Don't we all?

Fourteen

TOWERS TOPPLED

 As the sun went down over Firefall Keep, something shook the rooms where the two Summerstar lords stood with a few Purple Dragons, a cook, and the grim war wizard Broglan.

"What in the name of the Old Dragon of Cormyr was *that?*" Erlandar snarled as dust drifted down on their heads.

A dull, rolling boom resounded through Firefall Keep.

"Storm blasting the shapeshifter to little shifting bits?" Thalance suggested hopefully—and then winced as a second explosion flung him hard against the nearest wall. The goblet he'd been holding clanged off stone and rolled away into a corner, trailing its contents.

Abruptly, one panel of the barred double doors at the end of the room shivered and fell, hanging crazily from its hinge for a moment as a widening crack raced across the wall above it. The door collapsed with a rushing groan. Its bar bounced and clanged. The guards posted there cursed and scrambled to get clear—only to fling themselves on their faces when a pale creature streaked over them and flew down the room.

Broglan cursed and fumbled for his wand as blades flashed out of scabbards all around him. Suddenly, he was on the floor again, the wind knocked out of him. A nude woman, silver hair swirling around her, was curled up on his chest.

"Sorry," Storm said shortly, rolling off him, "but you were the only place left in here that didn't have a sword out! I had to materialize *somewhere!*"

Erlandar barked out a laugh. "Things are back to normal," he announced to the room full of staring men, "she's lost all her clothes again!"

"*Highly* amusing, my Lord Summerstar," Storm replied, snatching his blade from him. "I'll be needing this—I'm on my way to getting dressed. Gods, but that—that *thing* must have subsumed a lot of spells! He's blasting the Haunted Tower apart!"

"What?" Erlandar bellowed, laughter sliding into fury. "That's *our* Haunted Tower!"

Broglan, who'd been twisting on the floor struggling for breath all this time, found it at last—to laugh uncontrollably. "Do you . . ." he gasped, when he could, "know . . . how funny . . . that sounded?"

As a smiling Storm strode barefoot out of the room, and gestured rudely at the grinning guards who saluted her exit, the wizard on the floor finished a last guffaw and looked up. The room exploded with mirth.

It ended abruptly as the place rocked again, and a piece broke off the ceiling and fell. Dust descended in clouds, and the laughter turned to curses and coughing.

"Well," Thalance Summerstar said, as he snatched up a wineskin to replace his lost goblet, "this monster *could* dispose of us all by just bringing the keep down on top of us!"

"Did you have to say that?" Erlandar snarled as the room rolled underfoot again, and everyone fell.

* * * * *

Storm Silverhand went to her knees—*bare* knees, gods blast it—on the stones as the passage rocked around her. "I hope," she told the falling stones, "that he's *using up* the spells he's stolen!" A last stone fell in front of her and broke apart. "I won't be pleased if I hear otherwise." She got up and ran on.

The fallen rubble made barefoot running painful. As she mounted the stairs, she hurled a handsome load of curses in the direction of the Haunted Tower. Ten minutes ago, these corridors had been full of such wild magic that she'd dared not tarry here nor try to regain solid form. Now, the foe had gone so mad that he was pulling down the Haunted Tower on his very head!

"Goaded by the silver fire," she announced with grim satisfaction. At last reaching the right passage, she sprinted down it. "And not the first to suffer that fate, either."

Improbably, a door was open. Two fearful chambermaids were staring out at her as she sprinted past, hair streaming. They shrieked in chorus and flung their door closed with a boom.

"This whole vale is going crazy," Storm said with a laugh. She caromed sideways off the wall as the keep shook crazily once more. Somewhere ahead of her, something heavy broke and crashed down; amid the near-deafening booming, she heard the sharper sounds of stone cracking and rolling.

The Bard of Shadowdale ran across the passage to the door she knew and snatched it open. Dust rolled out. "Great!" she snarled. "Just great!" Coughing, she felt her way through the dust and dragged out her clothes. Defiantly, she sat down in the middle of the corridor, as the keep shivered and thundered around her, and got dressed. Slowly and carefully, she adjusted this and smoothed that, putting on her pectoral last of all, until she pronounced herself ready to receive company.

Ah yes, company: such as the room full of men she'd left so precipitously not long ago. Well, now: to rally them, or to confront a madman and dance to his spells as he happily tore apart the keep, and the moon rose over them?

The fortress shook again. Something even larger crashed down into ruin. Ahead of her, a curving staircase broke into chunks and dropped slowly out of sight, one piece at a time. A rolling, shattering sound arose from below. Moonlight shone down into the dusty air where the stair had been. The foe must be shattering the battlements above! Well, it wasn't as if she didn't know where he was. . . .

For the moment, the shapeshifter would keep. So much for grand schemes of spying out where he was and tracking him! Right now, she'd best get the few living men she'd need out of the place before he brought it down on their heads! What poison might fail to do, a nice heavy stone block might succeed at, all too well. . . .

"Why me? Mystra, all I ask is, why *me?*" Storm said as she started back down the passage.

As if in reply, the ceiling broke away and fell into the rooms beside her—and moonlight stabbed down from the open night sky above. *Two floors* that had been above her were gone!

Well, yes, Mystra, this *wasn't* the first time in her life that she'd made this very complaint. Sorry. Storm sighed and ran on.

* * * * *

"I am—I am—*Yes!*" And with that final, exultant shout, the man with three heads and eight arms flung his limbs up in triumph and hurled all the crowding chaos back where it belonged, clearing his mind at last. Balls of fire streaked up from two of those limbs, striking through the shattered stone and moonlight. Where they struck, a leaning turret broke away from the shattered stone around it and hurtled down into the open space that had not been there an hour earlier.

Down, down like a tumbling mountain, down to a crash that shook the entire vale and threw back echoes from the mountaintops . . .

Down to bury the place where the exultant many-limbed man had been standing, and on its way, scrape open an entire wall, and lay bare rooms and passages that had been walled away and hidden for many long years . . .

The ravaged wall creaked and buckled and bulged, threatening a great collapse. Leaning pillars held, and the slowly shifting stone ground ponderously to a halt, sending down only a little rubble. Out of one long-hidden cavity, something gleamed in the moonlight as it fell.

Something metallic and sticklike, with a single great eye as its head. The dragoneye scepter hit the rubble, bounced once, and slid to a stop, blinking up at the moon. Somehow, it looked angry.

* * * * *

Corathar Abaddarh clutched Dowager Lady Zarova's coronet and wished it would stop emitting little magical flashes. Was it going to explode, or burn him with lightning, or transport him somewhere unknown and perilous? Worse, would it attract the attention of the shapeshifter who was so busily blasting apart the keep on all sides?

The gods-cursed coronet was definitely flashing a

little brighter and faster than it had when he'd found its hiding place and snatched it into the light. Pearls and emeralds and gods-knew what else had spilled out with it in a glittering flood. He'd swept them all back behind the hidden panel and slammed it shut again. At least, he hoped he'd found them all. With the room shaking all around him, some of them had taken long and interesting journeys. And, of course, the tumult had shattered his lantern!

He wouldn't have dared keep it lit on the journey back, anyway. Not with a howling-crazed shapeshifter laughing like a loon and blasting everything that moved!

Corathar sighed. He felt his way cautiously forward in the darkness. The dowager lady, the boldshield, and the safety of the heavily guarded kitchen rooms were a long way off . . . and he was growing weary.

He'd been a little suspicious of this errand at first. The whole thing could have been just an excuse to send him out across Firefall Keep right into the clutch-es of this murderous shapeshifter. The boldshield, however, had assured him that ranking nobles did have such enspelled items. Some of them *were* best handled only by their rightful wearers or by war wizards, because of enchantments laid on them by Lord Vangerdahast or his predecessors. Well, all right, but what *about* those enchantments?

The cursed thing was flashing ever faster. He didn't see why he should die or be maimed just because some lazy noblewoman got all concerned over the fate of her coronet. After all, *she'd* left it behind. It was still in *her* castle, not out rolling around the countryside. Why couldn't it just have sat safe behind its stone panel until all this was over? Of course, there might not *be* a stone panel when this was all over, if—

Ahead, he heard a distant shout, and peered into the darkness. A many-armed figure was exulting in the moonlight, shouting and waving its arms in defiance at the night sky. Corathar swallowed and came to a hasty halt. This must be the foe!

Gods, if he looked over this way—! Corathar hastily cowered down, flipping up the tail of his robes to cover the winking coronet. There was a flash of fire from the distant figure—balls of fire, streaming up from those waving arms at some unseen enemy above. The bursts heralded a deep groaning that gave way to sharp cracking sounds . . . and then a growing, rumbling, thunderous roar.

The figure and the moonlight and all were gone as the world leapt and rocked all around Corathar. It flung him about like a child's ball. He gulped, grunted, cursed, and tried in the bruising darkness to keep the coronet and himself both unbroken.

At last his tumbling in the gloom came to an end, and he staggered to his feet and peered up and down the passage. The damned coronet was still blinking and winking. Where the moonlight had been he could see nothing—that way must be blocked.

"Mystra *spit* on it all!" he snarled, fear stoking fury.

He was trapped, and would have to go back into the cracked and lightless keep to dare one of the unsteady stairs and somehow find a way around all this. And was the mad foe dead? Or was the shapeshifter still lurking close by, in the dark—?

Something stumbled at him, and he shrieked and flung up the coronet in his hand. It flashed, obligingly. He briefly glimpsed a dust-smudged, wild-haired face, above a gown torn half off to reveal one gleaming white shoulder—and emerald eyes that were large and afraid and beseeching.

"Gods!" he swore hoarsely. It was the Lady Shayna Summerstar.

Or was it?

"Stay back," he shouted, in sudden, frantic fear,

holding up the coronet in front of him as if it was some sort of weapon.

"Who . . . who's that?" her quavering voice came out of the darkness—a weak and frightened voice that ended in a cough. It was followed by another, and another. Judging by the racking sounds, her coughing fit had taken her to her knees. Corathar stepped back and pulled a sleeve over the flashing coronet, unsure of what to do.

"Thalance?" she asked weakly, out of the darkness. It certainly *sounded* like the noble lady he'd watched down the feast table. . . .

Impulsively he stepped forward, wanting to see again the beauty he'd looked at so longingly that first feast night. He held out the coronet.

It blinked, and so did a pair of eyes very close to it— bewildered green eyes, that had trailed tears across the dust on her cheeks. That settled it. If this was the shapeshifter, it was an actor worthy of an easy meal.

"Lady?" he asked, reaching out into the darkness. "Will you tell me your name?"

The coronet flashed again, and he had another glimpse of her frightened, dirt-smudged face, eyes brighter now with hope.

"Shayna," she said. "Shayna Summerstar." The coronet winked. By its radiance he saw her lower lip tremble. She wiped dust and tears away from her eyes with one hand. "Who are you?" she asked as darkness descended again.

"Corathar, lady. Corathar Abaddarh; one of the war wizards."

"Wizards," she said slowly, as if it was a word she'd never heard before. "Not . . . Insprin?"

"Insprin is one of my companions, yes," he said eagerly.

He froze as a gentle hand tentatively touched him. It probed, ran up his arm—and the coronet flashed again, showing him fresh tears of hope. She looked up at his face, seeing him clearly for the first time, and opened her mouth to cry. He smiled at her reassuringly, and reached out.

"Thank the gods," she sobbed, clutching him, and dissolved into helpless weeping that shook them both. Corathar cradled her awkwardly, suddenly very aware of the gently spicy smell of her hair and of the softness of the body she was pressing against him.

She was a long time crying. She sobbed her way into silence and started trembling against him. He wasn't expecting the lips that found his, or the raw hunger with which she embraced him. He made a brief, wordless protest as he lost his balance and fell backward, but she clambered atop him, and the next flash of the coronet showed him her face as she bit her lip and tugged at his robes, panting.

"Corathar," she almost snarled. "Yes. *Yes.* Give me . . ."

Corathar reached out and gently set the coronet on her head. She responded by kissing him wildly and running her hands all over him, searching for buckles and lacings and openings, and . . .

Suddenly she stiffened, came to an abrupt halt with one delicate hand tugging her gown down and the other busily exploring its way down his bared chest. She sat up and pulled away from him.

"L-Lady?" Corathar whispered in sudden foreboding. "Have I . . . offended?"

The next flash of the coronet showed him a face that was somehow both sad and triumphant.

"No," she told him, in a voice that trembled a little. "No, you haven't. It's just—"

She was silent for so long that he dared to prompt her. "Just?"

Shayna Summerstar gave him a smile, and leaned close to him again. "I . . . you'll be my first," she whispered, eyes very close to his, "and there's a family tradition I must uphold. We must use my bed—and, as we won't be able to wed, you must claim a gift of me. There's a spellbook none of us can use in the strong chest under my bed; one of the treasures my father gave me. It shall be yours . . . if you can use your magic to get us to my bed."

Corathar sat up slowly. A spellbook! Was this truly happening?

"Where is your bed?" he asked, looking up and down at her slender, gowned beauty. Shayna pointed down the passage where he'd seen the roof come down . . . hours ago, it seemed, though it couldn't have been more than half an hour. . . .

"There," she said, and smiled weakly. "Or somewhere under there."

"Lady," the young mage said, his lust ebbing, "are you sure—"

"Corathar," she said, making his name a caress. The coronet flashed again. Her eyes were very large and dark. "Please? For me?"

She got off his legs, and he struggled to his feet. "Of course," he told her. "Yes. Just show me . . . I've a spell that can lift the fallen stones aside."

Soft hands stroked his cheek, and then took his arm. She leaned against him, and they walked together along the rubble-strewn passageway, moving slowly, her hip pressed against his with every step. "Do this for me," the noblewoman said softly into his ear, "and you'll always be welcome at Firefall Keep. Sometimes wizards need patrons. . . ."

"Lady Shayna," Corathar protested weakly, "I'm not a great wi—my magic's not that good." He cursed himself inwardly for a dolt. . . .

"And how do I know that?" she purred. "You are kind, and modest, and a mage who'll grow to be powerful and wise—what more can a woman ask for?"

What else, indeed? The coronet's flash became a

steady glow, now, and as Corathar cast a startled glance at it, she gave him an encouraging smile and pointed. "The bed must be just about there . . . about a dozen feet in, I'd guess."

"What if it's crushed?"

Shayna shrugged. "I don't think tradition demands that the bed be a certain size or condition—we'll make do." She flashed a dazzling smile, and then leaned close and whispered, "Hurry, my lord to be. Hurry."

Corathar smiled, nodded, and drew back his sleeves. "I'll need a little room," he said apologetically. She peeled herself away from his side and stepped back with another slow smile.

The youngest wizard of the Sevensash swallowed, collected his wits carefully, and then worked the most precise and exacting telekinesis spell he'd ever cast.

First that rock . . . no, think of Shayna's smiles later: rocks first . . . now that one . . . and that one . . .

Block after shattered block rose from where they'd fallen and swayed through the air off to one side, to clatter down into a shattered chamber beyond. About a score or so of rocks into this work, Corathar lifted a stone block that was almost intact, and thought he saw a hand lying under it. He blinking, feeling a sudden chill—but when he peered again at what he'd uncovered, it looked like the edge of the headboard. The bed!

He moved another stone, and another, with renewed eagerness, tumbling them out of the way, tossing and smashing them aside as sweat broke out on his brow— until a battered bed lay bare. With a flourish, he swept the last of the dust and rubble from its coverlet, and turned to the Lady Summerstar.

Shayna laughed delightedly and scrambled over the stones to reach it, coronet flashing. Corathar dismissed his spell and watched her, mouth suddenly dry. She reached the bed, lay down with slow grace, ran a hand up one hip of her gown, and beckoned to him.

"Come, my wizard," she called softly, opening her arms. Corathar obeyed.

His last memory was of how sweet her lips tasted as her eyes flashed in sudden triumph. The bed grew hands that sank iron-hard fingers into his throat, and strangled him.

He struggled for breath, but Shayna kept her lips pressed to his. It was from lower down that he felt sudden fire. He twisted, or tried to, and arched . . . and then a chaos of memories that were not his own flooded into and over him. With a despairing cry that he never voiced, Corathar Abaddarh rolled over into darkness, forever. . . .

* * * * *

"Spells, more spells," the man who was not Maxer muttered, and grew a tentacle to embrace the young woman beside him. WELL DONE.

He was so kind, Master. She sighed as she watched the husk fall back into ash and scatter on the rocks beneath them. The handsome head beside hers snorted and grew a long, long arm that reached up into a shattered room far above, and drew them up toward the moonlight.

"Kindness," the shapeshifter said aloud, scornfully. "Is that what you want me to give you?"

It would be a change, Master.

He stared at the young noblewoman in his arms, and suddenly shook with laughter. Gods, what spirit! He was beginning to feel the glimmerings of some respect for the nobility of Cormyr after all. 'Twas a pity, really, he'd have to destroy them all . . . including this one.

IF I HADN'T TOUCHED YOU WHEN I DID, he asked, suddenly and acutely aware that this young woman had chosen to rescue him from helpless death, and fought down strong urges and emotions to do so, WOULD YOU HAVE JOINED WITH THIS WIZARD?

She turned her head away from him, and he did not bother to grow an eyestalk to force a meeting of gazes. It was a long time before she said simply, *Yes.*

YOU HAVE MY THANKS, he told her gravely, wondering how soon it would be before he dared to destroy her. No one he might depend on could be permitted to survive. He must never lower his guard—and so, no one must be in a position to betray him . . . as she had betrayed another for him.

It was an even longer time before she said, in the depths of his mind, *You're welcome.*

She sounded so humble that he did not become alarmed at how deeply into his defenses she'd penetrated.

They sat together on the broken edge of a riven chamber and looked out over the moonlit rubble. The dust had largely settled, and they could see far into the Haunted Tower—and through it, trudging forward in answer to the master's call, the Hungry Man.

The Dark Master was in a hurry to transfer the puny spells he'd just subsumed to his mindless servant; the shambling husk hastened its tireless walk. It never saw what lay just beside one of its footfalls: a scepter whose metal shaft caught the moonlight and winked back from the watchful eye that surmounted it.

The dragoneye swiveled to watch the Hungry Man pass, and blinked once or twice as the shapeshifter stretched down his head so that two pairs of eyes faced each other from a pace apart—and blue-white beams of magic began to flow.

* * * * *

"Hold hard!" barked one of the guards at the doors, swinging a halberd up from the floor to menace her.

Storm raised an eyebrow. "To what?" she asked tartly. From somewhere beyond the ruined door at the guard's back, she heard Erlandar Summerstar laugh.

"It's her," the boldshield and the senior war wizard told the guard in unison, and he scowled and lowered his weapon.

"The way she came running up here . . ."

"You'd do more than run, man," Thalance Summerstar told him crisply, "if you were trying to make it through all those blasts and falls of stone!"

Broglan stepped forward a pace ahead of Ergluth Rowanmantle. "Are you—well? Did you meet with the foe?"

"I'm fine," Storm said, stretching. "Just a little weary—I'd grown unused to doing things without Mystra's power. No, I didn't see him, but I watched him bring down an entire turret, and it wouldn't surprise me if he didn't stop with just one, eith—"

She broke off and spun around. Someone was running toward them in the darkness, someone panting and not young and fit to begin with. Storm took two quick steps and put her hand on the guard's ready halberd, forcing its point down to the floor.

"What're you—" he snarled at her, straining with all his brawn to wrestle his weapon up again, and finding it as immobile as stone.

"Stand easy," Ergluth ordered gently, putting a hand on the Purple Dragon's shoulder.

Storm raised a hand. Everyone there fell suddenly silent as they saw a lone silver flame rise slowly from it. She held her palm up by her shoulder as if she held something she could hurl, and asked the darkness, "Who comes in such haste?"

The running steps halted, staggered, and then came on more slowly. "Insprin Turnstone, lady," a breathless voice called back.

"The dragon watches!" Broglan snapped.

"And never smiles," a reply came wearily out of the darkness. The speaker came forward into their torch-light. The senior war wizard relaxed; Insprin had obviously given the correct password to his challenge.

The older mage came up to them, still gasping for breath. He was covered with dust, and his sparse hair was in a wild twist of disarray.

"Are you all right?" Broglan demanded. "Did you see Corathar? Or Lady Shayna Summerstar?"

Insprin shrugged. "Corathar's out there some-where—we'd best look for him if we want to find him before the foe does."

He looked down at his hand, and held up what was still clenched in his fingers. Erlandar made a wordless sound as he recognized the tatters of Shayna's gown.

"I got *this* close to her," the old wizard said directly to the two Summerstar men. The guards around them drew back silently, watching the blood drain out of the nobles' faces. Insprin added quietly, "She tried to lure me into the Haunted Tower—but when we got there, she started to howl and bark like a dog, and then ran off—to *him*. I tried to hold her back, but . . ." He shrugged. "I dared not follow; if I fell with none of you knowing her fate, or that she belongs to the foe. . . ."

"No," Erlandar whispered hoarsely. "No." Then he spread his hands slowly, and turned around, gazing at all the grim men gathered there.

"If any hand must slay Shayna Summerstar," he said slowly, "let it be mine. None other must take her—not even you, Thalance. If you get out of this, it must not be with blood-guilt riding your shoulders for the rest of your days. Let it be bad old Uncle Erlandar."

To Storm he said, "Lady, I never thought to beg any woman for anything . . . but if you can bring our Shayna out of this—the Shayna we know—anything you ask shall be yours. The vale, the keep, all of it, if you want!"

Storm shook her head slightly. "I'll restore Shayna to you all, if I can. If, I said; Harpers don't make promises they cannot keep." She turned to the guard whose halberd she still held. "Bring all the torches."

Then she set off into the darkness.

"Storm—what're y—" Broglan began, and she turned around.

"How else do you expect to rescue our strayed ones?" she asked simply. "Come with me, all who will. Those who remain behind, be free in your choice and without shame."

Then she turned her head to lock eyes with Erlandar, and said, "One more thing, lord—if my hand does save Shayna, there will be no price. Saving things for their own sake is what Harpers do." She smiled faintly and headed back into the darkness.

There was a general roar as the men at her back scrambled to follow her.

Fifteen

CAT, AND MOUSE, AND DARK LORD

"Ah, they come at last," the man who was not Maxer purred. He perched on the broken edge of a room that was no more. "Full of fear that makes them desperate, willing to face even the fabled phantoms of the Haunted Tower—*we* know what makes them run, though, don't we?"

Shayna opened her mouth to reply—and closed it again in horror as the unmistakable voice of her grandmother Pheirauze came out of the shapeshifter's mouth. "Of course we do, Gallant One. Make them truly fear the Summerstars, so that none dare set foot in Firefall Keep without our leave! Let them taste the fire I did, my Dark Master!"

The laughter that followed veered sickeningly from the cold, brittle mirth of Pheirauze to the hearty bellow that was the shapeshifter's own.

"They call me the foe," he mused aloud, breaking off

his laughter abruptly. "Astonishingly apt." He smiled thinly, and said, "Yet if I am to prevail against them when they're finally sensible enough to come at me all together, I'll need to burn me another wizard or two."

He leapt up. His eyes went vacant, the way they looked when he was impressing commands on the Hungry Man. This time, no doubt, the Dark Master would be sending him away from the coming fray.

The shapeshifter swung around so that his lips could brush hers. "You, my pretty one," he murmured, "must be the lure that endangers Storm. Do not mind-speak to me unless she brings clear doom to you; she can hear when we talk so. Lead her on a dance—topple stones upon her, appear where she cannot follow, wear her out running . . . but take her away from the stalwart men of Firefall Keep, after I split them. Slay her not—for that is to be the finale of our feast."

"It shall be my pleasure, Master," Shayna whispered in his ear, and kissed it. He gave her a savage grin, slapped her shoulder, and growled, "Let us be about it, then! To war, for the bloody joy of it!"

He grew a tentacle that soared across the open area of his devastation. The limb snapped around the end of a roof beam. Another tentacle took her by the waist, and then the air was rushing past their ears as they swung across the emptiness of the night.

Shayna saw a few stars glittering above them, and then felt stone and tile under their feet again.

Her master said, "Don't mind-speak now, but heed: if you see Storm, cry out her name—sob, as if you're terrified—and run toward her. The moment you get behind cover, stop and dodge away. Once you're both away from the others, just try to stay ahead of her. I'll do the rest. Hold still."

He murmured something, touched her eyeballs with cool, feather-gentle fingertips, and said, "There. Now you can see in darkness."

She could. "How long does the spell last?"

He shrugged. "If it fails and Storm's close behind you, feign collapse, and I will free you when you awaken."

She looked down at her hands and her tattered gown. "Shouldn't I have a weapon? I—I'm all but naked."

"And that will be a weapon, if any of the men ever get close to you. Don't worry about who sees you. Save for Storm, none of them will see another dawn."

* * * * *

The torches wavered. One of the men cried out and swung his blade at something that moved in the gloom beside him. It faded away almost mockingly: a ghostly helm on the shoulders of a spectral warrior striding along a corridor that was no longer there.

"Easy," Ergluth said, his voice deep and calm. "We're in the Haunted Tower, now—there'll be other phantasms."

No one lowered a weapon. The two war wizards had their wands out, and only Storm walked barehanded, her blade riding ready on her hip.

The flickering torchlight showed them chaos ahead. Stone rubble was strewn everywhere, in some places heaped almost to the ceilings of chambers it had flowed into. The twisted, half-buried form of a chambermaid spoke silently of how swiftly and violently the collapse had come.

"Gods," one of the men muttered, "what're we fighting?"

"One who is insane," Storm told them all in level tones. "If he strikes, don't flee, but attack from all sides, repeatedly. We might push him howling over the edge, and he would cease to be a real threat."

"Is that a Harper's promise?" one of the armsmen asked almost slyly. There were hollow chuckles from those around him.

As if the mirth had been a cue, a sudden flash and roar came from above and ahead. The standing stump of a lone pillar toppled into their midst, showering jagged rocks in all directions as it came.

"Scatter!" Ergluth roared, scant seconds before the crash came. They all heard one agonized scream before the deafening thunder smote them.

Almost immediately, lightning cracked and snarled through the dust cloud above the tumbled stones of the pillar, reaching into the area the armsmen in the rear had fled to. There were more cries.

"Fall back!" Ergluth roared out of the darkness. "Back into the open hall—Redgarth Hall, where the stair had fallen!" He took two steps forward, holding his sword carefully upright so as not to stab anyone and reached down to where he knew a man lay.

His fingers encountered something shattered and sticky. He straightened with a sigh—only to stiffen, cold fear stabbing at his heart, as a voice said in his ear, "I'm the one he wants. I'll skulk off by myself and see if I can draw him away."

"Ye gods, woman!" he snarled. "Don't *scare* me like that! Why . . ." And then he fell silent. She was gone.

He stood still for a moment, breathing hard, staring around into the darkness and trying to see. There were no torches left alight hereabouts—only over there, beyond where the pillar had crushed a dozen men or more.

Time to start earning the tall stacks of coins a boldshield was paid—tall if they were coppers, at least.

As Ergluth turned that way, he saw under the shattered stone the agonized face of a veteran, a man he knew well. The armsman's back was broken; the pillar had crushed him below the waist, and now he was twisting and contorting in soundless agony, drumming one fist vainly against the ruined floor tiles.

Without hesitation, the boldshield said gravely, "You

shall be avenged," and drove his sword in deep through that gaping mouth, to end the pain.

Time indeed to start earning those coins.

* * * * *

Storm went forward like a soft shadow moving through the gloom. Her eyes could see as well as those of any cat. Sometimes it was useful to be a Chosen of Mystra. The foe had been above them, and just about ... there. If she took that stair—

The night behind her suddenly lit up with a burst of flame, and she heard more screams and groans. More Purple Dragons down. She set her teeth grimly. Still, if they'd stayed in the rooms by the kitchens, the shapeshifter could have strolled up and cooked them all at leisure by hurling that same spell into their laps ... At least this way the armsmen would die with swords in their hands. Still—they died.

There was a second flash, a little nearer. This one showed Storm a lone figure standing two rooms away, staring at her: Shayna Summerstar.

"Storm!" the young woman screamed. "Lady Storm! Save meeee!" She broke into a run, bare feet slapping on the stones in her frantic haste.

"Shayna!" the bard cried. She took twelve quick strides to the right, into deep shadow, and drew her sword.

It would be a bright sunset and a royal visit here, both, before she'd believe that lass was anything but a pawn of the foe.

She waited, still and silent. As long, wary breaths dragged by, she knew she'd been right. Shayna would have reached her by now if that terrified run had been genuine.

As if that thought had been a cue, there were scattered shouts from far off behind her, and one despairing wail. The foe was on the loose.

Storm glared into the darkness and then set forth like a panther on the hunt. If she let this go on, she might be the only defender still alive by the time the sun rose over the ruin of Firefall Keep. Yet she could do *nothing* to stop it that would not endanger her friends even more . . . and all this death was coming down on them because of her.

They died just as Maxer had died.

Sometimes it was a terrible thing to be a Chosen of Mystra.

Enough brooding. Somewhere off to the right should be the outermost passageway, and a stair that would take her up. Then she could circle back toward the foe. Shayna Summerstar, pretty little lure that she was, would have to start following, not lying in wait here, there, and everywhere.

A lance of ruby light split the darkness behind her. Storm threw herself headlong through a door, onto rubble, and smelled burnt leather from her right boot as the ravening radiance sang on down the passage. Calling up a shield spell, she stepped back out into the hallway. Ruby fire stabbed at her again.

She had a brief glimpse of Shayna's smiling face, chestnut hair plastered to an ivory forehead beneath a coronet whose upswept tips were emitting the ray— and then ruby death struck her shield, splashed out a spectacular shower of rosy sparks, and rebounded back down the hall.

There was a startled cry and then darkness and silence. Tasting her own weapon was not something a Summerstar heiress welcomed, it seemed.

"That's a Battlestar circlet," Storm murmured aloud. "Did she slay Zarova to get it?" She turned and ran lightly down the passage, heading for the stair she'd intended to use. No skulking. No little miss was going to dictate where she could go in this battle.

She was halfway up it when a rattle of tiny bouncing stones warned her. She threw herself sideways, slipped on stones, and ended up half over the rail. The wind was knocked out of her and she almost plunged over it.

A moment later, a statue as large as she was smashed into the steps above her. The impact showered her with jagged stone shards. The statue bounced past and slid to the bottom of the stair, leaving ruin in its wake. The rail under her shuddered, but the stair held.

"Bitch," she muttered to herself. "So it's toss the tower at Storm time again, is it?" She ascended the stairs at a run, lifting her voice merrily in the ballad "I Walk Carefree In the Moonlight."

A fist-sized stone whizzed past her nose. She grinned, somersaulted, and listened to another stony missile strike the floor and skitter away into the night. Aiming was not Shayna's strength.

Storm finished her song as she dodged forward in a series of zigzag runs at the place where Shayna must be—and was rewarded by a soft curse and the sounds of frantic fleeing.

Now we're getting somewhere. Run, little rabbit, and don't look back, because I'll be close behind you.

They burst out into an open gallery, running toward where the foe had toppled the pillar. Shayna was a pale, flitting form ahead. Storm put her head down and sprinted.

She was only a few paces behind when Shayna darted aside, into a chamber whose floor now formed a jagged bridge across an open, blasted ruined area.

Startled at how close Storm was, the Summerstar heiress called on her coronet again, splashing the bard—and the pillars on either side of her—with ruby fire.

Storm's shield held, but the pillars burst apart—and the Bard of Shadowdale had to leap for her life as the ceiling came down.

Mocking laughter echoed around Storm as she

rolled, came to her feet and ran on. She caught her
hand on a doorframe to spin around into that room—
and found the space no longer had a floor.

She fell hard, jarring her chin against her knees as
she struck loose rubble with both boots . . . and then
started to slide helplessly backward. Above her, ruby
fire flashed again. A larger explosion shook the loftiest
levels. Storm saw remnants of walls toppling slowly
down at her as she rode shifting rubble down. At last
she could roll over and find her feet again. Huge stone
blocks were crashing down all around her by then.

It was time to find another stair and do it all over
again.

"Shayna, dear!" she called gaily, "I'm coming for
you!"

Storm was rewarded with a hissed curse and ruby
death stabbing wildly down through an empty chamber behind her. As sparks danced and flew in the darkness, Storm found steps going up. She took them.

"Mystra, be with me now," she breathed. She
whirled around a landing and pounded up the next
flight. "If you like fun and folk making idiots of themselves with magic, you won't want to miss this!"

* * * * *

"Something moved, I tell you!" the Purple Dragon
snarled. He pointed with his sword. "Right—there!"

"Easy," Insprin Turnstone said from behind him,
raising his wand. "There's naught but death to be
gained from rushing off into the darkness hacking at
things!"

"What do *wizards* know of real war?" the armsman
spat over his shoulder. "Keep to what you know, mage,
and—"

His words broke off in a sudden gurgle.

To the warrior at his other shoulder, Insprin said

sharply, "Your torch! *Quickly!*"

They'd been cut off from the boldshield's rally by falling stones and spells that sent small, seeking balls of flame. We've not been cut off, but *herded*, Insprin thought bitterly. Now they were somewhere along the backstairs passage the servants called the Lower Run, well away from the Haunted Tower. The darkness around seemed a waiting, watching, menacing thing.

Now, as Insprin had feared, the darkness was beginning to grow tentacles. *Playing* with its prey.

The fluttering torchlight showed the black, glistening tentacle he'd expected. Purple Dragons shouted in disgust and rage all around the wizard and rushed at it, hacking and slashing.

And so, of course, they ran headlong into a waiting net of coiling arms, which fell on them from above. Insprin cursed, caught up a fallen torch, and threw it high and hard. It struck stone and spun away in a cloud of sparks, but it had shown him enough. The source of the tentacles was somewhere back *there*.

He aimed and fired his wand carefully—and was rewarded with a roar of pain. The armsmen suddenly bounced aloft in unison, kicking their boot heels, as the tentacles around their throats convulsed. One man slashed the tip of a tentacle. He fell, but scrambled up to stagger away. All the others came down atop him in a deadly rain of flesh, thudding against stone. The tentacles had made their victims into large, living flails to batter down the escaping man.

The Purple Dragons made wet, wordless sounds as their bodies were broken. Insprin cried out in his own revulsion and rage. He fired his wand—the tentacles quivered—and again. This time the tentacles withdrew, leaving a heap of blood-drenched, unmoving warriors behind. The war wizard backed away slowly, knowing he'd be next.

"Mystra watch over me now," he prayed aloud, "and

grant that I die well."

Mystra was hard of hearing, it seemed. The next thing he knew was the smashing strike of a tentacle leaping out of the darkness to send him flying into the nearest pillar. He struck it hard, and staggered away, trying to clear his wits of red pain. The next blow stung his fingers like fire, and snatched his wand away.

He watched a burst of radiance that must have marked the breaking of his weapon, and drew himself up. This must be his time to 'die well.' So be it; he'd not go to the gods weeping or pleading. He strode away from the pillar to take a stance where the floor was free of rubble, corpses, and blood, and asked sternly, as his hands began the gestures of a silent spell, "Have you no mercy?"

"Hah! Mercy! Kindness! The pursuits of fools!" came a laughing reply out of the darkness. Its source advanced slowly to gloat: a man whose skin was the same dusty blue-gray as the night around him, but whose eyes gleamed like those of a great cat. He smiled as he grew a tentacle that slid forward.

Insprin's eyes narrowed. He was suddenly surrounded by a glowing ring of spheres, the fruit of his spell—spheres of winking, dancing sparks. One sped toward the tentacle and burst, clinging to it with bright motes that burned and melted away the dark flesh.

The tentacle quivered, but slid on through the air, its tip questing for the mage. Insprin backed away and began to hurl the other spheres in a frantic stream—only to see the tentacle wriggle deftly through his dweomer.

"*Power* is a better goal!" the foe told him in tones of cold triumph.

"Mercy and kindness *are* power," Insprin replied firmly, weaving another spell as he backed away from the slowly advancing tentacle. "The slowest sorts to reward, but among the most mighty."

"What nonsense d'you speak?" the shapeshifter asked scornfully as Insprin spread his hands. Something that glowed drifted up from between them. "Tell me—how are they mighty?"

"They separate the truly just and noble from all others," Insprin replied softly, dodging away from the tentacle and drawing the dagger from his belt.

"And why," the foe asked, as his tentacle lashed out with the sudden speed of a striking snake and snapped around Insprin's throat, "would I want to do that?"

"What manner of monster are you?" Insprin gasped, feeling the coils tighten and knowing his dagger would be too little a fang to cut it in time.

The shapeshifter shrugged. "Once men worshiped me," he gloated, "and called me Bane."

Insprin Turnstone's face turned pale, and he closed his eyes.

The shapeshifter shook him by the throat as if he was a rag doll. "Hah! Not so noble now, are you, dead hero! I'll have your spells first, and then . . ."

Insprin opened his eyes again and gasped, "You . . . shall . . . *not*."

And from above Insprin, the glowing blade he'd wrought with his spell arrowed down to strike his own head.

Bright radiance burst in all directions, and the foe roared in pain as lightning spiraled down his tentacle. Hastily he severed it, reeling back as it dropped off to writhe and lash the floor like an agonized serpent.

"If that is what mortals mean by mercy," he croaked aloud, " 'tis a power yet beyond me!"

His voice twisted into the icy fury of Pheirauze Summerstar. "Stole his spells from me in the end, did he?" Tentacles grew hands and pointed in unison—and the reeling, headless body that had been Insprin flew apart in all directions, bloody bones clattering against the walls.

The man-thing who once might have been a small, twisted part of the god Bane did not wait to see the remains of his victim. He whirled about with a roar of rage that echoed back from the keep all around. Wings grew and took him racing down dark passages, seeking the last wizard. Like a loosed thunderbolt, he swooped.

Men cowered away in fear and shielded their guttering torches.

There'd be time to slay them later, when he was done hunting wizards. A wizard, Broglan Sarmyn—leader of these ineffectual dolts. A man who must have *some* spells worth hurling. A bit of a coward, who'd probably be somewhere near the boldshield and the largest band of Purple Dragons, a man who was . . . *there!*

Broglan saw death coming for him, and knew it for what it was. He fired his wand carefully, but did not wait to watch its blue-white bolts strike home. If any of the men around him were to survive, he had to get clear of them, and die—if Mystra willed it—alone.

He broke into a run, bellowing, "Ergluth, stay back! Keep your men *back!*"

Stones loomed up ahead of him, half-seen in the darkness; he leapt over them, stumbled on loose rubble, and ran on, staggering. Behind him he heard wild, triumphant laughter. He spun, fired his wand at a flicker of movement, and ran on. . . .

On into the Haunted Tower. In the distance, a pale phantom glided from doorway to doorway. Broglan shrugged and turned toward it, heading for a faint glow of moonlight. That must be the place the foe had blasted open to the sky.

Tentacles slapped at him and smote stones from the crumbling edge of a broken wall.

Broglan dodged desperately, his own breaths deafening in his ears, and kept going. An archway, a glimpse of Shayna Summerstar's face—wearing a crown?—from the gaping darkness of a chamber overhead, and he was clambering up a huge heap of stone.

A ball of fire burst ahead of him, hurling him back and blistering his face. He fell hard and tumbled on stones, losing his scepter somewhere in the fall.

He could see nothing but the afterimages of that flash. He was blind, and the foe was laughing somewhere nearer . . . and nearer. . . .

He struggled to sit up and clear his head, shaking it violently. It throbbed. The golden dancing radiances became red, fading ones, but still he could not *see!*

Something touched him. He dived away frantically, burying his face in sharp stones. Another touch, and another—tentacles! He rolled away, kicking at their rubbery, ropelike strength, fighting to get free. Bleeding fingers clawed for something to hurl at that cold, close laughter.

"Pitiful fool," the scornful voice of Pheirauze Summerstar said from above him. "I'll have your spells before you can waste any more of them. Farewell, Broglan Sarmyn, oh-so-capable leader of the Sevensash."

Tentacles came down like clubs upon his wrists, and ankles—and throat. Broglan bucked and wriggled, clawed frantically at the stones beneath him, and cried out for help.

All that came out was a hoarse rattle—but his fingers found something long, and cold, and hard. A poker? A mace-haft? He swept it up and thrust it desperately at a dark face above him—a dim face that was two red eyes and a gleaming, grinning mouth.

His improvised weapon seemed to have an eye of its own: a huge orb that winked at him knowingly as he thrust it out. Then its red eyes became two flames, and the flames lashed out.

As the real pain began, Broglan used the last breath in him to call on Mystra to claim his soul. He hoped she would hear him in time.

Sixteen

TO AWAKEN A DRAGON

 Flames seared Broglan Sarmyn like two needles driven into his eyes. All he could do was stare, unable even to blink. A whirling chaos of lights and sounds and flashing images rushed toward him.

The cold, cruel laughter of the foe laced every contorted image in the confused cacophony of shouts and cries and gasped words of agony and passion. The wizard could do nothing, nothing at all, as his thoughts, dreams, and memories were dragged away. In a another roiling moment, he would be gone, swept back into the stream of chaos and out of his own skull. . . .

"Storm," he struggled to say, with his last breath, "I have come to love and respect you—Mystra, please tell her thissss. . . ."

The stream sucked him down, past the place where he could speak and think and cling to anything he knew and loved.

Suddenly, though, its quickening rush stopped, eddying in confusion—broken by the calm, lazily blinking scrutiny of a dark eye as large as all the world. An eye that slid across to block the stream. . . .

The stream struck that eye and rebounded, something that *could not* happen, a raging voice within Broglan shouted. From somewhere nearby, the foe screamed.

The scream was long and raw and wild. It trailed off into howls of forlorn loss and agony, that in turn became wild giggling and sudden yips and barks and cries. This insane gibbering burst into screams once more when amber light flared into a sudden halo of flames around the dark eye, and a voice that echoed and re-echoed through the wizard's mind spoke.

AT LAST I AM AWAKE AGAIN. YOU HAVE MY THANKS, MAGE, FOR FREEING ME—EVEN IF YOU DO SERVE THE ACCURSED ONE.

"The Accursed One?" Broglan asked before fear told him silence might have been safer. Might.

SHE WHO IMPRISONED ME!

Mystra? Broglan gulped, and asked the question he had to: "Who are you?"

The eye seemed to twinkle as a laughter so deep that it hurt the ears boomed and rolled. DO YOU NOT KNOW ME?

Broglan had no defense but the truth. "N-No," he whispered.

THEN KNOW ME YOU SHALL!

The amber flames around the great eye suddenly flared to a blinding white radiance, and stabbed into Broglan far more keenly than the stream of chaos had done. This time, there would be no escape.

* * * * *

Storm turned toward the flash of white light. "What's *that?*" she murmured aloud. Elder magic, to be sure. Something of great power had just been awakened, back in the shattered heart of the Haunted Tower.

She broke into a run. She had to be there.

The stone hurled from above struck her so hard that she saw only dazzling golden sparks. Storm knew she fell sideways, but thought that she kept running—or at least her legs kept moving. . . .

When the sparks faded, she found she was lying on her side, and Shayna Summerstar was leaping down from a ledge above her, tossing aside an unnecessary second stone as she came. The Summerstar heiress was grinning maniacally, a tattered gown trailing behind her and the coronet askew on her tangled hair. A drawn dagger was gleaming in her hand.

On light feet, she danced toward the bard. A low chuckle of delighted anticipation rose from her throat as she came. Storm tensed, gathering herself for a desperate kick and roll. Shayna looked down at her and shook her head; she knew full well what the bard planned, and was enjoying the momentary taunt.

White light suddenly flared so brightly that it lit up the heart of the keep, and men cried out all over the fortress.

Shayna Summerstar threw back her head, the cords in her throat standing out like flesh-cloaked spines. She screamed in raw, rising agony. Her eyes rolled up in her head, her hands became claws that raked vainly at the air, and she shuddered so hard that the flesh along her ribs rippled in visible waves.

Then Shayna's head fell forward, and her body went limp. She whimpered, drew in a slow, tremulous breath, and seemed to see the blade in her hand for the first time.

She hurled it down in disgust, looked around wildly, a wordless quaver of fear rising in her throat. Her eyes fell upon Storm, and she cried, "Lady Storm! Lady

Storm! Lady Storm!" over and over again and went to
her knees, arms outstretched.

Storm rolled up to a sitting position and embraced
the terrified girl—who clung to her and burst into
wild, racking sobs. Her coronet fell off and rolled.
Storm stopped it with one outstretched foot, and
stroked Shayna's hair as the young heiress wept in
grief, remorse, and shame.

"There, there, little one," Storm said softly, hugging
the shuddering, heaving body. "You impressed us all."
Well, *that* was certainly true.

She went on murmuring reassurances as her eyes
went slowly from the coronet to the discarded knife
and back again. The white light at her back pulsed,
faded, and then brightened. Storm tried not think of
what it might herald.

* * * * *

Like an ungainly spider, the shapeshifter writhed
on his back. His many tentacles did an endless dance
around him. As he screamed and gibbered, the tendrils
whipped wildly against nearby stones, coiling and
shooting out to lash pillars and crumbling walls.

Their owner shrieked and babbled wordlessly as the
powers he'd subsumed were torn away. His linkage
with Shayna Summerstar was gone in an instant, and
spell after spell followed. His darkening mind became
a pitching place of spilling images. He clung grimly to
two things: awareness of who he had been—and would
become again—and the power to subsume. All he was
losing could be replaced some day, if he survived still
able to drink the knowledge, memories, and powers of
those he slew. . . .

Those Bane slew. Yes, Bane! The Black Hand would
rise again to smash all who stood against him! *"Bane!"*
he roared in a voice flung back at him by that the riven

innards of the Haunted Tower. "Fear Bane once more!"

The gigantic spectral eyeball floating above the scepter turned slowly to look at the howling shapeshifter. The white radiance around it flared to blindingly once more.

The man who had once, perhaps, been a part of Bane roared in fresh pain. Tentacles blazed up into nothingness or were sheared away by ravening fires that hurled him back, back. He tumbled end over end down a dark hall, trailing a helpless scream, until he came to the inevitable closed door.

There was a heavy, splintering crash, and the center of the door was suddenly gone. Shattered panels swung crazily and then fell. Stones clattered down to keep them company. Something tentacled rolled over once in the darkness, shuddered, and lay still.

* * * * *

The huge orb turned slowly to face him once more, trailing motes of magical radiance. Broglan Sarmyn trembled, but somehow could not move from the pose he had been swept into: kneeling as if in homage to a king, holding the dragoneye scepter upright as if it were a holy thing.

SUCH IS MY POWER.

Broglan swallowed. Was he supposed to speak?

IS IT NOT PARAMOUNT, MAN?

Forgive me, Mystra, Broglan prayed, *but to serve you, a man must betimes save his own skin.* "Y-Yes," he mumbled.

WITHOUT TREACHERY, I COULD NEVER HAVE BEEN MASTERED. The black eye drifted a little nearer. HAVE YOU GUESSED YET WHO I AM?

Helplessly Broglan shook his head. "No, Most Mighty One."

The eye drifted nearer still, ominously silent.

Broglan quivered, unable to move but desperately
wanting to scream and leap and flee, as fast and as far
as he could.

MOST MIGHTY ONE, the thunderous mind-voice
said slowly, as it was considering the sound of those
three words. MOST MIGHTY ONE! YES . . .

MOST MIGHTY ONE, INDEED! A FITTING
TITLE, MAGE! YOU HAVE OUR FAVOR!

Broglan set his teeth. He was leader of the
Sevensash wizards of war, and his duties in a situation
such as this were clear: find out all that can be learned
about any unknown magically powerful force or being.
"Who are you?" he asked again.

HER SHAME MUST HAVE DRIVEN HER TO
KEEP MY ENTRAPMENT A SECRET. . . . THAT
MUST BE WHY YOU KNOW ME NOT. MAN, I AM
DENDEIRMERDAMMARAR!"

"Den-Dendeirmerdammarar?" Broglan asked, wondering if he dared smile.

AYE. LORD OF THE THUNDER PEAKS. MOST
MIGHTY OF THE OFFSPRING OF ARNFALAMME
REDWING.

Something glimmered at the back of Broglan's
mind. The wisp of a memory, of reading that latter
name long ago in a lore tome in the court in Suzail, on
a hot and sunny afternoon. . . .

"You're a red dragon?" he asked.

OF COURSE, DOLT! NEXT YOU'LL BE ASKING
ME WHO BOUND ME INTO THIS SCEPTER!

"Well," Broglan heard himself saying, inner dread
growing with every foolish word, "ahem . . . yes."

THE ACCURSED ONE! THE SHE-MAGE! THE
WOMAN YOU SERVE!

The mind-shout almost bowled him over—but the
power of the radiant field held him where he was. His
trembling died away, and the brilliance forced him
back to the exact pose he'd been in before. 'Twas time

to try again. "Mystra?"

NAY, FOOL! The mind-voice was scornful. SEEK
NOT TO SHIELD HER WITH CLEVER TONGUE-
TRICKS! AMEDAHAST, THE ROYAL MAGE OF
CORMYR!

Amedahast! Gods above! The dragon had been in
the scepter for a long time. Seven hundred years, if
Broglan's memory of the royal mages held true. This
was probably not a good time to tell the freed sentience
that the woman he wanted vengeance on had been
dust—or, some among the war wizards whispered, a
kindly guardian and sometimes guiding spirit, as well
as dust—for five centuries or so.

Beings with power enough to be called Most Mighty
One are all too apt to lash out at whoever is handy
when something displeases them.

The eyes drifted ominously nearer. YOU ARE LONG
SILENT, O MOST BOLD AND CURIOUS OF
MAGES! DO YOU, PERHAPS, PLOT SOME FRESH
TREACHERY?

"Most Mighty One," Broglan answered truthfully, "I
lack the wits to successfully plan any treachery, great
or small, even if I had the desire to. It is all I can do to
serve my realm and my superiors, most times—and as
it is, I have failed my friends over and over again these
last few days. . . ."

The pupil of the huge floating eye seemed to expand.
A MAN WHO IS HUMBLE? AND TRIES TO SPEAK
TRUTH? HAVE MEN TRULY COME SO FAR IN THE
LONG TIME OF MY IMPRISONMENT?

Silence followed, and the dragon obviously expected
him to fill it. "I—I don't know what to say," Broglan
replied helplessly.

There was a rumble of what sounded like aston-
ished respect, and then the mind-voice said, THEY
HAVE. I BEGIN TO FEAR FOR THE FATE OF MY
KIN.

Trapped in immobility, holding the scepter and thinking of the tentacled thought-stealer that must be lurking somewhere beyond this great floating eye, Broglan began heartily to fear for the fate of his kin, too.

* * * * *

Ergluth Rowanmantle leaned wearily against a pillar and said hoarsely, "It shames me to say this, but I find my eyes closing, again and again. I've been too long without sleep."

Erlandar Summerstar shrugged. "Do not reproach yourself. We've all treated you like the ever-vigilant mountains above the vale—always there, never changing. 'Tis time, perhaps, we took charge of ourselves instead of leaving the vigilance to others."

"I would not see it as cowardice in any man to withdraw back to the kitchens now," Thalance said. One of his eyes was almost closed from the swelling of a great jagged gash on his brow—a gash that split his hair asunder, and spoke to all of how close the stone that made it had come to killing him. "We were all . . . overbold. Shapeshifters can be better hunted by daylight."

"Prudence would walk with you if you went back," the boldshield told him, "not reproach. Yet I will stay. The Lady Storm should not be alone here."

"She has the wizards to look after her," one of the armsmen said in the darkness.

"The wizards," another said in tones of disgust. "The Happy Dancing Mages—what use have they been so far? And just when will we see the tiniest flame of courage in any of their eyes?"

"Warrior, I saw who stood closest back there when that light burst forth, and the great eye appeared," Ergluth snapped. "It was the worried-looking one you lot have laughed so much about—the leader of the war wizards.

We fled back to greater safety, and even the shapeshifter ran, screaming; Broglan stood like a statue. I saw him. Sneer no more at wizards in my hearing."

"So because this willful half-goddess has to prove herself as much a man as any of us," a Purple Dragon veteran growled, "we must stay here, and get slaughtered."

"Aye," another agreed from beside him. "What odds that if she falls, Mystra reclaims her, and sets her back alive again to wiggle her hips at poor fools in some other realm? Mystra won't come down to succor the likes of us!"

The faintly glowing head of a phantom—the shade of a smiling court lady—rose out of the stones at the armsman's feet just then, and he jumped back with an oath. She went on smiling as she rose up, up into the ceiling above, and was gone.

"Still so sure you know every last detail of the doings of gods?" Ergluth Rowanmantle growled. "I say again: we are no men if we leave a lady in distress, nor Cormyreans if we let Harpers do our duty for us. I will stay, in case the Lady Storm needs me."

"Then I'll stay with you, to keep you awake," Erlandar Summerstar muttered.

"I'll stay, too," Thalance added quickly. "I'd rather die trying to rid our vale of this evil one than be struck down afraid, and hiding, and alone."

"Tarry it is, then," a young Purple Dragon said briskly. "Leave to snore, sir?"

There were snorts of amusement at this sally, and a few chuckles when their boldshield replied, "Only to windward, warrior."

The mirth stopped quickly when Thalance Summerstar asked the commander, "That eye—what do you think it is?"

Ergluth raised and lowered his shoulders in a slow, heavy shrug. "In truth, I know not. Some being of great wisdom and power . . . and yet not a godling or divine sending, I think. I've no proof, mind—just a feeling."

"And I think we're all going to die here," one of the older armsmen said sourly. "I can't prove that yet, mind . . . it's just a feeling."

* * * * *

Something moved in the lonely darkness. Slowly and stiffly, it rolled over. A single hoarse gasp of pain sounded in the chamber beyond the shattered door. A tentacle rose and flexed with a weary air, and then another uncurled slowly and tentatively. A face that had flowed like syrup rose up in dripping tatters, red eyes gleaming in the gloom. A jaw of wet fangs rose at the end of a fleshy tendril and retreated back into the face; a talon as long as a rack of swords wavered, shrank, and became a humanlike hand.

It was joined by another, and together the two hands traced a gesture in the air. And then another.

"Yes," a voice above them said in sudden, fierce determination. "So, let me . . ." The voice sank into mutterings and a short, rising chant.

Sudden radiance spilled out of one of those two hands, and the other suddenly held a scepter—a scepter topped by an eye. The swirling radiance formed an image of the astonished Broglan staring at his suddenly empty hand.

The motes that formed it flickered, faded, and died.

The scepter remained. Above it two eyes burst into sudden flame and bent forward greedily. Twin jets of flame lashed out, entwining the scepter. Around the immobile, intent head and hands, other tentacles grew claws that grabbed excitedly at empty air, or talons that slashed at stone. A mouth, swaying on its own stalk in the distant darkness, snarled to itself. A mind-voice rose to a thunderous, silent shout: GIVE ME.

YOU *WILL* GIVE ME . . . I WILL PREVAIL. I *WILL* PREVAIL. I—AHHHH . . .

The scepter blazed red-hot. Flames streamed around it, circling from one eye to the other. Then came a sharp crack, a flash of blue-white magic. The scepter broke into shards, which flew away into the darkness and crumbled to dust.

The shapeshifter stiffened and then rose into a larger bulk. His two eyes were now black orbs surrounded by white flames.

"Yes. *Yes.* Oh, yes. *Now* I have the power!"

White fire leapt out. The shattered door disappeared—along with most of the wall around it. Stones collapsed in a quickening roar, and out of the heart of their dust, cold laughter arose.

"Storm?" a voice called lightly. "Storm Silverhand? Your foe is *back!*"

Seventeen

MINDFIRE AND STORMLIGHT

Shayna clung to Storm, emerald eyes large with fear. "S-Stay with me," she begged. "Don't let him touch my mind again!"

"Be at ease, Shayna," Storm murmured. "Gently, now." She held the trembling heiress in her arms, drew in a deep breath, and reluctantly called on the silver fire.

She wanted only a little thing from Mystra. There was a power learned by—thankfully—few archmages since the days of Netheril, the ability to "hang" spells so that they waited, cast and ready to take instant effect, in an unseen, undetectable limbo. Storm used it now, soothing the terrified heiress while a spell of deeper slumber crafted by Azuth himself slowly unfolded.

When it was ready, she unleashed it on Shayna, kissing her to let the magic flow in.

With no more than a murmur, the noble went limp in her arms. Storm spun a ring of silver fire around her

to stop the questing mind of the foe. Then she laid the
sleeping girl against a pillar, curled up on her side, and
set three sloping timbers over her to turn away falling
stones. Storm carried the dagger and the coronet two
rooms distant and thrust them under a pile of rubble—
not a moment too soon.

As she set down the coronet, it blazed with sudden
fire. A faint echo of the foe's mocking laughter arose
from it. Storm stiffened and then hurriedly heaped
stones onto the circlet, being careful not to touch it
again. When it was safely buried, she selected a rock
as large across as a serving-platter, set her teeth, lifted the huge stone with a grunt of effort, and hefted it
into place atop the pile she'd made.

She turned again, looking back to where she'd left
Shayna. Bursts of silver fire, like snowflakes of light,
were winking and flaring out of thin air; her magic
was under attack. The foe was seeking battle again.

As the first gray glimmerings of dawn stole into
Firefall Keep, Storm, sword in hand, stalked through
its rubble-strewn heart. She'd tossed handfuls of dust
over her blade to keep it from gleaming, and was walking as quietly and alertly as she could.

Where was he?

Tendrils of smoke curled up from charred timbers
among the rubble. Dead armsmen lay everywhere,
crushed and half buried under falls of stone. The keep
sported an open central well it had lacked yestermorn,
an open bowl of death. The work of the ruthless foe, a
shapeshifter who could drink in and use the powers of
his victims. A shapeshifter who was beginning to seem
unstoppable. There were days of work, here, just to—

With a sharp clack, a stone struck the tiles behind
her and rolled away. Storm whirled around, looked up,
and had a brief glimpse of a smiling mouth and a cluster of three watching eyes, all on their own tentacles.
The mouth spat fire.

Storm dodged aside and pulled back her blade to save it from being destroyed. She called up silver fire to cloak her. The stones by her boots melted away, smoking, as the gout of flames struck them. Dragonfire! Where by the names of all the gods had he found a *red dragon* to subsume? This was starting to seem a proper nightmare!

The groaning behind and above warned her. Storm launched herself into a frantic headlong dive. She bounced and skidded painfully on stony rubble before rolling up and launching herself into another desperate dive. With ponderous, deadly momentum, the entire wall behind her broke loose and fell, crashing down in a mighty, ground-shaking river of shattered stone.

Cold laughter rolled around her as Storm struck the floor again and slid to collide with the staring corpse of a Purple Dragon. There was dust on his eyeballs, and his hands were frozen into claws, reaching vainly for his sword. Storm snatched it up. With steel in both hands, she looked up at the foe, a snarl curling her lips.

A row of bobbing mouths laughed at her in chorus. "Such defiance, little kitten!" one of them boomed cheerfully. The one next to it added with cold spite, "Do you know any other games, little trollop? I've seen running rabbits that were more amusing!"

Storm thought she recognized the voice of Pheirauze Summerstar in that last remark. She glanced quickly behind her and then all around to be sure no sneak attack was snaking up to lash at her while the mouths taunted.

The next moment, the smiling face of Maxer appeared at the edge of the room above, across from the mouths. It looked down at her. As hard as she could, she threw her newfound blade up at the face— just as the attack it had come to watch bore fruit.

The air shattered into four rushing balls of flame

that snarled into bright existence on all sides of her. Storm closed her eyes.

A moment later, the world went up with a roar.

Standing hunched, Storm felt the tatters she wore seared away from her, and whipped around her body in the blast of ravening fire. Her sword melted away and her hair lashed her face in a wild tangle as it sizzled and stank. A soothing coolness flowed through her. The powers laid on her long ago sucked the fiery assault into her and twisted it into beneficial energy. As it surged, she was healed and renewed. All weariness and discomfort washed away. Every dazed corner of her mind was relit. Still the energy came on.

She let it swirl around the forearm of her empty hand, and gathered the divine fire of Mystra. She called up that silver fire from within her and from around the keep, into something that snarled and thrummed in her with a fury all its own.

The fire raging around her abruptly faded away. Storm knew the foe would be looking down to see what his meteor swarm had wrought, unaware that it was one of the spells that could not harm her. She did not waste time looking up or pointing her arm grandly, but simply hurled the bolt of silver fire up where the false face of Maxer had been.

A tortured chorus of agonized screams was her reward. The row of mouths pitched and trembled in pain. Something black and shriveled trailed smoke as it staggered away. The silver fire had bored through it, the ceiling beyond, and the two floors above that one, to where the faint rosy fingers of approaching morning touched the sky.

Storm smiled tightly and ran from the scorched spot where she stood to a stairway that was still standing.

She was only just in time. Another burst of flame shattered the ceilings above where she'd been, hurling a ton of stone down onto the scorched floor—and through it. The floors collapsed into the cellars below and shook the stair she was racing up.

Glass shattered somewhere nearby. There were other, lesser crashes as shaken furniture pitched through holes in walls or floors, and tumbled down to crashing destruction.

As the echoes died away, Storm reached the next floor and raced through a scene of devastation. There were gaping holes and tumbled walls everywhere around her. She was seeking the tentacles that led to those mouths, hoping to get to them before they could wriggle away or be retracted . . . and to get to the foe at their far ends.

"Maxer?" she called in loud challenge, eyes flashing as she sought those tentacles. "Afraid to face me?"

Her answer came from a jagged hole in the ceiling. Jaws appeared, and then dragonfire. The stream went on and on, fanning across stone and fallen timbers as it sought her life.

Red ravening flames struck her. Storm staggered under their weight, planted her feet, and called on the silver fire again. Its shining stream split the roaring red flames asunder. With a savage smile, she turned her own fire up at the ceiling, seeking to strike through it at the unseen body of the foe above.

Stone, plaster, and wood collapsed amid the roiling flames and crashed heavily to the floor. Tiles buckled, spilling the debris down through it to the level below.

The dragonfire suddenly ceased. The jaws that had spouted it were gone.

Storm frowned, held back her outpouring of silver fire, and broke into a run, getting away from where she'd stood before the foe could trigger another ceiling collapse. She'd taken a bare dozen running steps when the floor heaved so hard it threw her to her knees. A deafening crash set her ears ringing. She was plucked up and flung on by tumbling timbers.

From the corner of her eye, she glimpsed the ponderous plunge of an entire turret, arched windows and
all, down from above, through the floor where she'd
been—and on, on down through all the levels below.

Storm struck a pillar, ribs shattering like dry twigs.
She spun around it with the force of her tumbling
flight, and fell to a now-tilting floor, roaring out her
pain like any dismayed warrior. She was still skidding
to a dusty stop when a sudden thought made her
chuckle.

"Apt name—Firefall Keep."

As the thunder of rolling stone died away, the tatter-
clad bard lay still and turned the energy inside her to
healing. One bloody end of a rib was protruding from
her flank; Storm frowned down at it and then grasped
it, set her teeth, and pulled it forth. Warm blood
drenched her fingers and she shuddered, let silver fire
burn both gore and bone fragment away to nothing,
and held her hand to her side.

"About now," she muttered, "he'll see the morning
sun and remember there's a kingdom out there he
could be despoiling—and it'll be 'rend the annoying
barrier' time again."

She laid her sword across her knees, made herself as
comfortable as she could, and closed her eyes, letting
the web of silver fire tell her where things were. The
morning sun fell through the shattered ruins of the
keep and laid bright fingers of sunlight across her
cheek. The warmth made Storm almost purr with
pleasure—an instant before the stabbing spells and
mind-thrusts at her barrier began. Then her gasps
became loud and quick and urgent. She rolled around
on the stones, clutching her half-healed gut and wondering if she could hold him back this time.

"Mother Mystra," she hissed, "be with me now!"

There was no answer. . . . Slowly, very slowly, the
floor beneath her started to tremble.

* * * * *

The sun on his cheek was bright and warm. Broglan
Sarmyn, war wizard of Cormyr, blinked at it. He slowly became aware that he was lying on sharp stones, in
stillness. The only sounds he could hear were some
tentative bird calls, though he dimly recalled the rubble beneath him shaking as sounds like thunder rolled
and crashed all around, not long ago . . . or perhaps it
had been a dream.

His last clear memory was a blinding flash from the
floating black eye, as it shuddered and blinked at him
almost beseechingly. That had come soon after the
scepter—and where had *it* come from, anyway?—had
disappeared. Now the eye was gone, probably con-
sumed in that flash of energy, and he was lying in the
rubble alone. Ah, well, even among wizards, the gods
rarely grant the sight and wits to know what's going
on.

Speaking of stumbling . . . Cautiously he got up, test-
ing his aching body. Bruises everywhere, some very
painful, but it seemed that Broglan Sarmyn was whole
and could walk unhampered. It seemed he would have
another chance to walk straight into his own waiting
grave.

Well, he'd best be about it. With a grunt of pain,
Broglan got up, made sure the dagger and the two
wands were still sheathed at his belt, and started a
cautious exploration.

This part of the keep was roofless: shattered walls
and rubble, rubble everywhere. It looked like a manor-
house he'd once seen after two wizards had dueled
each other to death in it: a rubble-choked shell. He
could scarcely recognize the bones of the proud old
family fortress he'd seen upon his arrival, only days
ago. Dead Purple Dragons lay everywhere, and here
and there a stray hand or bit of livery betrayed the

resting place of a luckless servant. It looked like the place had been fought through and then pillaged by victorious invaders.

Aye. Pillaged by one man.

Or rather . . . one monster. The foe was probably still alive. Broglan could not bring himself to believe that the shapeshifter was dead. Nor would he—not until he saw either the death or the remains with his own eyes.

The rubble here was almost roof-high, fallen across his path in drifts. He dug his boots into it and climbed, waving his hands awkwardly to keep his balance, trying to make no more noise than was necessary.

At the top of the pile he found the reason for its height: the stones had cascaded down a still-intact stairway, leading up onto the floor above. He ascended, rising warily into similar devastation to what he'd seen below. Still there was no sign of life.

Could he be the last one alive in all Firefall Keep? Gods, what would he tell Lord Vangerdahast?

For that matter, how would he find his speaking stone to tell Lord Vangerdahast anything?

He was crossing a room, that thought eating at him, when he saw Shayna Summerstar at the base of a pillar, under three fallen timbers. She lay curled up on her side, barefoot, wearing little more than dust, the tatters of a gown trailed from her limbs. It was a miracle none of the timbers had crushed—no, he saw, they'd been laid over her, to protect her against collapses.

He lifted them aside and peered at her. She was breathing slowly and deeply, but her eyes were closed. "Lady Shayna?"

There was no response. Broglan reached to his belt to take off his overrobe and lay it over her. His hands drew back. No, he needed the spell components his pockets bore.

He recalled a wardrobe fallen on its face a few rooms

back. Retracing his steps, he found it, failed in his attempt to overturn it, and used his dagger to lever its splintered back up.

It was full of women's clothes, all twisted together in dusty disarray. He found a gown and a night cloak. The next garment he lifted away uncovered the lifeless hand of a chambermaid who'd been crushed under the fallen furniture. Above the neck, she was only bloody pulp.

The wizard recoiled, shuddered, and hastily bore the two garments back to the Lady Shayna.

She'd turned on her back and flung her limbs wide, but was still sleeping soundly. Broglan looked at her bared limbs, swallowed, and then awkwardly dressed her. He lifted the limp, warm body to put her arms into the sleeves of the gown, slid its lower half underneath her, and then buttoned and tugged until she was more or less covered. He laid the fashionable light cloak over her, took hold of her shoulders, and shook her. "Lady Shayna?"

Nothing. Not even a flicker of her eyelids.

He slapped her cheek gently, once, and then again. She slept on, breathing steadily. He frowned. Magic? He rolled her over and slapped her behind so hard that his fingers stung and her body shifted on the stones. Still she slept.

Magic. He carefully cast his last, precious dispel.

Dusty lashes fluttered, and Shayna Summerstar looked up at him rather warily.

He waited, a wand raised to blast her face. When she recognized him, she managed a weak smile. "Sir Broglan? Who—what's befallen?"

"I know not, lady," Broglan said gently, lowering his wand. "This ruin around us is your home, 'tis morning, and since awakening I've found only death until I came upon you."

He put a gentle arm around her shoulders, and helped her sit up. "You are the heiress of House

Summerstar," Broglan told her gravely, "and my duty is to protect you as best I can. I hope to take you out of this place, find a horse, and get you to court, if we find none else alive."

Shayna looked around wearily, and then down at herself, and made a face. "Who dressed me?"

Broglan flushed. "Ah—I did, lady," he said carefully, fearing an angry response.

She merely nodded, and smiled thinly. "I thought so. You've put this gown on me back to front."

Broglan was relieved to find that he could still laugh, if hoarsely, and even more relieved to hear her merry laugh join his.

Cold laughter, which sounded like it was booming from the mouth of a nearby giant, drowned them out. It rolled around the stones of Firefall Keep and echoed back at them. Bolts of lightning started to flash through the keep, crackling down from the uppermost floor to an unseen target below.

Broglan was afraid that those bolts were seeking the life of Storm Silverhand. As he glanced at the avid face of the Lady Shayna, who was bent forward to get a better look at the distant leaping lightning, he was very much afraid he'd just awakened a willing hand of the foe.

* * * * *

Another man's scream broke off abruptly as the rolling pillar made a horrible wet crunch. The gathered warriors winced.

A grim Ergluth Rowanmantle looked up at the shuddering keep. Tiles and stone blocks tumbled all around. He said simply, "I was mistaken to think we could stay. We're getting out."

He walked steadily across a riven room and bellowed, "Follow!"

Ahead of him, a statue toppled from its plinth, struck the stony ground, and shattered as if it had been plaster. The boldshield ignored it, striding on through the tumult of booming, rolling stone.

"Where're we going?" Erlandar Summerstar called.

Ergluth did not turn his head, but every man there heard his deep roar of command. "To the dungeons under the gate tower—as far and as deep as I can get from this battle. Those two are like gods, smashing at each other up there. We go down and cower until they're done—and pray as we've never prayed before that Storm triumphs."

The keep shook and quivered around them as they ran on. The morning sky above was covered by a flickering curtain of rushing silver flames; men muttered, ducked their heads from this eerie sight, and hurried along. They were rushing down a dark, precipitous stone stair before the boldshield asked Erlandar, "Who've you got locked up down here?"

The eldest Summerstar shrugged. "No one, so far as I know."

Ergluth nodded and began to snatch down the unlit torches from each wall bracket they passed. When he couldn't see to go on he cried a halt and had an armsman light two of them.

Ergluth took one himself and ordered the other passed to the back of the group of grim warriors and fearful servants. He went on, selecting the deepest of the large cells.

Swinging the rusting but massive barred door wide, he boomed, "Our new home! In, everyone!"

Thereafter they sat in the close, dank darkness and together thought fearful thoughts. The keep shook and quivered above them. After what seemed a long time, a particularly violent blast made dust sift down on their heads, and was followed by a strange, hesitant series of louder and louder crashes.

Thalance Summerstar stepped out of the cell to see what could be causing the noise. In a moment, he scrambled in again and yelled at everyone to stand back.

Behind him, a boulder that was taller than a man came slowly crashing down the stairs, end over end. Advancing with the slow but inexorable stagger of a wounded giant, it came to a final thunderous halt against the bars of the cell, bending them inward as if they were mere threads.

"Gods," Thalance swore, "and the lady, she's up there, standing alone against him!"

The Purple Dragon commander nodded, his face as gray as the boulder. "And our only hope," he rumbled in a voice that made the crowded cell fall silent, "is that she defeats him." He turned his head to look at them all. "Keep only one torch lit, and gather the others to light from it, one by one; there's a bracket here. Those of you who aren't seeing to that can start praying."

Eighteen

TUMULT IN THE FOREST KINGDOM

The royal magician of Cormyr looked up at her. "Nothing until the moot at highsun? Good. Sit down, pray—we never have time enough these days to talk about things."

Lady Laspeera Inthré gave him a warm smile, patted his hand, and took the seat facing his. A tray that bristled with bottles and decanters of exotic liqueurs rose smoothly from the table to offer itself to her. His second-in-command waved a politely dismissive hand at it—and then chuckled and shook her head in surrender as she found a full glass of her favorite Old Rubythroat settling into her other hand.

"None of this nonsense about not drinking during the day," Vangerdahast told her gruffly. "You've been at that survey until I thought your finger'd wear through our best set of maps!"

Laspeera smiled. "Long work, yes, but 'tis done. The work was not all such drudgery, nor the end prospect so gloomy, that I can in all honesty claim any rightful need to *this*." She raised her glass.

"So stop protesting and drink it," Vangerdahast growled. "As if fine spirits needed an excuse to be drunk!"

She gave him another amused smile and obediently tilted the glass to her lips. The lord high wizard of Cormyr sat back in his chair, swirling smoking blue wine about the bottom of his own fist-sized glass, and gazed around Salantrin's Hall.

A moment of private peace was a rare thing for either of the two highest-ranking mages of Cormyr. Vangerdahast took care that few servants had both the keys and the knowledge to reach the luxurious inner chamber known as Salantrin's Hall. A tray floated obligingly into his lap. He cut a slab of sharp old bluelick cheese, with a smiling glance thanking Laspeera for her levitation. He sat back to enjoy the Tavilar Tapestry.

Said to have been given to his long-ago predecessor Amedahast, for her (unspecified) services to the elves, the hanging stretched along the entire north wall of the chamber. It was a glowingly vivid deep woodland scene whose lighting kept pace with the day outside, from bright morning through each day to the deepest gloom of night—though in the tapestry it was always summer, and never rained.

The magic of the tapestry often made birds and animals move through the scene, and from time to time, stags would bound through the trees, and a splendid elven hunt would ride soundlessly after them. It was a rare treat to see the shining white moment when a lone unicorn would appear and pause briefly to look out into the room. One was doing so now, and Vangerdahast raised his glass to it.

It turned its head toward Laspeera, for all the world as if it could really see both mages. She smiled and nodded. Then it tossed its head, and was gone.

"I love this," Vangerdahast said softly. "I could watch it for hours. Think you it shows us Evermeet?"

Laspeera shrugged, and daintily cut herself a rondelle of nutcheese. "Who can say?" She gave him an impish look. "Unless, of course, you craft a spell that'll let you step into it, and go see for yourself."

Vangerdahast made a rude sound. "Things have been quiet lately, but not *that* quiet." He sighed. "I take it the likelihood of any more powerful magic or mages being uncovered in the realm is decidedly slim now?"

Laspeera raised her shapely shoulders in another elegant shrug. "The noble houses, of course, have any number of magical toys hidden away that they don't want anyone to know about. Some of them were clever enough to reveal a few to me in hopes that I'd not think they had others. I can say that powerful spellwielders found in Cormyr in the years to come will either develop under our noses—or come in from outside . . . and I trust our vigilance is such that only a handful of the mightiest archmages are good enough to do that and remain undetected for long."

"Sarmyn did say he had Storm Silverhand on his hands up in Firefall Vale a few days back," Vangerdahast said idly.

Laspeera showed him the impish grin that wizards who were not her master or her husband were never allowed to see. "And did he enjoy it?"

"He hasn't yet said."

"Then he's *not* enjoying it," Laspeera concluded, watching a pair of stags leap frantically across the tapestry. A few moments later the expected hunt appeared in the distance, waving lances that glimmered from butt to tip with lazy runs of lightning. The wizards watched it rush pass, and raised their glasses to their lips in unison.

* * * * *

Lightning crackled hungrily around her, but Storm ignored it. Bolts and chain lightning were among the things she was immune to, by Mystra's grace; she kept her attention on the falling things dislodged by the laughing, glowing-eyed foe flitting above her. So far, nothing had crashed down on her head, but he was still trying.

A bolt veered away from her, toward the distant, startled face of Broglan Sarmyn.

"No!" Storm exclaimed in angry surprise. She raised her hand to slash the bolt with silver fire—but Shayna Summerstar rose up behind the mage, a chair-leg in her hand, and brought it viciously down.

The wizard fell out of sight. The young heiress capered in triumph; the bolt that might have struck her veered away of its own accord.

Sick at heart, Storm turned her attention back to the tentacled foe. "You'll pay for this. I swear it."

Their eyes met. The foe laughed maniacally before ducking out of sight onto the floor above. Storm sent a jet of silver fire into the ceiling above her—and as it punched through the stone, she was rewarded with his startled cry of rage and pain.

Furiously, the foe struck back, hurling the pieces of a shattered statue down at her.

Neither of them noticed a dust-covered figure rise from the rubble on the floor below Storm, and lurch toward the nearest ascending stair. The Hungry Man had forgotten some of its orders, but it knew to receive more, it had to be where strong magic raged.

* * * * *

Some overclever Sembians were stirring up trouble in Marsember again. The war wizard briefings and strategy sessions had been long and wearisome. As they walked together to the doors of Lionsrest Hall, Laspeera saw Vangerdahast put a hand to his mouth to conceal a yawn.

"Come in," she said gently, an offer that made his head turn quickly in surprise. "Aundable will be pleased to see you."

"He will? Having to kiss his wife in front of the royal magician of all the realm, and pretend the old gruff-nose isn't there? Strange man," Vangerdahast commented.

Laspeera wrinkled her nose, took him firmly by the elbow, and steered him into the parlor she shared with her husband, Aundable Inthré.

The seldom-seen subject of so much speculation among the magelings Laspeera tutored was bent over a tiny model of the fortress of High Horn. He frowned and glanced up at an image that hung in the air above it—a floating magical view of the castle. As they watched, he gestured with a fingertip, and one hillock shifted its position along the mountainside a trifle. Laspeera's husband nodded in apparent satisfaction, looked up, and broke into a broad smile.

Laspeera swept around the table and into her husband's arms.

"Lord Vangerdahast! A pleasure! What can I do to set you at ease?"

"Stop calling me 'Lord Vangerdahast' and try 'Vangey,' for a start," the old mage growled.

Aundable indicated that he'd heard Vangey's request by a wink, and was then rather busy with an affectionate, wordless greeting for the next four breaths or so. Vangerdahast hid a smile by taking up a decanter of amberfire wine and strolling over to glance at the miniature castle Aundable had crafted, on his way to the glasses.

"Ah, yes—please, make yourself at home," Aundable

said when he could speak again. "Like it?"

"I do indeed," Vangerdahast admitted, peering at the tiny windows and doors, and extending a cautious finger. Did they actually open? Say, th—

"If you'll excuse me," Aundable said, "I was just going to do my usual scry of the border lands, and then retire to bed."

Vangerdahast gave him a grave nod, and said, "And you shall not do so alone; I won't keep Laspeera more than a few breaths before wandering off in search of my own bed. Soon enough I'll be wandering the kingdom again, and sleeping out on wet, rocky ground under the stars. Aye, lass?"

Laspeera sighed. "Only you, in this entire palace, could get away with calling me 'lass'!"

"Oh, lass?" Aundable teased. "What's that you say?"

She reached out and playfully tweaked his nose.

"Urrgh!" he replied, intelligently and happily. He sat down at his scrying crystal. Few in the kingdom knew that a peerless master of strategy and foresight lurked in this back room of the palace, keeping watch over the realm—but Vangerdahast, for one, was glad he did.

Aundable waved away a proffered glass of amberfire wine, glanced at a map of eastern Cormyr, and ran a finger along the trails north and east of the Wyvernwater. There was the hold of Hawkhar, seat of House Indesm; Galdyn's Gorge, home of the Yellanders; and Firefall Vale, home to the Summerstars. . . .

The face of Shayna Summerstar swam into his mind. Aundable frowned and glanced at his wife. If he'd been one for the shining younglings, he could do worse, far worse, than the beautiful Shayna Summerstar.

His frown deepened as he bent his will to use that vividly remembered face as a focal point to target his scrying attempt. Wasn't Firefall where the Sevensash band had been sent, to see to some sort of minor trouble? Aundable leaned forward, peering into the depths of his scrying crystal, where small lights swam and wandered. . . .

* * * * *

It had been a long day. The sun set on Firefall Vale, and the shadows inside the riven keep grew truly dark. Storm wearily clenched her teeth and, with desperate speed, wove a web of silver fire, seeking to enclose the foe once more. Her barrier around the keep had gone long ago, sacrificed to save her own skin from the shapeshifter's vicious attacks.

Now he was teasing her, flying out from the battlements again and again, forcing her to snare him and drag him back. Each time she brought him back, he lashed her with spells that darted into her mind and sought to steal secrets and pry loose lore. This defense was grueling work. Storm was sweating and exhausted as she snared him for the fourteenth time.

This time he laughed and flew right at her, extending a finger that glittered.

Storm's heart sank. She knew what spell he must be using. Somewhere in the keep, there was an enchanted sword; if his extended digit struck her, the powers of that blade would injure her as if he wielded it directly.

"Bastard," she whispered, spinning three tongues of silver fire—two to fend off any tentacles he might decide to grow when he got close enough.

A head she had not expected to see again bobbed up from behind a broken wall, and magic missiles streaked through the air in a gleaming net of deadly force.

The enchanted bolts struck home, and the smiling foe spun sideways in startled pain, jerking his body repeatedly. He crashed into one of the few intact walls in the heart of the keep and tumbled along it—straight into the burst of magical ice that a grimly smiling Broglan hurled last.

Shards of ice sang and tinkled off stone. The foe fell with them, through a hole in the floor and out of sight. The war wizard gave Storm a cheerful wave, and pointed upward.

Storm looked. Shayna Summerstar dangled head down from the edge of a broken-off ceiling. Broglan's spells had made her gown into a gag, lashed her hands to her mouth, and transformed a cloak into the binding that held her ankles to a spar. The heiress hung, red-faced and helpless; if she struggled too much, she might plunge to the floor below and be struck senseless—or even swing herself out into a much longer drop, and almost certain death.

Storm grinned in appreciation, waved, and then set about using the time Broglan had bought her. She had to cast and hang three of her spells in a stasis-sphere, and make the sphere itself seem attractive.

She turned away from Shayna to obscure the young noble's view of what she was doing, and crafted a gleaming golden sphere about twice as large as her head. It floated, turning slowly as she pumped spells into it, casting them quickly and carefully: a ward-away, a manyjaws, and a blood lightning. In a few flickering instants, the silver fire triggered them, held them hanging, and closed up her sphere for her.

Two long-fingered hands rose from a distant rent in the floor and wove a spell of their own.

Part of Broglan abruptly became a spineless, glistening, pale-white mass of tentacles. The wizard's face went just as pale. He gasped, clutched at his heart, and collapsed back out of view behind the wall.

Shayna kicked and wriggled furiously in celebration, but the foe didn't notice her—or didn't care.

Storm slashed at the hands with a stream of silver

fire, but she didn't expect to strike them before they
vanished—and she didn't. She sent her silver down to
carve the floor in a neat line from the hole where the
hands had been toward where she stood, hoping to
reveal the foe beneath her.

She'd managed only a few feet of that work when
tentacles rose up all around her in a silent, sudden
forest.

Fast as those seeking tentacles were, Storm was
faster. She turned her hands straight down and used
streams of silver fire to blast herself up into the air,
seeking the floor above and hoping her little act would
work.

The golden sphere lagged behind. She gained her
footing in a shattered room, turned, put a look of
apprehension on her face as she saw the globe trailing,
and swiftly called on Mystra's fire to catch it and draw
it up to be with her.

The foe swallowed the bait. A tentacle shot out, its
tip glittering. He'd not dropped his fingerblade spell,
and was going to use it to slice open the sphere.

Storm yanked the sphere away from him, and then
seemed to lose her grip on it. Silver fire swirled, but
the sphere drifted free, moving slowly away. Like a car-
nival knife-thrower, she drew back her hand and
hurled silver fire after it, but the darting tentacle got
there first.

The sphere exploded in a spray of golden light—and
the very air boiled.

Storm felt the sudden tingling of the blood lightning
settling on her, just as she'd planned. Her gaze, however, remained intent on the foe. The shimmering of
the wardaway was already coiling down the tentacle,
but the shapeshifter had no time to worry about that.
Disembodied jaws were appearing all around him.
They streaked in to sink fangs into his ever-shifting
body. Storm leapt high, as she'd seen the witches of

Rashemen do when diving into pools from a height, jackknifed, and dived down into the heart of the foe, trailing silver fire behind her.

She protected her face and throat from the whipping tentacles, but left the rest of herself unshielded. Sure enough, a trio of tentacles that had suddenly acquired sawlike bony edges slashed across her breast and flank.

Blood flowed. The blood lightning burst forth, snarling angrily down into the struggling shapeshifter. Tentacles convulsed and flailed.

As she plummeted, Storm's hands spat silver fire in a dagger of ravening force. It punched right through the screaming foe.

She landed hard in a pile of rubble, rolling over and over and coming up with blood on her chin from a bitten lip, but there was a smile to go with it. At last the foe was tasting what he should have been feeling all the time, these last few days.

The roars of pain twisted very soon into wild, giggling laughter and a cacophony of gabbling voices shouting different things at once. The foe's overloaded mind was afire again.

Storm slipped away through the shadows, quietly rebuilding her barrier around the keep. He'd start blasting things soon enough, but she did not want to be the one to provoke him into wreaking more devastation. She was aching all over, limping slightly, and restlessly moving one arm to loosen a stiff, battered shoulder. Others in the ruins around her had fared far worse. Her time for healing and taking ease would come when this menace was ended.

The explosion she'd been expecting tore through a pillar not far behind her. A column of three rooms tilted slowly, turned—and with heavy grandeur fell down into the rubble below. The crash shook the entire fortress.

Shrill laughter arose above the din of clashing and rolling stone. A man with four arms capered amid the dust, Shayna Summerstar swinging high above him.

The mad shapeshifter threw out a blazing bolt of force that smashed through a wall. As stones sprayed and tumbled, shattering the room beyond, the foe bayed like a hound, punching the air with exultant fists. He stiffened, whirled around—and fired another bolt at a shard of wall that had been behind him.

The shard was narrow, but tall—a spindly fang of jagged rock that stretched up to where the battlements had been. It shivered, broke apart—and fell straight down on the shapeshifter, burying him.

Storm raced toward the spot, hardly daring to hope. Was he—?

Then, of course, Faerûn truly blew up around her.

* * * * *

Broglan was suddenly himself again, sobbing for breath, as a huge, roaring shaft of blazing power burst into being not far away. It smashed through all the floors of the keep, stabbed into the darkening sky, and hurled stones to the stars.

"Gods, what a stormlight," Broglan gasped, wincing at the sheer brightness of the blast.

The Bard of Shadowdale was flung end over end like a rag doll through the ruins. Her body flared with silver and white flames, then went dim, then blazed forth again, for all the world like a lantern flashed by sailors in a storm.

"I must go to her," Broglan muttered to the air.

He stumbled along the wall that had sheltered him . . . and then the bound body of Shayna Summerstar smashed down on him in a bruising tangle of bone. The world whirled its way into darkness and silence.

* * * * *

There came a flash of light, a scream of tortured crystal, and then the almost musical sound of shards whistling apart and tinkling off the table and the ceiling.

Aundable Inthré matched the scrying-crystal's scream and reeled in his chair. He struck its high back, bounced, and then slumped back again, his head lolling to stare at the ceiling.

"Aundable!" Laspeera shrieked, hurling down her glass and leaping toward him. The royal magician was close behind.

As they clambered past the furniture, smoke curled up from where the scrying-crystal had been. It was matched by two smaller plumes rising from Aundable's eyes.

"Gods above," Vangerdahast gasped.

* * * * *

Brightness gathered in the night sky above the darkened ruins of Firefall Keep. Motes of light danced like excited fireflies, spun, and flickered, drawing together into a cloud almost as fierce in its radiance as the shaft of energy that roared up in its midst.

As a few awed farmers gaped at it from afar, the cloud suddenly coalesced into the form of a dragon—a winged dragon with a mane, two backswept horns on its head, and scaly jaw winglets. It looked cruel and wise and utterly confident in its power. It lazily flapped its wings, watched its long tail uncurl smoothly behind it as it turned, and then gathered speed, beating its wings in earnest.

The gigantic, glowing phantom of the wyrm flew down Firefall Vale, swooping and darting like a gleeful dragonet at play. With a triumphant roar, it circled

near the mountains, and then soared up high into the
sky and raced southwest.

Cowering farmers watched it go, a bright and surging line among the winking stars, and wondered where
it was headed. If he'd been conscious to see its eager
flight, Broglan could have told them. It was bound for
distant Suzail, to bring down doom on the woman
who'd imprisoned it. She'd been dead for centuries, so
the war wizard worried about just what it would do
when it arrived. Lord Vangerdahast was not likely to
enjoy a peaceful evening.

* * * * *

At that moment, Lord Vangerdahast had hold of the
bodice of his second-in-command and was shaking the
hysterically screaming woman until her teeth rattled.

Laspeera bit the tip of her tongue, stared at him in
shock, and then fell to sobbing silently as the lord high
wizard snarled at her, "Stop that! I need your help, not
your tears!"

He thrust a decanter at her. "Pour that down his
throat, and work his chest to see that he swallows at
least some of it!"

Laspeera snatched the healing potion from him,
clawed the stopper out, and let it fly across the room.
Vangey thrust back his sleeves, went to a certain
carved panel near the door of the Hall, and did something to it. The square of wood swung open, and he
took a squat jar from the space behind the panel and
tossed it across the room.

"Catch, lass!" His snap of command seemed to
steady her; Laspeera snatched the hand-jar out of the
air without even looking at it. "Now daub some of that
over his eyes, and wherever he seems hurt. Cover each
eye entirely, but don't waste it."

Then he stepped back, closed his own eyes, calmed

himself, and carefully cast a spell he'd been carrying for a long time. When it was done, he stepped forward, touched Aundable's ear, and watched his body jump in the chair.

Laspeera looked up at him almost reproachfully. She'd long since smeared the ointment over her husband's face, and was visibly calmer. Only the edge of her lip, firmly caught between her fine white teeth, betrayed how upset she was. "And now?" she asked, her voice so low and quiet that it was almost a whisper.

"Mind-speak to him," Vangerdahast said briskly, handing her the other thing he'd taken from behind the panel. Laspeera recognized the circlet at once, donned it, gave him a thin smile of thanks, and bent over her husband's slack face.

Satisfied, Vangerdahast turned away and strode across the room to its door. Instead of opening it, he touched a certain spot in the relief carving of the mounted knight that adorned it, and then turned his head to watch a certain carving glow on another wall. Stepping smartly across the room to touch the lit spot before it faded, he spoke a word under his breath—and then turned again to face the door that was slowly appearing on a solid section of wall.

He ignored its handle, instead touching a bottom corner of the door with his hand as he muttered another word. The wall faded into invisibility, leaving a dark opening lit only by two gleaming, winking eyes. Vangerdahast stepped fearlessly straight into them. As they vanished, the hidden chamber beyond was flooded with light.

It was not an impressive place: a storeroom with a central table and walls covered with row upon row of shelves crammed with boxes, coffers, and chests of all sizes and descriptions. Vangey thrust the table aside to clear the floor area, selected seven boxes without hesitation, and from each one scooped out a crystal sphere similar to the one Aundable had been using, setting them in a ring on the floor around him.

Unless he was totally mistaken, Laspeera's husband would be fine; it was now Vangerdahast's pressing duty to see just what had attacked him so. He fished a slim, dark staff out of a recess behind the door-molding, touched each of the crystals in turn, and murmured a long-unused phrase.

The storeroom darkened. Glowing brightly, the seven crystals rose in unison around the old wizard. Vangerdahast closed his eyes to picture in his mind what he was about to scry.

Aundable had been looking at northeastern Cormyr, if the map he'd been running his finger over was any indication. So just what was it, in that forgotten and largely wild outlying arm of the kingdom, that had struck out at him?

Standing quietly among the scrying stones, the lord high wizard of Cormyr sent his awareness questing out through all of them. He was leaping north and east in little bounds, through the eyes of bats and awakening night birds and the bolder birds of the day, making their last flights as full night came down. . . . It was just a bit beyond Immersea that he saw something that flashed and glimmered through the sky on wings he could see through.

An onrushing dragon, wings spread in ghostly glory—a red wyrm, once, by its shape and the look of its head. The owl he was using wheeled away in mounting fear, and Vangerdahast ceased scrying to fix the sight of the high-flying dragon firmly in his mind.

He wheeled around and said, " 'Speera? Touch my mind."

Laspeera looked up, unsmiling. Her husband's head was cradled in her hands. She met her master's gaze squarely—and Vangerdahast's questing thought flashed between their eyes.

In a trice, he was in Aundable's mind, seeing what Laspeera saw, and giving his own warm greeting. The man was now unhurt, and completely fearless—but had totally forgotten what he'd seen or where he was scrying when he saw it.

Not for long: one glimpse of the dragon in the royal magician's mind made him cry out. Vivid memories flashed through the linkage. "That light!" Aundable cried aloud, half-rising from his chair despite Laspeera's restraining grasp. "Gods, what is it?"

"The ghost of a dragon, I fear," Vangerdahast replied, and withdrew from contact as he saw fresh tears course down Laspeera's cheeks again. There'd be forgiveness to be begged from her by the cartload when this was over, to be sure.

Right now, he had to see if the kingdom could be saved. Again.

Dragons didn't fly about Faerûn as ghosts . . . they just didn't. Something about their magical nature, he supposed. Wherefore this phantom dragon must be magically compelled, or shaped, or created . . . Vangerdahast's eyes narrowed.

His hand went to a certain shelf, and found something that he touched to the staff. Hitherto-hidden runes up and down its slim length gleamed. Vangerdahast patiently let the power build as he linked with the crystals again and searched along the line of his first scrying, until he found the phantom dragon again. When he could see it clearly, Vangerdahast unleashed the spell that would make it also able to see him.

Spectral eyes widened in fury and spectral jaws gaped to gout flame.

The floating head and shoulders of the royal magician said firmly, "Be as you were again. Go down."

His own sending faded and was gone, and the furious dragon craned its neck this way and that, looking for the mage who had appeared to it. The wyrm did not find him, but did not tarry to search.

Through his crystals, Vangerdahast watched it approach Suzail, slowly growing fainter and fainter, until at last it was . . . gone.

The royal magician of Cormyr let his crystals sink down, and shook his head to clear it of the spell, yawning wearily. There was Aundable to see to, and Laspeera to placate: he did not remain to see the last spark of the dragon's sentience falling to earth, a dragoneye gem once more.

A gem any citizen might prize, and take up, and keep hidden. Amedahast had always done good work.

* * * * *

Moonlight awakened him at last. Broglan Sarmyn was almost beginning to wish the gods would just take his miserable life instead of letting him waken into new nightmares—and more pain.

Stiffly, fearing something would be broken but again finding nothing, the war wizard sat up and looked around at the devastation. He was alone; either Shayna Summerstar had freed herself and left, or someone—something?—else had carried her off. The now-familiar rubble was everywhere, in this part of the keep that was more ruin than fortress. Moonlight lanced down in a hundred places, peering through holes to bathe the stone beneath.

Somewhere high in the mountains, a wolf howled mournfully. Broglan was suddenly and uncomfortably aware of the sweet stink of death, wafting faintly to him from the many corpses that lay among the rubble. He found himself staring at a certain pile of broken stone and fervently hoping the shapeshifter lay under there.

Or could the mad villain have somehow taken over

Lady Shayna's body, and be walking around the keep seeking more victims even now?

Broglan had to find out—and whatever the fate of the Summerstar heiress, he had to find Storm Silverhand.

Gods, *there* was a lady! A woman he'd follow to the end of his days and cheerfully serve as a drudge for every waking moment of them! To see her fighting on fearlessly, or laughing at them all unashamed of her nakedness, or joking with the two Summerstar men after all the rudenesses and cruelties the family had offered her . . . Broglan shook his head, the feeling of admiration ebbing as he stumbled through the rubble to where she must lie. His mind showed him that broken body tumbling end over end through the air. Who could live through that, Favored of Mystra or not?

He saw her at last, the silver swirl of her long hair spread out on the stones as she lay sprawled. One bare shoulder gleamed in the moonlight, mouth open in a last gasp of pain. She was dead . . . she must be.

Broglan shuffled toward her, grief rising within him—and then he froze in horror.

A shambling shadow moved in the darkness, stepping out to where he could see its slack-jawed, drooling face. No intelligence glimmered in those dead, dull eyes. Like black pits they seemed. The shuffling man swung around, sniffing at the sprawled bard as a dog might, and then stretched out what Broglan could only describe as a *paw* to prod her.

Storm's body rocked slightly but did not respond, and after a slow, cautious breath or two, the mindless thing advanced again.

Broglan stared at it, face pale and mouth soundlessly working. Deep within him red fury was building. He felt hot, and restless, and suddenly energetic.

Drawing himself up, he snapped out a word—and blue-white bursts of energy streaked from his fingertips to strike the shambling man.

It flinched and grunted as each magic missile struck, whimpering and cowering by the end of the barrage.

When no more came, however, it rose again, cautiously—and reached out for Storm again. Broglan quivered with rage and strode forward, shouting. "Get away from her! Just *get away!*"

The man turned a blank, expressionless face toward the source of the loud sounds, and then reached out again for the pretty thing.

Broglan was trotting now, knowing he had no useful spells left but determined to do *some*thing. His hurrying feet struck the legs of a crushed, half-buried table and sent one spinning. He hopped in pain for a moment, and then—whirled, snatched up the table leg, and ran on.

"Stop it! Leave her alone! *Leave her alone!*" he cried as the mindless man lifted Storm's limp arm and then plucked at her leg. It looked like he was going to tear her apart!

Broglan screamed out his revulsion and swung the table leg with both hands.

Bone cracked. The shambling man staggered back, roaring with astonishment and pain. He dragged the limp body with him, and shook it in bewilderment. How had the sleeping thing hurt him? How?

Broglan Sarmyn, leader of the Sevensash, leapt high into the air and swung his improvised club with all his might. The man flung up an arm, and the blow that might have crushed his skull glanced down and into his chest. He staggered back, winded but unhurt—and a furious Broglan brought the club back up under his chin.

The shambling man went over backward, letting go of Storm and consciousness at the same time. Back and down—down through a hole in the floor. He tumbled bonelessly to rubble far below.

For a long time, Broglan stared, panting, at the sprawled man. The fury slowly ebbed from behind his eyes. Wearily, he tossed aside the bloodied table leg. He turned back to Storm and took her gently in his arms.

She was so still, and so beautiful. . . . Grief rose like a choking lump in his throat. He lifted her in his arms, staggering under her weight. He almost fell twice in his first few burdened steps, but set his jaw and walked on through the moonlight. If he did nothing else right in this whole accursed visit to Firefall Keep, he would do this. He would carry this woman, who'd fought so hard for them all, to a place of greater dignity, where she could rest undisturbed by mindless men or hungry wolves. And he was going to tell Lord Vangerdahast how they all owed the safety of Cormyr to this one brave Harper.

The moonlight bathed Storm and the grimly staggering Broglan in blue-white glory. It also shone down into the hole where the shambling man had fallen. There, a broken, disheveled figure limped out of the shadows a few moments after Broglan had turned away. A half-naked man, somehow misshapen, lurched and crept forward to reach and touch the sprawled Hungry Man at last—with one anxious tentacle.

Nineteen
WHEN GODS DARE, HARPERS FALL

 SHAYNA.

The voice was a caress in her mind, an echo of its former self. Shayna Summerstar swallowed, wincing in pain as she rose, and looked around at the night-drenched keep.

SHAYNA, COME TO ME.

The voice sounded stronger. With it came the familiar hunger to be near him . . . to be part of something powerful again.

Yes, Master, she said firmly—and found herself trembling. *Where are you?*

GO DOWN. SEEK ME BELOW.

Shayna looked up regretfully at the blue-white moonlight and then turned her back on it, seeking an intact stair she'd seen earlier.

Since falling on—and killing, she hoped—the horrible war wizard, she'd remembered where one of her mother's robing rooms was, not far from here, and had been limping cautiously toward it. To get into proper boots again! Her feet were in ribbons from these stones, and she'd just *ruined* this dress. . . .

Rats around a partly buried armsman scattered reluctantly as she went past. She shuddered—and then, seeing his dagger lying by itself among rubble, she snatched it up. The stair was just ahead, here. . . .

* * * * *

By the time Broglan reached what was left of the courtyard, he was certain the woman in his arms was alive.

Twice Storm had murmured something. Once she'd twitched, just for a moment. He laid her down gently by the well, and then sat beside her, shaking with exhaustion; she was taller and probably heavier than he, and he was not overly young or overly fit.

When he could trust his arms and shoulders to stop trembling, Broglan drew up a bucket of icy water, drank, and then tried to get some into Storm. It gurgled between her parted lips but just sloshed there; he sat her up, and then held her hand in the bucket. It numbed his fingers to do it, but she did not react.

"*Storm!*" he hissed, not wanting to shout. "Storm—wake up!" He rubbed her wrists briskly, and then on an impulse pinched one arm. Nothing. Her head lolled as limply as ever. He dashed cold water across her face, and watched it run down her; she sat unmoving.

"Storm!" He slapped her gently, and then drew back his hand and stared at it. What was he *doing*?

What could he do?

He looked around wildly in the moonlight—and then remembered the box of leavings he'd found in the stables on his first survey of the keep. Rusty old bells, a lot of discarded purse-straps and single boots, filthy shreds of blanket—and an old, gnarl-stringed harp in a much-patched leather case. Gods willing, it was still there!

It was. With a feeling of triumph, he bore it out into the moonlight, undid the case, and drew it out. Three of the strings were broken, and he knew nothing about harping, but—

He brought his fingers down across the strings, strumming them as he sang, " 'Sleeping maidens wake! Lovers hearts do break! As for me, I seek—a love who'll . . .' oh, gods' spit, but I can't remember the rest of it!"

In lower, less exasperated tones, he added the observation, "And I can't sing, either, but—"

"You did well enough," the bard's voice said by his ear, soft and low.

"Storm!" he cried, flinging his arms around her and kissing her while tears of joy and relief sprang forth from his eyes. "You're awake! You're—"

His babblings were stopped by a firm kiss. Then two fingers were on his lips, bidding him be silent. She quietly finished his sentence: "—almost as glad to see you again as you are to see me!"

She gave him a smile and added, "By the grace of Mystra, I've been in fire trance, slowly coming back from, well, a sword's edge away from death. You've been carrying me and defending me, and Mystra knows what else." She gave him a smile of thanks and admiration, and squeezed his shoulder. Broglan winced; that shoulder had already been hurting.

The bard looked around. "So here we are, in the moonlight. How stand things in the keep?"

"Horrible," Broglan muttered. "The place is a ruin, with most everyone dead—except, I fear, the shapeshifter. Will you lower your barrier so I can call Lord Vangerdahast? If that . . . fiend is still alive, we'll need all the war wizards we can get here!"

"If we do that," Storm said quietly, "they'll be needed all over the realm, wherever they came from . . .

because our murderous foe will be there, and everywhere, on the loose. No, the barrier stays up."

"But what then do we *do*?" Broglan asked, almost pleading. "The moon'll go down soon, and we'll be at his mercy! We dare not hunt through the keep again, or we'll be slain!"

"We use me as bait," Storm told him, smiling weakly. "Care to light the lamps of a lady's bedchamber—and then wait in the closet like any young lover? They're sure to check under the bed. . . ."

Broglan rolled his eyes. "If we get out of this, I'll have tales to tell my grandchildren. . . ."

"If we get out of this, Sir Broglan, I'll send you Harpers to wed those grandchildren," Storm told him sweetly. "I take it by your tone that my bedchamber survives?"

"There's been no great damage at that end of the keep," he said, reaching out slowly to stroke her silver hair. Then he looked away, embarrassed.

"I'm sorry," he mumbled, "but I've wanted to do that for a long time."

Storm put her arms around him. "Go ahead," she said softly, "stroke my hair. Kiss me." Her eyes flashed. "Anything to stop you trying to play the harp!"

They clung to each other in the moonlight, laughing weakly, as the wolves started to howl again at the head of the vale.

* * * * *

SHAYNA, *NOW*.

The young heiress paused in the doorway of a wardrobe she'd happened upon, a new gown in her hands. She sighed, let the dress fall, and went back to the passage outside.

She found the Hungry Man standing there like a silent statue, his face vacant.

Master?

YOU HAVE A NEW TASK. TOO MANY PURPLE
DRAGONS ARE ABOUT. ELIMINATE THEM.

*I've been lucky thus far, but I can't use a sword, and
they're stronger than—*

BE THE LURE. MY HUNGRY MAN WILL DO THE
KILLING.

Yes, Master. Shayna Summerstar looked once at the
slack-jawed servant and then marched off down the
passage. There were armsmen to slay.

*　*　*　*　*

The moon had gone down by the time the master
called on her again. In the meantime, Shayna had gotten truly sick of killing. Her ribs burned where a
guard's sword had slid along them in the darkness,
and her hands were sticky with the blood of men she
did not know. The Hungry Man lurched tirelessly
along behind her; Shayna stole a glance at him and
shuddered. Together they'd sent nearly twenty men to
face the gods, and she was trembling with weariness.

There had been one bright thing. One of the guards
had been carrying the wand of lightning she'd seen
Corathar wielding before the master had claimed him.
It rested reassuringly in her hand, now, and—

SHAYNA, GO UP TO STORM SILVERHAND'S
CHAMBERS WITHOUT DELAY. BOTH OF YOU
SHALL RECEIVE MY ORDERS THERE.

Something inside the heiress of House Summerstar
almost broke at that moment, but she fought down an
inner scream, straightened, and smiled as she made
the mind-reply, *Yes, Master.*

Gods, would the slaying never end?

It was a long and rubble-littered way up to the
bard's guest room. The silence was eerie. This area of
the keep seemed undamaged, and someone had even

lit the torches along the walls.

Shayna's eyes narrowed. When she could see Storm's door, she stopped and looked at the Hungry Man.

He stared back at her. There was no comprehension in those dull eyes, but—as she'd expected—his orders drove him finally to shuffle past her and lay hands on the door himself.

There was a silent flash as he grasped its handle. The mindless man staggered back. Shayna watched him moan soundlessly as pain stabbed through him, but two breaths later, he was back at the door again.

This time it opened without incident, its magic gone. Flickering light spilled out into the passage. Shayna raised her wand and slipped soundlessly forward to peer through the doorway.

The Hungry Man was walking steadily toward the bed, obviously under the master's direct control, but Shayna could see past him.

The room was lit by many candles, and they seemed to have been arranged to display the room's lone occupant. Storm Silverhand lay asleep—or dead—on the bed, her body arranged under a linen shroud as if for burial.

"It's some sort of trap," the Summerstar heiress murmured, darting suspicious glances right and left at the corners of the room. The Hungry Man shuffled over to Storm and put his hands around her throat. Shayna expected him to twist his hands until she heard the crack of bone, but he froze.

Shayna swallowed. The bard was not dead, then; the mindless one was there to break her neck if she roused.

USE YOUR WAND. STRIKE UNDER THE BED, AND THROUGH THE CANOPY.

The master's mind was very loud; he must be near, Shayna thought, as she bent to send lightning under the bed.

* * * * *

At the back of the closet that led off the bedchamber, where he crouched under a heap of Storm's discarded gowns and hosiery, Broglan's fingertips tingled. Someone was hurling lightning bolts. Had it begun? He waited tensely in the darkness, straining to hear.

* * * * *

The canopy fell away in tatters as lightning crackled and smoked along the ceiling. There was no one there.

The noblewoman lowered her wand and looked down at the bard. Storm did not awaken. Shayna was close enough now to see the shallow rise and fall of the Harper's breast. The master must be coming to feed, and take the bard's life at last.

"Well done, Shayna," his compelling voice came from just behind her. "Go now and guard the door. Blast anyone who tries to enter or strike at us from outside."

Shayna gave the shapeshifter a weak smile. She moved mutely out of the way. On her way to the door, she looked back and saw him wrap two tentacles around the posts of the bed and haul himself up onto it almost impatiently. A delicate tentacle probed down, stroking the woman from knee to chin in what was almost a caress, drawing the shroud aside. There was no reaction.

"She's in a trance at last," he murmured aloud, and lowered himself to straddle her. Shayna took up her stance by the doors, crossed her arms, and then risked another glance back at the bed. What would it look like when the master subsumed the powers of someone who was almost a god?

The master's eyes gleamed with sudden fire. Shayna almost looked away—but suddenly Storm's own eyes were open. The Hungry Man's hands whipped up from her throat in a blur, reaching for the master!

The shapeshifter reared back with a choked, startled sound. The meaty smack of a fist striking flesh snapped across the room as the Hungry Man, tortured fury blazing in his own eyes now, punched his master with all his force.

The shapeshifter reeled. Storm's long legs rose up to hold him in a scissors lock. Tentacles flailed and grew bony spurs to stab with, but the Hungry Man surged forward, punching and throttling. . . .

SHAYNA! The thought was furious, clawing at her will almost frantically. Shayna brought the wand up without thinking, in fascination watching the unfolding battle on the bed.

Something washed over her like cool, perfumed water. She found herself blinking, a hazy picture of the war wizard Broglan's face floating before her eyes. The Dark Master's mind touch was gone! She was—free!

The shapeshifter grew tentacles in a frantic forest of eel-like wrigglings. The doors of the robing-room burst open, and Broglan emerged, his head adorned with a tangle of lacy lingerie and gauzy stockings. He ran grimly at the bed.

A tentacle shot out in a blur. Shayna found herself reeling back, head ringing from a slap that had almost broken her neck. Her fingers were burning where friction had stripped the flesh from them—from the blow that had shattered her wand. As she stared at them, its fragments spilled from her nerveless fingers. The tentacle reached for her again. Broglan laid on it a hand that blazed with sudden fire.

Smoke curled up from the eel-like member. The master roared out his pain, but dared not spare more attention to whatever was melting away his flesh. He had more pressing problems.

Through a bucking forest of tentacles, Shayna saw the shapeshifter and the Hungry Man staring at each other, nose to nose, muscles rippling and trembling as they strained to throttle each other.

Then flames raced out from the Master's eyes in a fiery plume.

Storm was twisting out from under them both as the flames roared, blinding-bright. When they died away, the Hungry Man was headless.

The body of the servant toppled, truly mindless now. Shayna screamed and ran, brushing past a startled Broglan, to get her own slim fingers around the shapeshifter's neck. She struck him from behind, digging in her nails to draw blood, howling, shaking him back and forth in a sudden frenzy of pain and rage and loss . . . but he was flowing out from between her hands, changing shape, his head melting away!

The master oozed across the bed, growing tentacles that reached back to tear her apart—only to stiffen and let Shayna fall away, sobbing in fear and anger.

The shapeshifter had locked eyes with a different foe, and his eyes were blazing again. So were hers.

Silver fire smoldered in Storm Silverhand's eyes as she faced him, and she coolly mind-spoke, *Time to feel the lash you've been using so cruelly on others.* It was followed by a knife-edged probe that slashed and tore at his mind even more viciously than the awakened dragon had.

Wild, insane laughter burst from the shapeshifter's mouth—but instead of hurling spells and babbling raggedly, the shapeshifter drew himself up to tower above them all. The flames curling out of his burning eyes deepened to a rich red hue.

"I AM THE LORD OF LORDS AND THE PRINCE OF DARK PRINCES. MY BLACK HAND SMITES FROM ONE END OF FAERÛN TO THE OTHER, AND BEYOND. BEHOLD ME, MORTALS, AND FEAR ME! FOR FEAR AND TYRANNY ARE MINE TO BESTOW, AND THE RUIN THEY DO IS MY

EXULTATION. I AM BANE THE UNDYING, AND NONE SHALL ESCAPE ME!"

As he shouted, red fire burst from the dark-skinned, many-tentacled figure that stood on the bed. The blaze seared draperies and clothing to hurl Shayna against the bedchamber wall. She struck it heavily, slid down it, and did not move again.

Storm and Broglan were thrown to their knees, and as they struggled to rise, thunderous laughter rolled around them, and that terrible mind-voice spoke again. STAY DOWN IN HOMAGE, WHERE YOU BELONG . . . FOR THE LAST FEW MISERABLE MOMENTS OF YOUR LIVES.

Twenty

TO BATTLE A MAD GOD

Bolts of black flame leapt from the outstretched palms of Bane and lanced about the bedchamber. Where they struck walls and furniture, they licked greedily but burned nothing, only coursed along surfaces. Where they struck mortals, they streamed into flickering fields around the bodies. Enshrouded in flames that did not burn, Storm and Broglan found themselves unable to move—except to tremble in time to the thrumming flow of unleashed power.

The revealed god stepped leisurely down from the bed, his face now almost unearthly in its beauty, his body jet-black, and his eyes two red flames. With lilting grace, he crossed the room to where Storm knelt, frozen with one open hand outstretched as if beseeching.

"I have waited so long for this moment," Bane said gently, reaching out to caress her hair. "Ever since I learned of your true power. Through you, my little

Stormling, and the other minions of Mystra I'll reach through you, I shall ascend once more!"

"Perhaps," Storm whispered as her eyes met his fearlessly. Silver fire shot out from them to strike the red blaze of Bane's gaze. All over the room, black flames fell away into curling, vanishing smoke as the air filled with surging silvery light.

Broglan cried out in awe and wonder. Bane cried out in pain and sudden despair. With a smile of relief, Storm reached up and touched the obsidian chest above her. At long last she was bringing down the full force of Mystra's divine fire on the foe, collapsing her barrier into his body.

Bane screamed, convulsed, and tried to turn away, to flee. As he struggled, writhing in the grip of silver flames that boiled up around him in racing, spiraling coils, he was lifted off the ground. Silver flames plunged through him to burst forth in ragged gouts from his every orifice.

The mad godling hung in the air above them, shuddering in the flames, his limbs flowing into scales and tentacles and feathers and soft suckers, but always being forced back into jet-black, human form. His screaming became raw and continuous as the black hue of the godly pretender fell away, and the naked body of a man began to take shape.

"You are no true god," Storm said, knowing she spoke truth, "but the twisted remnant of some unfortunate Bane took as an avatar—and abandoned later, leaving behind in a mortal body some dark shadow of himself as he went on to possess another. Shapeshifter . . . sorcerer . . . all powers stolen from victims, under the goad of Bane's madness. Who were you, at first? Who will you be, again?"

The flesh of the floating body flowed and swirled, becoming slowly clearer. It was hairy, muscular, and kind-faced. It was . . .

Tears welled up in Storm's eyes as she looked up at her beloved Maxer. Her cheeks were wet as she whispered, "I feared this, and it is so. Mystra . . . oh, lady fair, if you have ever loved me, do this one thing: grant me my Maxer back!"

She felt kindly, unseen eyes upon her—a regard that carried great but friendly weight. She cried out in wordless thanks . . . and an instant later, by Mystra's grace, Storm knew exactly what she had to do, and how to do it.

She smiled through the tears that streamed from her trembling jaw, and waved Broglan well back. She smiled because there was a way—and because it would not be easy, and Mystra was leaving it for her to take.

"Our choices strengthen us," she murmured aloud, "and we are changed by the accomplishments you leave to us. Thank you, Great Lady."

She bowed her head and bent her will to join with the silver fire surging through her—and rode it into the mind of the floating man, seeking the small, mad part of him that had once been Bane.

It was a long plunge into hot black-and-purple chaos. Her descent slowed as the silver fire encountered deeper and deeper gloom. Wild images of cruelty flashed before her, memories dragged from the dissolving mind of the foe. As she plunged through one after another, panting and gagging at what she saw, the revolting evil of Bane's deeds and schemes nearly overwhelmed her.

Shuddering with nausea, Storm almost lost her will to continue. As she floundered, retching and weeping, she felt a smile of sly triumph growing around her. . . . The foe was trying to shatter her mind with his images of torture and pain and mutilation!

Her anger almost doomed her again. Bane fed on rage, and could *twist* it in others to become a subtle slavery to his will. With icy determination, Storm tore free of his strengthening control and called the silver fire up protectively around her. She wrestled her way on into the dark caverns of the foe's mind, forcing it by sheer grim mental demand to yield up certain memories.

She tasted her own blood, and knew she was being hurt by this, lessened and changed forever. It was with her own flare of triumph, though, that a new welter of horrid visions began. The visions of her own choosing erupted around her.

Broglan saw the kneeling, silver-haired woman begin to pant and tremble ... and then to whimper and claw at herself with nails that left ribbons of blood behind. He almost broke his determination to keep back from her. Storm's eyes grew wide, and the blood drained from her lips until they became as white as those of any fish. She gasped in tiny whispers, "Ohohoh*n*onononono ..."

Her fingers clenched so hard that her nails drew blood from her palms. Suddenly her hands flew up, growing into talons as if she were a shapeshifter. She raked her own body frantically as she sprang up, drawing blood from deep slashes. She began to dance. Blood rained down around her.

Broglan had no magic strong enough to restrain her if she started to slay and blast in Firefall Keep. White-faced, he went to his knees and shouted a prayer to Mystra.

In that prayer, images of a kinder Storm—images that had once shamed him, even as they lit his night-dreams and made him long hopelessly for her caresses—blazed with sudden clarity in his memory. He remembered more. Too overwhelmed in wonder to give thanks to his goddess, Broglan received new visions, memories that were not his own: Storm Silverhand fighting at Maxer's shoulder, laughing in battle as their swords sang in unison; Storm dancing with her sisters on air, their bare feet well above the waters of a moonlit pool; Storm comforting a stricken Harper and giving of her own life-force to keep him alive; Storm playing with a child orphaned in battle, comforting the young girl as she deftly purged the worst horror from the infant mind and replaced it with the faces of kindly Harpers to be her new parents; Storm leaping in front of a young Harper in battle to take the sword-thrust that was meant to slay him; Storm . . .

Then the scenes became familiar—his own memories again, yet clearer, more vivid, and longer than he'd recalled them. Slowly, very slowly, Broglan Sarmyn of the Sevensash rose again to his feet as the memories faded, leaving him to watch the swaying, keening woman.

Storm's healing mind would later let her remember only a few of the memories of Bane she'd gone seeking. The first was the spicy taste of his satisfaction as he entered the body of the marilith and possessed her mind, crushing her will forever. He feasted on her memories, and found among them that one of her greatest triumphs was her recent rebuilding of the ravaged body of the mortal Maxer, to be her pleasure-slave.

Bane passed into Maxer, and saw what sustained and drove the risen man: his vivid memories of his beloved Storm Silverhand and her powers. Storm, a Chosen of Mystra!

Bane exulted, slaughtering hapless creatures at random in a wild orgy of death as he celebrated his glee. Storm would be for him a road to wounding Mystra and prying away some of her great power!

The Dark God decided that Maxer must be his new mortal form, to protect it fully. He used subsumption to drain the powers of the marilith into this new body.

He became Maxer—or rather, Maxer became Bane, mortal awareness dwindling as the god seized his form. A triumphant Bane set about scheming how to get at Mystra through Storm . . . and how to corrupt the Harpers to his will, whatever else befell.

Then came the disaster of the Fall of the Gods, and madness. Only the burning goal of regaining godhood kept this abandoned remnant of Bane from utter and irreversible insanity. Still, he was trapped in a mortal shell, with little more than the power of subsumption and the ability to see magic and living things in darkness and slumber.

Though firmly in thrall to the wandering mind of Bane, Maxer remembered Storm and yearned to be with her again. The twisted intellect that had once been a part of Bane, perceiving her powers, wanted to possess her . . . and so began the long journey and clumsy scheming that had led to Athlan Summerstar's murder in Firefall Keep.

Storm shuddered and surfaced, silver flames blazing briefly from her eyes and then curling away to nothingness. Did anything of Maxan Maxer survive? And how sane would the man she had loved—would *always* love—be after torment under a tanar'ri and then enthrallment under the awful weight of a god's mind?

No matter; what she must do was clear. Faerûn itself demanded it.

"Broglan!" Storm cried, turning to him. "Anchor me!"

The war wizard blinked. "How?" he asked, bewildered.

"Think of me—remember my looks, my voice, the way I move, what I've said—only keep *remembering!*"

Broglan nodded, a frown of concentration settling on his face. He reached out and took hold of her chin gently, holding her face so that he could look into it. Solemnly, he looked her bare body up and down, before nodding, clearing his throat, and saying roughly, "Do what you have to do, and may Mystra be with us both!"

Storm gave him a smile of thanks, and descended again into the darkness that had once been a part of Bane.

This time, madness was waiting for her—and it was desperate.

A sword of hatred stabbed into her, and fear lashed deep its blazing brands. She snarled and drove deeper, battered but determined, hurling silver fire wherever the darkness was deepest.

The pain of his attacks came again and again, always vicious thrusts that struck at what would disgust her—eyeballs and fingernails and worse. The silver fire surged and restored, but her mind grew steadily darker and angrier . . . and it was in her mind that the struggle would be won or lost.

The foe lurked, almost gloating, and slid away when she tried to smite, only to slash and goad from behind. Storm snarled and spun the silver fire about her like a cloak, so that to injure her, he must himself be harmed. Against every dark vision of cruelty, she set one of love, or sacrifice, or honor, calling on the long strivings for peace and justice, and friendship that she and her fellow sisters and Harpers had undertaken.

Those memories made her weep anew for friends gone and their noble deeds done. In answer to her raw heart, the silver fire began to burn here and there in the dark caverns that she traversed, brightening the mad mind.

Yet as Storm fought on through the abyss that had once been a part of Bane, silver hair swirling, she felt herself becoming slowly and inevitably as dark and serpentine and cruel as her foe, using her mind as viciously as he was using his—to slash and hack.

It seemed she was striking nearer and nearer to the oldest memories, and to the roiling rot of true madness. Madness had mastered him again and again in raging bouts of gibbering uncontrol. If not for madness, he would have won an easy victory over her in Firefall Keep. She fought closer to the shame and the trembling fear he so hated, that made him seek tyranny over others. This fear tasted like the tang of iron in blood, but came from a place weirdly different than Faerûn. The mortal who had become Bane, so long ago, had come from . . . somewhere else, and still had secrets that he was fighting wildly to keep from her, secrets that he would keep hidden at all costs.

At all costs . . . there was a sudden red roiling of disgusting, elongated internal human organs, bloated and wriggling, as the foe mentally turned himself inside out—and burned. He was slaying himself, to keep from yielding to her. He was dying utterly at last. He was . . . gone, a drifting wisp of smoke in the heart of the leaping silver fire.

The silver fire reached to a brightness above, a brightness that was calling Storm. She reached for it and rose to it . . . and slowly, very slowly, the light above her drew nearer.

Through her weary daze, Storm became increasingly ashamed of how twisted and besmeared the battle had left her. Yet she had prevailed, and was rising toward the light. New visions were coming.

Visions that had the warm, somehow *brown* feeling of Broglan's mind—visions of her beauty, impish outrageousness, and courage, laced about with awe and growing love. Faithfully, doggedly, and continuously replaying the vivid scenes that awoke in him both lust and love, Broglan was thinking of her.

The fouled, rising shadow seized on that anchor, and was suddenly Storm once more.

She saw the Realms around her again, and felt breezes moving over her body and something hard under her feet. She turned to look at Broglan, silver flames darting from her eyes.

Startled, the war wizard stepped back and raised

his hands to cast a spell if need be. His brow was dark with worry.

"Are you Storm?" Broglan asked gravely, almost formally, "or—someone else?"

She gave him a weak smile, and her eyes became the silver-laced blue he remembered. "I am Storm Silverhand," she said slowly, "thanks in large part to you, Broglan."

She looked over her shoulder. The body of Maxer was lying on a bed of silver flames. His face was peaceful, his hands at his sides, and his eyes closed. Storm bit her lip, turned back to the watching wizard, and took two quick strides forward.

"Thank you," she said fervently, as their lips met. Her next impassioned words were silent echoes in his mind. *Oh, Broglan, thank you. All the time you wrestled against loving me and then surrendered to it, and loved me, and aided me, and never forced yourself on me or demanded anything in return. The Lady needs more men like you. I needed you, though we were not for each other. I still need you. I revere you.* Then from her mind a gentle touch of silver fire reached out, and Broglan felt pleasure greater than he ever had before. It raised him up, gasping, to trembling heights of bliss. He was suddenly intensely aware of the beautiful woman he held in his arms, her bare skin against him in a hundred places, her sweet lips touching his own eagerly.

It was suddenly too much, and he murmured and broke free, feeling wild elation—and rising fear.

Broglan shook his head slightly as he gazed at her, tears in his eyes. When she reached for him again, he shuddered involuntarily and backed away, raising his hands to ward off danger.

She halted, and he looked at her in horror—horror at himself. White-faced, he looked slowly down at his treacherous hands and then back up at her, ashamed.

Storm reached out in a wave of forgiveness, and gave him a sad little smile. "Farewell, love who might have been," she said softly. "Know that you shall always be in my heart, and welcome. Come to see me in Shadowdale, as a friend . . . when you're ready. However long it takes, we'll"—she nodded toward Maxer's sleeping body—"be there. I hope."

"You hope?" Broglan asked, hesitantly.

"What was once a part of Bane is gone—destroyed, not driven out," Storm told him firmly, "but what is left behind could be a mindless thing, or something half-witted . . . or a Maxer who hates me for what I've done to him."

EPILOGUE

The hour was late, and the torches were guttering low. Storm watched them flicker toward smoky deaths. She glanced at the bedchamber door for perhaps the thousandth time.

Its closed surface told her nothing.

She sighed, struck a chord on her harp, and let her fingers wander gently over the strings in an old, old song of wistful hope. She'd long since played all of her favorite ballads, several times, and then all the others she could remember or half-remember, and was on to the tunes—or snatches of them—that her fingers remembered when her mind could not. This one had lyrics of the half-remembered sort; she sang the few words that came to her.

"In the morning when the mists steal away, I'll still sit and softly play. I sing for you, every night, every day, the long years through . . ."

She was groping for the refrain when the door

opened. Her fingers froze on the thrumming strings.

He stood there in a pair of her old breeches, barefoot and barechested, with one of her night cloaks thrown around his shoulders. He was smiling the way she remembered. His blue eyes were merry and bright.

Storm stared at him, unable to utter another sound.

"All these years you waited for me," Maxan Maxer said with a smile, his eyes shining. "I knew that, somehow, if I was ever set free, 'twould be my Storm that'd do it. Yes, my lady—'tis truly me, and not some last trick of the Dark One wearing my smile. Shall we carry on where we left off?"

Wordlessly Storm nodded, shaping his name with lips that trembled. She flung the harp down as if it were worthless kindling and leapt into his arms. Tears burst from her in a waterfall, and she could not speak.

"There, there," Maxer said soothingly, as he stroked her hair and shoulders, and felt her clinging to his ribs with bruising force. "Gods," he added huskily, a moment later, as his own eyes grew moist, "I've missed you. The feel of you, the smell of you. . . the warmth of your love."

They cried together for a time, and then looked into each other's eyes and laughed, and then cried again.

"Enough of this leaking all over the passage floor," Maxer growled after a time. "I'm much more interested in doing *this*." His lips met hers hungrily, and bore down.

Storm moved in his arms and murmured, and silver fire swirled around them as they embraced. Maxer cried out in wordless wonder at its cool, cleansing touch . . . and then it died away, and they were somewhere else.

Somewhere with cold flagstones under their feet, and a woman hissing, "Gods above!" in shock. A sword rang from its sheath.

Storm and Maxer stood with their arms around each other and smiled at Shaerl Rowanmantle, the

Lady of Shadowdale, who stared back at them in disbelief over the bright point of her drawn sword.

"Storm?" she asked, eyes narrowing. "*Maxer?*"

"Be at ease," said a musical voice from the empty air across the table. "They are truly what they seem to be. Welcome back, both of you."

Maxer stared around the low-beamed kitchen with a happy smile, scarce believing that he was in Storm's arms again, and would never have to leave. He cleared his throat several times before he managed to say, "My thanks, Syluné . . . and my apologies, Lady Shaerl, for our precipitous arrival."

Storm smiled at them with very bright eyes, and then buried her face in Maxer's chest again and cried. Wearing an expression of amazement, Shaerl watched her shaking shoulders.

"So success managed to find you again, Sister," Syluné said briskly. They saw the kettle lift from its hook by the hearth and head toward the pump. "There are scones in the warming-oven, and I suppose you'll be wanting tea."

"Tea," Maxer said slowly, and then one end of his mouth lifted in an impish grin. "And—zzar?"

"Of course," the unseen Witch of Shadowdale replied dryly. "It's in the cupboard behind you—*if* you can bring yourself to peel one inch of your flesh away from my sister for an instant or two."

The filled kettle drifted back toward the fire, and Syluné added briskly, "You can put away your steel and get me cups for six, Shaerl. There's nothing out and ready to carve up yet."

"Six?" the Lady of Shadowdale asked slowly, sliding her sword back into its sheath. "But—"

The end of the table she was facing glimmered suddenly, and Syluné said, "Ah, they're here—commendably swift of them!"

The glimmering became a flash that died away to

reveal a smiling, barefoot couple whose robes and hair were somewhat in disarray. The Simbul and Elminster nodded and smiled at the dumbfounded Shaerl and strode across the room to embrace Storm and Maxer.

The kitchen was suddenly a happy chaos of sobbing, laughing, and hugging folk. Shaerl stepped back and shook her head with a smile. She'd *never* get used to instant magical comings and goings, not if she lived to see two hundred winters or more!

A sudden aura of light surrounded Maxer's head, and he stiffened in Elminster's embrace. Storm turned quickly in the Simbul's arms to see what had befallen—and saw an identical aura gathering in the air about her.

"What—?" she began, and then fell silent as Maxer gave her both a rueful smile and a nod of reassurance.

"Sorry, lad," Elminster said gruffly, releasing Storm's beloved, "but we had to be sure."

"Of course," Maxer replied—as Storm felt the first swift darting of her sister's probe in her mind. She stiffened just as Maxer had, and then took a deep breath, forced herself to relax, and let the Simbul do her work.

"Sorry, Sister," the Queen of Aglarond said quietly, a moment later, releasing her.

"Acceptable, am I?" Storm asked teasingly, suddenly very weary. "Does that mean I can have tea?"

The Simbul smiled a little sadly, hearing the edge in Storm's voice, and impulsively hugged her sister from behind. Storm stiffened again, in astonishment this time; the Simbul *never* did such things.

"Mystra save us all," said the Queen of Aglarond fondly, "of course you can. Sit down, and cut some pie, and I'll just float those scones out. El?"

"Momentarily, m'dear," the Old Mage replied airily. "Ah . . . *now*." The glimmering at the end of the table began again.

This time the flashing magic brought three obviously startled arrivals: Ergluth Rowanmantle, still holding a bandage roll that he'd been wrapping his arm with; the worried-looking war wizard Broglan; and in his arms, smiling shyly, the Lady Shayna Summerstar.

All three blinked at the cheerful old stone kitchen around them, and Elminster gravely introduced it with a wave of his hand: "The farmhouse of Storm Silverhand, in Shadowdale."

Then the Old Mage staggered sideways, nearly bowled over in the Lady Shaerl's rush. "*Ergluth!*" she cried, leaping into the arms of her kinsman. "Oh, I've missed you! How's Cormyr these days, and the family? And when did you put on so much weight? However did you man—"

Ergluth Rowanmantle barked just two words over her head at Elminster: "Wine," and then, a few moments later, and a trifle more mournfully, "Help."

That was when Syluné, a spectral head floating above the table and trailing a long fall of hair, transported in the feast. Humming happily, she looked this way and that, and steaming platters began to appear by the dozens around her, on every horizontal surface save the floor, which was reserved for the arriving kegs.

Broglan and Shayna stared around in absolute amazement—and then stiffened in unison as auras of light came into being around them both. A third enveloped Ergluth as the boldshield wheeled around to stare at the sudden radiance.

"Right," the Simbul announced emphatically, "everything seems safe—let the revel begin!"

* * * * * *

In the wee, blue hours before dawn, when all the chatter and lights and revelry and those who'd partaken were gone again, three heads bobbed above the cool waters of the stream in the woods below the farmhouse.

One head floated above the water, surveying the other two critically. Syluné said, "There's a spell I think will suit you two just fine. . . ."

Maxer sighed. "If you don't mind," he said carefully, "I've had more than enough experience with magic these last few years—" He stopped speaking as the spectral head softly faded away.

"Oh," a ghostly voice said by his ear, just before he felt the soft touch of invisible lips, "this isn't that kind of magic."

"Syluné," Storm asked warningly, "what're you up to?"

"I just don't think you'll want to climb all the way back up to the loft, to find a bed—especially as Sir Broglan and Lady Shayna already seem to be using it. Will you want tea tomorrow, say around highsun?"

"Syluné!" Storm protested, laughter bubbling in her voice. "What're you up t—"

And then she fell silent, knowing she and Maxer were alone.

A moment later the spell took hold. They found themselves rising out of the water, as warm as if they'd been quite dry, and floating just above the gently tinkling waters. Maxer rolled over and lay on empty air, raising himself on one elbow to look at his beloved.

"Lady Storm," he said, admiring her frankly, "I like your sister's spells . . . but I'll take you over her any night."

"Why don't you do just that?" Storm asked, setting aside all her cares at last as she drifted gently through the moonlit air into his arms.

In the east, one more dawn was just beginning to creep into Shadowdale, but neither of them noticed it.

FANTASY ADVENTURE

Welcome to the FORGOTTEN REALMS®, the largest and most detailed of TSR's fantasy worlds.

Look out from the high walls of Waterdeep, the sprawling, cosmopolitan City of Splendors. Beyond lies the Savage Frontier: the rugged mountains and endless forests of the Sword Coast, wilderlands that cloak the crumbling ruins of fallen kingdoms.

Travel with the caravans that cross these dangerous lands, heading east toward the kingdom of Cormyr, fabled realm of ancient forests, land of chivalry and romance. Stop over in the Dalelands, home of the crusty old wizard Elminster and the birthplace of many heroes and heroines. Then continue onward to distant Thay . . . and beyond.

In your travels, you will encounter many folk from highborn to low. Among the beautiful and deadly Seven Sisters are Storm Silverhand, the silver-haired Bard of Shadowdale, and High Lady Alustriel, the gentle and just ruler of Silverymoon. A third sister is the Simbul, fey and wild-tempered Witch-Queen of Aglarond. There are four more sisters, each beautiful and powerful in her own way.

If you meet them on the road, do not meddle with the mysterious Harpers, who work to uphold freedom and the causes of good throughout the Realms. You may, however, share a drink with the eccentric explorer Volo, and pick his brain for a wealth of information about your next destination. Beware that sinister-looking fellow in the corner of the common room. He may be a Zhentarim agent, gathering information for a takeover of the Heartlands.

Should the surface world not prove exciting enough for you, make your way beneath Mount Waterdeep to traverse the miles upon miles of tunnels and caverns known as Undermountain—but beware its deadly traps and skulking monsters. If you survive these hazards, press on to the subterranean city of Menzoberranzan, home of the deadly drow and birthplace of the renegade Drizzt Do'Urden.

When you return to the light of the surface world, you may want to explore the crumbling ruins of Myth Drannor, a storehouse of lost magic and deadly monsters in the heart of the vast Elven Court forest.

From the dangerous sewers and back alleys of sprawling cities, to glaciers, deserts, jungles, and uncharted seas (above and below the surface!), there's a whole world to explore in the lands of the Forgotten Realms.